12-9-91

Dear Oliver,

We hope you enjoy

Somehow, I got the feeling
the author doesn't care too
much for women, but since
Alex read these when he was
a little boy, it probably
didn't matter a great deal to
him. We miss you and
send our love.

Alex & Ann

# The Caravan of Death

*The Collected Works of*
KARL  MAY

*Edited by Erwin J. Haeberle*

Series III  :  Volume 2

# THE CARAVAN
# OF DEATH

: *A Novel by* :

# KARL MAY

*Translated by*

MICHAEL SHAW

*A Continuum Book*

THE SEABURY PRESS : NEW YORK

1979 : *The Seabury Press*
815 Second Avenue : New York, New York 10017

*The present text is based on the volume, "Von Bagdad nach Stambul," published by Karl-May-Verlag, Bamberg. © 1951 Karl-May-Verlag, Bamberg.*

Printed in the United States of America

*Library of Congress Cataloging in Publication Data*

May, Karl Friedrich, 1842–1912.
The caravan of death.
(The Collected works of Karl May; ser.3, v.2)
(A Continuum book)
Translation of Von Bagdad nach Stambul.
I. Title.
PZ3.M45408Co     1977     ser.3, vol. 2     [PT2625.A848]
ISBN 0-8164-9361-8     833'.8s [833'.8]     79-1248

# Contents

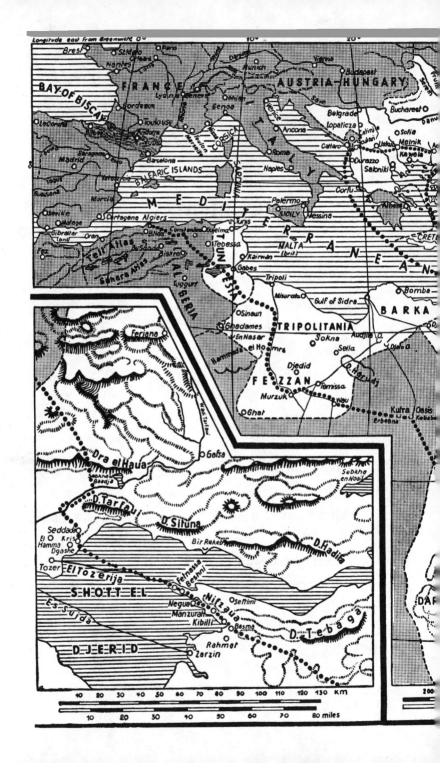

Kara Ben Nemsi in the Realm of the Padisha

Map of the Ottoman Empire about 1872

☐ Ottoman Lands
▒ other "
•••• Itinerary

This story takes place in the early 1870s.

# The Caravan of Death

# 1 : Along the Persian Border

South of the great Syrian and Mesopotamian desert lies the Arabian Peninsula, whose southeastern coast is washed by the stormy Arabian Sea.

A narrow but fertile coastal strip borders this land along three sides. It rises toward the interior and becomes an extensive, bleak plateau whose melancholy, confused stretches, especially in the east, are closed off by tall, impassable mountain chains of which the desolate Jebel Akdar is the most important.

In early times this region was divided into Arabia Petraea, Arabia Deserta, and Arabia Felix. Some geographers believe that the term *petraea* derives from the Greek word for *stone, rock*, and therefore call it *stony* Arabia, but this is a misconception. Actually the name should be traced to the old Petra, which was the capital of this northern province of the country. The Arabs call their native land Djesiret al Arab,* while the Turks and Persians refer to it as Arabistan. Opinions about the present political configuration differ, but for the nomadic inhabitants the only meaningful distinction is that between the various tribes.

---

* Arabic Island-land.

Arabia's sky is eternally cloudless, and at night the stars are clearly visible. The half-wild son of the steppe roams the ravines and the still partly unexplored desert plains on his magnificent horse or indefatigable camel. He is forever alert; save for the members of his own tribe, he lives in dispute and enmity with the rest of the world.

Joktan, the son of Eber, a fifth-generation descendent of Shem, is considered the ancestor of the real Arabs. His progeny settled in Arabia Felix and along the Tihama down to the Persian Gulf. Now, many tribes view it as an honor to be descended from Ishmael, Hagar's son. Legend reports that this Ishmael came to Mecca with his father Abraham and built the Kaaba there. But the truth is that the Kaaba was built or at least enlarged by the Kuraish. The well Zem Zem and the black stone that allegedly fell from heaven are the most famous memorials in that city. The various Arab tribes made pilgrimages there to enshrine their household and tribal gods, to sacrifice to them, and to offer their prayers. Mecca was thus the hub for the widely dispersed tribes. Since the Kuraish had custody of this important place, the tribe became the most powerful and respected in Arabia as it became the wealthiest, for the streams of pilgrims arriving from everywhere never came without gifts or valuable merchandise.

A member of this tribe, Abd Allah,* died in 570 A.D., and some months later his widow Amina gave birth to a boy who later was called Muhammad.† It is likely that the boy had another name before, and was only given the honorific Muhammad when his prophetic activity made him a man of eminence. His father had left him only two camels, five sheep, and an Ethiopian slave, so that he first had to rely on the protection of his grandfather, Abd al-Mutalib, and, after that man's death, the support of his uncle Abu Talib. But since the latter could not do much for him, the boy had to earn his livelihood herding sheep. Later he be-

---

* Servant of God.
† The Much-praised One.

came a camel driver and a bow-and-quiver carrier, which probably developed his warlike spirit.

When he was twenty-five he entered the service of Khadija, the rich widow of a merchant, and served her so faithfully that she became fond of him and made him her husband. But later he lost his wife's large fortune. Up to his fortieth year he was a merchant. On his extensive travels he came into contact with Jews and Christians, Brahmins and fire worshipers, and endeavored to understand their beliefs. He suffered from epilepsy and convulsions, and a resulting nervous ailment that made him highly susceptible to hallucinations, which his religious ruminations did nothing to cure. Finally, Muhammad withdrew to a cave on Mount Hira near Mecca. It was here that he had his first visions.

The circle of those that gathered around the Prophet originally consisted only of his wife Khadija, his slave Said, Osman and Abu Bakr, two men from Mecca, and his young cousin Ali, one of the most ill-fated of Islam's heroes.

Ali was born in 602 and was so highly esteemed by Muhammad that he was given the Prophet's daughter Fatima in marriage. When Muhammad formulated his credo for the first time in the family circle and then asked: "Who among you will be my follower?" all were silent except young Ali, who, enthusiastic about what he had just heard, called out with determination: "I will, and shall never abandon you." Muhammad never forgot this show of loyalty. Ali was a brave, daring fighter and had a considerable share in the rapid spread of Islam. But when Muhammad died without having made any final disposition, Ali was passed over and Abu Bakr, the Prophet's father-in-law, was elected caliph.* In 634, Abu Bakr was replaced by a second father-in-law of the Prophet, called Umar, who was succeeded in turn by Uthman, a son-in-law of Muhammad. Uthman was stabbed to death in 656 by one of Abu Bakr's sons. Ali was accused of having instigated this murder, and when he was elected

---

* Caliph means successor.

caliph by his party, many refused him homage. For four years he fought for the caliphate, and he was stabbed to death in 660 by Abd ar-Rahman. He was buried in Kufa.

The division in Islam between the Sunnites and the Shiites originates here. It is due less to Muslim tenets than to the question of successorship in the caliphate. The Shiites maintain that only Ali, not Abu Bakr, Umar, or Uthman, was entitled to become the first caliph. The disputes concerning the attributes of God, Kismet, the eternity of the Koran, and retribution that subsequently erupted between the two parties are to be considered less important.

Ali left behind two sons, Hasan and Husein. The former was elected caliph by the Shiites, whereas the adherents of the Sunna chose Muawija I, the founder of the Umayyad dynasty. Muawija moved the seat of government to Damascus, made the caliphate hereditary, and, while still governing, enforced recognition of his son Yazid. Husein could not maintain himself against Muawija and was poisoned in Medina, in 670. His brother Husein refused to acknowledge Yazid and is the hero of one of the most tragic episodes in the history of Islam.

The hand of Caliph Muawija lay heavily on the provinces, and his governors supported him to the fullest possible extent. Thus Sijad, the governor of Basra, for example, issued the order that under penalty of death no one must be seen on the streets after sundown. The evening after this order was published, more than two hundred people were seized outside their dwellings and immediately beheaded. The following day the number was considerably smaller, and on the third evening no one was found outdoors after dark. The most tyrannical of all statesmen was the governor of Kufa, whose bloody rule cost 120,000 people their lives.

During the time Yazid was caliph, Husein was in Mecca, where messengers came to call on him to go to Kufa, where he would be recognized as caliph. He followed this call, and it proved his undoing.

With barely a hundred loyal followers, Husein came to the gates of Kufa only to discover that the city had already been occupied by his enemies. He began to negotiate but without success. His provisions ran out, the heat of the sun evaporated what water he had, his animals collapsed, and pale death stared from the sunken, feverish eyes of his companions. In vain Husein called on Allah and the Prophet for help and succor; his doom was "written in the Book." Ubaid Allah, one of Yazid's commanders, attacked him near Karbela, massacred his escort, and also had Husein killed. When the troops found him he was already close to death from thirst but was shown no compassion. After vainly trying to defend himself with what strength he still had, the unfortunate man had his head cut off; it was then placed on a lance and carried about in triumph.

This happened on the 10th Muharram,* which has remained a day of mourning for the Shiites down to our time. In Hindustan, an image of Husein's head is carried about on a lance, as was done after his death, and with a horseshoe of precious metal the sound of his horse's hooves is imitated. On the 10th Muharram there is wailing in Borneo and Celebes, India and Persia, and as far as western Asia, where the Shia has only scattered adherents. On that same day there takes place in Karbela a turbulent ceremony in which despair attains a pitch I have never seen equaled anywhere. Woe to the Sunnite, woe to the Giaour† discovered by the raging Shiites on that day and in that city! He would be torn to pieces.

This historical introduction may help the reader to better understand what follows.

Not without difficulties and some hardship, we had made our way into the northern Zagros Mountains.

It was evening, and we had camped along the edge of a wood of chinars. The sky above us was of a purity found only in these regions. We were close to the Persian border, and the air of that country is famous for its transparency. The stars were so bright that I could clearly see the hands of my pocket watch although

---

* The first month of the Muhammadan year.
† Infidel.

there was no moon in the sky. Even constellations which normally can be seen only through the telescope, such as the seventh star of the Pleiades, could be made out without effort. The clarity of such a starry sky makes a profound impression on the mind, and it became comprehensible to me that Persia should have been the home of astrology, that unfree mother of a noble daughter who familiarizes us with those shining worlds.

Our situation made it advisable to spend the night out in the open. During the course of the day we had bought a lamb from a shepherd, and we now lit a fire to roast the animal in the skin, having previously cleaned and shorn it.

The horses were grazing nearby. During the recent past, much had been demanded of them and they should really have been allowed several days' rest, but unfortunately this was impossible. We were all well except for the Englishman, who had every reason to be terribly vexed.

Some days previously Sir David Lindsay had been attacked by a fever which had lasted for about twenty-four hours. Then it had disappeared again, but not without leaving its mark, that horrible gift of the Orient called the Aleppo boil, which afflicts not only humans but certain animals such as dogs and cats. It is invariably ushered in by a short fever, after which a large boil forms either in the face, on the chest, or along arms and legs. It discharges a fluid, lasts for almost a whole year, and leaves a deep, permanent scar as the swelling subsides.

I had seen this disfiguring boil more than once, but Lindsay's was of uncommon size. Not only did it shine in darkest red, but it had also been so insolent as to choose the poor Englishman's nose, of all places, a nose which was of exceptional size as it was. He humbly put up with this bane but betrayed his annoyance and impatience by outbursts that provoked the surreptitious amusement of the rest of us. Just now he was sitting by the fire, touching the brazen boil with both hands.

"Sir," he said to me, "look here."

"Look where?"

"What a stupid question! At my face, where else? Has it grown some more?"

"Yes, it's starting to look like a cucumber. Do you feel pain?"

"No."

"You are lucky."

"How long will I be walking around like this?"

"Certainly no less than a year."

"But that's terrible. Are there no medications? Can't it be cut off?"

"There's nothing to be done."

"But surely there are remedies for every disease?"

"Not for this one. The boil is not at all dangerous, but if one makes an incision, it can become quite serious."

"Does it leave any traces once it's gone?"

"That varies. The larger the boil, the larger the hole that remains."

"Hole? But that means I'll have to stay in this miserable country until . . ."

"Sidi,"* Halef interrupted him. "Don't turn around!"

I was sitting with my back to the edge of the forest, and it was immediately clear to me that the little Hadji must have noticed something suspicious behind me.

"What do you see?" I whispered.

"A pair of eyes. There are two chinars directly behind you, and between them a wild pear. Inside that shrub is the man whose eyes I saw."

"Can you still see them?"

"Wait."

Halef observed the shrub without seeming to, and meanwhile I admonished the others to continue acting normally.

I got up, pretending that I wanted to pick some dry kindling along the edge of the forest. I walked some considerable distance away from the camp, then entered the forest and crept back between the trees. No more than five minutes had passed before I found myself behind the two chinars, and I now had occasion to admire Halef's keen eyes. Between the trees and be-

* Master.

hind the shrub, a human shape was cowering, observing the activity around the camp fire.

Why? We were in an area where no village could be found for miles in any direction. True, various Kurdish tribes that fought each other lived round about, and it sometimes happened that a Persian nomadic tribe would cross the frontier to rob and steal. Besides, there were survivors of tribes that had been annihilated who were looking for the opportunity to join another.

Because I had to be careful, I softly approached the man and then quickly seized him by the throat. He was so frightened that he stiffened. Nor did he resist when I picked him up and carried him to the fire. There I put him on the ground and pulled out my dagger.

"Don't move, or I'll run this through you," I threatened him. I did not really feel that fierce but the stranger took my words seriously and folded his hands in supplication. "Mercy, master."

"If you lie to me, you are doomed. The choice is yours. Who are you?"

"I am a Turkoman from the Bejat tribe."

A Turkoman? Here? Judging by his garments, he could have told the truth. And I knew that at an earlier time there had been Turkomans between the Tigris and the Persian border. It was also true that they had been of the Bejat tribe. Luristan had been the scene of their raids. When Nadir Shah invaded Baghdad province, he had forced the Bejat to move to Khurasan. Because of its situation and nature he had called that province the "sword of Persia" and made an effort to people it with brave and warlike inhabitants.

"A Bejat?" I asked. "You are lying."

"I am telling the truth, master."

"The Bejat do not live here but in distant Khurasan."

"That is true. But when they were compelled to leave this region, some remained behind, and their descendents multiplied to such an extent that they now number more than a thousand warriors. Our summer pastures are near the ruins of Kizil Kharaba and around Kurucay."

I remembered having heard mention of this. "And now you are somewhere nearby?"

"Yes, master."

"How many tents?"

"None."

This was odd. When a nomadic tribe leaves its camp without taking its tents along, that usually means that it is either engaged in pillaging or feuding.

"How many men are there?"

"Two hundred."

"And women?"

"We have none with us."

"Where is your camp?"

"Not far from here, just beyond the edge of the forest."

"Then you must have seen our fire."

"We did, and the Khan sent me to find out who was here."

"Where are you going?"

"Southeast."

"What is your destination?"

"The area around Sinneh."

"But that's in Persia!"

"Yes. Our friends are holding a large celebration there, and we are invited."

That was curious. These Bejat lived near Kifri. But that town lay far southwest of the place we were camping that day, while Sinneh was somewhat closer, and in a southeasterly direction. Why hadn't the Bejat gone directly from Kifri to Sinneh? Why had they made such a pointless detour?

"What are you doing up here, and why did you choose a route more than twice as long as necessary?"

"Because then we would have had to ride through the territory of the Pasha of Sulaimaniya, and he is our enemy."

"But he also controls this region."

"But the Pasha isn't looking for us up this way. He knows we moved away and believes we are south of his capital."

That sounded improbable, and I still did not really trust the man, but I told myself that the presence of these Bejat could only be of advantage to us. Under their protection we could get as far as Sinneh without hindrance, and after that we had no further dangers to fear.

Now the Turkoman asked: "Master, won't you let me go? I did you no harm."

"You merely did what you had been ordered to, and are free to leave."

He sighed with relief. "I thank you, master. Where are you going?"

"South."

"Are you coming from the north?"

"Yes, from the land of the Berwari and Chaldani."

"Then you are courageous and brave men. What is your tribe?"

"This man and I are emirs* from Frankistan, and the others are our friends."

"From Frankistan!—Would you like to join us?"

"Will your khan receive us hospitably?"

"He will. We know that the Franks are great warriors. Should I go and tell him about you?"

"Go and ask if he will receive us."

He rose and hurried off. The others approved of what I had done and Muhammad Emin especially was pleased about this encounter.

"Effendi,"† he said. "I have often heard about the Bejat. They constantly war against the Djerboa, the Obeide, and the Beni Lam, and will therefore be useful to us. But we should not tell them that we are Haddedihn; it's better they don't know."

"Quite apart from that, we should be cautious because we don't know yet whether the khan will receive us in a friendly manner. Go get your horses and keep your weapons handy. We must be prepared for any eventuality."

The Bejat seemed to be holding an unusually long council about us, for by the time we saw them again our lamb had been roasted and eaten. Finally we heard steps. The Turkoman we had spoken to earlier was coming back with three companions.

---

* Chieftains.
† Sir.

"Master," he said, "the khan has sent me. You are to join us, and will be welcome."

"Go ahead then, and show us the way."

We mounted our horses and followed, holding our rifles ready. Having come to the far side of the forest's edge, we saw no camp site, but after we had passed through a strip of densely growing shrubs, we reached an open area that was surrounded by bushes on all sides. A large fire was burning. The site had been well chosen, for it could not be easily spotted.

Some two hundred dark shapes were lying about in the grass, and off to one side, near the flickering flame, sat the khan, who slowly rose as we came into view. We rode up to him and jumped to the ground.

"Peace be with you," I greeted him.

"I am your servant," he answered, bowing.

He had spoken Persian, perhaps to prove to me that he really was a Bejat, whose principal tribe lives around Khorasan. The Persians are called the French of the Orient. Their language is supple and euphonious and has for that reason become the court language of most Asian princes. But the polite, flattering, and often servile manner of the Persians has never made a favorable impression on me; I have always preferred the straightforward, rough honesty of the Arabs.

The others had also jumped to their feet, and any number of hands were stretched out to take our horses from us. But because we did not yet know if their intent was hospitable or treacherous, we held on to the reins.

"You can turn your horses over to my men. They will see to them," the khan said.

But I wanted to be sure, and therefore asked him in Persian, "Are you assuring me that we are safe?"

He bowed his head in assent and raised his hand. "I swear it. Sit down here and let us talk."

The Bejat took the horses and only my mount, Rih, remained with Halef, who knew my preferences. We sat down with the khan. The flames were bright enough so that we could see each other clearly. The Bejat was a man of middle age and a warlike appearance. His face inspired confidence, and the respectful distance his men observed suggested that their leader did not lack confidence in himself.

"Do you know my name?" he asked.

"No, O Khan," I answered.

"I am Heider Mirlam,* nephew of the famous Hasan Kerkush Bey. Have you heard of him?"

"Yes. He lived near the village of Djenija, which lies on the postal road from Baghdad to Tauq. He was a brave warrior but loved peace, and he protected the forsaken."

The Bejat had told me his name, and politeness required that I give him ours. So I went on: "Your scout will have told you that I am a Frank. I am called Kara Ben Nemsi . . ."

Although he had learned to control himself, Heider Mirlam could not suppress an exclamation of surprise. "Oh! Kara Ben Nemsi! Then this other man with the red nose must be the bey from Inglistan who wants to look for stones and documents."

"Have you heard of us?"

"Yes, Effendi. You gave me only your name but I know almost all of you. The little man who is holding your horse is Hadji Halef Omar, a person whom a good many big men fear?"

"You guessed correctly."

"And who are the other two?"

"Friends of mine who wish to remain nameless. Who told you about us?"

"A leader of the Abu Hammed. I saw him near Kifri, and he told me that it was your doing that the tribe must pay tribute. Be careful, Effendi! You will be killed if you fall into the hands of these men."

"I have been in their hands and they did not kill me. They couldn't hold me."

"I heard. You killed the lion, by yourself and in darkness, and then rode off with its skin.† Do you think that I too would be unable to hold you if you were my prisoner?"

This sounded ominous, but I remained calm. "You

---

* Mirlam the Lion.
† For this episode, see the first volume in this series, *In the Desert.*—Trans. note.

would, nor do I know how you would go about taking me prisoner."

"Effendi, there are two hundred of us, and only five of you."

"Khan, do not forget that there are two Franks among those five, and that those two count for as much as two hundred Bejat."

"You speak with a great deal of assurance."

"And you are being inhospitable. Would you want me to doubt the truth of your word, Heider Mirlam?"

"You are my guests, although I do not know the names of those two men, who will share bread and meat with me."

He smiled considerately and the glance he cast at the two Haddedihn* told me all I needed to know. Because of his magnificent snow-white beard Muhammad Emin could be recognized among thousands.

The khan gestured, and bread, meat, and dates were served us on square pieces of leather. When we had eaten a little, we were given tobacco for our pipes, which the khan himself lit.

Now we could consider ourselves his guests, and I gestured to Halef to leave Rih with the rest of our horses. Having led the animal away, he rejoined us.

"What is your destination?" Heider Mirlam asked.

"We are riding to Baghdad," I answered cautiously.

"We are going to Sinneh," the khan told me. "Will you ride with us?"

"Will you permit it?"

"I would be pleased to see you among us. Give me your hand, Kara Ben Nemsi. My brothers shall be your brothers, and my enemies your enemies." He offered me his hand, and I took it. He did the same with the rest, who shared my delight at having found a friend and protector in this man.

---

* There are two members of the Haddedihn in the group: Muhammad Emin, already introduced in *In the Desert*, and his son, Amad el Ghandur. In a volume in this series that has not yet been translated, the latter is rescued from a Turkish prison, and it is in the course of subsequent travels through Kurdistan that Kara Ben Nemsi acquires the dog Dojan, which is frequently mentioned in the present volume.—Trans. note.

"What tribes will we run into between here and Sinneh?" I asked.

"This territory belongs to no one; various tribes come here to graze their herds. The one that is stronger stays."

"What tribe invited you,"

"The Djiaf."

"You should be pleased to have such friends, for the Djiaf are the most powerful tribe in this land. All others fear them."

"Effendi, have you been here before?" the khan asked, surprised.

"Don't forget that I am a Frank."

"Yes, the Franks know everything, even what they haven't seen. Have you also heard of the Bebbeh tribe?"

"I have. It is the richest one far and wide. Its villages and tents can be found in the environs of Sulaimaniya."

"Your information is correct. Do you have friends or enemies among them?"

"No. I have never encountered a Bebbeh."

"Although we would like to avoid an encounter, you may get to know them."

"Are you familiar with the road to Sinneh?"

"Yes."

"How far is it from here?"

"A good horse will take you there in three days."

"And how far to Sulaimaniya?"

"You can reach it in two days."

"When are you setting out tomorrow?"

"At sunrise. Would you like to rest now?"

"If it is agreeable to you."

"The will of the guest is law in this camp, and you are tired, for you have already put your pipe aside. The man with the boil is closing his eyes. I do not begrudge you your rest."

"The Bejat have pleasant manners. Permit us to spread our blankets."

"May God give you sleep."

Heider Mirlam gestured, and some rugs were brought for him to sleep on. My companions arranged themselves as best they could, but I attached my lasso to my horse's halter, tied the end around my waist, and then lay down somewhat farther away. The horse could pasture and nothing would happen to it, especially since Dojan was watching by my side.

Some time passed.

I had not yet closed my eyes when someone approached. It was the Englishman, who put his two blankets on the ground next to me.

"Fine friendship," he grumbled. "There I sit, without understanding a word, expecting you to explain. And then you take off."

"I am sorry, Sir David. I really did forget you."

"Are you blind, or am I not tall enough?"

"No, no, you are striking, all right, particularly with that boil on your face. What do you want to know?"

"Everything. What did you discuss with this sheik or khan?"

I told him.

"Well, that's good news, isn't it?"

"To be safe for three days is preferable to being without protection."

"So you told him we were going to Baghdad? Is that really your plan?"

"It's what I would prefer, but it's impossible."

"Why?"

"We have to get back to the Haddedihn, since your servants are still there. Besides, I am finding it difficult to part from Halef. At least I will not leave him until I know he is safe and sound and back with his young wife."

"I agree! Decent chap! Worth a thousand pounds. I wouldn't mind going back there myself."

"Why?"

"Because of the winged bulls."

"You'll also find antiquities in the vicinity of Baghdad, in the ruins of Hilla, for example."

"Well, let's go there, then."

"That cannot be decided at this time. The main thing for now is that we get safely to the Tigris. Then we'll see."

"All right then. Good night."

Lindsay didn't realize that we would find ourselves in that area earlier than and under circumstances wholly different from anything he envisaged that evening. He wrapped himself in his blankets and could soon be heard snoring loudly. I also fell asleep, though not before I had seen four of the Bejat mount their horses and ride off.

When I woke up, it was getting light and some of the Turkomans were already busy with their horses. Halef was also awake, and he too had noticed the four men riding off the evening before.

After reporting it he asked, "Sidi, why are the Bejat sending out messengers if their intentions toward us are good?"

"I don't think those four men left because of us. We are in the khan's power in any event. Don't concern yourself, Halef." I thought it likely that the men had been sent ahead because the area was dangerous, and this assumption was confirmed when I questioned Heider Mirlam.

After a frugal breakfast of a few dates, we set out. The khan had divided his men into a number of troops which followed each other at fifteen-minute intervals. He was a smart, cautious person who took what measures he could to ensure the safety of his men.

We did not stop until noon. When the sun was at its zenith we interrupted the ride to give the horses some necessary rest. So far we had encountered no one and had found markings at certain spots, on trees, bushes, or the ground, which the four scouts had left to indicate the direction we were to follow.

But this direction puzzled me. Sinneh had been southeast from yesterday's camp site but we had been riding almost straight south.

"Aren't you on your way to the Djiaf?" I asked the khan.

"Yes."

"And that nomadic tribe is camping around Sinneh at this moment?"

"Yes."

"But if we continue in this direction, we will never reach Sinneh but come to Baneh."

"Do you wish to travel safely, Effendi?"

"Of course."

"So do we. And for that reason it is advisable that we avoid hostile tribes. We shall have to continue riding briskly until tonight, and then we'll be able to rest. For tomorrow we shall have to wait until the route eastward is open." This explanation didn't make sense to me, but since I could not very well refute the reasons he advanced, I said nothing.

After a two-hour rest we set out again. We rode at a good clip and I noticed that Heider Mirlam frequently had us zigzag. Obviously there were a good many spots the scouts wanted to keep us away from.

Toward evening we had to pass through a depression or actually a defile. I was at the khan's side with the first troop. We had almost come to the end of this passage when we encountered a horseman whose dismayed expression told us that he had not expected to come upon strangers at this point.

He urged his horse to one side, lowered his lance, and greeted us: "Es-selam 'aleikum! Welcome!"

"We 'aleikum es selam," the khan answered. "What is your direction?"

"Into the forest. I am deer hunting."

"What is your tribe?"

"I am a Bebbeh."

"Do you have a home, or are you nomadic?"

"We stay in one place during the winter but take our herds to pasture in the summertime."

"Where do you live during the winter?"

"In Nwisgieh. You can reach it in an hour. My companions will welcome you."

"How many of you are there?"

"Forty, but there are more with the other herds."

"Give me your lance and your rifle."

"Why?" the man asked, astonished.

"And your knife. You are my prisoner."

"Mashallah!" This was an exclamation of terror, and at the same time the man's eyes flashed. He pulled his horse up and around and rode off at full speed.

"Catch me!" we heard the quick-witted Bebbeh shout.

The khan picked up his rifle and aimed at the fugitive. I had barely knocked the barrel to one side when the shot went off. The bullet missed. The khan raised his fist but immediately thought better of it.

"What are you doing, traitor?" he exclaimed angrily.

"I am no traitor," I replied calmly. "But I do not want you to have someone's blood on your hands."

"But that Bebbeh had to die! If he escapes it will cost us dearly."

"Will you spare his life if I bring him to you?"

"Yes. But you won't catch him."

"Wait and see!"

I took off after the fugitive, who could no longer be seen. But when I had the ravine behind me I spotted him. A plain with white crocus and dianthus lay before me, and beyond it the dark edge of a forest became visible. If I let the Bebbeh reach it, he would be gone for good.

"Rih," I called, placing my hand between the horse's ears. The worthy animal had not been in peak condition for some time, but at this sign he flew over the earth as if he had been resting for weeks. Inside two minutes I had come to within twenty horse lengths of the Bebbeh.

"Stop!" I called out.

The man had courage. Instead of continuing his flight, or waiting, he reversed course and came toward me. Another moment and we would collide. I saw him raise his lance and seized my carbine. He pulled his horse slightly to one side, and we rushed past each other. The point of his lance had been aimed at my chest; I parried, but immediately pulled my horse around. The man had changed direction and was trying to get away. His animal was too valuable for me to shoot it, and I therefore took the lasso from my hip, fastened it to the saddle button, and looped the untearable strap. The Bebbeh turned around and saw me come closer. Presumably he had never heard of a lasso and did not know what evasive action to take. He seemed to have lost confidence in his lance, for he now picked up his rifle, whose fire could not be deflected. I measured the distance, and as the man raised the barrel, the strap whirred through the air. I had barely moved the horse aside when I felt a tug. There was a loud shout. I stopped, and the Bebbeh was lying on the ground, his arms pressed against his body. A moment later I was standing by him.

"Did you hurt yourself?"

Under the circumstances, my question could only sound sarcastic. The prisoner was trying to get his arms free and was gnashing his teeth.

"Robber!"

"You are mistaken. I am no robber but I want you to ride with me."

"Where to?"

"To the khan of the Bejat whom you escaped."

"The Bejat? So the men I encountered are of that tribe? And the khan's name?"

"Heider Mirlam."

"Now I know everything. May Allah destroy you, you thieves and rascals!"

"Don't be abusive! I promise you by Allah that nothing will happen to you."

"I am in your hands and must follow you."

I took his knife from his belt and picked up the lance and rifle. I then loosened the strap and quickly mounted the horse to be prepared, but the Bebbeh did not seem to be contemplating flight. He whistled to his horse and swung himself on his back.

"I trust your word," he said.

We galloped back alongside each other and found the Bejat waiting for us at the end of the depression. When Heider Mirlam saw the prisoner his face lit up.

"You really caught him, Effendi!"

"Yes, as I promised. But I gave him my word that nothing would happen to him. Here are his weapons."

"Everything will be returned to him later, but tie him now so he can't escape."

This order was immediately complied with. Meanwhile the second of our troops had arrived and the prisoner was turned over to it with instructions to treat him well but guard him closely. Then the ride continued.

"How did you overpower him?" the khan asked.

"I captured him," I answered tersely, for his behavior annoyed me.

: 19 :

"Effendi, you are angry. But the time will come when you will understand that I must act in this way."

"I hope so."

"This man must not let anyone know that the Bejat are in this area."

"When will you let him go?"

"The moment it is no longer dangerous."

"Consider that he really belongs to me. I hope you will honor the word I gave."

"What would you do if I didn't?"

"I would simply . . ."

"Kill me?" Heider Mirlam interrupted.

"No. I am a Christian and will kill only in self-defense. I would therefore not kill you but I would cripple the hand you gave me to confirm your promise. The khan of the Bejat would then be like a boy who could no longer wield a knife or an old woman whose words are ignored."

"Effendi, if someone else were to say that to me I would laugh; but I do not doubt that you are the sort of people who would attack me though my warriors surround me."

"We certainly would. None of us fears your Bejat."

"Not even Muhammad Emin?" the Turkoman asked with a smile.

Our secret was out, but I answered with equanimity, "Not even he."

"And Amad el Ghandur, his son?"

"Have you ever heard him called a coward?"

"Never. Effendi, if you were not men, I would not have received you among us, for we are traveling dangerous paths. I hope no mishap will befall us."

Evening came, and just as it was getting dark and high time to set up camp, we came to a brook pouring forth from a labyrinth of rocks. The four Bejat who had preceded us were camped there. The khan dismounted and walked up to them, talking to them for some time in a soft voice. Why was he acting so secretively? Did Heider Mirlam plan something that only they were allowed to know?

Finally he ordered his men to dismount. One of the four walked ahead and into the rocky maze. We led the horses and after some time reached an open, circular space surrounded by rocks. This was the safest hiding place that could be found, but much too small for two hundred men and their horses.

"Are we staying here?" I asked.

"Yes."

"But not all of us?"

"Only forty. The rest will camp nearby."

This answer had to satisfy me, but I wondered why no fire was lit although the site seemed safe. The same thought occurred to my companions.

"Nice place," Lindsay commented. "Small area, wouldn't you say?"

"Right."

"But it's cold and damp here by the water. Why not make a fire?"

"I don't know. Perhaps there are hostile Kurds around."

"What of it? No one can see us. I don't like the looks of this." He cast a suspicious glance at the khan, who was talking to his men, obviously anxious not to be overheard by us.

I sat down by Muhammad Emin, who seemed to have been waiting for this opportunity, for he immediately asked me, "Effendi, how long will we be staying with these Bejat?"

"As long as you wish."

"If you agree, we will leave them tomorrow."

"Why, sheik?"

"A man who hides the truth is no friend."

"Do you think the khan is a liar?"

"No. But I think he is a man who does not tell everything that goes through his mind."

"Heider Mirlam recognized you."

"I know. I could tell by the expression in his eyes."

"Does that worry you, perhaps?"

"No. We are the Bejat's guests, and they will not betray us. But why did they take this Bebbeh prisoner?"

"So that he would not give away our presence."

"Why should it remain a secret, Effendi? What do two hundred armed men with good horses have to fear when they have neither women nor children, no sick or old people, no tents or herds with them? Where are we now, Kara Ben Nemsi?"

"In Bebbeh territory."

"And the khan wanted to visit the Djiaf. It certainly hasn't escaped me that we were riding straight south. Why is he setting up two camps? I fear that this Heider Mirlam has two tongues, although he is being honest with us. Which route will we take tomorrow when we separate from them?"

"The Zagros Mountains are to our left, and I believe we are close to the district capital of Baneh. Ahmedabad is next. Behind that city there is a pass which leads through lonely gorges and valleys to Kisildja. One comes to the Bistan River, which flows into the Karatscholan Su near Karatscholan and then, together with it, into the Little Sab. If we can reach the plain near Tauq from Ahmedabad or Kisildja, we will be safe. Of course that is a difficult route."

"How do you know?" the Haddedihn asked.

"When I was traveling to Baghdad to see you there, I spoke with a Bulbassi Kurd who described that area to me so clearly that I was able to make a small map. I did not believe I would have any use for it; still, I drew it in my diary."

"And you think it would be advisable to take that route?"

"I also listed other localities and their mountains and rivers, but I think that is the best way. Otherwise we could ride to Sinneh, but that would be a considerable detour."

"Then it's settled: we separate from the Bejat tomorrow, ride through Ahmedabad and to the Karatscholan Su from there. And you think your map will not mislead us?"

"Not unless the Bulbassi did."

"Let's rest then, and sleep. And let the Bejat do whatever they please."

We watered our horses at the brook and gave them fodder. Then the others lay down to rest while I went to see the khan.

"Heider Mirlam, where are the rest of the Bejat?"

"Nearby. Why are you asking?"

"Because the captured Bebbeh is with them, and I should like to see him."

"Why do you want to see him?"

"It is my duty. He is my prisoner."

"He is not your prisoner, but mine. You turned him over to me."

"Let's not quarrel about it. I want to see how he is."

"He is well. When Heider Mirlam says so, it is true. Do not worry about him, Effendi, but sit down by my side so we can smoke a pipe."

I accepted his invitation to avoid making him angry but soon left to settle down for the night. Why should I not see the Bebbeh? He was not being treated badly; the khan's word guaranteed that. But it was clear that Heider Mirlam had a motive I was not ingenious enough to discover. I decided to release the prisoner early the following day and at my own risk, and then to separate from the Bejat. Then I went to sleep.

# 2 : Allo the Charcoal Burner

Even a person used to riding becomes tired when he keeps it up from dawn to dusk, and I was no exception. I slept well and soundly and certainly would not have awakened before morning if the growling of my dog had not roused me. When I opened my eyes it was pitch dark. Nonetheless, I realized that a man was standing near me. I reached for my knife.

"Who are you?" This question also awakened my companions, who took their weapons in hand.

"Don't you know me, Effendi? I am one of the Bejat," was the answer.

"What do you want?"

"Effendi, help us! The Bebbeh escaped."

I jumped to my feet, as did the others. "When?"

"I don't know. We were sleeping."

"Ah! A hundred and sixty men guarded him, and he got away?"

"But they aren't here."

"The hundred and sixty are gone?"

"They will be back, Effendi."

"Where did they go?"

"I don't know."

"Where is the khan?"

"He left with them."

I grasped the man by the clothing. "Are you by chance plotting some roguery against us? You would regret it."

"Let me go, Effendi! How could we harm you? You are our guests."

"Halef, find out how many Bejat are still here."

The night was so dark that it was impossible to see the site. The little Hadji rushed off to do as I asked.

"Four of us are left," the Bejat immediately explained, "and one is on guard at the entrance. Over in the other camp there were ten of us to guard the prisoner."

"How did he get away? On foot?"

"No. He took his horse and some of our weapons."

"That shows how intelligent and vigilant you are! But why come to me?"

"Effendi, catch him again!"

I almost burst out laughing at this effrontery but let it pass. "So you don't know where the khan and the rest have gone?"

"We really don't."

"But there must have been a reason for his leaving?"

"There was, but we are not supposed to tell you."

"Very well. We'll see who's in command here now, the khan or me . . ."

Halef interrupted me to report that there really were only four Bejat left.

"They are standing over there listening to us, Sidi," he said.

"Let them. Are your pistols loaded, Hadji Halef Omar?"

"Did you ever see them empty?"

"Take one, and if this man fails to answer the question I will now ask him for the last time, shoot him in the head. You understand?"

"Don't worry, Sidi. He'll get two bullets, not just one." The little fellow took his pistols from his belt and cocked them.

I asked the Bejat once more: "Why did the khan leave?"

He did not keep me waiting: "To attack the Bebbeh."

"The Bebbeh? So Khan Heider Mirlam lied to me. He told me he was visiting the Djiaf."

"Effendi, Khan Heider Mirlam never lies. He does intend to visit the Djiaf but only after the attack has come off."

Now I remembered that the leader of the Turkomans had asked me whether I was a friend or an enemy of the Bebbeh. He had taken me under his protection but had also wanted to keep me in the dark.

"Are you at war with the Bebbeh?" I asked.

"They are at war with us, Effendi. And so we will take their herds, their rugs, and their weapons today. A hundred and fifty men will take the booty home, and the other fifty will ride to the Djiaf with the khan."

"If the Bebbeh let you," I added.

In spite of the darkness I noticed that the Turkoman raised his head proudly. "Those Bebbeh? They are cowards. Didn't you see that this man ran today when he saw us?"

"Yes, he was one against two hundred."

"And you captured him by yourself."

"What of it? If necessary, I could also catch ten Bejat! For example: you and those four, the post out there and the nine over in the other camp, all of you are my prisoners. Halef, guard the exit. You will shoot anyone who enters or leaves this area without my permission." My brave Hadji left immediately.

The Bejat said timidly, "Effendi, you are joking."

"I am not! The khan did not tell me the most important thing, and you only talked because I made you. So you will have to guarantee my safety here. Come over here, you four!"

They complied.

"Put your weapons down at my feet." And when they hesitated, I added, "You have heard about us. If your intentions are honest, nothing will happen to you and your weapons will be returned. But if you refuse to obey, no jinni or sheitan can help you."

They did what I had demanded. I turned their rifles over to my companions and instructed Muhammad Emin how to conduct himself. Then I left to follow the brook out into the open.

Outside I found the guard among the rocks. He recognized me immediately.

"Why are you posted here?" I asked.

"So that Heider Mirlam will know as he returns that nothing is amiss."

"Very well. Go in there and tell my companions that I will be back right away."

"I am not allowed to leave."

"The khan knows nothing about that."

"But he will find out."

"Perhaps. But I shall tell him that I ordered you."

The man left. I knew that the sheik of the Haddedin would seize and disarm him. I had not inquired about the location of the second camp, but during the course of the evening I had heard voices nearby and therefore believed I would find the place quickly, as I did. I heard a horse paw the earth, and when I went in that direction I found nine Bejat sitting on the ground. In the darkness they took me for one of their own.

One of them called out, "What did the Effendi say?"

"Here he is," I answered.

They recognized me and got to their feet. "Oh Effendi, help us," one of them begged. "The Bebbeh got away, and if he is missing, we will fare badly when the khan returns."

"How did he get away? Hadn't you tied him up?"

"The Kurd was trussed but he must have loosened his fetters gradually, and while we were sleeping he took his horse and some rifles and got away."

"Get your horses and follow me!"

They obeyed, and I took them to our camp site. Amad el Ghandur had lit a small fire to illuminate the surroundings. The guard had already been disarmed and was sitting with the other Bejat. The nine men I was bringing were so downcast over the Bebbeh's escape that they surrendered their knives and lances without protest. I explained to the fifteen Turkomans that they had nothing to fear from us unless the khan should decide to commit an act of treachery. And I added that I could not possibly recapture the fugitive Bebbeh.

To the extent that his limited knowledge of the language permitted, Lindsay had been apprised of these developments by Halef during my absence. Now he came up to me. "Sir, what are we going to do with these Bejat?"

"We won't know until the khan returns."

"But suppose they run away?"

"They won't be able to. We'll keep an eye on them, and I'll post Hadji Halef at the exit."

"There?" the Englishman asked, and pointed to the passage leading out into the open. When I nodded, he added, "That's not enough. There's a second exit over there."

I looked in the direction he indicated. By the light of the fire I could make out a tall boulder with a bush in front of it. "You are joking, Sir David," I said. "Who could get over that boulder? It's at least five meters high."

"Hm. You are a smart fellow. But David Lindsay is smarter."

"Explain what you mean."

"Walk over and look at the boulder and the bush."

"I can't; that would attract the attention of the Bejat to that exit if it really exists."

"It exists all right. What you see there is not a single boulder but two, and the bush is covering the narrow gap between them."

"That might be of great advantage to us. Do the Bejat know about it?"

"I don't think so. They paid no attention to me."

"Is the gap very narrow?"

"You can get through it on horseback."

"And what about the terrain on the other side?"

"I don't know. I couldn't see."

This was important enough for me to investigate immediately. I told my companions what I was about, and left the camp. Because of the darkness I had some trouble finding the place where the bush was standing between the two boulders. The gap it covered was about two meters wide, and while there was a good deal of rubble behind it, it would not be difficult to guide a horse through it by daylight.

Since I could not know what might happen, I used my knife to make some cuts in the branches so that the bush would fall apart when one rode through it. I was careful not to attract the attention of the Bejat camping on the far side, and returned when I was finished. Halef was told to immediately report any approach to the exit.

"What did you find, Effendi?" Muhammad Emin asked.

"A splendid way out, should we have to leave suddenly. I made some cuts in the bush, and the moment a horseman rides through there, the bush will come down and those behind will have no trouble getting through. There are some large boulders lying about, but during daylight it will not be difficult to find one's way through them."

"Do you think we'll use that path?" the sheik of the Haddedihn wanted to know.

"I sense it. Don't laugh, Muhammad Emin, but since my childhood I have had a sort of intuitive perception and often know things that are about to happen."

"I believe you. Allah is great, and we should heed his warning."

My disquiet affected my companions. Our conversation became halting and we lay there wordless until dawn. No sooner had it become possible to see some distance when Halef came rushing in to tell us that he had spotted a good many horsemen. But he could not tell their precise number.

I walked up to my stallion, took the binoculars from the saddle pouch, and followed Halef. Even with the naked eye one could distinguish a good many dark shapes out on the plain.

"Sidi, who are they?" Halef asked.

"The Bejat are returning with their loot and herding the cattle of the Bebbeh. It seems that the khan and a detachment are in front, so he'll be here before the others."

I returned to my companions and reported what I had seen. They shared my conviction that we had nothing to fear from the khan. All we could reproach him with was his failure to inform us of his plan, and we agreed to receive him cautiously but politely. Fully armed, I went back to Halef.

The khan and his troops were approaching at a gallop, and no more than five minutes had passed when he pulled up before me.

"Selam, Effendi," he greeted me. "You must have been surprised not to see me here when you woke. But I had some urgent business to attend to. And we were successful. Look out there!"

I looked him in the face instead. "You have stolen, Heider Mirlam!"

"Stolen?" He sounded amazed. "Does taking from one's enemies what one can make one a thief?"

"The Christians would say it does, and you know I am a Christian. But why did you keep this secret from us?"

"Because otherwise we would have become enemies. You would have left us and warned the Bebbeh."

"I would not have searched them out, nor did I know which camp or site you were going to attack. But if I had encountered a Bebbeh I would have advised him of the danger threatening him."

"You see, Effendi, I am right! I had only this choice: either I must keep our plan secret from you, or I had to take you prisoner and detain you by force until this was over. Since I am your friend, I chose silence."

"During the night I went to the camp where you had left ten of your men," I answered him.

"What did you want from them?"

"To make sure they would not run off."

"Allah! What for?"

"Because I found out that you had left. I did not know what danger might be in store, and so I took these men prisoner. They were to guarantee my safety."

"Effendi, you are very cautious, but you could have trusted me. What did you do to the Bebbeh?"

"Nothing. I didn't even see him; he had escaped."

The khan paled. "That cannot be! It may ruin everything! Let me at those dogs who slept instead of keeping watch!"

He jumped from his horse and rushed through the rubble toward the camp. Halef and I followed. Once among his men the khan raged like a wounded boar, kicked some and beat others, and would not calm down until he had exhausted himself. I would not have thought the man capable of such an outburst.

"Moderate your wrath, O Khan," I finally begged him. "You would have had to release this man in any event."

"And so I would have," he stormed, "but not today, for my plan must not be betrayed!"

"What is your plan?"

"We took everything from the Bebbeh we could lay our hands on. Now, the good will be separated from the bad. All that has value will be sent to our tribe by roundabout but safe routes. Everything of inferior quality will be taken by those of us who are visiting the Djiaf. Along the way we will leave it here and there, to put our pursuers on the wrong track. The Bebbeh will believe they were attacked by a troop of Djiaf, and my men and their booty will get back safely to the camps and villages of the Bejat."

I had to admit that the plan was cleverly conceived.

"But as matters stand, we will fail. The Bebbeh we captured belongs to the group we attacked. He knows we are Bejat and will tell all he has seen. He probably suspected what we intended to do. The Kurd has a good horse. Suppose he used it to inform his friends hereabouts while we were launching our attack?"

"That would be disastrous for you and for us as well, since the Bebbeh saw us here," I answered.

"He also knows our camp site, and it seems likely that the Bebbeh know the opening into these rocks."

Heider Mirlam had barely finished when someone called loudly from the entrance, "Allah! There they are! Take all of them alive!"

We turned and recognized the escaped Bebbeh, who was leaping toward me, his eyes flashing wrath. Behind him a large number of men were bursting onto the site and a wild howl went up at the same time.

Rifle shots were fired. We had not observed what had been going on outside the camp and had even forgotten to have the entrance guarded.

But now I had no time to reflect, for the Bebbeh, probably a khan or a sheik, was coming toward me. Like his men he carried neither lance nor rifle, but the curved Afghan dagger sparkled in his hand.

I received this bold adversary with my bare hands. With my left, I quickly clasped his right, and I placed my right arm around his neck.

"Die, thief," he panted as he put all his strength into the effort to free the hand that held the dagger.

"You are mistaken," I answered. "I am no Bejat! I did not know you were going to be attacked."

"You are a thief, a dog! You took me prisoner and will now be mine! I am Sheik Gasal Gaboga, whom no one ever eluded!"

Quick as lightning the recollection flashed through my mind that I had heard of this man as one of the most courageous of Kurds. I must not hesitate.

"Take me prisoner then, if you can," I answered.

As I said this I let go of him and stepped back. Apparently he took this for an act of surrender, for he shouted with joy and raised his arm for a dagger thrust. This was precisely what I wanted. I plunged my fist into his armpit with such force that he lost his balance. His body described a wide arc and crashed to the ground some six feet away. Before he could pick himself up, I hit his temple with my clenched hand and knocked him unconscious.

"Mount your horses and follow me," I ordered my friends.

I took in our situation at a single glance. Some twenty Bebbeh had penetrated into the rock-bounded area and were engaging the Bejat. Lindsay had been set upon by two Kurds and was just ridding himself of one of them by a blow with his rifle butt. The two Haddedihn were standing side by side, their backs to the rocks, keeping their enemies at a distance, while little Halef was kneeling on an enemy, pounding his head with the handle of his pistol.

"Sidi, let's not flee. We can deal with them," he said.

"There are more enemies outside. The Bejat have been attacked. Move, quickly!"

I seized Gasal Gaboga's dagger, to at least have some souvenir of this day which was beginning so inauspiciously, and jumped on my horse. To give him space for a running start and my friends room to breathe, I pulled the stallion up and drove him right among the Bebbeh. Here I made Rih kick in all directions until I saw that my companions were mounted. I then had him jump into the bush, which he pulled down with his hooves.

The moment I was past the rocks and could see that all four had escaped safely, I spurred my horse and galloped out into the open plain. The others followed.

I looked around briefly to see what had happened. Gasal Gaboga was an intelligent man. Instead of merely warning his troop, which would have been too weak to put up a successful fight, he had alerted the entire area, and while the Bejat were unsuspectingly returning to the camp with their booty, it had already been encircled on three sides. The thieves could consider themselves lucky if they saved their own skins.

There was no time to try to determine how the Bebbeh had succeeded in approaching the Bejat outside the rocks. To our left I noticed an extended line of horsemen galloping toward the battleground, and to our right the entire area as far as the horizon was covered with moving dots. Those also were horsemen.

"Forward, Effendi," Muhammad Emin shouted. "Otherwise the Bebbeh will surround us. Were you hurt?"

"No. And you?"

"A little scratch."

The sheik was bleeding from the cheek but the small gash was not dangerous.

"Come closer," I said. "We'll form a straight line. Anyone seeing us from the side will think we are a single rider."

We executed this ruse but could not mislead the Bebbeh behind us and soon became aware that we were being pursued by a sizable horde.

"Are they going to overtake us, Sidi?" Halef asked.

"It depends on their horses. What's wrong with your eye, Halef? Is it serious?" His eye had swollen, although only a few minutes had passed since the attack.

"It's nothing, Sidi." The little fellow brushed aside my concern. "That Bebbeh was five times as tall as I, and he got in a blow. But I can assure you that that was the last time."

"You don't mean you killed him?"

"No, I know you don't want that, Sidi."

I was pleased that we had not killed any of the enemy. Even from the point of view of pure self-interest, that was reassuring, for should we fall into their hands there would at least be no cause for a blood feud. We continued riding rapidly for about a quarter of an hour. The battleground had long since disappeared from view but the pursuers were still behind us. They were no longer riding in formation. Those with good horses had come much closer while the rest had fallen far behind. The six farthest out front would not lose sight of us even if we rode all day, for their horses were excellent. This meant we had to kill those animals. I explained this to the Haddedihn, dismounted, and took my hunting rifle in hand. I asked the men to hold their fire until they could be certain they would hit the horses and not the men.

The pursuers were rushing toward us and already within range when they realized our intent. Instead of scattering, they stopped.

"Fire!" Lindsay ordered.

Although the Haddedihn did not understand the English term, they knew what it meant. We opened up—Lindsay and I firing twice—and saw immediately that none of us had missed. The six horses and their riders were lying on the ground in a tangle.

Shortly after we had got back into the saddle, all the pursuers had fallen far behind, and after a while we were alone on the plain.

But that plain soon ended. Mountains were rising in front of us, and on both sides the hills were edging closer. We stopped involuntarily.

"Where to?" Muhammad Emin asked.

"Hm," I mumbled. Never in my life had I been as uncertain about what direction to follow.

"We have some time now and can wind the horses, so try to think, Effendi," Amad el Ghandur urged.

"I might ask you to do likewise," I sighed. "I am uncertain where we are, but it cannot be far from Beitush. If we continued in this direction, we would get to Sulaimaniya . . ."

"We won't take that route," Muhammad Emin interrupted.

"In that case the only choice is the pass we talked about last night. We can stick to this course until we come to the Berazeh River, which we shall have to follow upstream for a day if we want to get into the mountains beyond Baneh."

"I am for that," Muhammad Emin said.

"That river has another advantage for us. It is the dividing line between Persia and the Ejalet, which means that we can cross and recross as our safety dictates."

We continued in a southerly direction. The terrain gradually rose, with valleys and mountains alternating more rapidly. By late afternoon we had penterated far into the mountains, and on a lonely, densely wooded height we came to a small hut. Smoke was rising from an opening in its roof. I dismounted and walked toward it. It was built of stones, the cracks between them packed with moss. The roof consisted of several dense layers of branches and the entrance was so low that a child would have had trouble getting in and out.

When my steps could be heard inside this simple structure, there appeared at the door the head of an animal I took to be a bear. But the voice of this hairy beast soon convinced me that it was a dog. Then a piercing whistling sound came from inside, and a second head came into view, though I could not tell immediately what sort of animal it belonged to. I saw nothing but a tangle of hair, a profoundly black, broad nose, and two flashing eyes that resembled those of an angry jackal.

"Good evening," I said.

The answer was a deep rumble.

"Do you live here alone?"

The rumble descended a few notes.

"Are there any other huts nearby?"

Now the rumbling became truly terrible, and the point of a spear appeared. It was being pushed forward, close to my chest.

"Come on out," I said politely.

Although this seemed hardly possible, the rumbling became deeper still, and now the point of the weapon was aimed at my throat. This was too much. I took hold of the spear and pulled. The mysterious inhabitant of the hut held on, but, not being as strong as I, he was pulled out of the entrance. First the tangled hair and the black, shiny nose, then two hands of the same color, with broad claws, a sack full of holes like those used by charcoal burners, two greasy leather sheaths, and finally two objects which I could never have identified had it not been for their contours, by which I immediately recognized them for the boots the Colossus of Rhodes must once have worn.

The moment these boots had cleared the door, the being straightened up and the dog also had room enough to show its full size. Like its master, the animal was incredibly shaggy, so that one could see nothing but a black nose and two eyes. Both creatures seemed afraid of me.

"Who are you?" I asked roughly.

"Allo," the creature mumbled.

"What are you?"

"A charcoal burner."

So this was the simple explanation for the black nose and hands. I saw that my severity was making an impression. The man was cowering and the dog had put its tail between its legs.

"Anyone else living hereabouts?" I asked.

"No."

"How far does one have to walk to find human beings?"

"More than a day."

"For whom do you make charcoal?"

"For the man who makes iron."

"Where does he live?"

"In Baneh."

"Are you a Kurd?"

"Yes."

"A Djiaf?"

"No."

"A Bebbeh?"

"No." As he gave this answer he cleared his throat and spat aggressively. I must confess that in the circumstances in which I found myself, this expression of sentiment had my hearty approval.

"What tribe do you belong to?"

"I am a Bannah."

"Look over there, Allo! Do you see those four horsemen?" He brushed the long strands of shaggy hair from his eyes to be able to see more clearly. In spite of the covering of coal dust on his skin, I noticed an expression of great fear in his face.

"Are they Kurds?" he asked worriedly.

Apparently I had got him to a point where he was talking freely. When I told him no, he went on, "What are they?"

"Three Arabs and two Christians."

He looked at me wide-eyed.

"Christians? What's that?"

"I'll explain later. We'll spend the night at your place."

Now the charcoal burner became even more frightened. "Don't do that, master."

"Why not?"

"There are evil spirits in the mountains."

"All the better. We've always wanted to meet spirits."

"And it rains at times."

"The water won't do us any harm."

"And occasionally there is thunder."

"That's part of things."

"There are bears around."

"We like eating bear meat."

"Robbers often roam these mountains."

"We'll shoot them dead."

When the Kurd realized that none of these subterfuges did any good, he told me frankly: "I am afraid of you."

"There is no need. We are no robbers. We want to sleep near your house and will move on tomorrow. We'll give you a silver piaster if you permit it."

"A silver piaster? A whole piaster?"

"Yes, perhaps even two if you are friendly."

"I am very friendly, master."

He was beaming, clapping his hands with delight. And this feeling seemed to be contagious, for his dog raised its tail and wagged it bashfully, playfully offering its paw to my Dojan, who paid as little attention to him as a mogul does to an urchin.

"Are you familiar with these mountains?"

"Oh, yes."

"Do you know the Berazeh River?"

"Yes, that's the border."

"How long does it take you to walk there?"

"Half a day."

"Do you know Baneh?"

"I go there twice a year."

"But you probably don't know where Bistan is?"

"I do; my brother lives there."

"Do you have to work every day?"

"I work when I feel like it," Allo stated proudly.

"Then you can leave whenever you like?"

"Why are you asking?"

This Stone Age man was a cautious fellow and I liked him for it. "I'll tell you why I ask. We are strangers here and don't know the paths through the mountains. So we need an honest man to be our guide. We'll pay two piasters a day."

"You will? I make ten piasters a year, and flour and salt. Do you want me to guide you?"

"We must get to know you first. If we like what we see, you'll make more money than you normally make in a year."

"Call those men here. I'll give them flour and salt and a pot for baking. I also have all the game you may want, and your horses will get as much grass as they can eat. There is a spring up there, and the ground you sleep on will be as soft as a divan."

I signaled to my companions, whose patience had been severely tested by our extended conversation. They marveled no less at the appearance of the charcoal burner than I had, and Lindsay was speechless. But the Bannah paid him back in kind, admiring Sir David's nose with a frankness that left nothing to be desired.

Finally the Englishman recovered his speech. "What the devil," he said. "Is that a gorilla?"

"No, he's a Kurd from the Bannah tribe."

"Oh dear," and, turning to Allo, he shouted: "Go and wash!" But since the poor fellow understood no English, the coal dust stayed where it was.

Meanwhile the horses had been tethered and blankets spread out on the moss. We sat down and I told Muhammad Emin about this man who would be our guide. Allo hauled a bag of coarse flour from the hut and brought us a clay vessel filled with salt. Then he opened a small rock-lined pit behind the house which contained his provisions of meat—two rabbits and part of a deer. We chose the latter, which was thoroughly washed. Then we made a fire, and while Halef watered the horses and the Kurd used his long knife to cut fodder for them, I spent my time turning an improvised spit.

When I started carving the roast, Allo was standing at the corner of his little hut, longingly licking the soot from his fingers.

"Come, Allo, join us," I invited him. In an instant he was by my side. I felt certain that from this moment on we would be the best of friends.

"How much is your deer?" I asked him.

"Master, I'll make you a present of it. I'll catch another."

"I'll pay you nonetheless. Take this."

I reached into the hidden compartment in my belt and took out two piasters for him.

"Oh, master, your soul is full of compassion. Won't you also roast the rabbits?

"We'll take them along tomorrow."

Lying near the hut was a large pile of foliage which the Kurd now dragged over to prepare a place for us to sleep. Using our blankets, he did such a fine job that the next morning we felt we had not slept as well for a long time.

Before setting out, each of us had a piece of the

remaining venison. Since the Haddedihn had agreed to our taking the Kurd along as our guide, I began questioning him once more.

"Have you ever heard of Ahmed Kulwan on the Karatsdolan Su?"

"I have been there."

"How far is it?"

"Do you wish to see many villages, or few?"

"We want to stay out of people's way."

"Then you'll need six days."

"Describe the route."

"From here you walk to the Berosieh and up the river to near Baneh. Then you cross and turn south until you reach Ahmedabad. Then, you take the pass through the mountains which will get you to Kisildja and Ahmed Kulwan."

I was pleased to note that this was the route I had marked down. The Bulbassi Kurd who had described this area for me had been an accurate reporter.

"Can you take us all the way?"

"Master, I can take you to the plain this side of Baghdad."

"How did you get to know those routes?"

"I was a guide for the merchants who come into the mountains with their wares and return when they are sold. In those days I was not yet a charcoal burner."

In spite of his filth, this man was a real find. He seemed a little dense but of an honest, loyal nature. So I decided to conclude an agreement with him. "You will take us to the plain, but not to the south but the west, and will receive two piasters a day. If you serve us faithfully we will also buy you a horse and make you a present of it when we separate. Is that all right.?"

A horse! This was enormous wealth for a poor Kurd. He took my hand and pressed it fervently to his beard. "Oh, master! Your amiability is greater than these mountains. May I take my dog along, and will you feed it?"

"Yes. We can shoot all the deer we need."

"I thank you. I have no rifle; when I want deer I must trap it. When will you buy me the horse?"

"As soon as possible."

Since the Kurd had salt, I told him to bring a supply of it along. How precious salt is one discovers only when one has to do without it for months at a time. For most Bedouins and many Kurds it is a rare luxury. Allo quickly made his preparations. He hid his flour and salt in the pit, took his knife and his horrendous spear, and put his dog on a leash that he roped around his hips. He had nothing to cover his head.

We set out on this journey with renewed confidence in our good luck. Our guide led us south until we reached the Berosieh river toward noon. Here we rested and bathed. Fortunately I was able to persuade Allo to do likewise. For soap he used the abundant sand, and he was a changed person when he left the beneficent waves.

We now took a southeasterly direction, but we had to make many detours to bypass the frequent settlements and shepherds' camps along the river. We spent the night on the bank of a stream which came flowing down the mountain to our right on its course toward the Berazeh.

The next morning we had hardly been riding for an hour when the Kurd stopped and reminded me of my promise to buy him a horse. He told me that an acquaintance of his was living nearby who had a horse for sale.

"Does he live in a large village?" I asked.

"There are just four houses."

I was glad to hear this, for I was anxious to attract as little attention as possible. Yet I could not let the Kurd go by himself, since I was not yet sure he would hold his tongue.

"How old is this horse?"

"It's still young. Fifteen, perhaps."

"Very well. We'll both go and inspect it, and the others will wait. Try to find a place where no one can spot them."

A quarter of an hour later we saw some houses down by the river.

"This is the village, Allo said. "Wait here, I'll hide your friends." He took them a little farther but returned in just a few moments.

"Where are they?"

"In a thicket where no one will pass."

"Don't tell those people down there who I am or where we are going, or that four men are waiting for us here."

"I won't say a word; don't worry."

I started down the slope and soon we found ourselves in front of a house with a number of pack saddles and riding saddles hanging under its projecting roof. There was a fenced-in pasture behind the house where a few horses were jumping about. An old, emaciated Kurd came toward us.

"Is it you, Allo?" he asked, surprised. "May the Prophet bless your coming and all your paths." And he added softly: "Who is this lord?"

Allo was intelligent enough to answer as I would have wanted him to. "This lord is an effendi from Kerkuk who wants to go to Kelekowa, where he will meet the pasha from Sinneh. I know the route, so I am to be his guide. Do you still have the horse that is for sale?"

"Yes," the man said as he eyed Rih admiringly. "It is behind the house. Come."

Because I did not want to leave the two, I quickly dismounted and followed. The animal in question was not one of the worst. I did not think it was as old as Allo had said, and since there were some other horses which seemed to be worth less, I wondered why precisely this one was for sale.

"How much is it?" I asked.

"Two hundred piasters."

"Put it through its paces."

He pulled the horse from behind the fence and had it walk, trot, and gallop. This aroused my suspicions, for it looked to be worth more than the price he had asked.

"Put the pack saddle and some weight on it."

He did, and the horse obeyed every command.

"Is there anything wrong with it?"

"Nothing at all," the old man assured me.

"It does have a flaw, and it would be better if you told me. This horse is for your friend Allo, and you wouldn't want to cheat him."

"I am not cheating him."

"Very well, then I'll try to discover what's wrong. Take off the pack and put on a riding saddle."

"Why, Effendi?"

"Because that's what I want," I said curtly.

He obeyed, and I asked him to get into the saddle.

"I can't, master," he excused himself. "I have rheumatism in my legs."

"Then I will try it myself."

I could tell from looking at the Kurd that I was about to discover the flaw. The horse let me approach, but the moment I raised my foot to place it in the stirrup, it moved to one side. I did not manage to get into the saddle until I had forced the animal close to the wall of the building. Now I swung myself on its back, but it immediately raised its hind legs so that I almost turned a somersault over its neck. Then it raised its front legs, bucking and jumping about so wildly that I took the first opportunity to jump down. Intentionally I did it in such a way that I fell to the ground as if I had been thrown.

"This horse isn't worth a para, much less two hundred piasters," I scolded. "No one can ride it. It has been ruined."

"Master, it is a good horse. Perhaps it simply doesn't like you."

"No, a bad rider has made it suffer, and an animal remembers that. Who is going to ride it now? It's no good except as a pack horse."

"Don't you need a pack horse?"

"No. Not until later."

"Then why not buy this one? You may not find one when you need it."

"Am I to burden myself with a nag that will only get in my way now?"

"I'll let you have it for a hundred and fifty."

"I'll give you a hundred, and not one para more."

"You are joking."

"Keep it, then! I'll find another in Baneh. Come along, Allo!"

I mounted Rih and the charcoal burner followed me, downcast. We had barely gone fifty paces when we heard the man call out to us: "Give me a hundred and thirty, master!"

I did not answer.

"A hundred and twenty!"

I rode on without looking back.

"Come back, master! I'll let you have it for one hundred."

I stopped and asked him if he also had a riding saddle and a blanket. When he told me he did, I rode back and bought a tolerable saddle and blanket for forty piasters. After I had paid him I saddled and bridled the horse and bade him farewell.

"We are leaving now. You were about to cheat your friend, but you will discover in a moment that he got this horse for a third of its value." The man did not answer but only smiled condescendingly. Allo also said goodbye to him and was about to mount the animal. His hairy face was shining with pleasure and joy at the thought that he would now be riding around on a horse, but the Kurd took him by the arm.

"Whatever you do, don't try to get on it! It will throw you and you'll break your neck."

"The man is right," I agreed. "Go get on my horse, it will carry you safely. I'll mount this one and show it that it must obey."

Absolutely delighted, Allo climbed on the back of my stallion, who put up with this indignity because he knew I was close by. For my part, I pushed the nag toward the wall and got into the saddle. Again the horse reared. For a few moments, I gave it its head but then tightened the reins and squeezed it. The horse was about to raise its front legs but no longer had the strength. It merely managed a few spasmodic movements and then became winded, with sweat coming from all its pores and foam dripping from its mouth in large flakes. Although I eased up, the animal stood still.

"The horse has been tamed," I said laughing. "Just wait and see how well it will obey, and don't try taking advantage of a friend again. May Allah be with you!"

I rode on and Rih followed the nag with noble modesty.

"Master," the charcoal burner asked, "is this stallion mine now?"

What a question! "No," I said, smiling.

"Why not?"

"Because he would throw you the minute I am no longer close. By tomorrow your horse will have become docile."

We came to the thicket where my companions had been hiding. Except for Halef, all were content with the bargain I had made.

"Sidi," Halef grumbled, "Allah will never forgive you for having Rih carry such a toad. Let the charcoal burner ride my horse and I'll take Rih."

"Let him be, Halef. Allo would be offended."

In the afternoon we came close to Baneh and crossed the Berazeh. Then we turned south. Later the pass opened ahead of us. Because the pathless heights had been a considerable strain for our horses, we wanted to rest them earlier than usual and pulled into a small but deep valley off to one side of the pass. Its sides were covered with densely growing small oaks. We had killed a deer, and after we ate we drew lots to establish the order in which we would stand guard. Here, near the pass, we felt that this precaution was especially necessary; news of the theft of the herd had certainly reached Baneh by now, and it could be assumed that we would also have been mentioned.

The night passed without disturbance, and as the day was dawning we entered the pass. We had chosen this time to be completely unobserved. Our way took us over bare heights and rock-strewn stretches, dark ravines and secluded valleys with hardly any water in them. One could see and sense quite clearly that this was soil no European had ever set foot on.

Toward noon we had to cut across a valley. Just as we had reached the far side, Dojan stopped and looked at me beseechingly. I knew his manner: he had noticed something suspicious and was asking permission to ferret it out. I had everyone stop and looked around but could see no trace of a living soul.

"Go, Dojan!" I called out, and the dog jumped into the bushes. A moment later, we heard a scream and then that brief sound which told me Dojan was standing over a human being.

"Halef, come along!"

We jumped off our horses and followed the dog. By the side of a growth that looked like a wild rose bush a man was lying on the ground, a rifle by his side. The dog was standing over him, his teeth on the throat of his startled quarry.

"Back, Dojan!" The dog moved away and the man got to his feet.

"Who are you?" I began interrogating him.

"I live in Suta," he answered timidly.

"Are you a Bebbeh?"

"No, master. We are enemies of the Bebbeh. I am a Djiaf."

"Where are you coming from?"

"From Ahmed Kulwan."

"That's quite some distance. What did you do there?"

"I tend the herds of the local magistrate."

"Where are you going?"

"To see my friends in Suta. The Djiaf are having an important celebration and we want to join them."

This was true. "Did the Djiaf invite guests?"

"I've heard that Khan Heider Mirlam is coming with his Bejat."

That was also true. The man did not seem to be a liar. "Why were you hiding from us?"

"Master, doesn't a person who is by himself have to hide when he sees six horsemen? Here in these mountains one never knows whether one is dealing with friends or enemies."

"Are you really alone here?"

"Absolutely, by the beard of the Prophet!"

"I'll take your word for it. Move!"

We returned to our companions, where he had to repeat what he had told me. They agreed with me that the man was not dangerous. His rifle was returned to him and he was given permission to resume his march. After he had thanked us and invoked Allah's blessings, we continued our interrupted ride.

I had noticed that Allo had observed the stranger thoughtfully and was still sitting pensively on the stallion. I was about to ask him what he was pondering when he looked up like someone who finally recollects something. He quickly came over to me.

"Master, this man lied to you! I knew him but had forgotten who he is. It's just come back to me. He is no Djiaf but a Bebbeh, and he must be a brother or a relative of Sheik Gasal Gaboga. I have seen both of them in Nwisgieh."

"I hope not! Are you sure you aren't mistaken?"

"Perhaps, but I don't think so."

I told the others what the charcoal burner had said, and added, I'm almost tempted to ride after the man."

But Muhammad Emin dismissed this idea. "Why waste time and turn back? If this fellow really were a Bebbeh, how could he know that Heider Mirlam was invited by the Djiaf? Things like that are kept secret from the enemy."

"Besides," Amad el Ghandur added, "what harm could he do us? He is going north, we are going south. Even if he told someone about us in Baneh, they would not be able to catch up with us."

These were persuasive reasons and I decided against turning back. Only the Englishman seemed dissatisfied.

"Why did you let that fellow go?" he asked angrily when I had explained things to him. "I would have shot the scoundrel. Would have been no great loss! Every Kurd is a rascal, no doubt about it!"

Some time later Lindsay reminded us that it was time for our noon rest. He was right. In spite of the bad road we had covered a fair distance, so we need not begrudge ourselves and the horses a well-deserved break. We found a suitable spot, dismounted, and went to sleep for a short while after posting a guard.

# 3 : A Surprise Attack

When we were awakened the horses were rested. I decided to see if the newly acquired animal would let the charcoal burner mount it. It did. It must have realized that we would not torment it. I could get back on my Rih, and this was fortunate, as I was soon to discover.

The heights, bare before, were now becoming increasingly wooded as we rode south where water was more plentiful. As a result our ride became more difficult. There was no road, properly speaking. At times there were steep hills to climb and descend again, at others we had to go between rocks, across swampy soil, or among half-rotten trees. Toward afternoon we entered a narrow valley which had a single meadow-like strip along its center and was otherwise bare except for an abundance of trees on either side. In the distance a tall mountain rose in a bluish haze. Together with its foothills, it looked as if it were blocking our path.

"Are we going to be able to get past that?" I asked Allo.

"Yes, master. We'll pass along its foot to the left."

"What's the fellow saying?" Lindsay asked.

"That our route goes past the foot of the mountain on the left."

"No need for us to be told that," he grumbled.

But the Englishman was soon to discover that our guide's remark was of the greatest imaginable importance to him, for I had barely opened my mouth to answer when a great number of shots was fired from both sides and more than fifty horsemen came galloping from under the trees on either side to surround us.

What an unpleasant surprise! My companions' horses had been hit, though not mine. This was intentional, as I was to hear later. The riders tried to get free of their stirrups and reach for their weapons. In a trice we were surrounded on all sides, and a rider was making straight for me. I recognized him: it was Sheik Gasal Gaboga. Only our horses had been shot at; we were to be taken alive. I therefore left the carbine dangling and reached for my hunting rifle.

"Worm, I have you now!" the sheik called out. "You won't escape me this time!" He raised his club to strike me down, but at the same moment Dojan leaped up and plunged his teeth into the enemy's upper thigh. The sheik uttered a scream of pain and the blow that had been intended for me hit the head of my horse instead. Rih neighed loudly and jumped into the air with all four feet. I had just enough time to bring my rifle butt down on the Bebbeh's shoulder before he dashed away, his pain making him deaf to my commands.

"Dojan!" I called back, for I did not want to lose that good animal, and a moment later a large number of lances were pointed at me. I swept them aside with my rifle, and that was all I knew. But as long as I live I shall never forget the ride that followed. No ditch was too deep, no boulder too tall, no crack too wide, no rock too smooth, and no swamp too dangerous. Everything—trees, shrubs, rocks, mountain, and valley—flew past me until I gradually regained control over the enraged horse. Then I found myself alone, in unknown territory. All I had been able to remember was the direction from which I had come, and the tall mountain we had been speaking of a short while before lay straight ahead.

What to do? Should I help my friends? That was impossible. It could be expected that the Bebbeh would now set out in pursuit of me. And how, I wondered, had they managed to penetrate the mountains this far? How had they discovered that we would follow this route? It was a mystery. For the time being there was nothing I could do for my companions. They were either dead or prisoners. Above all I had to stay in hiding and wait until tomorrow to see how the fight had developed. Only then would I be able to decide on a course of action.

First I examined Rih's head. There was a large bump. I led the animal to a nearby stream. Here I bandaged him as a mother would a sick child. Perhaps a quarter of an hour had passed when I heard a distant noise. It was a panting and snorting as if someone were running out of breath, and the next moment something came dashing toward me, uttered a loud howl of joy, and jumped at me with such vehemence that I fell over into the grass.

"Dojan!"

The dog was howling and whining, his joy irrepressible. Now he would jump at me, now at the horse. I could do nothing but let this outburst take its course until, gradually, he calmed down. He had received no injury whatever.

The intelligent animal soon seemed to understand why I was paying attention to the horse, for after he had watched me for a while he stood up on his hind legs and began carefully licking the bump. Rih suffered this quietly and even snorted amiably from time to time.

It was a long time before I thought it advisable to move on. Undoubtedly it would be best to make for the foot of the mountain the charcoal burner had spoken of, and so I got back in the saddle and rode the short distance toward that point.

The sides of the mountain were covered with dense forest. Only down in the valley through which our route would have taken us was there enough space to move freely. I noticed that the forest projected at one point and that the place would afford a view of anyone that might approach. I rode toward it and, having reached it, dismounted, my first concern being to find a secure hiding place for the horse. I had barely taken a few steps into the trees when Dojan gave me the familiar signal to indicate that he was scenting something suspicious. The situation was too precarious to leave him to his own devices. I therefore took him by the leash, tied Rih to a tree, and followed the dog, my rifle at the ready.

I seemed to be moving too slowly, for Dojan was tugging so vigorously that the leash threatened to break. Then, between two tall pines, he started barking. Several ferns were standing there close to each other, and as I thrust them apart with my carbine, I noticed a hole of about half a meter in diameter that had been dug into the ground at an angle.

Could there be an animal inside? Probably not. As I thrust the carbine into it, it felt as if it had encountered a body. Dojan's manner made clear that this could not be an enemy. I motioned to him to crawl inside but he refused, wagging his tail instead, and looking expectantly at the hole.

Without further ado, I stuck my hand inside and got hold of a very hairy head. The mystery was solved. It was the charcoal burner's dog that had hidden there. Presumably the animal had fled when it heard the shots, and its fear had led it to this spot.

"Eisa!" I called, for I had noticed that Allo used this name.

But all remained quiet, and not until I had repeated my call did I hear a cheerful grunt, and now Allo gradually emerged. What a pleasant surprise! If this man had escaped unscathed, the others might also have succeeded.

"Allo, what are you doing here? Where is your dog?"

"Crushed to death, master," he answered sadly.

"How did you get away?"

"When they were all pursuing you, no one paid any attention to me, and I jumped into the bushes. Then I came here because I had told you that we would have to pass this way. I thought you would come here if the Bebbeh did not find you."

"Who else got away?"

"I don't know."

"We will have to wait here and see if any of the rest make their way here. Find a hiding place for my horse."

"I know of a very good one, master."

"Then you must have been here before."

"I have burned charcoal here. Follow me, and bring the horse along!"

Allo led me up into the forest. After about a quarter of an hour we came to a rock wall covered by long, thick brambles. Pushing them aside at one place, he disclosed an opening large enough to accommodate a horse.

"This is where I lived at that time," he explained. "Tether the horse inside there. I'll cut him some fodder."

Inside the crevice several stakes had been driven into the ground. Perhaps they had served as table legs at an earlier time. I tethered the horse to one of them so he could not leave the hiding place. Outside, the Kurd was cutting grass.

"Go down there to the edge of the forest, master," he asked me. "One of our companions might arrive. I'll follow as soon as I have finished."

I took his advice and chose a spot where I could observe without being seen. Allo joined me a few minutes later.

"Is the horse safe?" I asked, and when he told me it was, I added, "Are you hungry?"

An uncertain grunt was the answer.

"I have nothing, unfortunately. We shall have to be patient until tomorrow morning."

Allo grunted again, and then said more distinctly, "Master, will I also get my two piasters for today?"

"You'll get four!"

Night came, and as the light of day was about to fade I had the impression that on the far side of the narrow clearing, to our left, a figure was skipping past the trees. Although it was getting dark, I had seen this so clearly that I got up to make sure. The Kurd was instructed to stay with my rifles, which would have encumbered me. I took the dog by the leash and crawled forward.

I had to pass the deep cut the clearing made, and had not yet covered half the distance when I saw the same figure dashing across the open space. A few quick leaps brought me to the point it had to pass. Now it emerged within reach. I was about to stretch out my hands when Dojan prevented me, barking joyfully. The shape heard him and stopped.

"Who's there?" Two long arms came toward me.

"Sir David! Is it really you?" I exclaimed.

"Ah yes. It's me all right." Lindsay was overcome with joy, and so surprised that he disconcerted me a little, for he embraced me, clasped me to his breast, and tried to kiss me although his infected nose got in the way.

"I would never have thought I'd run into you here, Sir David."

"Why not? The gorilla—no, I mean, the charcoal burner said we would have to come this way."

"You see how providential that was. But tell me how you saved your skin."

"Things went quickly. My horse was shot from under me, I worked myself free, saw that they were all after you, and jumped off to one side."

"That's exactly what Allo did."

"Is he here too?"

"He's sitting over there. Come along."

I took the Englishman to our observation post. The Kurd was very pleased to see another of his companions safe.

"How did you fare?" Lindsay asked me.

I told him.

"And Rih wasn't injured?"

"Nothing except for the bump on his head."

"My horse is dead. Poor animal! I'll shoot these Bebbeh, all of them, depend on it!"

"Then you still have your rifle?"

"My rifle? Do you think I'd abandon that to them? It's lying over there."

"So you have every reason to be pleased. It would have been irreplaceable."

"And I also have my knife, revolver, and cartridges in my belt."

"What luck! But you have no idea if any of the others got away?"

"No one did. Halef was lying under his horse, and the Haddedihn were surrounded by the Bebbeh."

"Then all three are lost."

"Let's wait and see, Kara Ben Nemsi. Allah Akbar— God is great, as the true believer says."

"You are right, Sir David. Let's hope for the best. And if we should be mistaken, we have to do everything in our power to free them."

"Quite! But now I want to sleep. I am tired, I had to do a lot of running. And there's no blanket! Miserable Bebbeh! Miserable country!"

Lindsay and the Kurd fell asleep, but I stayed awake for a long time and later laboriously climbed the height to look after my horse. Only then did I try to get some rest, leaving the faithful Dojan to watch over us. I woke up because someone was vigorously shaking my arm. It was dawning.

"What is it?"

Instead of answering, the Kurd pointed past the trees toward the edge of the bushes on the far side. A stag had appeared there, on its way to the nearby water hole. We needed meat, and although a shot might give us away, I fired.

The report woke Lindsay, who sat up, bolt upright. "What is it? Where is the enemy?"

"Over there, Sir David."

"Ah, a buck! Splendid! Comes in very handy. Haven't eaten since yesterday noon."

Allo ran off to pick up the animal, and a few minutes later a fire was burning in a protected spot and the succulent meat was roasting over it.

During the meal we came to the decision to wait until noon and then investigate what the Bebbeh were up to. As we were talking Dojan suddenly got up to look into the depths of the forest. For a few moments he seemed uncertain, but then he leaped away without so much as a glance at me. I quickly got to my feet to pick up the carbine and take off after him but stopped again immediately, for instead of the shout of fear I had expected, the dog was barking loudly and happily.

A moment later my little Hadji Halef Omar, without his horse but fully armed with rifle, pistols, and knife, emerged before our eyes. "Hamdulillah, Sidi, that I found you, and that you are alive," he greeted me. "I was concerned for you, but the knowledge that no enemy can overtake your Rih consoled me."

"How did you get away, Halef?"

"The Bebbeh shot our horses," he began his report. "Mine also fell, and my legs got caught in the stirrups. But the Bebbeh did not bother with us. All they wanted was you and your Rih. So Allah struck them blind, and they did not see this Kurd and the Englishman escape. I finally extricated myself, took my weapons, and ran off."

How careless the Bebbeh had been! They had aimed only at the horses to catch the riders alive, and then had let them get away.

"Did you see what happened to the two Haddedihn?"

"As I was running I saw that they were taken prisoner."

"Then we mustn't waste any more time but set out right now."

"Wait, Sidi, let me finish! When I had got safely away, it occurred to me that it might be more intelligent to stay and observe the enemy than to go on. I climbed a tree and hid in the foliage. I remained there until evening. Only after it had become quite dark could I come down again, and so I noticed that the Bebbeh have no intention of leaving. They have set up camp. I counted eighty warriors."

"What sort of camp?"

"The Kurds have put up huts made out of branches, and the Haddedihn, with their hands and feet tied, are in one of them. I didn't sleep but stalked the camp during the night because I believed I might perhaps get to the prisoners. But unfortunately that was impossible. You might be able to do it, Sidi, for you have mastered the art."

"Wasn't there something to suggest why the Bebbeh are staying? I cannot understand why they shouldn't have left again right away."

"Nor can I, Sidi. I could find out nothing."

"By the way, Halef, I have to praise you for having come so close to us without our having noticed it. What made you think I would be here, of all places?"

"Because I know the way you go about looking for a spot where you cannot be seen and yet observe everything that goes on, Sidi."

"Get some rest now. I want to consider what we should do. Allo, water my horse and give it fresh grass!"

The charcoal burner had not yet got to his feet to do as I asked when the dog growled. At the uppermost point of our narrow horizon, a rider approached. He quicky drew closer and trotted past us.

"Well, Mr. Kara, why don't I lay him low?" Lindsay asked.

"Under no circumstances!"

"But he's a Bebbeh!"

"Let him go! We are no assassins!"

"But we'd get a horse that way."

"We'll get horses all right."

"Hm." He smiled. "Not assassins but scoundrels! So you are going to steal horses, eh?"

This single Bebbeh made me wonder. Why had he left his companions, and where was he going?

After perhaps an hour the mystery was solved, for the Kurd was now coming back and riding past us, unaware that we were so close.

"What did that fellow down there want?" Lindsay asked.

"He's a messenger."

"From whom?"

"Sheik Gasal Gaboga."

"To whom?"

"To the Bebbeh detachment that has taken up positions half an hour down that road."

"How do you know?"

"I assume it. Somehow the sheik has found out that we will come, and so he has blocked the road at two points. Then the second unit can catch those that get past the first."

"Nice idea, sir, if true."

That was something I had to determine. We agreed that the Englishman and Allo would remain behind in Rih's hiding place while Halef and I went reconnoitering. Should I not have returned by noon of the following day, Lindsay would take my horse and have Allo guide him to Bistan, where he would wait for me for fourteen days. He would stay with Allo's brother.

"If Halef and I should not get there during that time," I added, "it means that we are dead, and you, Sir David, will be my heir."

"Heir? What's there to inherit?"

"My horse."

"I don't care for it. If you are dead I hope this whole country will go down, including all its horses. And all the oxen, sheep, and Bebbeh besides. Everything!"

"That's all you have to know," I said, putting an end to his maledictions, "and all that remains for me to do is instruct the Kurd."

"Be sure you explain things clearly! I can't speak a word with him. What fun! I might as well have stayed in England!"

I had to abandon Lindsay to his muted despair. After giving Allo all necessary instructions, I shouldered the two rifles and entrusted myself to Halef's guidance. He led me back to the path he had taken in the morning and showed that he had been a good student. He had used all available cover, judged the terrain intelligently, and been so cautious that even an Indian would have found it difficult to follow his trail without having to stop now and then.

We walked along under the trees but made sure that we kept the open terrain in view. I had taken the dog along, and since we were moving against the wind, there was no need to worry that we might be taken by surprise.

Finally we came close to the site of the attack, and I ordered Halef not to accompany me any further.

"Should I be taken prisoner," I told him, "you know where to find Lindsay. For now, it will be best if you climb one of those pines. They stand close enough to each other for their branches to hide you. You can distinguish the report of the hunting rifle or the rapid cracks of my carbine from the voices of other guns. Only if you hear me fire will I be in danger."

"And what do I do then?"

"Stay where you are unless I call your name loudly. Get up there now!"

I pulled the dog close to me and crawled on. After a while I saw the first hut through the trees. It had been made of branches in pyramidal form. I pulled back and first described a wide half-circle around the place, for I had to determine whether there might be Bebbeh in the depths of the forest, in which case they would be behind me and could easily discover me.

I crawled from tree to tree, always picking the most massive ones, straining my ears in the silence of the forest. I soon realized that my caution was not superfluous, for I thought I could hear human voices, and Dojan nudged me at the same moment. The magnificent animal knew that he must keep utterly still and only gazed at me with his intelligent eyes.

Continuing in the direction from which the sounds had come, I soon spied three men under a tree which was surrounded on three sides by cherry laurel bushes about one and a half meters high. The place was ideally suited for eavesdropping. And since I assumed that yesterday's events would not fail to be discussed, I circled the three, lay down, and crawled up to the bushes where I could hear every word distinctly.

I soon recognized that one of the men was the Kurd whom Dojan had pulled to the ground, and whom I had let go because he had identified himself as a Djiaf. Dojan also recognized him; there was a hostile glimmer in his eyes. So Allo had been right! This Kurd was a Bebbeh and must have been standing guard to report our passage. He must have had a horse hidden off to one side, and ridden on ahead of us while we believed he had turned north.

"All of them were stupid," he was saying. "But the man that rides the beautiful stallion was the stupidest of all."

How flattering!

"If the stranger had not made prisoners of the Bejat that remained behind, and if he had not insulted them, they would not have told us what they had heard him say, and we would not have known which route to follow."

So this was the solution to what had been baffling me. When the Bejat were taken prisoner they had betrayed our escape plan to curry favor with the victors.

"And it was also stupid of the Frank to let you take him in," the man sitting next to the speaker added.

"But Sheik Gasal Gaboga was also unintelligent to order us to spare the horsemen and the black horse. The stallion would have been a great loss, but why worry about the men? Now four of them have got away, including their leader."

The three Bebbeh had been gathering mushrooms, which they were now cleaning before taking them back to camp, and this afforded them the time and occasion for a confidential exchange.

"What has the sheik decided to do now?" the third man asked.

"He's sent off a messenger. The second unit is to wait until the sun reaches its zenith. If none of the fugitives has been found by then, they are to abandon their position and rejoin us, for it will mean that they have made good their escape. And we are returning today."

"What is going to happen to the two prisoners?"

"They are important people, it seems. So far they haven't said a word. But they will have to tell us who they are and pay a heavy ransom if they don't want to die."

I had heard enough and pulled back carefully. The three had almost finished their work and could easily spot me when they got up to leave.

So I was stupid, the stupidest of all of us! Unfortunately there was nothing I could do about this bit of flattery at the moment. But that did not trouble me. What did, however, was the fact that these men intended to break camp by noon. So the Haddedihn would have to be rescued by then. But how?

The three Bebbeh got to their feet. The one who had called himself a Djiaf told the others, "Go on, I'll look after the horses."

I followed him at a distance. He led me to a depression which had a small stream running along its bottom. More than eighty horses had been tethered here to trees and bushes, sufficiently far apart to have enough green to eat without getting in one another's way. The place was sunny, and the distance from the first to the last horse was perhaps eight hundred paces.

I could observe everything closely. There were magnificent horses among them, and mentally I was already picking the six best. I was especially pleased that only one Kurd was watching the animals; it would be easy to overpower him.

My unsuspecting guide was busying himself with a chestnut which was perhaps the finest of the lot. It seemed he owned it, and I decided to repay his charming flattery by giving him the opportunity to walk back home on his own two feet.

He exchanged a few words with the guard and then walked toward the camp. As I followed him I became convinced that I would encounter no one along its approaches. There was thus no reason not to move in close. In a careful scrutiny of the camp I counted sixteen huts which had been set up in a half-circle under the trees. It seemed likely that Sheik Gasal Gaboga's would be the largest one, from whose top an old turban was fluttering in the wind. It had been placed at the innermost point of the half-circle and I expected no difficulty edging up to it. Next to it was the one housing the prisoners, for two Kurds, their rifles cradled in their arms, were squatting in front.

I could now return to Halef. He was still sitting in the tree and climbed down when he saw me. I explained to the little fellow my plan for freeing the Haddedihn and then we hid at a spot from which we could survey the path. Impatiently we awaited the time to act.

About two hours had passed when we saw a single horseman. "He was probably sent to report the arrival of the other troop," Halef said.

"Perhaps. Did you notice the tall oak above the depression where the horses are?"

"Yes, Sidi."

"Crawl there and wait for me. I want to hear what this rider has to say. Take Dojan along; I have no use for him now. And take the rifles as well."

The little fellow left with the dog and the guns while I hurriedly moved close enough to the sheik's hut to hear what was being said. I had just taken cover behind a tree when the horseman came galloping up and jumped from his horse.

"Where is the sheik?" I heard him ask.

"In his hut."

Gasal Gaboga came out and walked toward the man. "What news?"

"The warriors will be here shortly."

"So you saw none of the fugitives?"

"No. We watched all night long, until just now. We occupied all the side valleys, but we saw no one."

"Here they are!" someone was shouting outside the camp.

As they heard this call, all the men ran out into the clearing, and even the two guards left their post. They knew that the two Haddedihn were fettered.

This presented a more favorable opportunity than I had hoped for. With two leaps I stood behind the prisoners' hut. Two cuts with my knife, and I was inside. The men were lying side by side, their hands and feet tied.

"Muhammad Emin, Amad el Ghandur, up! Quickly!"

Cutting the ropes was a matter of seconds. "Come quickly!"

"Without arms?" Muhammad Emin whispered. "They are in the sheik's hut."

I stepped outside and looked around. No one was guarding the camp. "Follow me!" I rushed to the sheik's hut and darted inside, the Haddedihn at my heels. They were in a state of feverish excitement. Their weapons were hanging here, and there were also two inlaid pistols and a long Persian rifle, obviously the sheik's. I took the pistols and the rifle and looked out again. We were still unobserved. We crawled out and ran toward the depression. It was some five minutes away but it took us no more than two to reach Halef.

"Mashallah!" he cried out.

"To the horses!" I urged the men.

The guard was sitting at the bottom of the depression, his back turned toward us. At a signal the dog jumped down; a second later the man lay on the ground. He had uttered a scream but apparently had not had the courage for another.

I pointed to the six best horses and called out to Amad el Ghandur, "Hold on to them for a moment! Halef, Muhammad Emin, quickly, take the rest into the forest!"

They understood me immediately. Just then, as we were jumping from horse to horse, cutting the ropes, loud shouts of welcome could be heard behind us. Amad el Ghandur was finding it difficult holding on to his six horses; I had to shoulder three rifles and put two pistols in my belt. Then I mounted the bay and took a second horse by the reins.

"Move! It's high time!"

Without turning to look, I urged my horses up the steep slope, and then the sheltering forest hid us from view. Here the terrain was difficult and we made slow headway, especially since a detour was necessary.

Soon, however, we came to a better path and could increase our pace.

Just then we heard loud shouts behind us, but there was no time to waste guessing about their cause. We had to move.

We had to describe a wide arc, and at the distant point where that arc began we now saw two riders. When they spotted us, one of them turned back while the other pursued us.

"Full speed, or I'll lose my stallion," I shouted at my companions. "In a moment the Bebbeh will be at our heels!"

We had made a good choice; the horses turned out to be first rate. Soon the corner of the forest came into view. We reached it and stopped behind some trees. I saw only Allo.

"Where is the Frank?" I asked.

"Up there with the horse."

"Here's a rifle for you. Get on this bay, it's yours!"

I gave Allo the sheik's rifle and ran uphill toward the cave. It was a quarter of an hour away, but I believe it took me no more than five minutes.

Lindsay was sitting on the ground. "Back already, sir? How did it go?"

"Fine, fine. But there's no time now, they are after us! Run down as quickly as you can, Sir David! There's a horse for you."

"They are pursuing us? Splendid!"

He rushed down the hill. I untethered my stallion and led it down the slope. Unfortunately this took more time than I would have wished. When I had reached level ground the others were already mounted, and Halef was holding on to the sixth horse.

"That took a long time, Effendi," Muhammad Emin remarked. "Look, it's already too late!" The sheik of the Haddedihn pointed.

The first pursuer had just become visible. I recognized the man. "Do you know who he is?" I asked.

"Yes, Sidi," Halef answered. "It's the Djiaf we ran into yesterday."

"He is a Bebbeh, and betrayed us. Let him pass, and he'll be ours."

"But suppose the others come in the meantime?"

"They need more time. Sir David, we'll ride ahead and take this man between us. If he resists, we'll knock the weapons out of his hand."

"Splendid, Mr. Kara."

The Bebbeh was disappearing behind the next bend us from our pursuer. He heard us and turned, recog- say and I reached that bend, only fifty paces separated us from our pursuer. He heard us and turned, recognized us immediately, and became so frightened at our appearance that he involuntarily stopped his horse. He had assumed we would be ahead of him and now discovered us at his back. Before he could regain his composure, we had seized him.

The Kurd reached for his knife. I grasped his fist and squeezed it so tightly that he let the weapon drop. While Lindsay was taking his lance from him, I cut the strap by which his rifle hung over his shoulder; it fell to the ground. He was disarmed, and his horse was galloping at full speed alongside ours. He had submitted to his fate.

We kept moving south, and when we felt we had a sufficient head start we slowed down and Allo took the lead.

"What are we going to do with this Kurd?" Lindsay wanted to know.

"We'll punish him."

"Good idea! Pretended to be a Djiaf. What punishment?"

"I don't know. We'll deliberate."

"Fine. How did you free the Haddedihn?"

I told him briefly. When I was about to describe how we had caught the guard napping, I suddenly interrupted myself. "Oh, no! What have I done!"

"But everything went well!"

"I was in such a rush I forgot to call my dog away from the fellow."

"Too bad. But he'll rejoin us."

"Never! He's dead right now, and so is the guard."

"Why dead?"

"The moment Dojan is threatened, he will bite through the throat of the man lying under him. So the Bebbeh will shoot him. I'd be ready to return for the sake of the dog and risk any danger whatever. But unfortunately that would be pointless."

Halef was also dismayed at the loss of this faithful, intelligent animal, and I spent the rest of the afternoon profoundly disturbed. When evening came we stopped, and only then did we tie up the Bebbeh. In spite of our haste, Halef had taken the time to fasten the remains of the buck to the riderless horse, and so we had more than enough food.

When we had eaten the prisoner was interrogated. Up to this time he had not spoken a single word. The reason for his submissiveness was obviously the hope that his companions would soon appear and free him.

"Who are you?" I began. "Djiaf or Bebbeh?"

He made no reply.

"Answer my question."

The man remained immobile.

"Halef, take off his turban and cut off his lock!"

This is the greatest imaginable dishonor for a Kurd. As the Hadji, the knife in his right hand, was reaching for the prisoner's hair with his left, the man implored me, "Master, leave me my lock; I'll answer!"

"Very well. What is your tribe?"

"I am a Bebbeh."

"You lied to us yesterday."

"One does not have to tell the enemy the truth."

"You swore to your statements by the beard of the Prophet."

"An oath sworn to an infidel doesn't count."

"You also called me a fool."

"That's a lie, master!"

"You said that all of us were stupid, but that I was the stupidest. That's the truth, for I heard it with my own ears—behind the camp, when you were cutting mushrooms. I was lying behind a bush, listening to you. Then I took your prisoners and your horses. So you judge for yourself if I am really so stupid!"

"Forgive me, master."

"I have nothing to forgive you, for that term, coming from you, can never offend an Effendi from Frankistan. Yesterday I let you go because I felt sorry for you. Today you are again in my hands. So who is the more intelligent of us? Are you a brother of Sheik Gasal Gaboga?"

"I am not."

"Hadji Halef, cut off his lock!"

This command turned out to be a prompt remedy. "Who told you I am?" he asked.

"Someone who knows you."

"What ransom do you demand?"

"You were going to demand ransom for these two men," I said, pointing at the Haddedihn. "You are Kurds. I never take ransom, I am a Christian. The only reason I took you prisoner was to show you that we have more intelligence, courage, and skill than you think. Who was the first today to notice that the prisoners were gone?"

"The sheik."

"How did he discover it?"

"He walked into his hut and saw that the prisoners' weapons and his own as well were missing."

"I took them."

"I thought Christians didn't steal?"

"That's true. A Christian never takes what is not his by right, but he will allow no Kurd to steal from him, either. You shot our horses, which we were fond of; in exchange I took six we do not care for. We had many things in our saddle pouches which were essential to us. You caused their loss; I took the rifle and the pistols of the sheik. We made an exchange. But you started this exchange by force, and I ended it the same way."

"Our horses are better than yours were."

"That is no concern of mine, for when you killed ours you didn't ask whether they were good or bad. Why wasn't my horse shot?"

"Because the sheik ordered us not to."

"Did he really believe he would get hold of the stallion? And even if he had, you can be sure I would have recovered him. Who discovered today that the horses were missing?"

"The sheik. He ran into the prisoners' hut, and when he found it empty he ran to the horses. They were gone."

"Didn't he notice anything?"

"The guard with the dog standing over it."

"What happened to the guard?"

"They let him lie where he was to punish him for not having been watchful."

"Terrible! Are you human beings?"

"Those were the sheik's orders."

"And what will happen to you, who weren't alert either? I sat behind the berry bush, one step away from you. Then I followed you to the horses, for I did not know where they might be, and I also followed you to the camp."

"Master, don't tell the sheik!"

"You needn't worry. You are the only person I am concerned with. Now I am going to translate your answers for my companions, who will pass sentence on you. You will not be judged by the two of us who are Christians but by these four men of your own faith."

I proceeded to translate my conversation with the Bebbeh into Arabic.

"What are we going to do with him?" Muhammad Emin finally asked me.

"Nothing," I answered calmly.

"Effendi, he lied to us, deceived us, and delivered us into the enemy's hand. He deserves to die."

"And what weighs even more heavily, he swore by the beard of the Prophet! He deserves to die three times over," Amad el Ghandur added.

"What do you say, Sidi?" Halef asked.

"Nothing for the time being. You go on and decide what is to be done with him."

While the four Muslims were deliberating the Englishman asked me:

"Well? What about that sham Djiaf?"

"I don't know. What would you do with him?"

"Hm. Shoot him."

"Do we have the right?"

"Of course!"

"The proper legal procedure would be this: we make a complaint to our consulates which is forwarded to Constantinople, whereupon the Pasha of Sulaimaniya will be ordered to punish the evildoer— unless he's told to reward him."

"What a procedure! What law!"

"But it is the only one permissible to us as citizens of our respective countries. And furthermore: as a Christian, what will you do with this enemy?"

"Spare me those questions, sir! Do what you please!"

"And suppose I let the Kurd go?"

"That's all right too! I'm not afraid of him, so he doesn't have to be shot on my account. It would be better if you could arrange for him to get my nose. That would be the best punishment for this fellow for having put something over on us."

Meanwhile the Bebbeh seemed to be losing patience. "Master, what is going to happen to me?"

"That depends on you. Whom do you want to judge you? Those four men you call believers, or the two you so often insult by calling them 'Giaour'?"

"Master, I pray to Allah and the Prophet that only the faithful judge me!"

"You shall have your wish! Both of us would have forgiven you and allowed you to return to your companions tomorrow. I wash my hands of you, and may you never regret having doubted the word of a Christian and rejected his compassion."

Finally the others came to a decision. "Effendi, we are going to shoot him," Muhammad Emin announced.

"Under no circumstances!"

"He dishonored the Prophet."

"Are you to judge him for that? That's something he must settle with his imam, with the Prophet, and with his conscience."

"He acted the spy and betrayed us."

"Did one of us lose his life because of it?"

"No. But we lost everything else."

"We took something better in exchange. Hadji Halef Omar, you know my views. I am saddened to see you so bloodthirsty."

"Sidi, I didn't want to go along," he excused himself anxiously, "but the others insisted."

"Then it is my opinion that the Bannah has no voice here. He is our guide and is paid for it. Change your sentence!"

They started whispering again, and when they were done Muhammad Emin informed me: "Effendi, we will let him live, but he shall be dishonored. We shall cut off his lock of hair and lash his face. Anyone with such welts has lost his honor."

"That is more horrible than death."

"But a while ago you yourself were about to have his lock cut off."

"No, I would not have done that. That was just a threat to make him talk. In any case, why do you want to embitter these Bebbeh even more? They feel they are in the right because they believe that we were allies of the Bejat. They cannot know that I told Khan Heider Mirlam to his face that I would have warned the Bebbeh if I had had a chance. They came upon us when we were in the company of robbers and now treat us as such. We have been fortunate and got away; perhaps they will leave us alone now. Do you want your cruelty to force them to continue pursuing us?"

"Effendi, we were their prisoners and must avenge ourselves."

"I also have been a prisoner, more often than you, yet I did not avenge myself."

"Effendi, you are a Christian, and Christians are either traitors or women!"

"Muhammad Emin, repeat what you said just now and our ways will separate this very moment! I have never reviled your belief, so why are you reviling mine? Have you ever seen me or David Lindsay act like women or traitors? It would be easy enough for me to abuse the Muslim faith. I could say: Muslims are ungrateful for they forget what Christians do for them. But I won't, for I know that while a few may let themselves be carried away by their passion, there are many more who can control themselves!"

The old man jumped up and stretched his hands out to me. "Effendi, forgive me! My beard is white and yours still dark, but although your heart is young and warm, your understanding has the ripeness of age. We shall let you have this man. Do as you please with him!"

I was moved. "Muhammad Emin," I answered, "I thank you! Does your son agree?"

"I do," Amad el Ghandur assured me.

I turned to the prisoner. "You have lied to us before. Will you promise me to tell the truth today?"

"I promise."

"If I now take off your fetters and you promise not to escape, will you keep your word?"

"I will."

"Well, then. These four Muslim gave you back your freedom. Today you will stay with us, and tomorrow you may go wherever you wish."

I undid his fetters.

"Master," he said, "I am not to tell you any lies, and now you are lying yourself."

"How so?"

"You say that these men gave me my freedom. That's not true. You won it for me. Your companions first wanted to shoot me, then whip me and take from me the ornament of the believer, but you took pity on me. I understood everything, for I know Arabic. And I also know from what you said that you did not help the Bejat but were well intentioned toward the Beb- beh. Effendi, you are a Christian. Up to now I hated the Christians; today I came to know them better. Will you be my friend and brother?"

"I will," I said, yielding to a sudden impulse.

"Will you trust me and stay here, although your pursuers will be here tomorrow?"

"I trust you. But will my companions also be safe?"

"Everyone that is with you. You did not demand ransom for me; you first saved my life and then my honor. You and your men will be safe from all harm."

So we were rid of all our worries. To celebrate this event I took out what remained of my tobacco. It wasn't much but the aromatic smoke created a mood of peace. We went to sleep in good spirits and were even bold enough not to post a guard.

The following morning things looked a bit less ro- mantic than they had the evening before by the warm glow of the fire. I decided nonetheless to show the Bebbeh that I trusted him.

"You are free now," I told him. "There's your horse, and you will find your weapons on your way back."

"My fellow tribesmen will find them. I shall remain here," he answered.

"But what if they don't come?"

"They will," he said with conviction. "And I will make sure that they see us."

We had spent the night in a small side valley whose entrance was so narrow that even during the day we would not have been noticed from the main valley. The Bebbeh walked toward the mouth and sat down at a spot which permitted him to see far in the direction from which we had come. The rest of us tensely awaited developments.

"What if he should deceive us again?" Muhammad Emin asked worriedly.

"I trust him," I answered. "He knew that his freedom would be returned to him and did not have to admit that he had understood every word of our conversation. I really believe he is sincere."

"But if he should deceive us nonetheless, I swear by Allah that he will be the first to be struck by my bullet, Effendi!"

"In that case he would deserve no better."

Lindsay also seemed unhappy. "Sir, there the Kurd is, sitting at the entrance. If he lies again, we will really be in a very tight spot. I hope you won't mind if I check my new horse and my weapons."

It was true that I had assumed considerable responsibility, and I freely admit that I did not feel altogether at ease. Fortunately, the decision was not long in coming.

We saw that the Bebbeh had risen, was shading his eyes with his hand and looking attentively into the distance. Then he went to his horse and quickly mounted it.

"Where to?" I asked.

"The Bebbeh are coming," he answered. "Permit me to prepare them, master."

"Go on!"

As he rode off, Muhammad Emin commented, "Effendi, I wonder if you haven't made a mistake."

"I hope I did right. We made peace, and if I had acted distrustfully that might have been the very thing to make him our enemy once more."

"But he was in our hands, and was to serve as hostage."

"You can be sure he will come back. Our horses are close, we can jump into our saddles. Keep your weapons ready but don't make a show of it."

"What's the good of that, Effendi? The enemy is more numerous and you always want us to shoot at the horses, not the riders."

"Muhammad Emin, I am telling you that if this Bebbeh is intent on betraying us, we will not save ourselves by shooting the horses, and I would be the first to fire at the riders. Stay where you are. I'll post myself at the entrance, and you can take your cue from me."

# 4 : Sheik Gasal Gaboga

Leading my horse, I walked toward the narrow passage by which one entered the valley, mounted, and took carbine in hand. When I bent forward I had a view of the open field. At some distance I could see a troop of horsemen which had stopped to listen to someone talking to them. This was the sheik's brother. After a while two riders separated from the rest and came toward the valley. I recognized Gasal Gaboga and his brother and knew that we no longer had anything to fear.

When the sheik had come close and saw me, he stopped. The expression on his sunburned face was unfriendly, and his voice sounded almost threatening as he asked, "What are you doing here?"

"I am receiving you," I answered curtly.

"Your reception is not very polite, stranger."

"Do you demand that an effendi treat you with greater friendliness than you show him?"

"You are very proud. Why are you on horseback?"

"Because you are."

"Come with me to my companions. This man here, my father's son, wishes me to determine if we can forgive you."

"Then you should come with me. My companions

also intend to deliberate whether you should be punished or pardoned."

This was too much for the sheik. "Frank!" he called out. "Consider who you are, and who I am!"

"I am considering it," I said with sangfroid.

"There are just six of you."

I smiled, and nodded.

"And we are an entire army."

I nodded again.

"Then obey, and let us enter!"

I smiled even more pleasantly and urged my horse aside to let the sheik and his brother through the narrow entrance. Should the sheik decide to continue hostilities against his brother's will, we would simply take him prisoner. We had won.

Both rode toward my companions, dismounted, and sat down. I followed slowly.

"Is he hostile or friendly, sir?" Lindsay asked eagerly.

"I don't know yet. There is something I should like you to do."

"Of course."

"In a minute or so, get up and in the most casual manner walk to the entrance to stand guard. If you see the Bebbeh out there starting to move in our direction, call out, and if one of these two wants to leave without my permission, shoot him down!"

"All right. I'll take my rifle. I am in no mood for jokes."

The two Bebbeh had heard but not understood our exchange. "Why are you taking in a foreign language?" the sheik asked suspiciously.

"Because that brave bey from the Occident speaks only the language of his people," I answered as I pointed at Lindsay.

"Brave? Do you really believe that there is one among you who is brave?" And with a contemptuous gesture he added, "You fled from us!"

"That is true, sheik," I answered with a laugh. "We got away from you twice because we are more daring and braver than you. There are only a few of us, and you yourself have stated that you are an entire army. But that army was unable to hold us. Is that our disgrace, or our honor? It's not because we are cowards that we avoided fighting you. We spared you and wish to continue doing so. But we also demand that you be intelligent enough to understand the situation in which you find yourself."

"I understand it," Gasal Gaboga said sarcastically. "It is the situation of the victor. I expect you to ask my forgiveness and surrender everything you stole."

"Sheik, you are mistaken, for it is you who finds himself in the situation of the vanquished. It is not we but you who must ask for forgiveness, and I expect you to do so now."

Speechless with surprise, the Bebbeh stared at me; then he burst out laughing. "Stranger, do you take the Bebbeh for dogs, and their sheik for the bastard of a bitch? I yielded to my brother's request and came to you to study the magnitude of your crime with the eyes of mercy. Your punishment will be lenient. But since you refuse to understand what serves your salvation, the call of enmity will continue to resound between us, and you will learn that it takes only my command to crush you."

"Give that command, Sheik Gasal Gaboga," I answered coldly.

Now his brother intervened for the first time. "This stranger from the Occident is my friend. He saved me from dishonor and death. I gave him my word that there would be peace between him and us and I shall keep it."

"Keep it, if you can do so without me," the sheik grumbled.

"A Bebbeh never breaks his promise. I will remain by my protector's side as long as he is in danger, and I should be surprised if the warriors of our tribe dare attack men who have turned to me for protection."

"Your protection is not that of the tribe. Your foolishness will be your undoing, for you will die with these men." The sheik rose and walked to his horse.

"Is that your decision?" his brother asked.

"It is. If you remain here, there is nothing further I can do for you except to give the order not to shoot at you."

"That order will be pointless! I will kill everyone who threatens my friend, including you, and then I will not be spared either."

"Do as you please. Allah has permitted you to lose your mind. May he hold his hand over you when I can no longer protect you. I am going."

While his brother stayed where he was, the sheik mounted his horse to leave the valley. But now Lindsay raised his rifle and aimed it at his chest.

"Stop, old boy," he ordered. "Dismount, or you are a dead man."

The sheik turned back to me and asked, "What does he want?"

"To shoot you. I have not given you permission to leave here."

Gasal Gaboga could tell from my rigid expression that I meant what I said. He also saw that Lindsay had his finger on the trigger. He turned his horse and said angrily, "Stranger, you are a scoundrel!"

"Sheik, if you say that once more, I signal the guard and you are a corpse."

"But your conduct is an act of betrayal! I came here as the emissary of my tribe and am entitled to safe passage."

"You are not the emissary but merely the leader of your tribe! The rights of an intermediary are not yours!"

"Do you know the law of nations?"

"I do, but it is obvious that you are ignorant of it! You may have heard talk about it, but your mind was not sufficiently mature to understand it. The right you are talking about commands honesty in combat. It commands that the enemy be informed of the intent to attack him. Did you? No! You fell upon us like the vulture that tears apart the dove. And now you are surprised that you are being treated as a bandit. You came here because you thought we were cowards who would fear your escort, but you will discover that the opposite is the case. You will leave this place when I decide you may. Any attempt to force your way will cost you your life! Dismount and rejoin us! But remember that I expect politeness from you, and that your death is inevitable, should your Bebbeh dare attack us here."

Gasal Gaboga slowly complied with this order but could not refrain from remarking threateningly, "My men would avenge me."

"You have already seen that we do not fear their revenge, and you will have other occasions. But now let us calmly discuss the matter that brought you to us. Speak, Sheik Gasal Gaboga, but avoid all insult!"

"You are our enemies because you joined the Bejat to rob us . . ."

"That is an error," I interrupted. "We encountered the Bejat at a place where we were spending the night, and Heider Mirlam invited us to be his guests. He told us that he was on his way to a festivity of the Djiaf, and we believed him. The khan took your herds while we slept, and when I became aware of the truth I made no secret of my anger. You attacked us and then pursued us. We spared you for we only shot your horses. We escaped. Then you ambushed us. We captured your spy and showed him mercy. Then you attacked and we spared your lives. I entered your camp and freed my companions. I did not shed a drop of blood. You pursued us. We took your brother prisoner and not a hair on his head was touched. Try to think, sheik, and to understand that we did not act as enemies but as friends toward you. And the thanks we get are insults! Instead of asking our forgiveness, you demand that we implore yours. May Allah judge between you and me. We do not fear you. And do not try to discover whether you have reason to fear us."

The Kurd had listened with only half an ear, and now he said sarcastically, "Your speech is very long, stranger, but all you say is false!"

"Prove it!"

"That's easy. The Bejat are our enemies. You were with them and are therefore also our enemies. When my men pursued you you shot their horses from under them. Is that friendship?"

"Was it friendship to pursue us?"

"You hit me on the head so that I lost consciousness. Is that friendship?"

"You were attacking me, so I knocked you down."

"And finally, you took our best horses yesterday. Is that friendship?"

"I took those horses because you had shot ours. All your reproaches are baseless and false. We have neither the time nor the inclination to let our patience be abused any longer. Tell us briefly what your demands are, and I shall give you my answer!"

The sheik now stated his conditions: "I demand that you come to us. You surrender your horses, your weapons, and everything you carry with you. Then you may go wherever you please."

"Is that all?"

"Yes. You can see that I am merciful, and it is my hope you will consent to these demands."

"I won't! You are in no position to make any, and I would advise you to let us go without interference! That's the best . . ." I stopped, for a shot had been fired outside, and it was quickly followed by others.

I turned to the Englishman. "What's up, Sir David?"

"Dojan!" he called back.

I jumped to my feet and had reached the entrance a moment later. It really was the greyhound. The Kurds were chasing him but he was intelligent enough to move around them in an arc. Unfortunately this maneuver did not seem to be successful. The animal was so worn out that the small, shaggy horses of the Bebbeh outran him. Aware that he was in great danger of being shot, I jumped toward my horse.

"Sheik Gasal Gaboga, now you will see the kind of weapon an effendi from the Occident owns. But take care not to pass the entrance! You are my prisoner until I return!"

I mounted the stallion and rode out into the field. With my outstretched arm I signaled to the Kurds to desist from their pursuit of Dojan. They saw me but did not obey. The dog also noticed me and, instead of following his original path, came straight toward me. This took him closer to his pursuers. I could not tolerate having this courageous animal which I had believed lost and now had almost recovered shot at the last moment. I therefore stopped Rih and showed him the barrel of my hunting rifle. He stood motionless. I raised the rifle, fired twice, and felled the horses of the two Kurds closest to Dojan, who could now pass un-hampered, but the Bebbeh raised a furious outcry and came dashing toward me.

In his joy at having found me, the dog took a single leap and landed next to me on the back of the horse. But I immediately pushed him down again, fearful that he might hinder my freedom of movement.

"Over here!" I heard someone call at the entrance to the valley. It was the sheik, who wanted to use this opportunity to escape from his unpleasant situation.

The Kurds heard his shout and urged their horses on, brandishing their weapons. As I reached the entrance I saw Gasal Gaboga lying on the ground and Halef and Lindsay fettering him. His brother was standing next to them. No one had laid a hand on him, and I could tell by his stance that he did not wish to involve himself in this fight.

"Master, spare my fellow tribesmen," he asked.

"If you will guard the sheik," I replied.

"I shall, master."

I dismounted and ordered my companions to take up positions behind the rocks by the entrance. "Aim only at the horses," I reminded them.

"Is that the way you keep your word, Effendi?" Muhammad Emin asked angrily.

"The sheik's brother means well," I reminded him. "The first salvo only at the horses. Then we'll see!"

All this had happened so quickly that the Bebbeh had by now come within range. Having fired both barrels of the hunting rifle, I picked up the carbine. We began firing.

"Look at them tumbling," the Englishman rejoiced. "Five, eight, nine horses!"

He rose from his kneeling position to reload while I continued firing. Allo had been using the sheik's rifle and wounded a Bebbeh. The others were better marksmen. The first salvo kept the attacking Kurds at bay until we could reload; the second stopped them in their tracks.

"Let's get them!" Lindsay shouted. "Let's move out and kill those dog catchers!"

He had seized the barrel of his rifle and was really about to charge, but I kept him back. "Have you gone mad, Sir David? Do you want to risk that handsome nose of yours? Stay where you are!"

"Why? This is as good an opportunity as any!"

"Nonsense! We are safe here, but not out there!"

We were interrupted by the sheik's brother, who laid his hand on my arm and said, "Effendi, I thank you. You could have killed more of them than there are horses lying out there, but you didn't. You are a Christian, but Allah will protect you!"

"Do you see now that our weapons are superior to yours?"

"I do."

"Then go out and tell the Bebbeh!"

"I will. But what about the sheik?"

"Gasal Gaboga stays. I'll give you a quarter of an hour! If you aren't back by then with a message of peace, the sheik will be hanged. Don't doubt it! I am tired of fighting an irrational enemy."

"And what if I bring peace?"

"Then I shall release the sheik."

"And what about his demands?"

"I will not meet them. Gasal Gaboga is responsible for the attack we just beat back. He has no right to expect consideration. We are the victors."

He left, and my first task was to reload my rifles. Dojan was lying at my feet, barking with joy although so worn out that his tongue was hanging from his mouth.

"What do you think, Effendi?" Amad el Ghandur asked. "Did your dog bite the guard to death?"

"I hope not. I must assume that Dojan left the man when he was tired of waiting. He guarded him all afternoon and all night, and the poor creature is exhausted. Halef, give him something to eat—but no water just yet."

The sheik was lying on the ground, fettered and utterly silent, but his eyes followed our every movement. There was no chance now that he would ever be a friend of ours.

We tensely awaited the decision of the Bebbeh. They had clustered together and we could tell from the liveliness of their gestures that the deliberations were stormy. Finally the sheik's brother returned.

"I am bringing peace, master," he said.

"What are the conditions?"

"No conditions."

"I had not expected that. You must have pled our cause with fervor. I thank you."

"Be sure you understand me correctly before you thank me. I bring peace, but the Bebbeh also will accept no conditions."

"Ah. And they call that peace? Very well, so I'll have to protect myself. Tell them that I will take the sheik, your brother, as a hostage."

"How long will you keep him?"

"Until I am certain I am not being pursued. Then he will be released unharmed."

"I believe you. Permit me to inform my men."

"Go and tell them to pull back to the mountains that edge the prairie. The moment I notice that they are following us, Gasal Gaboga dies!"

He left, and soon we saw that all the Bebbeh, both on horseback and on foot, were slowly moving north. He himself returned for his horse.

"Master," he said, "I was your prisoner. Are you releasing me?"

"Yes. You are my friend. Here, take your brother's pistols. It is not to him but to you that I am returning them. The rifle remains the property of the man to whom I made a present of it."

He waited until the sheik had been tied to his horse and we were ready to move out. Then he took his leave. "Farewell, master. May Allah bless your path! You are taking with you a man who is your enemy and who now is mine as well. Yet I commend him to your kindness, for he is my father's son." He followed us with his eyes until we had disappeared, but the sheik had not deigned to look at him once. It was clear that the two brothers had become enemies.

We continued south. Halef and Allo had taken the sheik between them, and apart from a few brief comments that were occasionally necessary, we followed our route in silence. I could tell that my companions did not approve of my conduct during the past few days. While nothing was said about it, that much was obvious from their sullen manner. I would have preferred a frank exchange to their taciturnity. And the landscape in which we found ourselves was no friendlier. We rode over desolate mountaintops, along bare slopes, and through dark ravines. Toward evening it became as cold as wintertime, and the night we spent between two sheltering rocks did nothing to change our mood.

Shortly before daybreak I took my carbine to stalk some game. After searching for some time I managed to bag a miserable badger, the only catch I brought back to camp. A glance Halef gave me surreptitiously told me that something had gone on during my absence.

I did not have long to wait to find out more about what had happened, for I had barely settled down when Muhammad Emin asked, "Effendi, how long are we going to burden ourselves with this Bebbeh?"

"If you intend to say something important," I answered, "remove the prisoner; he probably knows Arabic as well as his brother."

"Let Allo see to him."

I took Gasal Gaboga some distance away and entrusted him to the charcoal burner, impressing on him the need for the greatest possible vigilance. Then I returned to the others.

"No one will overhear us now," Muhammad Emin said, "and I shall repeat my question: how long will we burden ourselves with this Bebbeh?"

"Why do you ask?"

"Don't I have that right, Effendi?"

"I don't dispute it. I am going to keep the sheik until I can be certain that we are no longer being pursued."

"How can you make sure?"

"By observation. We will continue on our way until noon. Then you will pick a suitable place to spend the night while I ride back. I am convinced I'll see the Bebbeh if they should be behind us. Tomorrow morning I'll rejoin you."

"Is such an enemy worth all that trouble?"

"No, he isn't, but our safety demands it!"

"Why not make things easier for yourself and for us?"

"How?"

"You realize that the prisoner is our enemy . . ."

"Even a dangerous one."

". . . who repeatedly tried to kill us?"

"Of course."

"Gasal Gaboga even betrayed us when he was in our hands, for he called on his men to attack when you had left the valley to defend your dog."

"That is also true."

"According to the laws of the Shammar tribe, he has done more than enough to deserve to die."

"Are those laws valid here?"

"They are valid wherever a Shammar has to pass judgment."

"Oh, so you want to judge the prisoner? Apparently you have already arrived at a sentence. What is it?"

"Death."

"And why haven't you executed that sentence?"

"How could we do that without you, Effendi?"

"You are not courageous enough to do so without me, but you have passed sentence without my participation. Muhammad Emin, you are taking a false path, for the prisoner's death would also have been yours!"

"Why?"

"Very simple! Here sits my friend Lindsay Bey, and there my brave Hadji Halef Omar! Do you believe they would have permitted you to kill the Bebbeh in my absence?"

"These men would not have stopped us. They know we are stronger than they."

"It's true that you are the bravest heroes among the Haddedihn, but these men don't know the meaning of fear. What do you suppose I would have done when I saw what you had been up to?"

"Then it would have been too late to do anything."

"That's true, but you would have died. I would have thrust the knife into the earth before your feet and would have fought you as the avenger of the man who was murdered though he stood under my protection. Only Allah knows whether you could have vanquished me."

"Effendi, let us not talk about such a thing. You see that we are asking you before taking action. Gasal Gaboga deserves to die. Let's deliberate about him."

"Deliberate? Don't you know that I promised Musafi to release his brother unharmed the moment I am persuaded we are not being pursued?"

"That was a rash promise. You gave it without consulting us. Are you perhaps our lord that you should now be making it a habit to act on your own?"

This was a reproach I had not expected. I remained quiet for some time to examine my conscience, and then I answered, "You are right when you say that I have occasionally acted without consulting you. But I did not do so because I consider myself the most important person but for other reasons. You do not understand Kurdish and I was the only one who could converse with them. Was I to translate every question I asked or every answer I gave? When a quick decision has to be made or something must be done on the spot, is there the time or the opportunity to deliberate with one's companions, not all of whom even speak the same language? Has it not always been to your advantage to do as I advised?"

"Since we encountered the Bejat, your advice has never been good."

"That's something I am unaware of, but I will not quarrel with you. I am not Allah but a human being who may err. Up to now you gave your free consent to my leadership because you had confidence in me. Since I see that this confidence is gone, I will step back. Muhammad Emin, you are the eldest, and no one will begrudge you the honor of taking over from me."

Neither he nor his son had expected this, but my last statement flattered the old sheik too much for him to reject my offer without discussion. "Is that your firm resolve, Effendi? Do you really believe I could be your leader?"

"Yes, for you are as wise as you are strong and brave."

"I thank you. I do not speak Kurdish."

"I will be your interpreter. Besides, we will soon enter territory where only Arabic is spoken."

"Do the others go along with your proposal?"

"Hadji Halef Omar will do as I ask, and I shall consult the Englishman."

When I explained the situation to Lindsay he remarked drily, "Make no mistake, I have long since noticed that something was troubling the Haddedihn. We are Christians and much too humane for their liking."

"You are probably right! But I am supposed to ask you if you will accept Muhammad as our leader?"

"Yes, provided he knows the way. In any event, I don't need a leader! I am an Englishman and do as I please!"

"Do you want me to tell Muhammad Emin that?"

"By all means! Tell him whatever you like. I have no objections, even if this charcoal burner Allo should want to play the lord and master."

I informed the Haddedihn of this view. Muhammad's brows contracted a little. His position, barely assumed, was already being undermined.

"Those who trust me will have reason to be satisfied with me," he said. "But now let's talk about the Bebbeh. He deserves death. Is he going to be shot or hanged?"

"Neither. I already told you that I vouched for his safety."

"Effendi, that no longer counts, for I am the leader now, and what the leader says must be done!"

"No, I will not allow my word to be broken."

"Effendi!"

"Sheik Muhammad Emin!"

Little Halef drew one of his pistols and asked, "Sidi, do you want me to put a bullet in someone's head? By Allah, I wouldn't hesitate!"

"Hadji Halef Omar, leave your weapons where they are, for we are friends, although the Haddedihn seem to be forgetting it," I told him calmly.

"Effendi, we are not forgetting it," Amad el Ghandur defended himself. "But neither should you forget that you are a Christian who finds himself in the company of true believers! Here the laws of the Koran apply and a Christian must not keep us from acting in accord with them! You have already shown the Bebbeh too much indulgence. Why do you keep ordering us to fire at the horses, not the riders? Are we boys who were given their arms for mere play? Why should we spare traitors? The teaching you follow will ultimately cost you your life!"

"Be silent, Amad el Ghandur, for you are certainly still a boy although your name means 'hero.' Learn what men are before you speak."

"Effendi," he flared up, "I am a man!"

"No, for then you would know that a man will never allow anyone to force him to break his word."

"You are not being asked to break it; it is we who will punish the Bebbeh."

"I forbid it!"

"And I order it," Muhammad Emin shouted angrily as he rose.

"Is it your place to give orders here?"

"And is it yours to issue prohibitions?"

"Yes, my solemn pledge entitles me to that."

"Your pledge means nothing to us! We are tired of permitting a man who loves his enemies to dictate to us! You have forgotten what I did for you. I took you in as my guest, I protected you and even gave you the horse that is worth half my life to me! You are an ingrate!"

I felt the blood draining from my cheeks but managed to control myself. "You will retract that word," I said coldly as I also rose.

I gestured to Halef, walked to the spot where the sheik of the Bebbeh was being guarded by the charcoal burner, and sat down.

Less than a minute later the Englishman had joined me. "What happened, Mr. Kara? My God, you are crying! Whom should I shoot or strangle?"

"Anyone who dares lay hands on this prisoner!"

"Who would that be?"

"The Haddedihn. Sheik Muhammad Emin has reproached me for being ungrateful. I am returning Rih to him."

"You must be crazy to give back a horse like that once it's yours. I hope something can still be done."

Now Halef joined us. He was leading two horses, his and the supernumerary I had stolen from the Bebbeh. It was carrying my saddle, which Halef had taken off the stallion.

My little Hadji also had a tear in his eye, and his

voice was trembling. "You acted correctly, Sidi! The devil has got into those Haddedihn! Should I take my whip and drive it out again?"

"I forgive them.—Let's leave here."

"Sidi, what do we do if the Haddedihn want to kill the Bebbeh?"

"We'll shoot them down."

"That suits me. May Allah stone those scoundrels!"

Gasal Gaboga was once more tied to his horse and our little train started moving. We passed by the Haddedihn, who were still sitting in the grass. Perhaps they had believed that we would give in, but when they saw that we meant what we said, they jumped to their feet.

"Effendi, where to?" Muhammad asked.

"Away," I answered.

"Without us?"

"As you please."

"Where is the stallion?"

"Over there."

"Mashallah! Rih is yours!"

"He is yours once more. May Allah give you peace!"

I spurred my horse and we trotted off. But we had barely covered a mile when the two came after us. Amad el Ghandur had mounted the stallion and was leading his former mount by the halter. It was impossible now for me to take Rih back.

Muhammad Emin came up beside me while his son hung back. "Effendi, I don't understand you. I wished to punish the Bebbeh who took me and my son prisoner. What did I do to you?"

"O Sheik, you have lost the love and esteem of three men who risked their lives for you and your son, and who until today would not have hesitated to give them for you."

"Effendi, forgive me!"

"I am not angry with you."

"Take the stallion back!"

"Never!"

"Will you punish my old age with dishonor, and shame my white beard?"

"Precisely your age and the snow of your beard

should have taught you that nothing good ever comes of wrath."

"Is it going to be said among the Beni Arab that the sheik of the Haddedihn had his gift returned to him because he was unworthy of bestowing it?"

"That's what people will say."

"Effendi, you are cruel! You are bringing disgrace on my head."

"You yourself did that. I was your friend and loved you, and even now I forgive you. I know what will be said when you bring the stallion back to your tribe. I should like to help you, but I cannot."

"But you can. All you have to do is take Rih back."

"I would, but it has become impossible. Look."

At a loss, the old sheik turned. "What do you mean, Effendi?"

"Don't you see that the stallion already has an owner?"

"I understand, Effendi. Amad el Ghandur will dismount."

"Nonetheless I will not take the horse. Your son put his saddle on him and mounted the animal. That means that you took Rih back. If you were to return the stallion as I left him, unsaddled and untouched, I would assume that we were friends, and I could remove this disgrace from you. But you have made that impossible for me."

"Allah! What a mistake we have made!"

I could not understand what had suddenly got into these normally so reasonable men. Perhaps the seeds of this conduct had started growing in them long since and had been nourished by my demand that our enemies be treated with compassion. But my sparing the two Bebbeh had been the straw that broke the camels' back.

The Haddedihn was riding silently alongside me. Finally he asked hesitantly, "Why is your anger so sustained?"

"I am not angry, Muhammad Emin, but sad that you should be so bloodthirsty."

"Very well, I will make good this error."

He reined in his horse. Lindsay and Halef were riding behind me, followed by Allo and Gasal Gaboga, with Amad el Ghandur in the rear. I did not look back because I assumed Muhammad Emin wished to speak to his son.

But suddenly I heard the loud voice of the Haddedihn: "Ride back, and be free!"

My first glance showed me that he had cut the fetters of the prisoner, who immediately spurred his horse and galloped off.

"Sheik Muhammad Emin, what have you done?" Halef exclaimed.

"Damn it! What's got into the Arab?" Lindsay shouted indignantly.

"Did I act correctly, Effendi?" Muhammad Emin asked.

"You acted unthinkingly," I said angrily.

"I wished to be conciliatory and do your will," he excused himself.

"But who told you that I wanted to release Gasal Gaboga as quickly as that? Now we have lost our hostage and are in danger once more!"

"May God forgive him," Halef said. "Let's pursue the Bebbeh!"

"We won't catch him," I objected. "Our horses are no better than his. "Only the stallion is faster."

"Amad, after him!" Muhammad Emin ordered his son. "Bring him back or kill him!" Amad el Ghandur turned Rih and rode off at full speed.

He had barely gone five hundred paces, however, when the stallion refused to continue carrying him. But Amad was not the sort of person to simply let himself be thrown. He forced the animal forward. Now he had disappeared behind a bend in the road, and when we had reached that point we saw him struggling with the noble animal in the distance. He used all his strength and skill, but in vain, for finally he was thrown and Rih turned back, came up to me, and stopped by my side, rubbing his beautiful head on my thigh, snorting gently.

"Allah akbar—God is great!" Halef commented. "He gives a horse greater devotion than many a person. What a pity, Sidi, that your honor makes it impossible for you to take the stallion back!"

Amad el Ghandur had taken a serious spill and had trouble getting up again, but when I examined him it turned out that he had sustained no injuries. "Rih is a devil," he said. "He used to carry me often."

"You forget that he carried me after you," I explained, "and I have always known how to accustom a horse to me."

"I'll never mount that sheitan again!"

"It would have been intelligent if you had not done so earlier," I said. "Had I been in the saddle, Gasal Gaboga would not have escaped us."

"Why don't you get on him now, Effendi, and take off after him," Muhammad Emin asked me. "Otherwise the Bebbeh will get away!"

"Unfortunately, but that is no one's fault but yours."

"Terrible," Lindsay moaned. "How stupid, how unpleasant!"

"What do we do, Sidi?" Halef wanted to know.

"To recapture the Bebbeh? Nothing. I would have sent Dojan after him if the dog didn't mean so much to me. But we must come to a decision now." And turning to the Haddedihn, I asked, "Early today, when I was gone shooting the badger, did you discuss the route we were going to take in the presence of the Bebbeh?"

Both hesitated with their answer, but Halef said, "Yes, they did."

"But only in Arabic," Huhammad Emin excused himself.

Had he not been such a venerable figure I would have rebuked him severely. Instead I forced myself to be calm. "You did not act intelligently! What did you say?"

"That we are going to Bistan."

"Is that all? Try and remember! It is essential to recall every word that was spoken. Any insignificant detail you fail to mention can do us great harm."

"I said that from Bistan we might ride to Ahmed Kulwan, but that we would certainly go to Kisildja to get to the Karatscholan Su."

"You were a fool, Sheik Muhammad Emin. It is fairly certain now that Gasal Gaboga will pursue us. Do you still think you could be our leader?"

"Effendi, forgive me! But I am convinced that the Bebbeh will not catch up with us. He has too far to go to rejoin his men."

"You think so? I have been among many peoples and come to know their character, and so it is not so easy to deceive me. The sheik's brother is an honest man, but he is not the leader of the Bebbeh. All Musafi could obtain from them was safe conduct for us, and I am willing to wager my head that the Kurds followed us without letting themselves be seen. As long as the sheik was our captive we were fairly safe. But now we have to be on our guard. They will want to avenge themselves for everything, including the loss of their horses."

"We need not fear the Bebbeh," Amad el Ghandur said consolingly. "Just because of those horses not all of them can pursue us. And when they do come we'll receive them with our rifles!"

"That sounds fine, but it isn't the way things are. The Bebbeh have realized that we are their superiors in a pitched battle. They'll ambush us again, or attack at night."

"We'll post guards."

"There are just six of us, and we'd need at least that many guards to feel tolerably safe. No, we have to think of something else!"

Our guide, the charcoal burner, had kept some distance away from our group. He was embarrassed, expecting to be reproached for not having prevented the sheik of the Haddedihn from freeing the prisoner.

"How far south do the Bebbeh roam?" I asked him.

"All the way down to the Kara Dag," Allo answered. "They know every mountain and every valley between Karkik and Mik, Nwisgieh and the Kara Dag, as well as I do."

"We will have to change our route. We must not go west. How far east is it from here to the principal chain of the Zagros Mountains?"

"Eight hours, if we could ride through the air."

"But since we have to stay on the ground?"

"It all depends. I know of a pass farther down. If we ride east, we can spend the night in a safe forest and reach the Zagros Mountains tomorrow, when the sun is in its zenith."

"That's where the Persian border must be."

"Yes. Kurdish Teratul borders on the Persian district of Sakis, which is part of Sinneh."

"Are there Djiaf Kurds in that area?"

"Yes, and they are very warlike."

"Perhaps they'll be hospitable toward us since we have done them no harm. It is also possible that Khan Heider Mirlam's name may serve as a recommendation. Lead us to the pass you mentioned. We'll ride east."

This conversation had been carried on in Kurdish. I translated for my companions and they agreed to my plan. When Amad el Ghandur had put his saddle back on his own horse and mounted it, we moved on. Muhammad Emin took Rih by the reins.

A considerable time had been wasted with these unpleasant debates and it was almost noon when we reached the pass. By now we were in the mountains and we turned east, having first made sure that no hoofprints would betray this change of direction.

Only an hour later the terrain began to descend, and when I asked him Allo told me that a fairly sizable valley would have to be crossed between here and the Zagros Mountains.

The dispute had profoundly upset all of us, and my face probably showed this quite clearly. I had to avoid glancing at my stallion. True, the bay was not bad, but the Kurds ruin their horses. Sitting in the saddle I felt like a beginner.

Toward evening we reached the forest where we intended to settle down for the night. So far we had not encountered a soul, but we had come across some game and so had something to eat. We had our meal in oppressive silence and then bedded down for the night.

I had the first turn at guard duty and was sitting some distance away from the others, leaning against a tree. Halef came up to me, bent down to me, and asked softly, "Sidi, you are grieved. Does your horse mean more to you than your faithful Hadji Halef Omar?"

"No, Halef. I would trade ten such horses for you."

"Then console yourself, my dear Sidi, for I am with you and will remain with you, and no Haddedihn will make me leave you." He placed his hand on his chest and stretched out alongside me.

The following morning we continued on our way. Allo had not been mistaken, for even before midday the heights of the Zagros rose into view and we could let our tired horses rest for a short while. We let them graze and ourselves lay down in the tall grass, which was fresh and succulent because the valley, whose steep walls seemed inaccessible, was watered by a small brook.

Lindsay was lying near me, gnawing on a bone and mumbling incomprehensibly. He was in a bad humor.

Suddenly he propped himself up on his elbow and pointed behind me. I turned and saw three men slowly coming toward us. They were dressed in thin, striped cloth, wore nothing on their heads, and were armed only with knives. Such pathetic creatures did not warrant our taking weapons in hand. They stopped before our small group and saluted respectfully.

"Who are you?" I asked.

"Kurds from the Mir Mahmalli tribe."

"What are you doing here?"

"We have a blood feud and escaped to look for a tribe that will grant us asylum. Who are you, master?"

"Strangers," I said evasively.

"What are you doing here?"

"Resting."

The speaker did not seem to mind my laconic answers but went on, "There are fish in this brook. Will you permit us to catch a few?"

"But you have neither rod nor net."

"We have learned to catch them by hand."

I had noticed that there were trout, and since I was curious to see how they would go about it, I agreed. "I have told you that we are strangers here. We cannot forbid you to fish."

Immediately the Kurds began to cut grass. When they had a sufficient quantity they gathered rocks to dam the brook at two places. The water drained, and it was easy enough to seize the fish that were now lying on dry land. Since the procedure was entertaining in spite of its simplicity, we tried our hand.

The catch was ample, but because the slippery fish kept getting away from us we paid more attention to them than the three Kurds, until our guide shouted loudly, "Master, watch out, they are stealing!"

I looked up and saw the three already sitting on our horses. One of them had taken Rih, the second my bay, the third Lindsay's horse. Before my companions could recover from their surprise they had galloped off.

"There goes my horse!" Lindsay said.

"Allah kerim—may God protect us! The stallion!" Muhammad Emin shouted.

"After them!" Amad el Ghandur roared.

I remained calm. We were dealing with neither experienced horse thieves nor clever individuals, for otherwise they would have left no horses behind.

"Stop, wait!" I said. "Muhammad Emin, will you admit that the stallion is your property once again?"

"Yes, Effendi."

"Very well. I could not take him back as a gift but I can borrow him. Will you lend him to me for a few minutes?"

"But Rih is gone!"

"Tell me quickly if you are lending him to me?"

"Yes, Effendi."

"Then follow me slowly!"

I jumped on the closest horse and took off after the scoundrels. What I expected had already happened. Some distance away one of the Kurds was desperately trying to stay on the horse, which was bucking wildly to throw the thief. I had not yet reached Rih when the fellow fell to the ground. The stallion came back and stopped when he heard my call. I quickly jumped into the saddle, left the other horse where it was, and urged Rih on.

The Kurd had picked himself up and was trying to get away. Galloping past him, I bent down and hit him on his bare head with the butt of my pistol. He collapsed. I put the weapon back in the holster and took the lasso from my hip.

Noticing the other two thieves far below, I placed my hand between Rih's ears. "Rih!"

He flew along, quicker than a bird through the air. In less than a minute I had reached one of them. "Stop, get off the horse!" I ordered.

He turned. Though startled, he did not obey me but urged Lindsay's horse on. I drew level with him and threw the lasso as I sped past. There was a tug. I pulled the thief along for some distance and then stopped and jumped off my horse. The man was lying motionless on his back. Because of Rih's speed he had been dragged over the ground for a considerable distance and had lost consciousness.

I gathered up the lasso, made another loop, left the Kurd where he lay, got back on the horse, and took up the pursuit of the third. It did not take me long to reach him. The terrain was favorable since he could turn neither left nor right. I also ordered this man to stop, but in vain. Again I threw the lasso. It wrapped itself tightly around his arms, pulling them close to his body. Rih continued running a short distance before I reined him in. The Kurd was lying on the ground like his companion, though still conscious.

I jumped down and finished tying him. Then I set him on his feet. His horse had stopped and was shaking.

"So those are the fish you wanted to catch?" I asked roughly. "What's your name?"

He did not answer.

"Then stay here until the other two are brought." I gave him a push and he fell stiffly to the ground.

Since I saw my companions coming, I also sat down. Within a rather short period of time we had recovered our horses and caught the thieves. Better still, Allo had been smart enough to take the blanket off his horse to wrap the fish while we were chasing the Kurds. He had brought them along and we now dug a hole in the ground and lit a fire over it.

Lindsay had recovered his good humor, but those poor devils who had looked forward to a ride that had been so abruptly terminated were all the more downcast. They did not dare raise their eyes.

"Why did you want to steal the horses?" I asked them.

"Because we desperately need them," one of them answered.

This was an excuse I was inclined to accept, especially since stealing horses is not considered a dishonorable trade among Kurds. "You are still young. Are your parents living?"

"Yes, and so are those of my companions. This one has a wife and child."

"Why don't your accomplices talk?"

"They are ashamed."

"And you aren't?"

"Doesn't one of us have to answer you?"

"You don't seem such a bad fellow, and since I feel sorry for you I'll try to put in a good word for you with my companions."

But that turned out to be a vain endeavor, for all of them, including Halef and the Englishman, insisted that punishment was called for. Lindsay wanted to see them whipped, but he gave up that demand when I told him that that would be inflicting dishonor whereas stealing horses was considered a courageous act.

"So we don't whip them. Instead we can singe their mustaches. We've never tried that before."

I had to laugh, and when I told the others of Lindsay's proposal they immediately agreed. The three men were held, and within two minutes their beards and been reduced to a thin brush, after which they were allowed to go. None of them resisted or said a word, but the glances they cast us as they left startled me.

Some time later, as we were getting ready to set out again, Muhammad Emin approached me. "Effendi, I'll lend you the stallion for today."

How clever! He thought he had found a way of reconciling me and returning the horse. "I don't need him," I answered.

"But any moment may create a situation in which you will, as you did just now."

"Then I shall ask for him."

"There may be no time for that. Ride Rih, Effendi, since no one else can."

"Provided he remains your property."

"I agree." I felt conciliatory and so acceded to his wish, although I was determined never to take the horse back. I did not suspect that things would turn out quite differently.

# 5 : Fallen in Battle

We followed the course of the valley, which took us almost straight south. Then we crossed some green heights and finally, when the sun was about to set, we came to a tall, isolated rock that would shelter us for the night. First we circled it. I was riding out front and just turning a ledge when a young Kurdish woman carrying a small boy on her arms suddenly appeared before me. She was profoundly startled. Nearby, at the edge of some bushes, I saw a stone building which appeared to be the residence of a well-to-do person.

"Don't be frightened." I addressed her kindly. "May Allah bless you and your boy! Whose house is this?"

"It belongs to Sheik Mahmud Mansur."

"Of what tribe?"

"The Djiaf."

"Is he at home?"

"No. The sheik is rarely here, for this is his summer residence. He is far up north at the moment, attending a celebration."

"I have heard about that. Who is in charge during his absence?"

"My husband, Djibrail Mamrash, the caretaker."

"Will he permit us to spend the night in his house?"

"Are you friends of the Djiaf?"

"We are strangers who come from far away and don't know the Djiaf at all."

"Then wait. I'll talk to my husband."

The woman left and we dismounted. In a little

while a man came toward us. He was somewhere in his early forties, had an open, honest face, and made an excellent impression on us.

"May Allah bless your arrival," he greeted us. "You are welcome if you care to enter."

He bowed to each of us, and this politeness indicated that we were already on Persian soil.

"Do you have room for our horses?" I asked him.

"Both room and feed. They can stay in the yard and will be given barley."

The property was surrounded by a high rectangular wall. Inside were the house, the courtyard, and the garden. As we entered we noticed that the house was divided into two sections that even had separate entrances. The door leading to the men's quarters was in front, while that to the women's could be entered only from the rear. The man took us to the former, which was some twenty paces long and ten wide. There were no windows, but under the roof spaces had been left between the beams to make up this lack. A matting of reeds covered the floor and along the wall were small pillows, an amenity for men who had been riding for weeks.

We had to sit down on these cushions, and then our host opened a chest standing in one of the corners and asked, "Do you have pipes with you?"

How describe the effect this question had on us? Allo had remained outside with the horses. Not counting our amiable host, there were thus five of us, and ten arms and all fifty fingers now reached for our pipes while we sounded a loud chorus "yes."

He brought us some of the weed we had done without for so long. It was contained in those well-known square red packages used for the fine tobacco that is grown in Basiran, along the northern edge of the Persian desert of Lut. In no time at all the pipes had been filled, and the aromatic smoke was drifting toward the ceiling when the woman appeared with some Mocca— which often bears no resemblance whatever to real Mocca but tasted very good to us since we had not enjoyed any for a good many weeks. I felt so much at peace and so contented that I would have accepted not just one but ten or even twenty stallions, had Muhammad Emin wished to make me a present of them.

I drank three or four small cups and then stepped out into the yard to look after the horses. When Allo saw my burning pipe he grunted so longingly that I immediately went back in to ask for a little tobacco for him. When I brought it to him he did not fill his pipe but put it into his mouth. His taste was not ours.

Since the surrounding wall was more than man-high, our horses would be safe when the large, heavy gate, the only entrance, was closed. Satisfied, I went back in, where our host had joined his guests and was conversing with them in Arabic. Soon his wife brought in some paper lanterns, which spread a pleasant half-light, and then we had dinner, cold fowl and flat barley cakes.

"This region seems to have an abundance of birds," Muhammad Emin commented.

"That's true. The lake is not far away. It is called Seribar."

"Ah, the 'Lake of Birds,'" I interrupted, "on whose bottom lies the sunken city of sin which was built of pure gold."

"Yes, Effendi. Do you know the story?"

"Its population was so godless that they mocked Allah. So the All-Powerful sent an earthquake that buried the entire city."

"You heard the truth. On certain days, at sundown, one can see the palaces shining deep down in the water, and those who are divinely inspired can also hear the voice of the muezzin proclaiming the hour of prayer. Then one sees the drowned streaming toward the mosque, where they pray until their sins are atoned."

"Have you seen and heard this?"

"No, but my wife's father told me about it. He was fishing on the lake and told us what he saw. But permit me to leave and lock the gate. You must be tired and long for rest."

"Decent fellow," Lindsay said.

"No doubt! He asked neither our names, nor where we come from nor where we are going. That's real oriental hospitality."

"I'll give him a good tip."

Now our host returned with pillows and blankets.

"Are there also Bebbeh living among the Djiaf in this area?" I asked.

"Only a few. The Djiaf and the Bebbeh don't care for each other. But you won't find many Djiaf, for a tribe of the Bilba has moved up here from Persia, and they are the fiercest bandits imaginable. People believe they are planning an attack, so the Djiaf left with their herds."

"And you are staying behind?"

"My master ordered me to."

"But the bandits will rob you of all you have."

"They'll find the walls, nothing more."

"Then they'll avenge themselves on you."

"They won't find me either. The lake is bordered by swamp and reeds. There are hiding places there which a stranger will never discover. But permit me to retire now so I won't deprive you of your rest."

"Will this door remain open?" I asked.

"Yes. Why?"

"We are used to taking turns standing guard by the horses, so we would like to be able to move in and out."

"You won't have to stand guard; I shall be your guard."

"You are very kind, but I ask you not to sacrifice your sleep."

"You are my guests and Allah commands that I watch over you. May he grant you sleep and pleasant dreams."

Nothing disturbed our enjoyment of this friendly Djiaf's hospitality. When we set out the following morning he advised us not to continue riding east since we might encounter the thieving Bilba in that direction. He considered it best to make for the Diyala and ride along its banks until we came to the southern plain. I did not really feel inclined to take that advice, for I was thinking of the Bebbeh whom we might encounter if they should be pursuing us. But the suggestion appealed so strongly to the two Haddedihn that I went along without comment.

We gave ample presents to our host and his wife and set out, a troop of Djiaf horsemen escorting us.

After some hours of strenuous riding we came to a valley west of the heights of the Auroman Dagh. The famous Shamian route which constitutes the link between Suleimaniya and Kermanshah passes through this valley. We stopped by a small brook.

"This is the Tschakan Su, also called Garran," the leader of our Djiaf escort told us. "You are on the right road. Just follow this small river which flows into the Diyala. May Allah be with you!" He and his men left to return home, and we were on our own once more.

The following day we reached the Diyala, which flows down to Baghdad, and settled on its bank for a midday rest. It was a bright, sunny day that I will not forget as long as I live. To our right the waves of the stream were rustling, and off to one side there was a hill covered with acorns, chestnuts, plane trees, and cornels. Behind it we saw the gradual rise of a narrow ridge whose jagged peak resembled an old castle. The small quantity of provisions we had taken along had come to an end, and I picked up my carbine to hunt something edible. I followed the ridge for perhaps half an hour but encountered no game and turned back toward the valley. I had not yet reached it when I heard a shot to my right, which was immediately followed by another. Who could have shot here? I hastened my steps to reach my companions, but when I came to the camp, I only found Lindsay, Halef, and Allo.

"Where are the Haddedihn?" I asked.

"They went to hunt some game," Lindsay answered. He had also heard the shots but assumed that it had been the two Haddedihn. Again we heard two, three reports and a few more a short time later.

"For heaven's sake, on your horses quickly!" I shouted. "Something terrible is happening!"

We mounted and set off at a gallop. Allo followed somewhat more slowly with the animals of the Haddedihn. Again two shots were fired, and then we heard the sharp report of a pistol.

"A battle, a real battle!" Lindsay exclaimed.

We stormed over the meadow that edged the river, turned around a bend in the ridge, and now were so close to the scene that we could intervene without delay. Along the Diyala some camels were lying in the grass, and nearby several horses were grazing. Alongside the camels I noticed a covered sedan chair, and to the right, by a rock, six or eight strangers were defending themselves against a numerically superior group of Kurds. Straight ahead of us, Amad el Ghandur was fighting off a horde of enemies with the butt of his rifle. Directly next to him Muhammad Emin was lying motionless on the ground. I galloped into the midst of the Kurds after having fired my carbine a few times.

"There he is—spare his horse!" a voice cried out. I turned and recognized Sheik Gasal Gaboga. He had uttered his last word: Halef rode toward him and shot him down. There now developed a struggle whose details I cannot recall. I only know that I was bleeding, that shots were fired and flashed past my eyes, that I defended myself against blows and jabs and that a shape alongside me was constantly busy fending off strokes I had not seen. It was my loyal Halef. Then my horse reared because it had been wounded in the neck by a jab aimed at me. Rih rose on his hind legs and somersaulted. That was all I heard, saw, or felt.

When I woke up I was looking into Halef's eyes; they were full of tears.

"Hamdulillah—Allah be praised, he's alive! He's opening his eyes!" he exclaimed, beside himself with delight. "Sidi, are you in pain?"

I wanted to answer but couldn't. I was so fatigued that my eyelids closed.

"What a disaster," I heard him wail, then I lost consciousness once more. Later, it was as though I was dreaming. I had to struggle with dragons, against giants and monsters. But suddenly these wild, disquieting creatures had disappeared, a sweet scent was wafting about me, gentle sounds like angels' voices reached my ears, and soft, warm hands were touching me. I opened my eyes. The mountain heights beyond were glowing in the last light of the sun, and twilight was already spreading over the valley. But it was still light enough to recognize the beauty of the two female heads that were bending over me from either side.

"Ah me," I heard in Persian; the veils dropped over the faces and the two women fled. I tried to sit up and succeeded. I noticed that I had been wounded below the clavicle. Later I heard that I had been jabbed by a lance. And my entire body was aching. The wound had been carefully bandaged and the scent I had smelled earlier was still about.

Halef approahced and said, "Allah kerim—God is merciful. He returned your life to you. May he be blessed in all eternity!"

"How did you fare?" I asked weakly.

"Very well, Sidi. I was shot in the left thigh; the bullet passed through."

"And the Englishman?"

"He was grazed, and two fingers of his left hand were cut off."

"Poor Lindsay! Go on."

"Allo received some blows but lost no blood."

"Amad el Ghandur?"

"Uninjured, but not talking."

"And his father?"

"Dead. May he enter paradise!"

He fell silent, and I also said nothing. The news of my old friend's death shook me profoundly.

After a long pause I asked, "What about my stallion?"

"Rih's wounds are painful but not dangerous. You don't know yet what happened. Shall I tell you?"

"Not now! I'll try to join the others. Why am I lying here, so far away from them?"

"Because the women of the Persian wanted to bandage you. He must be a rather prominent and wealthy man. We have already lit a fire; you will find him there."

Getting up caused me some pain, but I managed with Halef's help and found I could walk. Not far from where I had been lying a fire was burning. As Halef led me to it the tall figure of the Englishman came toward me.

"Well, Mr. Kara. You have taken quite a tumble! You must be solidly built. We thought at first you were dead."

"How are things with you? Your head and left shoulder are bandaged."

"I got a scratch on my head. Any number of hairs and a piece of bone are gone. But it's of no consequence. And then I lost two fingers, and that's something I could have done without."

A second figure had risen with the Englishman. This was a well-proportioned man of proud bearing, dressed in long and very ample trousers of red, with a shirt of white silk and a tight vestlike garment extending below the knee. Over that he wore a dark blue coat and an outer garment of delicate wool of the same color. From a cashmere wrapped around his hips there hung a valuable saber, next to which the golden handles of two pistols, a dagger, and a curved sword were gleaming. He had on riding boots and his head was covered by the widely used Persian cap of lambskin around which he had wound a valuable blue-and-white scarf.

He stepped up to me, bowed, and addressed me in Persian: "You are my lord."

"You are very kind," I answered with a suggestion of an equally polite bow.

"Sir, you are brave!"

"And you are a hero!"

"I am your brother."

"I am your friend."

We shook hands.

"I have already heard your name," the Persian continued in Arabic. "Call me Hassan Ardshir-Mirza and consider me your servant." The title 'Mirza' indicated an important person.

"I also am at your command," I answered politely.

"Not at all. These eight men are my servants. You will come to know them," and he pointed at eight figures who were standing there respectfully. Then he went on: "You are the master of the camp. Take a seat."

"I will obey your wish. But first permit me to console my friend." Muhammad Emin's body was lying near the fire. Alongside it, and with his back turned toward us, his son Amad el Ghandur was sitting motionless. I walked up to him. The venerable sheik of the Haddedihn had been shot through the forehead and his long white beard had been colored red by the blood from a gaping neck wound. I knelt down beside him, speechless with grief.

After some moments, when I had mastered my emotion, I placed my hand on Amad's arm. "Amad el Ghandur, I grieve with you."

He did not stir. I tried hard to elicit some response, but in vain. It was as if his grief had turned him into a stone sculpture. I returned to the fire, and as I was about to sit down next to the Persian I almost stumbled over the charcoal burner, who was lying on his stomach moaning softly. I examined him. He had not been shot but had received a few blows and jabs which were apparently causing him some pain. I consoled him.

Hassan Ardshir-Mirza was unscathed but his men had been badly mauled. Yet none of them showed the pain he felt.

"Effendi," the Persian began when I had sat down next to him, "you came at the right moment! You are the savior of us all."

"I am pleased to have been of service to you."

"I shall tell you what happened."

"First permit me to inquire about some essentials. Did the Kurds flee?"

"Yes. I sent two of my servants to observe them. There were more than forty enemies. They lost a good many men while we mourn only one, your friend. What is your destination, Effendi?"

"The pastures of the Haddedihn, on the other side of the Tigris. We had to make a detour."

"I am going south. I have heard that you have been in Baghdad before."

"Only briefly."

"Do you know the way there?"

"No, but it is easy to find."

"And the way from Baghdad to Karbela as well?"

"Yes. Are you going to Karbela?"

"Yes. I intend to visit Husein's grave." This piece of news found me very sympathetic. Like the overwhelming majority of his countrymen, this Persian was a Shiite, and I secretly wished I could make the journey with him.

"Why are you traveling through the mountains?" I asked.

"To evade those thieving Arabs who lie in wait along the normal pilgrims' route."

"And so you fell into the hands of the Kurds. Are you coming from Kermanshah?"

"From farther away. We had been camping here since yesterday. One of the servants had gone into the forest and saw the Kurds from a distance. They noticed him as well. They followed him and thus came to our camp, which they attacked. During the battle, which we felt we would lose, the courageous old man lying there appeared. He quickly shot two Kurds and rushed into the fray. His son followed. He is as brave as his father. Nonetheless, we would have been overcome had it not been for you. Effendi, my life and everything I own are yours. Let your path be mine for as long as you can."

"I wish that were possible. But we have one dead and are wounded. The old sheik of the Haddedihn must be buried with dignity. And we have to remain here because we will soon be suffering from traumatic fever."

"I intend to stay also, for my servants are wounded."

At this moment, right in the middle of the conversation, it suddenly occurred to me that Dojan was nowhere to be seen. I asked the Englishman about the dog, but he could tell me nothing. Halef had seen him during the mêlée but could give me no further details.

The Persian's servants approached with ample supplies and a meal was prepared over a fire. Afterward I got up to reconnoiter around the camp and look for the dog. Halef accompanied me. Rih had not only been wounded by a lance but had also been grazed by a shot, and Halef had bandaged him. The five camels were resting nearby. It was already too dark for me to look at them carefully. Their burdens lay next to them, and the sedan chair, the present shelter of the two women who had fled when I regained consciousness, was standing some distance away.

"You saw me fall, Halef. What happened then?"

"I thought you were dead, Sidi, and that gave me the strength of wrath. The Englishman also wanted to avenge you, and so the enemy could not stand their ground. The Persian is a very courageous man, and his servants are like him."

"Did you capture nothing?"

"Weapons and some horses which you did not notice in the darkness. The Persian had the corpses thrown into the water."

"Do you suppose there were wounded among them?"

"I don't know. After the fighting was over I examined you and noticed that your heart was still beating. I wanted to bandage you but the Persian would not permit it. He had you carried to the place where you regained consciousness, and then the two women bandaged you."

"What did you find out about those two women?"

"One of them is the wife, the other the sister of the Persian. They have an old female servant who is squatting over there by the sedan chair and constantly munching dates."

"And the Persian? What is he?"

"I don't know. The servant won't tell me. She must be forbidden to say what her master's position is, and I think . . ."

"Wait," I interrupted, "listen!"

By now we had walked farther than the noise from the camp could carry, and during Halef's last words it had seemed to me that I had heard a familiar sound. We stopped to listen, and now the angry barking which indicated that the greyhound had seized an enemy was quite distinct. But the direction from which it had come remained uncertain.

"Dojan!" I called loudly. A very clear answer came from the bushes that covered the slope. We slowly climbed it. To make sure, I called out occasionally, and the dog answered every time. Finally we heard the short, whistling noise by which he showed his joy, and this led us to him. A Kurd was lying on the ground and Dojan was standing above him, ready to bite him to death. I bent forward to look at the man but could not recognize his features. The warmth of his body meant he was still alive, although he did not dare move.

"Get back, Dojan!" The dog obeyed. I ordered the Kurd to rise and then began interrogating him. He called himself a Kurd from the Soran tribe. Since I knew that the Soran are mortal enemies of the Bebbeh, I suspected that he was a Bebbeh pretending to be a Soran to save his skin.

"How is it you are here and in this situation if you really are a Soran?"

"You seem to be a stranger in this land to be asking such a question. The Soran were once powerful and great. They lived south of the Bilba and Harir, the noblest town in Kurdistan, was their center. But Allah turned his back on them so that their vigor left them and passed to their enemies. They had planted their last banner in the region of Koi Sanjak. Then the Bebbeh came and tore it down. Their herds were stolen, their daughters and women led away, their men, youths and boys, killed. Only a few saved themselves to scatter far and wide, or to hide in solitude like me. I live there among the rocks. My wife is dead, my brothers and children have been murdered. I don't even own a horse and have only a knife and a rifle. Today I heard shots being fired and came down to watch the skirmish. I saw my enemies, the Bebbeh, and picked up my rifle. Hidden behind some trees, I shot down more than one; you will find my bullets in their bodies. I killed them out of hatred and because I wanted to acquire a horse. But this dog saw the flashes from my gun, took me for an enemy, and attacked me. My knife had dropped to the ground and my rifle had not been reloaded. I tried to keep him away with the barrel, but finally he threw me to the ground. I knew he would tear me apart if I moved, and so I lay quietly until just now. Those were terrible hours."

I could tell that the man was being truthful, but I had to be cautious. "Will you show us where you live?"

"Yes. It is a hut of moss and branches, with leaves to sleep on. That's all there is to see."

"Where is your rifle?"

"It must be lying somewhere near."

"Look for it." He walked away while the two of us waited.

"Sidi," Halef whispered, "He'll run away!"

"Yes, if he is a Bebbeh. But if he really is a Soran he will come back, and then we can trust him."

We did not have long to wait until we heard a voice from further down the slope: "Come down! I found both the knife and the rifle!"

We rejoined him. The man seemed honest, as I had thought. "You will accompany us to the camp," I told him.

"Gladly, master. But I will not be able to talk to the Persian; I speak only Kurdish and Arabic."

"Do you have a complete command of Arabic?"

"Yes, I have traveled as far as the sea and the Euphrates and know those regions."

It seemed a piece of good luck to have found this man. At the campfire he created a stir. Amad el Ghandur was the most affected, for he no sooner saw the Kurd than he shook off his mental paralysis. The young Haddedihn took the Soran for a Bebbeh and reached for his dagger. I placed a hand on his arm and told him that the stranger was an enemy of the Bebbeh and under my personal protection.

"An enemy of the Bebbeh? Do you know them and their ways?" he hastily asked the Soran.

"I do."

"I'll speak to you later."

Having said this, Amad el Ghandur turned and sat down by the corpse again. I then explained to the Persian how we had found the Kurd, and he agreed to his staying in our camp.

Some time later the servant returned and reported that the Bebbeh had ridden south for a considerable distance and then turned right, toward the Kara Dag. It seemed that we had nothing further to fear from them, and the Persians settled down to sleep after we had jointly taken the necessary precautions.

I searched out Amad el Ghandur and entreated him not to deny himself some rest.

"Rest?" he answered. "Effendi, only one person is at rest, and that is this dead man here. Unfortunately he will not be buried in the land of the Haddedihn or laid to rest by the children of his tribe mourning his loss. He will lie in these alien mountains over which Amad el Ghandur's curse hovers. My father had set out to bring me back home. Do you imagine that I shall see that home again without avenging his death? I saw both the man who stabbed him and the one who shot him through the forehead. They got away, but I know them and will send them to the devil!"

"I understand your wrath and your grief, but I ask that you remain calm. You mean to pursue the Bebbeh to avenge your father's death. Have you considered what that means?"

"The blood feud commands it, and I must obey." He was silent for a while, then he asked, "Will you accompany me in the pursuit of the Bebbeh, Effendi?"

I said I would not, and he lowered his head. "I know that Allah created a world where true friendship and gratitude do not exist."

"Your idea of friendship and gratitude is false," I answered. "Think back and you will admit that I was your father's true friend, and that I have been yours since I freed you. I am ready to risk my life to accompany you to the pastures of the Haddedihn. But as your true friend I must keep you from incurring dangers which will unfailingly lead to your death!"

"Effendi, you are a Christian and act like one. Even Allah wants me to avenge my father, for through you he created an opportunity tonight. And now I ask you to leave me."

"I will fulfill your wish, but first I demand that you undertake nothing before discussing it with me."

Amad el Ghandur turned away and did not answer. I sensed that he had made a decision and feared that I would keep him from carrying it out. For that reason I determined to keep a close eye on him.

When I woke the following morning the young Haddedihn was still keeping vigil. The Soran Kurd had just approached him and they were talking animatedly. Everybody else was up and about, and the Persian was sitting by the sedan chair talking to the veiled women.

"Effendi, I wish to bury my father. Will you help me?" Amad el Ghandur asked.

"Certainly. Where is he to be buried?"

"This man says that there is a place up there among

the rocks which the sun greets early as it rises and in the evening when it sets. I want to have a look at it."

"I'll go with you."

The Persian had no sooner noticed that I was up than he came to wish me good morning. When he heard of our plan he offered to come with us. Up on the height we found a huge boulder and decided to use its smooth surface as the site of the grave. Nearby was the wretched hut of the Kurd, and a little farther on we found an enclosed space that was suitable for a camp site, especially since it had a spring. We agreed to move there.

This caused some difficulties, but we managed. While those who were unscathed or had suffered only minor injuries addressed themselves to the heavy labor of making the grave, the rest set up a hut for the women which was separated from the men's area by an impenetrable wall of branches. The horses, which could not tolerate the odor of the perspiring camels, were tethered some distance away from them.

By noon everything in the camp had been put in order. The Persian had ample supplies of flour, coffee, tobacco, and other essential provisions. There would be no difficulty in finding game and thus no reason to fear that we might suffer want.

The burial site was not ready until some time later. It consisted of a cone of rock almost three meters high, with a hollow space to accommodate the body, which was to be buried at the time of the Moghreb.* Amad el Ghandur prepared the corpse for burial.

The sun was about to set when our small group of mourners approached the site. Following the splendid Muslim custom, all the men present took turns carrying the dead on a bier made of branches. The opening of the grave faced west southwest, which was precisely the direction of Mecca, and when the dead man had been placed inside his face was turned toward those regions where the Prophet of the Muslims had received the revelations of the angels.

Amad el Ghandur came toward me and asked,

---

* Prayer held at sunset.

"Effendi, you are a Christian, but you were in the holy city and know the Sacred Scripture. Will you pay your dead friend the last honors and recite the Sura of the Resurrection?"

"Gladly."

"Then let us begin."

By now the sun had reached the western horizon, and all of us sank to our knees to pray the Moghreb. Then we rose again and formed a half-circle around the opening in the stone.

It was a solemn moment. The dead man was sitting erect in his final abode. Dusk was spreading purple rays over a face that was as pale as marble, and strong breezes made his white beard tremble.

Amad el Ghandur turned in the direction of Mecca, raised his hands, and recited the Exordium:

"In the name of Allah, the Compassionate, the Merciful. Praise be to Allah, Lord of the Creation, the Compassionate, the Merciful, King of Judgment Day! You alone we worship, and to You alone we pray for help. Guide us to the straight path, the path of those whom You have favored, not of those who have incurred your wrath, nor of those who have gone astray."

I then raised my hands as he had done and recited the seventy-fifth sura, the Sura of the Resurrection:

"In the Name of Allah, the Compassionate, the Merciful. I swear by the Day of Resurrection, and by the self-reproaching soul.

"Does man think We shall never put his bones together again? Indeed, We can remold his very fingers!

"Yet man would ever deny what is to come. 'When will this be,' he asks, 'this day of Resurrection?'

"But when the sight of mortals is confounded and the moon eclipsed; when sun and moon are brought together—on that day man will ask: 'Whither shall I flee?'

"No, there shall be no escape. For on that day all shall return to your Lord. On that day man shall be informed of all that he has done and all that he has failed to do. He shall become his own witness; his pleas shall go unheeded.

"Yet you love this fleeting life and are heedless of the life to come.

"On that day there shall be joyous faces, looking towards their Lord.

"On that day there shall be mournful faces, dreading some great affliction.

"But when a man's soul is about to leave him and those around him cry: Will no one save him? When he knows it is the final parting and the pangs of death assail him—on that day to your Lord he shall be driven. For in this life he neither believed nor prayed; he denied the truth and, turning his back, went to his kinfolk elated with pride.

"Well have you deserved this doom; well have you deserved it. Well have you deserved this doom: too well have you deserved it!

"Does man think that he lives in vain? Was he not a drop of ejected semen?

"He became a clot of blood; then Allah formed and molded him and gave him male and female parts. Is He then not able to raise the dead to life?"

Now Allo and the Kurd stepped close to the grave. I was about to say something when the Persian signaled to me. He moved forward and spoke a few phrases from the eighty-second sura:

"In the Name of Allah, the Compassionate, the Merciful.

"When the sky is rent asunder; when the stars scatter and the oceans roll together; when the graves are hurled down; each soul shall know what it has done and what it has failed to do.

"Yet you deny the Last Judgment. Yet there are guardians watching over you, noble recorders who know of all your actions.

"The righteous shall surely dwell in bliss. But the wicked shall burn in hellfire upon the Judgment Day: they shall not escape.

"It is the day when every soul will stand alone and Allah will reign supreme."

The opening in the stone was closed now, and a final prayer was required.

Halef stepped forward. Tears were sparkling in the eyes of the brave little Hadji and his voice trembled as he said, "I shall pray." He raised his hands and began: "You have heard that Allah will gather all of us on the day of Judgment. Over there the sun has set, and tomorrow it will rise anew. In like manner we shall arise up there when we have died on this earth. Oh Allah, grant that we be among those worthy of your mercy, and do not separate us from those we loved. You are the All-powerful and can also grant this prayer!"

All of us turned our head to the right, then to the left, and intoned: "Es-selam 'aleikum we rahmetulla." Then all passed the palms of their hand across forehead, face, beard, and chest. The service was over.

What a curious burial! A Christian, two Sunnites, and one Shiite had spoken by the grave of the dead, but Muhammad had not sent down a bolt of lightning. Speaking for myself, I did not feel that I was committing a sin by taking leave of my friend in the language he had spoken. But the participation of the Persian was proof that he was intellectually and spiritually far superior to the ordinary Muslim. And I could have embraced Halef for his brief, simple words.

We were about to leave the boulder when Amad el Ghandur drew his dagger, struck a piece from one of the rocks of the site, and put it away. I knew what this meant and was convinced now that no human being would be able to dissuade him from his revenge. During the course of the evening he neither ate nor drank, did not join in our conversation, and showed no inclination to speak to me, however briefly. He responded to only one remark.

"You know that Muhammad Emin took the stallion back," I told him. "It is yours now."

"Then I have the right to give it away again?"

"No doubt."

"I give it to you."

"I will not accept Rih!"

"Then I shall force you to keep him."

"How?"

"You will see! May you spend a pleasant night." Amad el Ghandur turned away and left me standing.

It occurred to me that the time had come to double my vigilance as far as he was concerned. But things were to turn out differently. It was a sad, indeed a dismal evening. The Persian had withdrawn behind the branches, his men were squatting about, and

Halef, Lindsay, and I were silently sitting by the spring, trying to cool our burning wounds. Muhammad Emin's death had affected each of us more than we cared to admit. Occasionally I felt a flash of coolness in my feverish body, the approach of traumatic fever. Halef was already feverish. I spent an uncomfortable night but, having a strong constitution, did not have too serious an attack. It was as if I felt every single drop of blood coursing through my veins. Half awake, half dreaming, I tossed back and forth, spoke to all kinds of people my imagination conjured up, yet knew that all this was an illusion. Not until morning did I begin to sleep more soundly, and then I did not wake until evening. The scent I mentioned before had enveloped me again, but instead of two beautiful pairs of eyes, I saw the huge Aleppo boil on the Englishman's nose shining above me.

"Back to the living?" he asked.

"I believe so. But what's this? It's almost evening!"

"You should be pleased, sir. The two ladies have been nursing you. They sent some medicine for your wound, and Halef applied it. Then one of them came in person and poured something between your teeth. I don't imagine it was porter."

"Which one?"

"One of them. The other stayed where she was. But then again, it may have been the other one, I really couldn't say."

"I mean, was it the one with the black or the one with the blue eyes?"

"I saw no eyes. They are wrapped up as tightly as a package!—You seem all right!"

"Yes, I feel refreshed and in good spirits."

"Same here. Do you want something to eat?"

"Is there anything? I'm very hungry!"

"Here you are." A silver pan with cold meat, sour bread, and some delicacies had been set next to me. Alongside it was a pot containing a nourishing broth.

"The ladies seem to have known that I would wake up before the broth got cold," I said.

"Oh, no! This pot has been sitting here since noon. Every time it got cold they had that old woman pick it up and reheat it. You seem to be a favorite of theirs."

I looked around more closely. Halef was lying nearby, asleep, but otherwise I saw no one.

"Where is the Persian?"

"With the women. He left this morning and came back with a mountain goat, and it's goat broth you are drinking."

"Served by such hands, it always tastes delicious. What about Amad el Ghandur?"

"He went riding early this morning."

That startled me. "What? That was terribly rash!"

"He left with the charcoal burner and the Kurd." Now I knew what Amad el Ghandur had meant when he said that Allah had sent him a means for his revenge. The Kurd, a mortal enemy of the Bebbeh, was to act as his interpreter. I felt sorry for the vengeful Haddedihn. The odds were ten to one that he would never get back to his tribe. But to go after him was out of the question. To begin with, he had too much of a head start. Besides, I was wounded. Nor could we allow another's blood feud to involve us in murder.

"I assume he is riding the stallion?" I asked.

"The stallion is here." More bad news. Amad el Ghandur was in effect compelling me to accept the horse as a present. At that moment I was uncertain whether to be pleased or annoyed.

"So Allo left with him? What about his wages?"

"He didn't take them, and that bothers me. I don't like accepting presents from a charcoal burner."

"Console yourself, Sir David. He has the horse and a rifle, and that's ample payment. Besides, who knows what the Haddedihn promised him. How long has Halef been sleeping?"

"As long as you."

"Sleep is a potent medicine. But I want to eat now!"

I had no sooner started when I was interrupted by the Persian. I wanted to get up but he pressed me down. "Stay where you are, Effendi, and eat!" he said amiably. "That's most important now. How do you feel?"

"Quite well, thank you."

"Your fever won't return. But now I want to give you a message. Amad el Ghandur came to see me. He told me a great deal about you and himself, so that I really got to know you as well as he does. The Haddedihn set out after the Bebbeh and asks that you forgive him. He doesn't want you to follow him but hopes you will return to the Haddedihn, and that you will meet again there."

"Thank you. His departure grieved me, but I must abandon him to his fate."

"Where will you go now?"

"That's something we still have to discuss. My friend and servant Hadji Halef Omar has to return to the Haddedihn, for his wife is there. And this bey from Inglistan left two of his servants with the tribe. But it is possible nonetheless that we will first ride to Baghdad. The Englishman has a ship there on which we could sail down the Tigris to the pastures of the Haddedihn."

"Then go ahead and discuss things with your companions, Effendi. Should you go to Baghdad, I ask that you keep me company. You are brave warriors. I already owe you my life and I should like to show you that I have become fond of you. We will remain here until we can leave without endangering your health. Now you should eat and drink. I will send you more; you are my guests. May Allah be with you!"

He left, and a bare two minutes later the old servant woman arrived with a second tray of food. "Take this. The master is sending it," she said.

"Do you have a fire by the hut?"

"Yes, and a small tripod, so we can prepare meals quickly."

Just as the old woman was about to waddle off, Halef started yawning and then opened his eyes. Surprised, he looked around and sat up. He seemed confused as he asked, "Mashallah! There's the sun! Did he turn or was it me?" He could not imagine that he could have slept all this time, and he was even more astonished when he heard that Amad el Ghandur had left us. "Did he really go? Without parting words? By Allah, that wasn't right! But what do we do? Now you are rid of your obligations and no longer have to return to the pastures of the Haddedihn, Sidi."

"On the contrary, I think I still have them. Do you think I would leave you without being sure that you will return safely to Sheik Malek and Hanneh, your wife?"

"Sidi, the two are well and will have to wait for me. I love Hanneh, but I will not abandon you until you return to the land of your fathers."

"I cannot ask such a sacrifice of you, Halef."

"It is not my sacrifice but yours for you to keep me with you, Sidi. Decide whatever you please and I shall follow, unless you should be cruel enough to send me away."

The Persians brought an ample quantity of fish from the river and we prepared our evening meal. Since I had already eaten, I went up to the boulder to watch the sunset from the grave of the Haddedihn. I felt sadness, an inner emptiness, as if part of my own being had died with the dead. Yet one should never mourn at the grave of a decent man. Death is God's messenger who only draws near to lead us back to those luminous heights of which the Savior told his apostles: "In my Father's house are many mansions . . . I go to prepare a place for you." Life is a battle. One lives to fight and dies to achieve victory.

The wooded heights below me resembled a green sea over whose frozen waves dusk was slowly spreading its advancing shadows. I felt the evening wind sweep across the nearby crests, and the treetops gently bowed in the breeze. The shadows darkened, the distance faded, the evening light waned, and now even what was close was veiled in darkness. If I could only travel with the sun and follow it far, far to the West, where its light was still bright and warm as it fell on my native land. Here, on this lonely height, I felt that homesickness no responsive person can ever be immune to. "Ubi bene, ibi patria"* is a maxim whose cold indifference is echoed only in the lives of callous drifters. The impressions acquired in youth can never be wholly effaced; memory may lie dormant but it never dies. It returns when we least expect it, and with it comes that longing whose pain can so grievously unsettle the mind.

---

* Where it is well with me, there is my country.

# 6 : A Persian Fugitive

I returned to camp by a roundabout way and found everyone already asleep. Although it was late, I lay awake for a long time, and some birds were already chirping when I finally fell asleep. I woke toward noon and heard from Halef that the Englishman had gone hunting wood grouse with the Persian. They had taken Dojan with them.

Some time later the men returned with an ample bag. The Persian greeted me with unfeigned cordiality, and then joined the women. Sir David sat down beside me.

"You just got up?" he asked.

"I must admit I slept late again."

"This is Cockaigne, but how long will it last?"

"Until we leave, no doubt."

"A brilliant answer! And where are we going?"

"Baghdad. Are you coming along?"

"Suits me! I'd like to get out of these mountains. And where are we going after Baghdad?"

"We'll have to see. In any event, it isn't certain yet whether I really want to go to Baghdad itself. I just meant we'd be going in that direction."

"No matter, as long as we get out of here."

The old woman emerged to turn the wood grouse over to the servants for plucking. Behind her was her master, who gestured to me and then left the camp slowly. I followed him. At a place shaded by two oaks he sat down in the moss and asked me to settle by his side.

When I had done so he began: "Effendi, I trust you, so listen to me. I am a fugitive. Don't ask me the reason. It's a political matter, though I do not mean an intrigue and base lust for power but—as far as I am concerned—something that involves the well-being of my people, whom I consider spiritually enslaved and prevented from developing freely and healthily. And do not ask me who my father was. He died a sudden, violent death and his friends whispered secretly that he had been killed because he stood in someone's way. I, his son, avenged him and had to flee with my family. But before that I loaded all the valuables I could save on some camels and sent them ahead across the Persian border, in the custody of a man who is loyal to me for a variety of reasons. We followed along a different route. I knew we would be pursued and therefore misled my pursuers by riding through Kurd territory. And now, Effendi, tell me if you will accompany me for as long as your route is the same as mine. But consider carefully that I am a fugitive."

There was no reason to hesitate. I liked this Persian. He was clearly a generous individual who had failed in some sort of reform attempt. I had already decided that I would take him under my wing, and so I said, "I will escort you as long as that will be of use to you and yours."

"I thank you, Effendi. And your companions?"

"They will go where I go. May I ask what your destination is?"

"Hadramaut."

This name quickened my interest. Hadramaut was an unexplored, dangerous city. All fatigue, all moroseness were suddenly gone, and I asked eagerly, "Are you expected?"

"Yes. I have a friend there whom I advised by messenger of my arrival."

"May I accompany you as far as Hadramaut?" I asked.

"All that distance, Effendi? I cannot ask for such a sacrifice."

"It is none! I'd gladly accompany you."

"Then you are welcome. Stay with us as long as you please. But I should tell you that before going to Hadramaut I must visit An Najaf."

"Ah, we are at the end of Rabi II, and Jumada I is about to begin. And the fifteenth of that month is the anniversary of Caliph Ali's death."

"Yes. I must go to An Najaf to bury my father on this

Shiite holiday. So you can see that it is almost impossible for you to accompany us."

"Why? Because I am a Christian? I have already been to Mecca, and only Muslims are admitted there."

"You might fare badly if you were recognized in An Najaf!"

"I was also recognized in Mecca—and am still alive!"

"Effendi, you are a bold man. I know that my father is resting in Allah's hands, whether his corpse be buried in Teheran or in An Najaf. I would never make the pilgrimage to Karbala, An Najaf, or Mecca, because Muhammad, Ali, Hasan and Husein were people just like you and me. But I must fulfill my father's dying wish. He wanted to be buried in An Najaf, and for this reason I shall join the death caravan going there. If you wish to stay with me, it is not I that would betray you. My family would also keep the secret, but my servants do not share my views about the teachings of the Prophet and would be the first to kill you."

"Let that be my worry. Where do you pick up your camels?"

"Do you know Kadhimain, near Baghdad?"

"The Persian city? Yes, it lies on the right bank of the Tigris, opposite Muazzam. It is connected with Baghdad by horsecar."

"That's where my camel drivers are expecting me. They also have my father's body with them."

"So I will first accompany you there, and then we will see. But tell me, will you be safe in Kadhimain?"

"I hope so. It's true that I am being pursued, but the pasha of Baghdad would not hand me over to my enemies."

"Trust no Turk, trust no Persian! You were careful when you decided to travel through the Kurdish mountains! Are you going to abandon that wise caution now? You can reach An Najaf without joining the death caravan."

"I don't know of any way."

"Then I shall guide you. Allah gave me the ability to orient myself in unknown regions."

"I like your proposal, Effendi, but it won't be possible. I must join my people in Kadhimain."

"Then go there secretly and avoid Baghdad and the death caravan."

"Effendi, I am no coward. Are my men to think I am afraid?"

"I understand: you also are bold. That's good, for it means we are suited to each other. We will travel together."

"I agree, Effendi, but there is one condition. I am wealthy. I demand that you take everything you need from me."

"Then I am your servant who is being paid a wage."

"No, you are my guest, my brother, whose love permits me to provide for him. I swear by Allah that I will not ride with you unless you accept."

"You force me to fulfill your wish. You are showing me great kindness and trust although you do not know me."

"You think I don't? Didn't you save us from the Bebbeh? Didn't Amad el Ghandur tell me about you? We will stay together, and for the little I can offer you I will receive treasures I have always searched for in vain because I found no one who had them—treasures of the spirit. Effendi, I am not an uneducated person, but I cannot hope to rival you. I know that in your country a boy has more knowledge than an adult in mine, that you revel in possessions whose names we don't even know. Compared to yours, our land is a desert and the poorest of your people has more rights than the vizier of Farsistan. There are many other things I know and I also know the reason: You have mothers, women; we have neither. Give us mothers, and our children will soon be able to compete with yours! A mother's heart is the soil in which the child's spirit strikes root. Oh, Muhammad, I hate you, for you took the soul from our women and made them the slaves of sensual passion! Thus you took away our strength, petrified our hearts, turned our lands into a desert and cheated all your followers of true happiness."

He had risen and was shouting his accusation of the

Prophet. It was fortunate that none of his men was listening! Only after a lengthy pause did he turn back to me. "Do you know the route to Baghdad?"

"I have never traveled it but will not lose my way. We have the choice of two directions: one leads southwest, to the Djebel Hamrin, the other will take us along the Diyala south of Baghdad."

"How far do you think it is from here to Kadhimain?"

"If we take the first route, we will arrive in five days, but we will need only four along the second."

"Do these routes pass through inhabited areas?" he asked.

"Yes, and that's precisely the reason they seem best to me."

"Then there are others?"

"Yes. But we would have to journey through stretches where no one but thieving Bedouins roam."

"Are you afraid of them?"

"Afraid? No. But a cautious person will always choose the better of two routes. I have a passport from the sultan which is respected along the Diyala and west of that river, but not by the Bedouins."

"And yet I would prefer the less traveled route, since I am a fugitive. I don't want to be caught this close to the Persian border."

"Perhaps you are right. But consider that going through the steppe, where the heat of the sun has now withered all vegetation, will be quite laborious for your family."

"The women fear neither hunger nor thirst, neither heat nor cold. Their only fear is my capture. I have skins filled with water and provisions for at least eight days."

"Are you certain you can rely on your men?"

"Completely."

"Very well, then we'll ride through Bedouin territory. Allah will protect us. Besides, once we have reached the plain we'll advance rapidly; your camels are having trouble in this mountainous terrain. So we are agreed and have only to wait until our wounds are sufficiently healed."

"Now please do me one favor," he said hesitantly.

"When I set out, I provided myself with all necessities. On long journeys clothes wear out, and I also took a supply of garments along. Yours no longer befit you, so I request that you take from me what you need."

This offer was not unwelcome but perhaps not quite appropriate. The Persian was right: we could not let ourselves be seen in any civilized place without being taken for vagabonds. But I also knew that the Englishman would accept no gifts, and it was a point of honor for me not to tax the Persian's friendship excessively. In any event, I did not much care whether Arabs saw me in my less than presentable attire. A real Bedouin judges a man by his horse, not his coat, and no one would fail to envy me Rih. At most a son of the desert might take me for a horse thief, but that would be more of an honor than a disgrace in his view.

"I thank you," I said. "I know you are well intentioned toward us, but please let us postpone discussing this matter until we reach Kadhimain. For the Bedouins, all garments are good enough, and I think I can continue wearing mine during the few days it will take us to get to the vicinity of Baghdad. I think we . . ." I stopped, for it seemed to me I had heard a noise in the mulberry bush behind the two oaks.

"It's nothing," the Persian said. "Perhaps an animal, a bird, a lizard, a grass snake."

"I know every kind of forest sound," I contradicted him. "That was no animal but a human being."

With long leaps I circled the bush and seized a man who was just about to flee. It was one of the Persian's servants.

"What are you doing here?" I barked at him.

He said nothing.

"Talk, or I'll make you!"

He opened his lips but uttered only an incomprehensible noise.

The Persian came closer. When he saw the man he said, "It's Saduk. He cannot answer, he is mute."

"What is he doing in this mulberry bush?"

"He will tell me, I can understand him." And turning to the servant he asked, "Saduk, what business do you have here?"

The man opened his hand, in which he held a few

: 121 :

herbs and mulberries, and tried to convey his meaning by gestures.

"Where did you come from?"

Saduk pointed in the direction opposite the camp.

"Did you know we were here?"

He shook his head in denial.

"Did you hear what we discussed?"

He made the same sign.

"Go then, but don't ever disturb us again!"

Saduk left, and his master explained, "Saduk was ordered by the old servant woman to gather mulberries, leeks, and herbs to be used in preparing the grouse. He did not mean to come close to where we were standing."

"He was eavesdropping," I countered.

"But you saw that he denied it."

"I don't believe him."

"There can be no question of Saduk's loyalty."

"I don't care for his physiognomy. A man with angular, broken jawbones is always false. That may be a prejudice but I have always found it confirmed. Was he born this way?"

"No."

"How did he lose his speech?"

The Mirza hesitated but then said, "Saduk no longer has his tongue."

"Ah! So originally he could speak. Then it was cut out?"

"Unfortunately," the Mirza admitted reluctantly.

I thought with horror of the formerly common cruelty of punishing the tongue by cutting or even tearing it out when talk had caused a crime. This barbarity was especially widespread in the Orient and the North American slave states.

"Hassan Ardshir-Mirza," I began again. "I see that you are loath to discuss the matter. But I don't care for this Saduk. I could never trust him, and his presence during our conversation seems suspicious to me. I am not inquisitive, but it is my custom in dangerous situations to pay attention to even the most trivial detail. I am asking you to tell me how Saduk lost his tongue."

"I have tested him, Effendi; he is loyal and honest.

Nonetheless, you will hear what prompted my father to punish him in this fashion."

"Your father? That's important."

"You are mistaken, Effendi, it is irrelevant. Listen to what I have to tell you: in his youth, Saduk was my father's archer and, as such, his duty was to convey his orders, messages, and other dispatches. He frequently visited the house of the mujtahid* and saw his daughter. She pleased him, and Saduk was a handsome man. He jumped over the garden wall when she was standing by the flowers and dared speak to her of his feelings. The mujtahid, who was nearby but had not been seen, had Saduk arrested. Out of consideration for my father, he did not turn him over to the Urf tribunal, which would have sentenced him to death. But Saduk had sinned with his tongue, and the mujtahid insisted that my father remove it. My father had to accommodate this man, and so he ordered an apothecary who was also a famous physician to cut out the archer's tongue."

"That was almost worse than death! Has Saduk been with your father since that time?"

"Yes. And he bore his pain with patient resignation, for he is gentle and submissive. But there was a curse on the deed."

"How so?"

"The mujtahid died of poison, the physician was found murdered at the door of his pharmacy, and the girl drowned when the bark of a masked man capsized hers."

"That's very odd! Were the three murderers never found?"

"No. I know what you are thinking, Effendi, but you are wrong. Saduk was often ill, and on the very days when those three died, he lay sick in his room."

"And your father did not die a natural death either?"

"He was attacked when he was out riding. Saduk and a lieutenant were accompanying him. Only Saduk saved himself—he had been wounded and was bleeding. The other two were dead."

---

* A legal scholar with the authority to make autonomous decisions.

"Hm. Didn't Saduk recognize the murderer?"

"It was dark. He recognized one of the attackers by his voice—it was my father's greatest adversary."

"On whom you avenged yourself?"

"The judges acquitted him—but he is no longer alive."

The Mirza's face made clear how that man had died. He threw up his hand contemptuously and added, "That's over and done with. Let's return to camp."

Hassan Ardshir-Mirza left, but I lingered for a while. What I had just heard made me wonder. Saduk was either a wholly selfless individual, and they are few in number, or a rare scoundrel. He would bear watching. When I returned to camp later, the noon meal was being prepared. I told the Englishman that I would like to accompany the Persian to Baghdad and then to An Najaf, and he immediately agreed to come along on that dangerous journey.

My wound had stopped bothering me. I felt well and picked up my carbine in the afternoon to look about a bit. I took Dojan but told Lindsay, who wanted to accompany me, that I preferred being by myself. Following a habit of many years, I first wanted to make certain that the camp was secure. Above all, one must hide one's tracks and then see if one can find those of a possible enemy. I circled the camp several times until I reached the river below. Here the grass had been trampled down, and that struck me as odd. I was about to approach the spot when I heard branches rustling behind me.

At once I moved behind a dense bush and crouched down. Someone was walking close by, and now the mute Persian came out of the bushes and looked around. Believing himself unobserved, he went to the spot along the river which had just attracted my attention, stamped on the grass, and then went back quickly. Before he had reached the edge of the bushes he cast a careful glance at two places. He was about to dart past me when I seized him with my left hand and slapped him so vigorously with my right that any resistance would have been pointless.

"Traitor, what are you doing here?" I burst out.

The incomprehensible sounds he uttered were due more to his fright, I had no doubt, than to any intent to explain his activity.

"You see this rifle?" I threatened him. "If you don't immediately follow my order, I'll shoot you. Take your cap, scoop up some water, and pour it on the trampled grass so it will stand up again. You'll speed things up by using your hands as well!"

Saduk made some gestures, perhaps in a show of resistance, perhaps to excuse himself, but when I raised my carbine he obeyed, looking at the weapon with one eye and his work with the other.

"Come along now," I ordered him when he had finished. "Let's see what you went out of your way to look at."

I scanned the two spots he had glanced at and noticed small tufts of grass on each of two bushes, which were some seven meters apart. "So it's a sign! That's really something! Take that grass down and throw it into the Diyala." The mute obeyed. "And now we are going back to camp. Move! If you try to run I'll shoot you or my dog will tear you limb from limb."

My foreboding had not misled me: this Persian was a traitor, although the exact circumstances still had to be brought out. When we got back to the others, I sent a servant for the Persian.

"What is it? Why are you holding on to Saduk?"

"Because he is my prisoner. He is plotting your destruction. You are being pursued, and he secretly shows your pursuers where we are. I surprised him when he was trampling down the grass along the bank of the Diyala, and there were tufts of grass hanging from the branches to indicate where one must pass through the bushes to get into our camp."

"That's not possible!"

"I say it is! Interrogate him if you can understand him."

Hassan Ardshir-Mirza propounded a number of questions to the prisoner but could gather nothing more from all his signs and gestures than that Saduk had no idea what I wanted from him.

"You see, Effendi, he is innocent," the Mirza said.

"Very well, I'll act in your place. I hope I shall be

able to convince you that Saduk is a traitor. Go get your rifle and follow me. But first tell your men that my companions will shoot down anyone who makes an attempt to free Saduk. My friends are not accustomed to being toyed with. Until we return, let someone stand guard by the edge of the bushes so he can report the approach of any danger."

"Do we ride or walk?" the Persian asked.

"How far is it from here to the site of your last camp?"

"We rode over six hours."

"Then we won't be able to reach it today. We'll walk."

He fetched his rifle while I gave Halef and the Englishman some necessary instructions. They bound up the prisoner and placed him between them. He was in good hands, and I could leave without worry.

We first turned down the valley toward the Diyala. Halfway along this short walk I stopped in surprise, for on a small copper beech there hung a tuft of grass similar to those I had made Saduk throw into the river.

"Stop, Mirza! What is this?"

"Grass," he answered.

"Does grass grow on trees?"

"Allah! Who put it there?"

"Saduk. Come here to the right, where I suspect we'll find another sign."

Surprised, the Mirza followed me. My guess was confirmed. "But wasn't that there before we got here?" The Persian was still skeptical.

"Hassan Ardshir-Mirza, it is a good thing that I am the only one to hear your words! Don't you see that this grass is still new and fresh? Come down to the Diyala, where I found the first signs. This rascal has marked a wide path from the river to the camp. We would have been attacked and killed there, just as your father, the apothecary, the mujtahid, and his daughter had to die."

"I dread to think you may be right."

"I am. Are you a good walker, and do you think you can find the way by which you came from your last camp?"

He answered both questions affirmatively and we

started walking upstream. Soon we got to the place where we had camped before coming to the help of the Persians. We had been riding south. Here the small stream turned east and we followed that direction. We had already passed the bend when I noticed a large willow to our right. Two strips of bark had been cut from its trunk.

"In what order did you normally ride?" I asked him.

"With the sedan chair carrying the women in the middle, and the men divided into two groups, one behind, the other ahead of me."

"Where was Saduk?"

"He was always with the section behind me. He often stayed back; he loves flowers and herbs and enjoys looking at them."

"Saduk hung back because he wanted to leave secret signs to guide your pursuers. He's really quite clever. Let's go farther."

A quarter of an hour later the Diyala had become nearly three times as wide. As a result, it was shallower and there was a ford where we could easily wade across.

Mirza stopped there and pointed at a young birch which had been broken a short distance below its crown. "I suppose you take that for a signal too?" he asked with a smile.

I examined the small tree. "Of course it is. Look at the trunk, and also at those of the other trees. Then see the direction in which the heights run, and you will discover that the only wind here will be from the west. No wind from anywhere else would be strong enough to break the crown of this slender tree. But broken it is, and in such a way that it points west. Doesn't that strike you?"

"It does, Effendi."

"And now examine the break. It is still light-colored, and can only date from the time when you passed here. During the last few days there has been no storm heavy enough to cause it. The crown points west, which is the direction you took. Come with me."

"Are we going to swim? We came across by this ford."

"Perhaps swimming won't be necessary; the river is

shallow. Let's wade across and you will see that we will find more signs where you rode into the water."

We tied our garments into bundles and placed them on our heads. The water was soon above our knees but only once reached my chest. On the other bank Mirza soon discovered that I had guessed correctly. Several vines had been bent together and connected in such a way that they symbolized a gate.

"Did Saduk have the time for this when you passed here?" I asked.

"Yes. I remember that the camels did not want to go into the water and gave us trouble. Saduk left his horse here to take one of them across and returned by himself to get his horse when the rest of us were already on the other side."

"How clever! Do you still refuse to believe me?"

"Effendi, I am beginning to agree with you. I wonder what kinds of marks he left in the plain, where there was nothing but grass."

"We'll find out. What direction were you coming from when you arrived here?"

"East. Over there . . . Effendi, what's that?" He was pointing, and as my eyes followed the direction of his arm I noticed a dark line that seemed to be coming toward us. "Are those horsemen?" he asked.

"They certainly are! Quickly, back across the river; there is nowhere for us to hide on this side. Over there we'll find rocks and bushes."

We quickly retreated and looked for a safe hiding place from which we might observe the approach of the riders. Only then did we find the time to put our clothes back on.

"Who could those people be?" the Mirza asked.

"Hm. This is no trading route, though the ford might be known to others. We'll have to wait."

The horsemen were approaching slowly and arrived at the opposite bank. They were so close that we could see their faces.

"This is serious," Hassan whispered. "Those are Persian troops."

"Here, on Turkish soil?" I asked skeptically.

"But you can see that they are dressed like Bedouins."

"Are they Ihlats or militia?"

"Ihlats. I know the commanding officer. He was my subordinate."

"Who is he?"

"Captain Maktub Aga, the son of Aijub Khan."

We saw that the officer was inspecting the vine. Then he turned to his men, pointed at it, and led his horse into the river. The others followed.

"Effendi," the Mirza whispered excitedly. "You were correct in everything you said. These men have been sent to capture me. I also see the Najib Omram, who is Saduk's nephew. What if they see us? Your dog won't give us away?"

"No. He'll keep quiet."

There were thirty of the pursuers. Their leader, a real daredevil, had stopped by a birch and was laughing. "Bravo!" he exclaimed. "Come here, Najib, and convince yourself that we can rely on your father's brother! Here's another mark. We will ride downstream. Let's move!"

The Ihlats passed without noticing us.

"Well now, Mirza, are you convinced?"

"Completely. But there is no time for talk. We have to act."

"Act? There's nothing we can do except follow your enemies and be careful."

We left our hiding place and cautiously scurried after them. Fortunately they were riding slowly. After a quarter of an hour the pursuers reached the camp site from which Muhammad Emin had rushed to his death. They stopped to examine the footprints. We turned off toward the right, entered the bushes, and hurried along as quickly as we could. The distance we had to cover normally took about ten minutes, but we reached camp in half that time. I was perspiring, the Mirza panting. A glance told me that everything was normal.

"Keep quiet, enemies are approaching," the Persian ordered his men, and then we leaped downhill and found the man we had posted there.

After barely a minute the pursuers appeared and stopped opposite us. "A good place to camp," their leader said. "What do you think, Omram?"

"It's getting late, master," the Najib answered.

"Very well, we'll stay. There's grass and water."

I had not expected this dangerous decision. While we had effaced all other traces of our presence, at the spot where we had camped the first night the grass had been burned and the earth blackened, something we had not been able to hide completely. I also noticed that the grass Saduk had trampled down had not yet risen again.

"Now what shall we do?" Hassan whispered.

"We'll stalk them. But three of us can be discovered easily. One is enough, so I'll do it. Take the dog, return to camp, and prepare for battle. If you hear this revolver being fired, you can stay where you are. But if you hear the voice of the carbine, it will mean that I am in danger and you will have to rush to my aid. In that case have Hadji Halef Omar bring my hunting rifle."

"Effendi, I cannot abandon you in this danger."

"I am safer here than you are up there. You are of no use to me here."

With his servant and Dojan the Persian climbed the height. It was better that I should be by myself than hampered by someone with no experience. The only danger was that the officer might have the bushes searched. But this Persian captain was no Indian chief; that was perfectly evident from the casual way he let his men set up camp. The horses were unsaddled and left to themselves. They immediately rushed toward the water and scattered. The horsemen threw their lances aside, placed their possessions carelessly on the ground, and then stretched out in the grass.

Only the Najib inspected the terrain and thus came to the place where our fire had been. He bent down to have a look and exclaimed, "Pay attention!"

"What is it?" his commanding officer shouted and jumped up.

"There was a fire here! They spent the night in this place."

When the captain had convinced himself of the correctness of that observation he asked, "Is there a sign?"

"I don't see any," the lieutenant answered. "Perhaps Saduk did not have a chance to leave one. We'll find something tomorrow. We can also light a fire here. Bake some bread!"

When I observed the unconcern with which the soldiers attended to their tasks, I realized I had no reason to fear them. They started a huge fire, mixed flour and water until it became a thick paste which they squeezed, pressed, rolled, and finally stuck on the points of their lances to hold over the fire. While it was still hot, and half burned, they tore it apart and devoured it greedily. That was their evening meal. When dusk fell they prayed and then moved closer to the fire to tell each other the fairy tales from the "Thousand and One Nights" for the thousand and first time. Clearly I was superfluous here.

I crawled noiselessly back to camp. No fire had been lit there. Everyone was sitting at his place, ready for battle. Saduk was still lying between Halef and the Englishman, but he had been tied more securely, and gagged.

"How does it look, Effendi?" the Persian asked.

"Fine."

"Have they left?"

"No."

"Then how can things be fine?"

"Because these Ihlats and their commander are terrible fools. If we keep quiet during the night, they will leave early tomorrow without bothering us in the least. Halef, is your leg well enough so you can climb down there?"

"Yes, Sidi."

"Then go down and keep watch until I relieve you."

"Where are you going to look for me?"

"The soldiers have a fire and there is a crooked old pine tree directly above it. I'll meet you there."

"Very well, Sidi. I'll leave my rifle here. My knife is sharp, and if one of those fools should dare climb that tree, he'll have an opportunity to think of Hadji Halef Omar as he roasts in hell."

He scurried away quietly and his neighbor, the Englishman, took me by the arm. "Sir, what's going on? I am sitting here and can't understand a word being said. All I know is that a bunch of Persians is down there. Suppose you tell me what's up."

I briefly set forth the state of things, but the Mirza felt that my explanation was taking too long. He interrupted me. "Effendi, couldn't I have a look at the Ihlats?"

"Can you move soundlessly over roots and foliage, or through branches?"

"I should think so. I'd be careful."

"Have you learned to suppress coughing and sneezing?"

"That's impossible!"

"It isn't. It's not even difficult provided one has practiced it. But we'll take a chance. Perhaps we can listen in on them and find out something important. If you feel a tickle in your nose or throat, put your mouth firmly on the ground and cover your head. While stalking an enemy one must never breathe through the nose; then one won't sneeze. If one has to cough while the enemy is near, one must cough toward the earth and with one's head covered. At night one should imitate the hoot of the eagle owl. But an experienced hunter will never cough or sneeze. Let's go."

I took the lead, trying to move everything out of Hassan's path that might get in his way. We reached a spot off to one side of Halef's post, by the edge of the bushes where it was easy to hide in the deep shadows of the foliage. The fire was burning a mere twelve paces ahead. The two officers were sitting near it while the others had formed a three-quarter circle around it.

Hassan did not say a word, but I could tell from his breathing that he was in a state of excitement. He was unquestionably a courageous man and experienced in the use of arms, but he had never found himself in a comparable situation. My heart had also beaten audibly when I stalked my first enemy, but practice had made me calmer.

The Ihlats seemed convinced that no one else was about, for their conversation was so loud that it could have been heard on the other side of the river. Just as we were coming to our hiding place, the lieutenant was asking his superior, "Are you going to bring him back alive?"

"I am no fool. Tell me, men, do you want him dead or alive?"

"Dead!" they all shouted.

"Of course! We have been ordered to pursue the Mirza and to bring back his head if we cannot capture him alive. If we bring him back alive, we'll have to turn over all his possessions. But if we bring his head, no one will bother about anything else."

"I hear he transported his money and valuables," the lieutenant said.

"Yes, that son of a cursed general is very rich. He loaded eight or ten camels with his treasures. There'll be valuable booty for us to share."

"And what will you do if the Mirza places himself under the protection of a sheik or a Turkish official?"

"What if he does? But if that should happen we mustn't let on that we are Persians, you understand? In any event, Hassan won't have the time to seek out such protection, for we'll capture him tomorrow or the day after. We'll leave here at dawn and continue finding those marks which show us the way. That fool thinks Saduk is harmless because he can't talk. He forgets that he knows how to write. What Saduk left for us is as clear a form of writing as his papyrus strips. Settle down now, there is not much time left for sleep."

In addition to the obvious benefit, our eavesdropping brought me another: I knew now that the Mirza's father had been a general and felt sure that he himself had also held a high post in the Persian army. Those whose revenge he was trying to escape had to be people of considerable importance.

When the Ihlats had wrapped their blankets around them, we soundlessly crawled away. "Effendi," the Persian said angrily when we were out of earshot, "I heaped all sorts of benefits on that captain and that lieutenant. Those two must die!"

"They are unworthy of your notice," I calmed him. "They are dogs sent out to harry you. It is not they but their masters who deserve your wrath!"

"Those ingrates want to murder me and steal all I own."

: 133 :

"But they won't succeed. We'll discuss it when we get back. Go on by yourself now, I'll be back in camp soon."

The Mirza left reluctantly. When I could no longer hear his quiet movements, I scurried over to Halef and whispered some necessary instructions. I then described an arc around the camp of the Ihlats so that I reached the edge of the bushes and the Diyala to the right of them, and then walked on in a southerly direction. After about two minutes, I bent a small alder so that its crown pointed south, and five or ten minutes later I repeated that same procedure twice. At the point where I left the last sign, the river made a sharp bend, and that suited my intentions admirably. Then I returned to camp.

My short excursion had taken about half an hour, and both the Persian and Sir David had felt some anxiety about me. The Englishman asked, "What are you doing, running all over the place? I am sitting here like an orphan no one is bothering with, and getting a little tired of it!"

"Calm down. There will soon be something for you to do."

"Very well. Are we going to kill those scoundrels?"

"No. But we are going to have a chance to thumb our noses at them."

"It would be better still if we could give them mine. Who'll be in the party?"

"Just you and me."

"All the better. When do we start?"

"Shortly after daybreak."

"Not until then? In that case I'm going to catch a few winks." With perfect sang-froid, Lindsay wrapped himself in his blanket and soon fell asleep.

Hassan was anxious to council with me, and close to the branches that separated the women's quarters from ours I saw the three women, clearly driven by anxiety and eager to listen to our conversation.

"Where did you go, Effendi?"

"I wanted to give you time to calm down and reflect. An intelligent man does not consult his wrath but his reason. I imagine your anger has abated, and you can tell me now what you plan to do."

"I am going to attack those Ihlats with my men, and kill them."

"Those thirty, healthy men with your wounded?"

"You and your companions will help us."

"No, we won't. I am no barbarian. My belief permits me to defend myself when I am attacked, but otherwise I am commanded to respect my brother's life."

"Then you won't help me, Effendi, although you are my friend?"

"I am your friend, and shall prove it to you. But I ask: Will Hassan Ardshir-Mirza turn into a cowardly assassin?"

"Never, Effendi!"

"And yet you wish to attack the Ihlats in their sleep. Or do you propose waking them first so that the skirmish is fought fairly? If so, you would be done for."

"I do not fear them!"

"I know that. But a wild, undisciplined bravery resembles the fury of the buffalo which blindly rushes to its death! Let us assume you kill ten or fifteen of these Ihlats; twenty or twenty-five will be left to engage you. In that case you will have given yourself away, and they will stick close to your heels until you are destroyed."

"Your speech sounds wise, Effendi, but sparing my pursuers is an infallible way of delivering myself into their hands! They will seize me today or tomorrow, and you have heard what will happen then!"

"Who says that you should deliver yourself over to them?"

"Isn't that the way it would be? Or do you imagine you can persuade them to let me continue my journey?"

"That's precisely what I will do. Just now I was down by the river and broke off some small trees. When the Ihlats notice that, they will continue on their way. I will ride ahead of them and leave signs which will mislead them. And if they should discover our camp before setting out, you will defend it. I will hear your fire and return immediately."

"What good will it do to lead them away from our trail if they find us again later?"

"Let me worry about that. I will see to it that they won't. Do you have parchment with you?"

"Yes. And we also found parchment in Saduk's possession."

"He used it to send messages to the Ihlats. Did you ask him about it?"

"Yes, but he admits nothing."

"We don't need his confession. Give me his parchment and go to sleep. I shall wake and watch, and rouse you when the time has come."

The women disappeared and the men settled down. Saduk had heard every word of this exchange. He must have been on pins and needles. I checked his bonds; the ropes were strong enough and, though firmly gagged, he could breathe.

Just before dawn, I woke the Englishman. The Persians were also stirring, and the Mirza came toward us. "Are you leaving now, Effendi? When will you be back?"

"The moment I am convinced that I have misled the enemy."

"That may not be until tomorrow."

"True."

"Then take some flour, meat, and dates along. And what should we do until you return?"

"Keep quiet, and leave this area as little as possible. Should some danger arise, consult with my Hadji Halef Omar. He is intelligent and experienced."

I scurried back down to tell Halef of my plan. When I returned, Lindsay was ready and I saw that our pouches had been filled with provisions. After a brief farewell we set out.

Since it was dark, it was quite difficult and time consuming to lead the horses past bushes and trees down the slope, and we had to make a detour to avoid being detected. Finally we reached the valley, mounted, and trotted off. Because mist lay over the water, it was not possible to see very far, but in the east it was already getting light and a gentle morning breeze indicated the coming of daylight. After barely five minutes we reached the bend in the river where I had left the last mark. I dismounted.

"Why are we stopping?" Lindsay asked.

"We have to wait here to see if the Persians go on immediately, or first reconnoiter and possibly engage our friends."

"Very clever. That way we'll be sure to be there. Did you bring tobacco along?"

"I'll check." Hassan had been very attentive; he had placed a small quantity of Persian tobacco among the provisions.

"All right, let's light a pipe. Splendid fellow, that Mirza!"

"Wait. The mist is lifting and in two minutes we'll be able to see the Ihlats. We have to move to the other side of the bend, otherwise they'll notice us and we'll have muffed our chance."

We hid behind the sharp bend of the river valley and waited. Finally I saw through my binoculars that all thirty Ihlats were coming down at a trot. We mounted and galloped away. After a mile, I cut a strip of bark from a willow.

"Those fellows would have to be very stupid not to notice that this is of extremely recent origin," Lindsay mumbled.

"Yes, that captain is no Hadji Lindsay Bey. You notice that the river seems to be forming a very wide arc? It must be turning back in this direction near the mountains in the south, which would mean an arc whose chord is at least eight miles long. Why not lead the Persians into the water?"

"I'm willing. But will they follow us?"

"Of course."

"And will they believe that the Mirza crossed the river at this point with his camels?"

"That's exactly what I want to determine. If their commanding officer does, he will also be duped by all our other tricks."

I tied the branches of a pipe shrub to form a very conspicuous arch, had my stallion prance about to cover the ground with prints, and then made him enter the water. The Englishman followed. Because we rode upstream, the current, though strong, did not keep us from reaching the corresponding spot on the opposite bank, where I bent the tips of some bushes to indicate a southerly direction. Fortunately the ground was grassy here; the water we were dripping would not be noticeable.

We galloped on. The Persians were sure to reach this place in half an hour, and if they were not wholly inexperienced they would recognize that the hoof-prints in the grass had been made no earlier than that morning. This jeopardized the success of our under-taking but was a chance I had to take. We continued riding for two hours in the same direction, across short plains and low hills, and through shallow valleys with small streams running through them. Then we found ourselves on the bank of the Diyala once again, as I had assumed, and crossed to the other side. It goes without saying that we left signs at appropriate spots. I now pulled out a piece of parchment.

"Are you going to do some writing?"

"Yes. I want to see if parchment will have the same effect as those marks we left."

"Let's see what you are putting down."

"I'd rather tell you, you wouldn't be able to decipher it. It is Persian and reads from right to left. The words are: 'Keep moving down.' I am curious to see if our pursuers will follow these instructions."

I pulled two branches of a shrub together and at-tached the parchment so that it could not be over-looked. We then followed the course of the river until we found a spot from which we could observe our last crossing without being seen. Here we dismounted to have something to eat and to let the animals drink and graze.

We had to wait considerably more than an hour before we finally noticed some movement along the river above us. A look through my binoculars showed that our plan had succeeded. Pleased with ourselves, we rode on. I did not make another sign until shortly before noon, and another toward evening, by the cor-ner of a valley running west from the Diyala. This was the first opportunity to carry out the second part of our enterprise, which was to guide the Persians off to the right, for up to now the terrain had not been suit-able for that purpose. At the entrance to the valley we settled down for a night of well-deserved rest.

The following morning I left a second piece of

parchment which indicated that the route would now be leading west for some time. In the course of the morning I placed a third sign to advise our pursuers that Hassan had become suspicious because he had seen me (i.e., Saduk) make one. At noon I made the fourth and last, which stated that the Mirza intended to ride to Kifri or even to Djumeila. His suspicion, I wrote, had increased to such an extent that he had put me in the van so that he could constantly keep an eye on me. It would therefore not be possible to go on leaving signs.

Our task was accomplished. I did not consider it necessary to make sure that we would really be followed this far; judging by everything that had happened up to this point, we had every reason to believe that our ruse was working.

At an angle to the direction we had been following, we now set out on our return journey, passing through territory that could have been visited only rarely. Many detours and bends had to be followed, yet we reached the Diyala long before evening. We rode some distance upstream until darkness obliged us to stop for the night. Having left early the following morning, we reached camp by noon.

Before we had entered it, Halef came rushing down the height toward us. "Allah be praised, Sidi, that you return unharmed. We were very concerned; you stayed away two and a half days. Did something unexpected happen?"

"No, on the contrary, things went very smoothly. We did not come back earlier because we weren't certain whether we had really misled the Persians. How are things in camp?"

"All right, although something did happen that shouldn't have: Saduk escaped."

"How could he?"

"He must have a friend among the other servants who cut his bonds."

"When did he get away?"

"Day before yesterday, early, in broad daylight."

"How could that have happened?"

"You had left with the Inglis, and I was on guard here. The Persians left the camp, one after the other, to see what the Ihlats might do. They moved out, but when our Persians returned to camp, the prisoner had disappeared."

"That's very serious. Had it happened a day later there would have been no reason to worry. Come, lead Rih."

Up on the height everyone hastened toward us, and I could see how worried they had been. Then the Mirza took me aside and reported Saduk's escape.

"Two things are to be considered," I said. "First, if Saduk catches up with the Ihlats, he will bring them back quickly. Second, he may be somewhere near here, to revenge himself. In either case it is certain that we are no longer safe here. We must leave immediately."

"Where to?" the Mirza asked.

"To begin with we'll cross the river. There is no ford down here, so we'll return to the place where you crossed. This will also give us a margin of safety, for it won't be assumed that you went upstream. If Saduk has remained somewhere nearby, he will not dare come close during daylight hours. I could try using my dog to find his trail but that would be time consuming. Give the order to get ready to break camp, and show me the cut ropes. From now on don't ever let your servants know what you intend to do."

The Mirza went into the women's hut and returned with two ropes, a strap, and the piece of cloth that had served as a gag. All four had been cut. The cloth gave me the most trouble, since its many folds were difficult to reconstitute. Finally I succeeded and then examined the places where it had been cut.

"Order your men to line up," I told Hassan.

They obeyed his call without knowing what was up, but then they saw the bonds lying at my feet.

"Give me your knives and daggers," I commanded.

While each was handing me what I had asked for I surreptitiously observed their faces, but I noticed nothing out of the way. I carefully examined the cutting edges of the weapons and said as though in passing, "All these things have been cut by a three-edged dagger; I shall soon know who did it."

Altogether, there were only two such daggers, and I

saw that the owner of one of them suddenly paled. At the same time he was raising one foot like someone about to leap.

I said casually, "The guilty one is about to flee. He should not take that chance, for that would make matters worse for him. He can only save his skin by a frank confession."

The Mirza looked at me in surprise, and the three women, whose heads had appeared above the partition, were whispering softly to each other through their veils.

I had now completed my examination and knew what I had been looking for. I pointed at the man with my finger and said, "This is the one! Seize and tie him!"

I had barely uttered these words when the evildoer started off, leaping toward the bushes. The others were about to take up the pursuit.

"Stay where you are!" I commanded. "Dojan, go get him!" The dog dashed into the bushes—we heard a loud shout and the dog's barking.

"Halef, go get the fellow!"

"How can you tell from the knives who did it?" Hassan asked.

"That's easy. A flat blade will not make the same kind of cut as a three-edged one, which is more suitable for thrusting. Since the cut surfaces had been pushed far apart, the cut had not been made by a thin blade. And look at this: where these cut surfaces begin, they are not smooth but torn and turned inside out. The blade is nicked. And now examine this dagger: it is the only one with a nick."

"But how did you know the man was going to run?"

"Because he first went pale and then raised his foot. Who is going to interrogate him, you or me?"

"You do it, Effendi. That way, he won't lie."

"Then tell your men to disperse so that his confession will be easier for him. Here, return their knives to them. But I stipulate that you allow me to pass sentence."

Hassan consented readily.

Now Halef arrived with the sinner. For a few moments I fixed my eyes on his face. Then I said, "Your fate lies in your hands! If you confess what you did, you may expect mercy. But should you deny it, prepare yourself to enter hell!"

"Sahib, I will tell you everything," he answered, "but call the dog away."

"No. He will remain in front of you until we are finished. At a signal from me he will tear you apart. Now, tell me honestly, was it you who freed Saduk?"

"Yes."

"Why did you do it?"

"Because I had sworn it to him before we set out on this journey."

"I don't understand. Tell me the whole story."

"Saduk and I were sitting in the courtyard," he began hesitantly, "and he wrote on a small piece of parchment to ask if I was well intentioned toward him. I said 'yes' because I pitied him for having lost his tongue. He then wrote that he felt the same toward me, and that we should be friends. I agreed and we swore by Allah and the Koran that we would never abandon each other but help each other in all dangers."

"Are you telling the truth?"

"I can prove it to you, Effendi. I still have the parchment."

"Let me see it."

He gave it to me. It was quite dirty but the writing was still decipherable. I passed it to the Mirza. He read it and nodded.

"You were very careless," I told the man. "You swore loyalty to Saduk without examining whether that might not bring you harm."

"Effendi, everyone believed he was honest. I never thought that Saduk could be a scoundrel, and so I felt pity for him when he lay there bound up. I remembered my oath to help him if he should be in trouble and believed Allah would punish me if I did not keep it. So I waited for a moment when everyone was gone and freed him. He got up and ran into the bushes."

"In which direction?"

"Over there," and he pointed away from the river.

"You have become disloyal toward your master and have betrayed us because you wanted to keep an oath you swore thoughtlessly. Guess what your punishment will be."

"Effendi, you will have me killed."

"It is true that you deserve to die, for you freed a murderer and thereby endangered us all. But you confessed and so I shall permit you to ask your master for a more lenient punishment. I do not believe that you are a scoundrel at heart."

The sinner was weeping profusely. He threw himself on his knees before Hassan and the severe countenance of his master became milder. "Do not speak," he said, "for I know you will implore me, but I cannot help you. I have always been satisfied with you, but your fate no longer rests with me. Only the effendi can now determine it. Address yourself to him!"

"Sahib, did you hear?" the man stammered.

"So you think a good Muslim has to keep his oath?" I asked. "Could you break your oath?"

"No, even if it should mean my life."

"So that if Saduk came back to you secretly, you would help him again?"

"No. I set him free. I kept my oath. That suffices!"

What a curious way of judging the validity of an oath, though a view that suited my purpose.

"Would you like to make your master forget your error by being faithful and devoted to him?"

"I swear by Allah and the Koran, and by the caliphs and all the saints who ever lived!"

"Very well then. You are free and will continue serving Hassan Ardshir-Mirza!"

The man was beyond himself with joy and happiness, and I could tell that the Mirza endorsed what I had done. But we did not discuss the matter, for we had our hands full with our departure.

# 7 : Mirza Selim

Leaving the camp, we had considerable trouble with the camels. Those stupid animals were used to the extensive treeless plains and could not find their bearings among rocks, trees, and shrubs. We had to carry all our possessions as far as the river and pull the beasts down to the bank. And we also had difficulty getting them across the Diyala.

During this entire trek both Halef and I always stayed behind to efface our trail carefully.

It was not our intention to set out for Baghdad immediately. We simply wanted to leave a site where we no longer felt secure, and look for another where we would not have to fear being discovered by Saduk and the Ihlats. Toward evening, when we had long since turned south, we came upon a deserted hut which presumably had served as shelter for some lone Kurd. Its rear wall abutted against a rocky ledge and on the other three sides it was surrounded by bushes and shrubs. Beyond those bushes one had a distant view. Our animals were put up inside this area, and we also set up camp there, going no further than simply to spread our blankets on the ground. At evening time we were done, and the three women immediately got busy preparing a good supper. Because of the strenuous activity during the last three days, I was tired and soon settled down.

I must have been sleeping a few hours when I felt someone touch me and opened my eyes. The old servant woman was standing before me, gesturing. I rose to follow her. Only the Persian who was standing guard was still awake. He was sitting by the bushes and therefore could not see us.

The old woman led me to one side of the house, where dense elderberry was spreading its many clusters. Here I found Hassan. "Do you have something important to discuss?" I asked.

"It is important for us since it concerns our journey. I have been thinking about what I should do, and I would be glad to have your approval of my plans. Forgive me for having interrupted your slumber."

"Tell me what you have decided."

"You have been to Baghdad before. Do you have friends or acquaintances there, Effendi?"

"Some superficial acquaintances. But I have no doubt that they are well disposed toward me."

"Then you could stay with them without worry?"

"I can't think what danger there would be, especially since I stand under the protection of the sultan and could even place myself under that of a European power."

"In that case I have a request. I have already mentioned that my people are expecting me in Kadhimain. After everything that has happened to me recently, after Saduk's betrayal and the appearance of the pursuers under the command of former subordinates, I have come to feel that I would not be safe there. So I should like you to go and settle my affairs."

"Gladly. What would you like me to do?"

"The camels you will find there carried those possessions of mine which I could save. They will hamper me as I continue my journey, and I shall sell everything. Will you take charge of this sale?"

"Yes, if you repose such trust in me. But one thing does concern me. You have indicated that you turned your property over to an agent who is loyal to you. Won't this man feel offended and slighted when I suddenly appear in Baghdad and usurp his place, as it were?"

The Persian shook his head pensively. "Your misgivings are justified. Let me be quite frank and show you things in their true light. The man we are discussing is called Mirza Selim. Like my father and me, he served in the shah-in-shah's army and belonged to that group who were—well—dissatisfied with certain conditions in the country, like my father and me. Mirza Selim is an ambitious man; he is also audacious and ruthless when circumstances require. The fact that he could have the title 'Excellent Horseman' conferred on himself testifies to that. I became aware of his aspiration to marry my sister Benda and exploited it to create a certain dependence on me. I must admit that, so far, he has proven himself."

"And now?" I asked.

"Now, Effendi, I have changed. My recent experiences have made me suspicious, and that suspiciousness extends to Mirza Selim. I should tell you that Saduk was his confidant, as the captain and the lieutenant were. He certainly never loved me. He served me only to pursue his ambitious goals, and it is possible that Benda also was merely to be a means to an end. Effendi, everything suddenly presents a gloomy picture to me, while before I was as credulous as a child. Do you understand? I should like to rid myself of him cautiously to spare myself further disappointments."

"And what if you do, and make still another enemy?"

"I hope you will be intelligent enough to avoid that."

"Hm. What good is all my intelligence if this man is driven by his ambition and will not voluntarily give up his rights?"

"Should that be the case, you would have to proceed ruthlessly, for wouldn't that prove that he is not selfless? I hope, of course, that this matter can be brought to a satisfactory conclusion. I will send one of my men along and give him a letter that will establish your identity. You will sell everything, including the animals. Then you can pay the men and dismiss them. I know you will discharge this commission better than anyone else. And there is a second reason why I am giving it to you. Will you find an apartment in Baghdad right away?"

"I'll have the choice of several."

"Good. For I wish to entrust not only my possessions but also my family to you."

"Hassan, your plan embarrasses and surprises me. Consider that I am a man and a Christian!"

"It is a matter of indifference to me whether you are a Christian or a Muslim. When you saved my life, you didn't stop to ask what I was. I have to try to evade my pursuers. They must not know where I am, and that is the reason I entrust you with both my possessions and my family. You will protect them during my absence. I know you will respect my wife's and my sister's honor."

"I will not insist on either seeing or talking to them. But what do you mean when you talk about your absence?"

"While you are in Baghdad, I shall go to An Najaf with Mirza Selim and bury my father."

"You are forgetting that I also plan to go there."

"Effendi, give up that idea! It is too dangerous. It's

true that you were in Mecca without having paid for it with your life. But consider the difference between Mecca and Ali's resting place! In Mecca you have devout, calm Muslims, but in An Najaf you will run into fanatics whose fervor reaches such a pitch that it becomes a madness, a delirium which sometimes does not even spare true believers! If just one of them suspects that you are no Shiite, that you are not even a Muslim, you would suffer a very cruel death! Do as I say and abandon that plan!"

"Very well. I won't decide until I am in Baghdad. But whether I go or stay, you can rest assured that your family will be safe."

We stayed five more days at this spot and did not leave until we were firmly convinced that everyone had regained his strength. The ride through the mountains was uneventful, and the plain also was crossed without a hostile encounter with Arabs.

On the far side of Khan Beni Sad, four hours northeast of Baghdad, we stopped by a canal. From here I was to ride to Kadhinaim to talk with Mirza Selim. Our small troop had chosen a spot where we seemed safe from all interference. I first helped set up the camp and was then given Hassan's letter which was to serve as my attestation.

The Englishman observed our preparations for the journey, and said, "Are we going to Baghdad? I'm coming along!" I had no objections, but Halef also wanted to join me, and this was impossible since the protection of the camp required his presence.

We set out and three hours later had reached the third bend of the Tigris, above Baghdad. That is where Kadhinaim is, though on the opposite bank. We crossed the postal route that leads to Kirkuk, Erbil, Mosul, and Diyarbakir, rode past a large brickyard, and were ferried across. Passing through pleasant palm gardens, we reached Kadhinaim, which is inhabited exclusively by Shiite Persians.

This place stands on "sacred" soil, for the imam Mussa Ibn Djafar lies buried here. This famous man accompanied Caliph Harun al-Rashid on his pilgrimage to Mecca and Medina. In Medina the imam saluted the grave of the Prophet with the words "Hail to you, Father," while the caliph merely said: "Hail to you, Cousin!" "How dare you claim to be more closely related to the Prophet than I, his successor?" Harun exclaimed angrily, and from this time on he hated his confidant as profoundly as he had esteemed and preferred him before. Mussa Ibn Djafar was thrown into a dungeon, where he died. But after his death a magnificent mosque with a gilded cupola and four beautiful minarets was built over his grave.

Kadhinaim is noteworthy for other reasons, for it has a horsecar line whose starting point is the arsenal in Baghdad. It was constructed by the progressive Midhat Pasha, who later died so horribly in Arabia. Had this man not been recalled from his post as governor of Iraq, Mesopotamia would have had a railroad connecting the regions along the Euphrates and Tigris with Constantinople by way of the more important Syrian towns.* The Persians living in Kadhinaim are mostly traders and merchants who visit Baghdad daily to carry on business. To find Mirza Selim here I had to go to a caravanserai; they are plentuful in Baghdad and can also be found in Kadhinaim.

It was around noon, and in July, and the heat was above forty degrees celsius in the shade. The air over the city was opaque and all those we saw had their faces veiled.

We found ourselves in an alley as a man in luxurious Persian dress came toward us. He sat on a white horse which was wearing one of those valuable harnesses only the wealthiest can flaunt. Compared to him we looked like petty thieves.

"Out of the way!" he barked at us, making a gesture of loathing.

I was riding alongside the Englishman, but the alley was wide enough for the Persian to pass easily. Nonetheless, I would have done as he asked had it not been for that gesture. "You have more than enough room," I answered. "Move!"

Instead of passing us, the man blocked our path. "Sunnite swine, don't you know where you are? Yield, or my whip will show you the way!"

---

* The railroad, the Baghdad Railway, has been built since then.

"You would not dare!"

The Persian drew his camel whip and raised it above his head but missed, for my stallion leaped past him while I pushed my fist into his face with such force that even his Persian saddle did not keep him from being thrown.

I was going to keep riding without bothering with the fellow, but then I heard him curse, and the servant the Mirza had sent with us exclaimed, "For God's sake, it is Mirza Selim!"

I turned immediately. The man was already back on his horse and had drawn his curved saber. Only now did he recognize the servant.

"It's you, Arab!" he exclaimed. "What are you doing in the company of these scoundrels whom Allah will curse?"

I did not give the servant a chance to answer. "Be still! Are you really Mirza Selim?"

"Yes," he answered, momentarily dumfounded by my tone.

I urged my horse close to his and said in a low voice, "Hassan Ardshir-Mirza sent me. Don't attract attention, and take me to your house."

"You?" he asked in surprise, and scrutinized me. Then he turned to the servant: "Is that true?"

"Yes," Arab answered. "This sahib is Kara Ben Nemsi Effendi. He is the bearer of a letter from my master to you."

Arrogantly Mirza Selim looked us over once again. "I will read the letter and discuss the blow you gave me. Follow, but keep your distance. You offend me."

So this was the "Excellent Horseman," the Faithful One, who had resigned his commission in the Persian army, to whom Hassan had entrusted his possessions, and who had even won Benda's heart! Poor girl. There seemed little chance that she would be happy with this ruthless individual who struck me as a fool on top of everything else. If he really was an extraordinary horseman, he should be able to judge a man by his horse, and in that respect neither Lindsay nor I was a beggar. Nor was it particularly intelligent of him, a fugitive, to make such a display and to show an arrogance which would not have been becoming even in a much more highly placed person. I could see no reason why I should encourage his imperiousness, and so I gestured to Lindsay and we took him between us.

"You son of a dog," he threatened, "fall back, or I shall have you whipped."

"Be silent, you fool," I answered calmly, "otherwise I'll give you another blow on the nose. It's easy to play the lord and master when one rides the horse of one's superior. You will have to learn politeness."

He did not answer but rearranged his veil, which was hanging askew because of his fall. Because he had been wearing it the servant had not recognized him sooner.

We rode through a number of narrow streets and then Mirza Selim stopped by an opening in a low wall. After a man inside had removed the crossbars and let us in and we had entered the courtyard, I saw a number of camels lying on the ground, chewing ostrich-egg-sized cakes of barley and cotton seed, the fodder customarily given these animals in Baghdad. Some indolent individuals were lolling about, but the moment they saw Selim they bestirred themselves. It seemed this little mogul had been able to assert himself.

He turned his horse over to one of these men while we entrusted ours to Arab. Then Mirza Selim took us to the house, whose wall formed the rear end of the courtyard. We went down a staircase into one of those underground rooms which, because of the prevailing heat, is the preferred living quarters of the local population. It was square, with soft, thick cushions along the walls. A magnificent rug covered almost the entire floor. A silver coffee service had been placed on one of the cushions, and next to it I saw a costly hooka.* Equally valuable weapons and some tshibuks for guests were hanging from the walls. An antique vessel of Chinese porcelain, shaped like a dragon, contained some tobacco, and a lamp filled with sesame oil was suspended from the center of the ceiling by a silver

---

* A Persian water pipe, something between a nargileh and a tshibuk.

chain. By local standards these were truly princely furnishings, and I thought it unlikely that all these objects were Mirza Selim's property.

He settled down on a cushion and clapped his hands. Immediately one of the men I had seen in the courtyard came in. His master gestured him to light the hooka. This was done with typically Oriental slowness and conscientiousness, and during the entire solemn procedure we were standing by the door like foolish boys.

Only when this difficult feat had been accomplished and the servant had left, presumably to post himself behind the door to eavesdrop, did Mirza Selim feel that the time had come to grace us with his attention. He exhaled some clouds of smoke, and asked, "Where do you come from?"

A superfluous question since he had already heard from Arab. But to avoid more friction I answered calmly, "We are messengers sent by Hassan Ardshir-Mirza."

"Where is he?"

"Near the city."

"Why doesn't he come himself?"

"He is being cautious."

"Who are you?"

"Two Franks."

"Giaours? What are you doing in this country?"

"We travel to look at the towns, villages, and people."

"You are very inquisitive. Only an unbeliever would be that rude. How did you happen to meet the Mirza?"

"We met him."

"I am aware of that. Where did you meet him?"

"In the Kurdish mountains. We were with him until we came here. I have a letter for you."

"It is very reckless of Hassan Ardshir-Mirza to let you know his name and to entrust a letter to people such as you. I am a believer and not allowed to receive it from you. Give it to the servant. I shall call him."

That was more than insolent, but I said quietly, "I do not think the Mirza is reckless and would ask that you tell him so yourself. I should add that he never required an intermediary to receive something from us."

"Be silent, Kafir! I am Mirza Selim and do as I see fit. Do you know all the people with Hassan Ardshir-Mirza?"

I told him we did, and he asked whether any females were accompanying him, and how many.

"Two ladies and a servant," I answered.

"Did you see them?"

"Of course."

"The eye of an unbeliever must never rest on the garment of a woman."

"Why don't you tell the Mirza that?"

"Silence, you insolent fellow! I have no need of your advice. Did you also hear the voices of the women?"

This lout was testing my patience too severely. "In our country one does not inquire so brazenly about the wives of others. Isn't the same true here?"

"How dare you!" he snapped. "Take care. There is still your attack to be settled between us. Now hand over the letter." He clapped again. The servant came in but I ignored him. I took the letter from my belt and offered it to Mirza Selim.

"You give it to that man," he ordered, pointing at the domestic. "Did you understand me?"

"Very well, then I shall leave. Farewell, Mirza Selim." I turned and the Englishman followed silently.

"Stop! You are staying!" the Persian called out, and he ordered his servant: "Don't let them out!"

I was already at the door when the man seized me by the arm. This was too much. Lindsay had not been able to follow our conversation but could tell from the tone and our facial expressions that we were not exchanging pleasantries. He took the slightly built servant by the hips, picked him up, and threw him across the room. The man fell on top of Selim and pulled him to the floor.

"Did I do right, Mr. Kara?" he asked.

"Fine!"

Selim immediately jumped to his feet and reached for his saber. "Sons of dogs! I'll cut off your heads!"

The time had come to teach this man a lesson. I

walked toward him, gave him a blow on the arm so
that he dropped the saber, and took him by the shoulders. "Mirza Selim, our heads are not at your disposition. Sit down now, and obey. Here is the letter. I
order you to read it this instant."

I pushed him down on a cushion and pressed the
letter into his hands. He looked at me in utter surprise
but did not dare resist. The courageous servant had
preferred to beat a hasty retreat. When I clapped, he
barely stuck his head through the opening.

"Come in," I told him.

He did but stayed close to the door, ready to jump
back out.

"Bring pipes and coffee now."

He looked at Selim questioningly, but I took him by
the arm and pushed him toward the place where the
pipes were hanging on the wall. This seemed to make
an impression on him, for he took down two filled
pipes, put them into our mouths, and lit them.

"Now get some coffee, but be quick about it, and be
sure it's good." He left hastily.

Smoking, we sat down and waited for Mirza Selim
to finish the letter. He was certainly taking his time
about it. The message seemed so incomprehensible to
him that he had trouble understanding it.

Mirza Selim was indisputably handsome, as I noticed now that I had a chance to observe him. But
around his eyes there already lay those deep shadows
that indicate the waste of time and energy, and as I
examined him more closely I was struck by something
repellent in his expression. Had I been in Hassan's
place I would never have put my trust in this man.

The servant returned with small cups set on openwork golden saucers shaped somewhat like our egg-
cups. Instead of just two, he had brought half a dozen
so that he would not have to linger.

Meanwhile Selim seemed to have taken hold of himself. He looked at me darkly and asked, "What is your
name?"

"I am called Kara Ben Nemsi."

"And the other?"

"David Lindsay Bey."

"I am to turn everything over to you?"

"Those are the instructions Hassan Ardshir-Mirza gave me."

"I refuse!"

"Do as you please. It is not up to me to give you orders."

"You will return to the Mirza now and convey my answer."

"I am not going to do that."

"Why not?"

"Because it is not up to you to give me orders either."

"Very well. Then I shall send a messenger and remain in this house until an answer arrives."

"Your messenger will not find the Mirza."

"But Arab, who accompanied you, surely knows where his master is?"

"He does. But he is not leaving here."

"Why not?"

"Because I say so. Hassan Ardshir-Mirza asked me to take charge of all his possessions, and to send you and Arab to him, and that's precisely what I will do. Arab will not return to his master except at your side."

"Would you be brazen enough to try to force me?"

"Brazen? Where's the risk? If we were equals I would use a very different tone. But you are just a little aga from Farsistan! And you have not even learned to deal with men of consequence. Out on the street you demanded room as if you were a chamberlain. Here you offer us neither coffee nor tobacco. You insulted us. Yet you are a mere worm compared to us and your master. I will fight a lion, but I won't interfere with a worm that enjoys crawling about in the filth. Hassan Ardshir-Mirza turned his possessions over to me; so I am staying! And you are free to do as you please."

"I am going to complain about you," Selim hissed venomously. "I won't turn anything over to you!"

"Nor is that necessary, for here I sit, and have already taken charge."

"You will not lay a hand on anything that was entrusted to me!"

"I will touch everything that has been turned over to

me. Should you interfere I will inform the Mirza. In any event, what is of consequence here is neither you nor me, but only the best interest of your master. And now I suggest that you order a good meal for us, for I am not only a guest but the master of the house."

"It belongs neither to you nor to me!"

"But you certainly rented it. Don't be difficult. I am being indulgent when I permit you to give orders here. If you refuse, I shall see to it that we get what we need."

Feeling cornered, Selim got to his feet.

"Where to?" I asked.

"To order you a meal."

"You can do that here. Call the servant."

"Am I a prisoner?"

"Pretty much. You refuse to respect the Mirza's rights. So I have to prevent your leaving this room because you might do something I cannot approve!"

"Effendi, you don't know who I am!" This was the first time he had addressed me as "Effendi." He no longer felt sure of himself.

"I know very well," I answered. "You are Mirza Selim, and that is all."

"I am Hassan Ardshir-Mirza's confidant and friend, and have sacrificed everything to follow him and save his fortune."

"That is very nice and very commendable. But don't forget that henceforth your fate is closely tied to his. The moment you think only of yourself you are done for. I hope you are willing now to accompany me back to the Mirza."

"I am. He will decide."

"My companion will remain here and you will see to it that he has everything he needs. The rest will be settled by Hassan Ardshir-Mirza himself."

I told the Englishman what I had proposed. He welcomed my suggestion, for in the house he could rest comfortably while I had to go back out into the heat. After Selim had given some essential instructions we entered the courtyard, where he wanted to get back on the valuable horse he had bought with the Mirza's money in Kadhinaim.

"Take another animal," I told him.

He looked at me in surprise. "Why?"

"To avoid attracting attention. Your servant's horse will do." Selim submitted and Arab followed us.

To mislead possible observers we asked to be ferried to Muattam, which lies opposite Kadhinaim, and then turned north by a roundabout route. Muattam is a good-sized place on the left bank of the Tigris, an hour north of Baghdad. It is here that Imam Abu Hanifa, the founder of the Four Rites of Islam, is buried. The legal code and the ritual of the Osmans are his work. Because he hated him the caliph al-Mansur poisoned Abu Hanifa. Originally there was a mosque on his grave which Malik Shah, the Seljuk prince, had built in his honor. But when the great Osman ruler Sulayman the Magnificent subdued recalcitrant Baghdad, he constructed a fortified castle around the site. Now thousands of Shiites stream to his grave.

It took us two hours to reach the place where Hassan Ardshir-Mirza had set up camp. He was clearly surprised to see me again but received us with great amiability.

"Why are you coming back yourself?" he asked me.

"Ask this man," I answered, pointing to Mirza Selim.

"Tell me," he commanded the latter.

Selim took out the letter and asked, "Master, did you write this?"

"I did. You know my seal; why are you skeptical?"

"Because you are ordering me to do something that I neither expected nor deserve."

The women were standing behind some bushes to see Selim and to listen to our conversation.

"What is it you did not expect?"

"That I should turn everything I saved over to this stranger."

"This effendi is no stranger but my friend and brother."

"Am I not also your friend?"

The Mirza hesitated, and then answered curtly, "You are an ally whom I trust. We pursued a bold, proud plan together and have both failed for the time being. Our salvation was flight, and I am doing everything in my power to make it succeed. Are you going to sacrifice a great goal to petty ambition? I don't understand you, Selim. This effendi is so selfless, he is willing to sell all I own without attracting attention. That will give you and me the means to proceed. Why are you creating difficulties for him?"

Mirza had spoken with great seriousness. Selim was embarrassed, particularly because he had seen the women, and he was searching for a weighty excuse. "This man gave me a blow when he ran into me," he said.

"Why did he strike you?"

"We were coming toward each other on the street and I commanded him to make way. He didn't, and struck me in the face with such force that I fell from my horse."

"Is that true, Effendi?" the Mirza asked me.

"More or less. I did not know Selim when we met, and your servant Arab could not recognize him because he wore a veil. He was riding a magnificent white horse, like a great man. He ordered us to move aside although there was room enough, and his tone was that of a padisha. You know me, Mirza. I do not mind in the least being polite, but I demand the same of others. So I called his attention to the fact that he could pass quite easily. In answer he took hold of his whip, called me a swine, and was about to strike me. The natural consequence was that he found himself lying on the ground a moment later, and then, when it was unfortunately too late, I found out that he was the man you had sent me to. That's all I have to say. I suggest you speak to him and call me when you need me." I went over to the horses to chat with Halef.

Half an hour later Hassan came up to me. His face showed profound annoyance. "Effendi," he said. "This affair is very embarrassing to me. What am I to do? I cannot make an enemy of Selim. Will you forgive him his rashness?"

"Gladly, if that is your wish. What have you decided?"

"He will not return with you."

"I expected as much."

"Here is a list of everything I turned over to him; he had it with him. You will have all these things appraised and then sell them. I approve in advance whatever you may do, for I know that it is difficult to find buyers on such short notice. You will then discharge my servants and give them the amount I indicated here. I have already placed the money in your saddle pouch. When do you think I should leave for Al Najaf?"

"Today is the sixth, and the festivities are on the fifteenth. You will need four days to get there from Baghdad, and will want to be there a day ahead of time, which means that the tenth of this month would be best."

"Am I to stay in hiding here for another four days?"

"No. It should be possible to find some place in the city where you and your family would be safe. Let me see to that. Do you intend keeping everything you now have with you?"

"No, all this should be sold too."

"Then it might be better if you let me have whatever you can spare, and tell me the price. There are wealthy people in Baghdad. Perhaps I can find a Parsi or an Armenian who will take the lot."

"That would require a fortune."

"No matter. I will protect your interests as if they were my own."

"I trust you. Come with me, we will have a look at everything I have here."

The packages were opened and I was astonished. Never in my life had I seen treasures and valuables in such abundance, or of such quality. A list was made and the Mirza set a price which, though low when measured against the real value of these things, yet came to a sum one could only call a fortune.

"And what are you going to do with your escort?"

"I will give them presents and discharge them as soon as you have found a place for me to stay."

"For how many people?"

"For Selim, the women, their servant, and me. Then I intend to hire a domestic who does not know me."

"I hope I shall find everything you want. Have these things put on the camels."

"How many camel drivers will you be taking?"

"None. Halef and I can do what needs to be done."

"Effendi, I don't want you to do that work yourself."

"Why not? Am I to burden myself with men who will get in my way in Kadhinaim or Baghdad?"

"Do as you think best."

The camels were loaded and tied to each other to form a single line. We were ready to leave.

"Now you should give me some kind of authorization that will prove to your men that I am acting on your behalf."

"Take my signet ring."

The Persians were amazed when our transport reached the courtyard. I called them together, showed them their master's seal, and told them that I was taking Mirza Selim's place and that they would now have to obey my orders, a change which did not seem to grieve them greatly.

They told me that the owner of the house was a wealthy trader who lived on the other side of Baghdad in the western suburbs, near the university. The goods Selim had had in his charge had been stored in a first-floor room of the building, and I had the things I had just brought taken there. Because I was tired I decided to postpone a careful examination to the next day.

When I looked into my saddle pouches, I found the money Hassan Ardshir had put there. It consisted entirely of handsomely minted tomans and was at least four times the sum I had been asked to pay out. Leaving Halef in charge of the servants, I went to look for Lindsay.

He had stretched out on the soft cushions in the serdab. His nose was moving rhythmically as he breathed, and a loud snore came from his wide-open mouth.

"Sir David!"

Immediately awake, he jumped up and drew his knife. "Oh, so it's you? How are you, Mr. Kara?"

"Look at this perspiration. What hellish heat!"

"Well, lie down and join me."

"We have things to attend to. But I must eat first," I said.

"Just clap your hands and the servant will come."

"Did you try that?"

"Yes. Unfortunately he didn't understand me. I asked for sherry and he brought dates. Awful!"

I clapped my hands, and immediately the same domestic who had served Selim appeared. "Sahib, tell me how I am to address you."

"You will call me effendi, and this man is a bey. Get me something to eat."

"What would you like, Effendi?"

"Whatever there is. And don't forget some fresh water. Are you the chef?"

"Yes, Effendi. I hope you will be satisfied with me."

"How did Mirza Selim pay you?"

"I advanced the amount needed and he reimbursed me every other day."

"We'll follow the same procedure. You can go now."

A short time later he brought me a selection of the principal foods Baghdad has to offer, and Lindsay Bey helped himself a second time.

"Are you rid of this Selim, sir?" he asked.

"Yes. He is staying with Hassan for the time being. I'm afraid he's thinking of revenge."

"The man is a coward! You know what we might do after we have eaten? We could go to Baghdad by horsecar and buy some clothes."

"We could certainly use some. And that will also give me a chance to make some inquiries which are even more important. I am looking for a buyer for Mirza's valuables. I just brought back a few camel loads of them."

"What kinds of things?"

"Magnificent objects which are to be sold for a fraction of their value. If I were wealthy, I would buy them all."

"For example?"

I took out the list and translated for him.

"How much?" he asked.

I told him the amount.

"Are they worth that much?"

"I'd say they are easily worth twice that."

"Fine, very good. No need to look. I know someone who will buy."

"Who?"

"David Lindsay, that's who!"

"Do you mean it? That would relieve me of a great

worry! But where are you going to get the money? The Mirza wants to be paid immediately."

"That's no problem."

"What luck! So that's settled. But that still leaves the things that were entrusted to Selim."

"Is it a great deal?"

"We'll have to see. I have another list here, and tomorrow I am going to have the crates opened and the contents appraised. I won't know until then how much money I must get out of them."

"Are they beautiful things?"

"Of course. Here you have three Saracen coats of mail, a rarity in any collection. Swords of Lahore steel which are even more valuable than the genuine Damascus blade; many bottles of rose oil, gold and silver brocade, magnificent rugs, Persian scarfs of Kerman wool, whole bales of the rarest silks, and so on. There are antiques here of almost inestimable value. If one were to buy these things and sell them piece by piece in Europe, one could make a great deal of money."

"Make money? Why bother? I'll take it all."

"All? You mean you will also take what is on this second list?"

"Why not?"

"But consider how much that will come to!"

"It may be a lot to you, but not for David Lindsay. Do you know how much I'm worth?"

"No. I have never inquired about your circumstances."

"Well, no need to talk about them now either. I am very well off."

"But even a millionaire should think awhile before spending such a sum for a hobby."

"Perhaps, but there is value here. I don't have enough cash to pay for everything but I know some people in town. I'll make out a document, sign my name, and get the money. We'll have a look at those things tomorrow."

"Very well. I'll be conscientious, for you are as much my friend as the Mirza is. I will have some experts come and appraise the lot. Then we can negotiate."

"Fine. But now let's go into town and get some decent clothes on our backs."

"Take a pipe along, Sir David. We'll go to the market as Muslims."

After I had told Halef that we would probably return before nightfall, we went to the horsecar. It was in dilapidated condition. The windows were broken, the cushions had disappeared from the seats, and the bones of the two nags—moving skeletons—actually rattled as they pulled the coach. But we reached Baghdad without incident.

# 8 : In Baghdad

We first went to the clothes bazaar, which we left as though newborn. I had not been able to prevent the Englishman from paying for my things. He had also bought Halef a new suit and entrusted it to a young Arab who had offered his services when he saw us leave the store with the package.

"Now where to, sir?" my companion asked.

"Wine, raki, coffeehouse," I said, imitating his manner.

Lindsay agreed with a friendly smirk, and after some looking we found an out-of-the way place where we had some aromatic Mocca, smoked some Persian tobacco, and were also shaved and beautified.

Our porter had sat down by the door. He wore nothing but a loincloth but his bearing was royal. He had to be a free-born Bedouin. How did it come about that this son of the desert was working as a porter? His appearance fascinated me so strongly that I gestured to him to come sit next to me.

He accepted my invitation with the decorousness of a person aware of his value and took the pipe I had someone offer him. After a while I began: "You are a free Ibn Arab. May I ask how you came to Baghdad?"

"On my feet and on horseback."

"Why do you carry things for others?"

"Because I must earn a living."

"Why did you leave your tribe?"

"Because of a blood feud."

"Are you being pursued by an avenger?"

"No. I am the avenger!"

"And your enemy fled to Baghdad?"

"Yes. I have been searching and waiting for two years."

"From what country did you come?"

"Master, why are you asking so many questions?"

"Because I am visiting all Muslim countries and would like to know if I have also been to yours."

"I come from Kara, where the Wadi Montish and the Wadi Kirbe meet."

"You mean where the Ssajban live, in the Belad Beni Issa? I have never been there but I plan to visit that country."

"You will be welcome if you are a faithful son of the Prophet."

"Since you have been here in Baghdad for two years, I imagine you know the city well?"

"Yes, master."

"Do you know of a house where one would be sheltered from the heat and, above all, live pleasantly and undisturbed?"

"I can show you such a house."

"Where is it?"

"Not far from where I live, in the palm gardens in the southern part of the city."

"Who is the owner?"

"A devout Talib who lives in seclusion and would not disturb a tenant."

"Is it far from here?"

"A donkey would carry you there quickly."

"Then go and order three. You shall be our guide."

"You will need only two, for I shall walk."

A few moments later two donkeys and their drivers were standing outside. They were white, as many donkeys in Baghdad are.

Up to now the Englishman and I had been sitting back to back because the beautification procedure required it. Finally my barber was finished, and the one who had been attending to Lindsay also clapped his hands to indicate that the great work was completed. We turned toward each other at the same moment, and two faces can rarely have contrasted as vividly as ours at this moment. Sir David uttered a shout of surprise and I couldn't help laughing out loud.

"What's there to laugh at, sir?" he asked.

"Tell him to bring you a mirror."

"What's the word for it?"

"Mirat."

"Well!" He turned to the barber. "A mirat, if you please."

The man held it out to him and I wonder if anyone could have kept a straight face as he observed my companion's expression. The reader should try to visualize a long, narrow face, shrunk by the heat of the sun, with a very pale reddish beard, a wide-open mouth, a long nose, three times its normal size because of the Aleppo boil, and, above it, a cleanly shaven head with a whitish sheen on whose crown a single little tuft had been left standing. Even the Bedouin could not refrain from smiling and barely suppressed his laughter.

"Terrible, devilish," Lindsay exclaimed. "Where is my revolver? I'll shoot the fellow."

"Don't excite yourself, Sir David. This good man has no idea you are an Englishman, after all. He took you for a Muslim, and so he only left you that little coil."

"That's all right. But this face! What a horror!"

"Console yourself! The turban will cover everything, and before you get back to England your fur will have grown back."

"Fur! Why do you look so well although you have no more hair than I do?"

"That's a matter of race. Germans feel too much at their ease, wherever they are."

"True enough. All right then, what do we owe?"

"I am paying ten piasters."

"Ten piasters? Are you mad? A mouthful of bad coffee, two puffs of stinking tobacco, and a ruined head—ten piasters!"

"Remember that we resembled savages. And now look at you!"

"Very well then. But let's get out of here! Where to?"

"To rent an apartment in some residence outside the city. The Bedouin will take us. We will ride the two white donkeys out there."

"Off we go!"

We left the coffeehouse and mounted the small but very sturdy and tireless animals. My feet were almost dragging the ground and Lindsay had pulled his pointed knees up to his armpits. The Bedouin preceded us, remorselessly using his stick on anyone who threatened to get in our way. The two of us, hunched like monkeys on camels, followed him, and the owners of the animals were behind, yelling hoarsely as they applied their sticks to the hindquarters of their beasts. We scurried through lanes and alleys until the streets came to an end and houses became infrequent.

Before a high wall the Bedouin stopped and we dismounted, to wait by a gate as our guide vigorously worked its knocker. It took a very long time until someone opened the gate.

The first thing we saw was a long, pointed nose and then a pale face. "What do you want?" the person asked.

"Effendi, this stranger wishes to talk to you," our guide explained.

A pair of small gray eyes fixed on me and then I heard a trembling voice: "Enter, but only you."

"This bey will come with me," I answered as I pointed at Lindsay.

"Very well, but only because he is a bey."

We entered, and the gate closed behind us. On his skinny feet the man wore a pair of gigantic slippers, and so he shuffled through the magnificent garden above which palms were swaying. He stopped in front of a pretty little house.

"What do you want?" he asked.

"Are you the owner of this splendid garden, and do you have an apartment for rent?"

"Yes, do you want it?"

"Perhaps. But we must see it first."

"Come along.—Pisa Krew, damn, where's my key?"

As he was searching through the folds of his garment I had a chance to recover from my surprise. This man, ostensibly a Turk, had sworn in Polish!

Finally he found the key between the bars of a window and opened the door. "Enter."

We came into a pretty foyer with a stairway at the back. There were doors to right and left. The man opened one on the right and gestured us into a large room. For the first moment I thought it had green wallpaper, but then I noticed that tall frames had been placed all along the walls from which green curtains were hanging. As I cast a glance at the long table in the middle of the room I could guess what they might be hiding. The table was covered with books and directly in front of me lay an open illustrated Nuremberg bible. I quickly moved closer and put my hand on it.

"The Bible!" I exclaimed in German. "Shakespeare, Montesquieu, Rousseau! What are these books doing here?" Those were just a few of the many works I saw scattered about.

The master of the house stepped back, clapped his hands, and asked, "What? You speak German?"

"As you hear."

"Are you German?"

"I am. And you?"

"I am a Pole. And the other gentleman?"

"He is English. My name is . . ."

"Please, no names just yet," the Pole interrupted. "Before we start using names we should get to know each other."

He clapped his hands, as the local custom was, but had to do so several times before the door finally opened and there appeared a shape of such shiny fatness as I had rarely seen.

"Allah akbar, not again?" was the sigh that issued from between two sausagelike lips. "What do you wish, Effendi?"

"Coffee and tobacco."

"Just for you?"

"For everyone."

"Lots of beans?"

"Be gone!"

"What an effendi!" With this exclamation the mysterious creature waddled out again.

"Who is this monster?" I asked, perhaps somewhat impertinently.

"My servant and cook."

"What a misfortune!"

"It is. He takes the lion's share of everything, and I get what is left over."

"That's too bad."

"I am used to it. He was already my servant when I was still an officer."

"An officer?"

"In the Turkish army."

"And now you live here by yourself?"

"Yes."

The profound melancholy in the Pole's face aroused my sympathy. "Do you also speak English, by chance?"

"I learned it in my youth."

"Then let's use that language so my companion doesn't get bored."

"Gladly. So you really came to look at my house? Who told you about me?"

"No one said anything about you, only about your house—the Arab, who brought us here. He is your neighbor."

"I don't know him. I have nothing to do with anyone. Are you looking for a place just for yourselves?"

"No. We are part of a group of five men, two women, and a servant."

"Five men, two women? Sounds romantic."

"And so it is. I'll explain as soon as I have had a look at the apartment."

"It will hardly be spacious enough for that many.— But here's the coffee."

The fat servant, his face cherry colored, had come back in. On his hands a large tray with three steaming cups, an old pipe, and a quantity of tobacco barely sufficient to fill a pipe once, was swaying back and forth. "Here," he croaked, "here is coffee for everyone."

We had sat down on a divan and we relieved him of the tray, since he was unable to bend down to us. His master was the first to taste the coffee.

"Is it good?" the fellow asked.

"Yes."

Now the Englishman had a sip.

"Is it good?" the servant repeated his question.

"Fie!" Lindsay spat out the dishwater, and I simply put my cup aside.

"No good?" the servant asked me.

"Why not try it yourself?" I countered.

"Mashallah, I don't drink that sort of brew," he said ingenuously.

Now the Pole reached for his pipe. "There is still ash in it," he said reproachfully.

"I just used it a little while ago."

"Then you should empty it."

"Give it to me."

The servant pulled the pipe from his master's hand, knocked the ashes out of it in front of the door, and came back. "Here. Now you can fill it, Effendi."

The master obeyed his servant but apparently remembered as he was filling it that we had not yet had anything. He decided to offer us his most exquisite possession. "Here is the key to the cellar," he told his servant. "Go down there!"

"What do you want me to get, Effendi?"

"The wine."

"The wine? Allah kerim! Will you sell your soul to the devil? Will you let yourself be sent to the deepest abyss of hell? Drink coffee or water! Both will keep your eye clear and your soul devout! But anyone who drinks wine will fall into profound misery and ruin."

"Go!"

"Effendi, don't afflict me with the certain knowledge that the devil will seize you in his claws."

"Be still and obey! There are three bottles left. Bring them!"

"Then I must obey, but Allah will forgive me. I cannot be blamed for your damnation." And with these words the fellow shuffled out of the room.

"Curious character," I said with a faint smile.

"But loyal, although he pilfers the provisions. The wine is the only thing he can't get at. He is only given the key when I want to drink some, and as soon as he has brought me the bottle he must surrender it again."

"That's very wise, but . . ."

I could not continue because the servant was already back, puffing like a locomotive. He had one bottle under each arm and the third in his right hand. He bent forward as far as he could and placed them at his master's feet. I had to bite my lips not to burst into ill-mannered laughter: two of the bottles were completely empty and the third barely half full.

His master looked at him nonplused. "Is that the wine?"

"The last three bottles."

"But they are empty!"

"Almost completely empty," the fellow confessed, his eyes rolling.

"Who drank the wine?"

"I did, Effendi."

"Have you gone mad? To drink two and a half bottles now, within a few moments, when my guests and I are waiting for it?"

"Now? At a single sitting? Effendi, that's not so, I am innocent. I drank the wine yesterday, the day before yesterday, a week, a month ago. I wanted a glass every day."

"Thief, scoundrel! How did you get into the basement? The key stays with me day and night. Or did you steal it while I was sleeping?"

"But, Effendi! I already told you that I am perfectly innocent."

"But how did you get into the locked basement?"

"But, Effendi, the basement wasn't locked! I never locked it when you had wine in it."

The Pole cursed.

"Master! Cursing in a foreign language doesn't make things any better! There is still enough for you and your guests."

The Pole picked up the bottle and held it against the light. "What does this wine look like, eh?"

"Effendi, it won't do you any harm. There was just half a glass left! That wouldn't have been enough for three men, so I added a little water."

"Water? Here, take your water!" Our host raised his arm and aimed the bottle at the servant's head. But his intended victim ducked more quickly than one might have thought possible, and the bottle flew over him and hit the door, where it broke and its contents spilled on the floor.

The servant clapped his hands in a gesture of regret. "For Allah's sake, what are you doing, Effendi? Now that beautiful water is gone, and yet it could so easily have been drunk as wine. And all this broken glass! You will have to pick that up yourself, I cannot bend over that far." And he tramped out of the room.

I would hardly have believed such a scene possible had I not witnessed it myself. But what surprised me most was that immediately after his unsuccessful throw the Pole recovered his calm. This extraordinary indulgence by a master of a stupid and insolent servant had to have a deeper cause. The man was a mystery to me.

"I am sorry," he said now. "This kind of thing won't happen again. Perhaps I will tell you why I am so lenient with this man. He has rendered me important services. Fill your pipes."

I took out my own tobacco, and when the pipes had been lit our host said, "Come with me, I'll show you the apartment."

He took us to the second floor, which consisted of four rooms with locks, rugs in the center, and small cushions along the walls. Under the roof were two additional small rooms which could also be locked. I liked the place and asked about the price.

"But no," the Pole protested. "We must treat each other as compatriots. You and your friends will be my guests."

"I won't reject your kind offer, especially since it is a contract I can terminate at any time. The most important thing for me is to be unobserved and undisturbed by the world outside."

"Here you will be. How long do you think you will stay in my house?"

"Not long, unfortunately. A minimum of four, a maximum of fourteen days. Perhaps you will permit me to tell you a little adventure that will explain my situation?"

"Why not? Let's sit down. The seats here are just as comfortable as downstairs."

I told him as much of our circumstances and my encounter with Hassan Ardshir-Mirza as I thought necessary. He listened attentively and jumped to his feet when I finished. "Sir, you should feel no hesitation about moving in here with me. No one here will importune, let alone betray you. When are you coming?"

"Tomorrow, at dusk. But there is one thing I forgot: we have several horses and two camels. Do you have room for those animals?"

"Yes. You haven't seen the courtyard behind the house. Part of it is roofed and ample for your needs. But I do expect you to provide your own servants."

"Of course."

"Tomorrow, when you get here, ride around the garden wall. Along the side opposite the small gate you will see a large one, where I shall look for you."

Satisfied with our success, we took leave of the Pole and returned to town with our guide.

We moved in the following evening. Hassan Ardshir-Mirza was wearing female dress to mislead possible watchers. His men had been paid and dismissed and only Selim was still with him. The Arab, who had been our guide the previous day, took the place of the servants.

When I again raised the question about his journey to An Najaf with the Persian, I was sorry to see that the Mirza resolutely refused to take me with him. I could not blame him. He was a Shiite, and his faith forbade him under penalty of death to visit the sacred places in the company of an unbeliever. The only concession he made was that he gave me permission to ride with him as far as Hilla, where we would have to separate temporarily and then meet again in Baghdad. Originally he had planned to leave the two women here, but they would not consent to this arrangement and were so insistent that he finally gave in.

I was thus relieved of the responsibility of having to act as their protector.

Even now many pilgrims were passing through Baghdad to continue westward, but it wasn't until the tenth of the month that we heard that the death caravan was approaching the city. Without delay, Lindsay, Halef, and I set out to enjoy this curious spectacle.

Enjoy? It was a dubious pleasure, to be sure. The Shiites believe that every Muslim whose body is buried in Karbala or An Najaf will enter Paradise immediately. It is therefore every Shiite's fervent wish to be buried at one of these two places. Since the transport of bodies by caravan is very costly, however, only the rich can afford it. The poor who want to be buried at these sacred places say farewell to their family and make their way begging over considerable distances until they reach Ali's or Husain's grave, to there wait for death.

Every year hundreds of thousands of pilgrims set out for those places, but the numbers are greatest when one of the important anniversaries of the Shia draws near. At those times the death caravans of Persian, Afghan, Baluchistan, Indian, and other Shiites come down from the Iranian plateau. Corpses are brought from everywhere and even transported down the Euphrates. Frequently the bodies have been lying ready for months before the journey begins; the caravan has far to travel and makes only slow headway. The heat of these southern regions broods with frightening intensity over the distance that must be covered, and the horrible stench spread by such a caravan can easily be imagined. The corpses lie in coffins which burst in the heat, or they are wrapped in felt blankets which are destroyed by the processes of putrefaction. It is thus not surprising that the hollow-eyed specter of the plague on its skinny nag follows closely behind. Those encountering such processions veer far to either side and only the jackal and the Bedouin come close, the former because the stench attracts it, the other because the treasures carried by those caravans to be turned over to gravekeepers at the end of the pilgrimage lure him. Vessels decorated with precious stones, cloth embroidered with pearls, valuable weapons and implements, inestimable amulets, and huge quantities of gold coins are transported to Karbala and An Najaf, where they disappear in subterranean vaults. To mislead Bedouin robbers all this is hidden in coffinlike cases, but experience has taught the enterprising Arab tribes, and such measures no longer avail. During an attack they open every coffin and thus find the treasures they are looking for. Afterward the battleground offers a chaotic picture of fallen animals, dead humans, the scattered remains of corpses, and stinking fragments of coffins. To escape the breath of the plague and the danger of infection, the solitary wanderer steers clear of such sites.

Safety demands that the death caravan must not come close to any city. At an earlier time it was permitted to pass through Baghdad, entering the city by the eastern gate. But it had barely left by the western one when the miasma spread over the city of the caliphs and the plague began to rage. Thousands fell victim to Muslim indifference, which could only advance the empty consolation that "everything is written in the Book." In more recent times this has changed, and the much admired but equally controversial Midhat Pasha in particular has set aside the old customs. Now the death caravan can come no closer than the northern city limits and must then cross the Tigris on the upper pontoon bridge. It was here that we saw it.

An unbearable effluvium wafted toward us as we approached the place. The head of the long procession had already arrived and was making ready to settle down. A tall banner with the Persian coat of arms (a lion with the rising sun behind it) had been planted and was to form the center of the camp. Those who had arrived on foot were sitting on the ground, and the riders had dismounted from their camels and horses. But the coffins were not taken off the mules, an indication that the stay would be only temporary. Behind these groups, the interminable train drew near, like a snake crawling over the ground in a straight line. Brown shapes, baked by the heat of the sun, were hanging exhausted from their animals or shuffling along on tired feet. But their dark eyes glowed with fanaticism as, indifferent to the crowd of spectators, they sang their monotonous pilgrims' chant.

We were standing in the immediate vicinity of the pilgrims, but as more of them arrived, the stench became so infernal that Halef covered his nose with the tip of his turban.

One of the Persians noticed this, stepped up to him,

and shouted, "Why are you covering your nose, you dog?"

Since Halef did not know the language, I answered in his place: "Do you think that the emanation from these corpses is the scent of paradise?"

The man gave me a contemptuous sidelong glance. "Don't you know what the Koran proclaims? It says that the corpses of believers smell of ambergis, roses, jasmin, musk, juniper, and lavender."

"That's not in the Koran at all, but in Ferid Eddin—Ather's Pandnama. Remember that! And why did all these people cover their noses?"

"They may have, but I didn't."

"Then why not complain first to your countrymen, and then come to us? We have no business with you."

"You sound proud. You are a Sunnite and caused the real caliph and his son great grief. May Allah send you to the darkest depth of hell!"

He turned away with a threatening gesture, an example of the irreconcilable hatred between the Sunna and the Shia. This man had not hesitated to insult us amidst thousands of Sunnites, and I wondered how someone who was recognized as not being a Shiite would fare in Karbala or An Najaf.

I would have liked to wait until the tail of this seemingly endless procession arrived, but caution drove me away. I had decided to travel as far as Karbala, should the obstacles not be unsurmountable, and so it was not advisable to make a spectacle of myself here, among the Sunnites. I might easily attract attention and be recognized later. The Englishman readily agreed to turn back. He claimed he could no longer bear the stench, and even the ordinarily brave Halef eagerly sought refuge from the horrible odors which made the camp of the Persians intolerable.

When we returned to the house, Hassan Ardshir-Mirza informed me that he would not join the caravan but would postpone his departure until the following morning. He had already told Mirza Selim of this decision before Selim left to have a look at the Persian caravan.

I cannot say why Selim's departure struck me as suspicious. Surely there was nothing disquieting in his desire to see the caravan. But I felt a kind of ill-defined worry. When we went to sleep the man had not yet returned. Halef was also missing; he had gone for a walk in the garden after dinner and had not come back. It was not until midnight that I heard soft steps stealthily passing our door. About ten minutes later it was opened almost inaudibly. Someone was coming toward me.

"Who is it?" I asked softly.

"It's me, Sidi. Get up and come with me!"

"Where to?"

"Be still! Someone may be listening."

"Should I take my weapons?"

"Only the small ones."

I picked up my knife and revolvers and followed him on my bare feet. He walked to the rear gate, where I put on my shoes. "What's up, Halef?"

"Come with me, Sidi. We must hurry and I can tell you everything as we walk along."

We left the garden gate slightly ajar. Surprised that Halef did not turn toward the city but toward the south, I followed silently, waiting for him to begin.

"Sidi, forgive me for disturbing your rest. But I do not trust this Selim."

"What about him? I heard him come back some time ago."

"I'll tell you. When we returned from the caravan camp and I unsaddled the horses, I ran into our host's fat servant. He was annoyed and swore like a fox that let a lizard get away."

"What about?"

"Mirza Selim. He had left instructions to keep the gate open for him, saying that he might be coming back late. I don't like this fellow because he does not care for you, Sidi. The servant had watched him as he left and noticed that he was not turning in the direction of town but south. What business did the Persian have outside the city? You will understand my curiosity, Sidi. I went back inside, said my prayer, and ate, but could not get Selim out of my mind. The evening was beautiful, the stars were shining and I could do what the Mirza had done. I also went for a walk, and in the same direction. I was thinking of you, of Sheik

Malek, my wife's grandfather, of Hanneh, the flower of women, and did not notice that I had already come a considerable distance. I was standing by a dilapidated wall. I stepped across the rubble and then proceeded slowly until I came to a place where I saw trees and crosses. It was a cemetery for unbelievers. The crosses were shining in the light of the stars and I moved softly. Their souls must not be wakened by loud steps, for then they become angry and pursue the intruder. Now I saw figures sitting on a grave. They were not ghosts for they were smoking their pipes and talking. Nor were they from the city, since they were wearing Persian dress. Only a few of them were Arabs. And some distance from the graves, I heard tethered horses pawing the ground."

"Did you hear what the men talked about?"

"They were a fair distance away from me, and I only heard them mention a lot of booty they would capture, and that only two Persians would be left alive. I also heard an imperious voice saying that they would wait in the cemetery until dawn. One of them rose to take his leave. He passed close by me and I recognized Selim. I followed him to our house and then it occurred to me that it might be well to know who these men are with whom he spoke. So I woke you."

"We'll look into it. You are probably talking about the English cemetery. I know it from my first stay here. It is not far from the Gate of the Blind and won't be difficult to approach unobserved."

We walked along rapidly until we came to the opening in the surrounding wall. I told Halef to wait for me there so that he might cover my retreat, should that become necessary, and moved on cautiously. Not a breeze was stirring and no sound broke the silence of the night. Unobserved, I reached the entrance facing north; it was open. As I entered, I heard a horse snorting off to one side. The animal belonged to a Bedouin, for only horses that live out in the open snort in this curious, frightened, trembling manner which is intended as a warning. Because the sound could betray my presence and become dangerous, I quickly turned to the other side and crawled forward.

Soon I saw something shimmering through the bushes. I recognized this white, it was the color of an Arab burnous. I moved closer and counted six men lying on the ground, sleeping. They were Arabs; there was no Persian. It seemed unlikely that Halef had made an error; either the Persians were farther off to one side or they had left. To make certain, I crawled on, but I came close to the horses without noticing anyone else. Although I was now approaching them from the other side, the animals again became restless. I could not let this stop me. I had to know how many horses there were. I counted seven. But I had counted six Arabs; where was the seventh? Resting on my hands and knees, I was about to scan the terrain when a man threw himself on me, pressing me to the ground. Here was the seventh! He had been guarding the horses. And this fellow was no weakling. He lay on me with his full weight, roaring like a lion.

Should I chance a struggle? Should I quietly surrender because I might perhaps discover what had brought these men here? No! I jerked upward and threw myself on my back so that my attacker came to lie underneath me. Apparently he had not expected this or had injured his head. In any event, his arms fell away. I jumped to my feet and hurried toward the exit. But directly behind me I now heard the steps of my pursuers. Fortunately my clothing was light, my weapons almost weightless, and they did not catch up with me. At the opening in the wall I drew my revolver and fired twice into the air, and when Halef fired his pistol as well, the white shapes behind me disappeared.

"Did you let yourself get caught, Sidi?"

"Unfortunately. Those Arabs were smarter than I thought. They had posted a guard."

"Allah kerim! that could have turned out badly. Those men are up to no good. But all that ran after you were Arabs."

"The Persians you saw were no longer there. Didn't the man in charge, whose voice you heard, look familiar to you?"

"I couldn't see him clearly; it wasn't light enough and he was sitting among the rest."

"Then we wasted our time, although I still suspect that they were Hassan Ardshir's pursuers."

"Could they have got here already?"

"Yes. They turned west because of the signs we left, but they may well have assumed that Hassan would go to Baghdad and retraced their steps. We had the women with us; our progress wasn't as rapid as theirs."

We returned to our apartment, where I informed the Persian of our experience and my fears, but he made light of this news. He could not imagine that his pursuers were in Baghdad and he thought it equally improbable that the words Halef had heard referred to him. I urged him to be careful and to ask the pasha for an escort, but he also rejected that proposal.

"I am not afraid," he said. "There is no reason I should fear the Shiites, for during the celebration hostilities are suspended. And it is equally certain that I will not be attacked by the Arabs. You and your friends will accompany me as far as Hilla, and it is only a day's journey from there to An Najaf. There are too many pilgrims along that route for bandits to show their faces."

"I cannot force you to take my advice. I assume you will leave everything you won't need here in Baghdad?"

"I will leave nothing here. Am I to entrust what remains of my possessions to strangers?"

"Our host seems to be an honest man."

"But he lives in a secluded house."

There was nothing further for me to say. I went back to sleep and did not wake until late the following morning. The Englishman had left for town, and when he returned it was in the company of four men, three of whom were carrying hoes, shovels, and other excavation implements.

"Why these men?"

"To work," he answered. "Three of them are sailors from England who have been paid off here, and the fourth is a Scotsman who knows some Arabic. He'll be my interpreter when I start the dig. I need him since you are going to An Najaf."

"Who found them for you?"

"The consulate."

"You saw the consul without telling me?"

"Yes. I picked up some mail, sent off some letters, and got hold of enough money to settle with Hassan. Everything has been discussed. The consul will send all valuables to England. I didn't tell you because we are no longer friends."

"Why?"

"Anyone who goes to An Najaf without taking me along need not bother with my affairs. So there!"

"But, Sir David, what has got into you all at once? Your presence would only endanger both of us."

"I have accompanied you so far and not been harmed. Two fingers are gone, but that doesn't count —and to make up for that, my nose is twice as long as before."

Lindsay turned away to talk to his men. I let him be; I knew him well enough to realize that he was not seriously angry. He was too good-natured for that.

# 9 : The Death Caravan

In the afternoon, when the worst heat was over, we said a cordial goodbye to our Polish host and his fat servant. We were leaving Baghdad. Our guide, whom Hassan Ardshir-Mirza had hired, took the lead with some mule drivers whose animals were carrying those of his possessions that had not been sold to Lindsay. This seemed an incomprehensible carelessness to me. Hassan Ardshir and Selim were riding alongside the camels that were carrying the women's sedan chair. Halef and I kept together, and the Englishman brought up the rear, supervising the men with whose help he planned to force the ruins of Babylon to yield their hidden treasures. The old female servant was sitting on a mule, and the Arabic servant had stayed in Baghdad.

This was not the way I had conceived of our expedition. The order was wrong. Perhaps that was my own fault, but recently it had become difficult for me to discuss an opinion thoroughly. It seemed that I had recovered from my wound but its effects were still making themselves felt; besides, I had gone through more anxiety, excitement, and strain than any of my companions. I felt very weak and depressed without being able to discover the cause.

We were riding upstream along the Tigris on our way to the upper pontoon bridge. There I stopped to cast a glance at Harun al-Rashid's former capital. It lay before my eyes in the light of the sun, in all its splendor and magnificence but also with all the ineffaceable traces of decay. In the left foreground was the garden behind which the horsecar goes north, and farther back the quarantine station. Beyond that lie the tall castle and the governor's residence, whose base is washed by the waters of the Tigris. To the right, the suburb with its largely Arab population and the Medresse Mostansir, the only structure of the oldest quarter created by Caliph Mansur that survives to this day. And behind these buildings a vast comglomeration of houses with stylish minarets and the glazed cupolas of perhaps a hundred mosques towering above them. Here and there the beautifully outlined crown of a palm was swaying back and forth, its green forming a soothing contrast to the haze and the clouds of dust that always lie over the city of the caliphs.

Here Mansur had welcomed a mission sent by the Frankish king Pepin the Short to negotiate a treaty against the Umayyads who gave rise to such fears in Spain. Here the famous Harun al-Rashid had lived with the beautiful Subajda, who shared his piety and extravagant love of splendor. They repeatedly went to Mecca and had the road there covered with the most valuable rugs. But where today is that precious golden tree with its fruit of diamonds, emeralds, rubies, sapphires, and pearls that shaded Harun's throne?

This caliph was called al-Rashid (the Just), and yet he was a crafty tyrant who had his loyal wesir Djafar murdered, his sister and her child entombed alive, and who butchered the noble family of the Barmecides. The luster the fairy tales of "A Thousand and One Nights" impart to him is a lie, for history has long since shown that the real Harun was not the same as the Harun of legend. Driven away by his own people, he fled to Rakka and died in Rhages in Persia.

Here lived Caliph Mamum, who denied the divinity of the Koran and worshiped "eternal reason." Under him, wine flowed in abundance and under his successor Mutasim, things became worse. In a desolate, bare region he built the city of Samarra, a paradise, but on this paradise the public treasure of entire generations of rulers was squandered.

How different from this is contemporary Baghdad! Filth, dust, ruins and rags are everywhere. Even the bridge where I had stopped was damaged and its miserable woven railing was hanging down in shreds. Instead of "Dar el Caliphet" or "Dar el Sallam," the city now would be much more appropriately named 'Dar el Ta'un.* Although it is still a splendid sight, a third of the terrain within the walls consists of cemeteries, miasmic fields, swamps, and decaying rubble haunted by vultures and riffraff. The plague recurs every five or six years and destroys thousands. Even in the face of such disasters the Muslim shows his calamitous indifference. "Allah has sent it, we must do nothing about it," he says. During the horrible outbreak of 1831 the English representative did all he could to initiate comprehensive protective measures. But the mullahs rose up against him, alleging that this attempt went against the Koran. He was forced to flee, with the result that day after day up to three thousand died of the plague.

As I reflected about this, I felt as if I myself had been infected. In spite of the heat, a cold shudder went down my spine. I shook myself and quickly followed the others to get out of the city.

Between the road to Basra on the left and that to Deir on the right, we passed brickworks and the grave of Subajda, crossed the canal, and now found ourselves on an open field. To reach Hilla we had to cut across the narrow spit which separates the Euphrates from the Tigris.

The sun was still burning hot in the sky and the air seemed full of the traces of the caravan which had crawled past here yesterday. I felt as I might in an

---

* House of the Plague.

unaired hospital ward. And this was not my imagination; Halef made a similar remark, and the Englishman sniffed about ill-humoredly in the polluted air with his gigantic nose.

Now and then we passed an old pilgrim who wished to be buried in sacred soil but had dropped back from exhaustion, and there were groups which had burdened some poor mule with several corpses. The animal panted along, sweating, with the men marching alongside, their noses covered. In their wake the deadly breath of putrefaction streamed toward us. A beggar, naked except for a narrow loincloth, was sitting by the wayside. To give expression to his grief for the murdered Husain, he had made a nauseating spectacle of himself: his thighs and upper arms were pierced by sharp knives and he had driven long nails into his lower arms, his calves, his neck, nose, chin, and lips; iron hooks with heavy weights attached to them had been sunk into his hips and stomach, and since all other surfaces of his body were dotted with needles, there was not a single spot the size of a penny anywhere that was free of these painful wounds. The man was a ghastly sight.

"Dirigh-a. Waj Muhammad," he shrieked in a repulsive voice and stretched his hands out to us to beg for alms.

I would have preferred giving this fanatical and stupid fellow a good slap, for the unreason that invents such horrible tortures to celebrate the anniversary of someone's death was incomprehensible to me.

Hassan Ardshir-Mirza threw him a gold toman.

"May God protect you," the monster shouted, raising his arms like a priest.

Lindsay took ten piasters from his pocket.

"Merciful God," the ogre said, already much less polite, identifying Allah, not Lindsay, as the giver of the gift.

I took out a piaster and threw the coin at his feet. The Shiite saint made first a surprised, then an angry face.

"Miser," he exclaimed, and then added with a gesture of abhorrence and very rapidly, "You are a miser, you are five misers, you are ten misers, you are a hun-

dred, a thousand, a hundred thousand misers!" He
stepped on my piaster, spat on it, and showed a fury
meant to inspire fear.

"Sidi, what is he saying?" Halef asked.

"He is calling me a miser."

"Allah! And how do you say miserable beggar?"

"Bisaman."

"And vagabond?"

"Djaf."

Little Halef now turned to the Persian, stretched the
palms of his hands toward him, wiped them on his
thighs in a gesture that is considered an enormous
insult, and shouted, "Bisaman! Djaf! Djaf!"

At these words the rhetoric of the Shiite became an
overwhelming flood. This "holy martyr" had a vocabu-
lary of insults I cannot possibly put down here. We
bowed to his superiority and moved on.

The air was not getting better. We could see the
traces of the caravan, and the numerous foot- and
hoofprints far off to one side showed that the military
escort which had accompanied it from Baghdad to
protect it against bandits had kept at a prudent distance to escape the effluvia from the coffins.

I proposed to Hassan Ardshir that we leave the
caravan route and continue in the same direction but
at a respectable distance. But because it does the pilgrim great credit to ride through "the breath of the
dead," he rejected my suggestion. He told me that
while he set no store by such rules, he owed it to his
dead father to obey the law of the Shia as he accompanied him on his final journey. Fortunately, I could at
least persuade him not to spend the night in a khan
where the pilgrims had rested, but to set up camp at
some distance from it.

We were in dangerous territory and could not leave
the camp. Before we settled down for the night, it was
decided to overtake the caravan the following day, to
reach Hilla, and to spend the night at the "Tower of
Babel." Then Hassan wanted to let the caravan pass
and catch up with it later while the rest of us awaited
his return.

I was very tired and felt a dull pain in my head,
although I normally never have headaches. It was as if

a fever were coming on. I therefore took some medicine I had bought in Baghdad. In spite of my fatigue I was unable to fall asleep for a long time, and when I did I was disquieted by ugly dreams which woke me time and again. Once I seemed to hear the muffled step of a horse, but, being still half asleep, I took it to be part of a dream.

Finally my restlessness drove me to my feet, and I stepped outside the tent. It was beginning to dawn. Once the eastern sky becomes light in these regions, full daylight is not long in coming. I scanned the horizon, and toward the east I noticed a point that was rapidly increasing in size. After just two minutes I recognized a horseman who was approaching rapidly. It was Selim. His horse was steaming when he jumped out of the saddle. He seemed rather embarrassed when he saw me, greeted me briefly, tethered his horse, and was about to pass me.

"Where were you?" I asked him tersely, though my tone was not unfriendly.

"What concern is that of yours?" he returned defiantly.

"It is very much my concern. People who travel in company in a dangerous area owe each other information."

"I went to get my horse. It had broken loose and run away."

I examined the rope. "This was not broken," I said.

"The knot had loosened."

"Thank Allah if the noose that will be placed around your neck one of these days holds no better than this one."

I was going to turn away but he came toward me and asked, "What are you saying? I don't understand you."

"Then think about it!"

"Wait! You can't leave like that! You must tell me what you meant!"

"I wanted to remind you of the English cemetery in Baghdad."

Selim paled a little but had such control over himself that he could answer calmly, "The English cemetery? What does that have to do with me? I am no

Englishman! You were speaking of a rope around my neck. I have nothing to do with you and will complain to Hassan Ardshir-Mirza. He will teach you how to treat me!"

"Tell him or not, it's a matter of indifference to me, but I will treat you as you deserve."

Our loud exchange had roused the sleepers. Preparations for our departure were made, and we continued our journey. As we rode along I saw Selim agitatedly speaking to Hassan, and soon the latter dropped back.

"Effendi, will you permit me to discuss Mirza Selim with you?" he asked.

"Of course. I know he complained about me."

"He did. He feels insulted. Since I have given Selim to understand that he no longer enjoys my complete confidence, he has tried very hard to prove his devotion. Now you have suggested that he deserves to be hanged. Tell me, Effendi, is the fact that a horse runs away a reason for hanging its owner?"

"No. But it is reasonable to hang someone who rides off because he passes on information about his companions."

"Effendi, I have noticed that your soul is sick and your body tired, and so you see evil everywhere. Your speech is bitter as the juice of the aloe. You will get well again and judge everything more calmly, including Selim. Remember that he sacrificed everything for me."

"And what about his visit to the English cemetery?"

"That was harmless. He told me about it just now. It was a beautiful evening and he went for a walk. He came to the cemetery by chance, and didn't know that people were there. They were peaceful wanderers who were telling stories of robberies and also talked about capturing booty. That much is true."

"Do you really believe his horse ran away today?"

"I don't doubt it."

"And do you also believe that Selim is the man to find a runaway horse in the dark?"

"Why not?"

"Even if it has run some distance? The animal was covered with froth and perspiration."

"To punish it, Selim rode it very hard. He explained that to me too: you see, there is no basis for your suspicions. Please think better of Selim than heretofore."

"Gladly, if he attempts to act less secretly than heretofore."

"I shall urge him to. But you should consider that a human being makes mistakes. Only Allah is omniscient." And with this admonition he ended our conversation.

What was I to do, or, more precisely, what could I do? I was convinced that Selim was plotting some sort of mischief and felt certain that he had just met those men with whom he had already talked in the cemetery. But how could I prove that? I was worn out; I felt as if my bones had become empty, as if my head had turned into a large drum on which someone was producing hollow sounds. I noticed that my will power was ebbing away, and that I was becoming indifferent toward things which normally would have called forth whatever energy I had. That was also the reason I reacted to Hassan Ardshir's request, which was really almost a reproach, quietly and merely decided to be as vigilant as possible.

Our animals were carrying us rapidly across the level ground. We were passing more and more pilgrims, the nauseating stench became ever more unbearable, and it was not yet noon when we saw the long line of the caravan appear on the western horizon.

"Do we ride around it?" I asked.

"Yes," Hassan said, and gestured to the guide to take us out of its wake. We were alone on an open plain. The air had become purer and we inhaled it with pleasure. I would have enjoyed our quick ride, had it not been for the great quantity of ditches and canals that slowed us down. Because of my headache, these obstacles caused me considerable pain and I was glad when we dismounted around noon to wait for the greatest heat to pass.

"Sidi," said Halef, who had been observing me steadily. "Your face is gray and there are rings under your eyes. Do you feel very sick?"

"It's just a headache. Give me some water and the vinegar!"

"I wish I could take those pains into my head."

What a decent fellow Halef was! He had no idea what he himself was in for.

Finally, during the late afternoon, we saw the ruin of El Himaar appear ahead of us on the right. It is only a little over a mile from Hilla. We rode through the gardens of that city on the left bank of the Euphrates and crossed a rather rickety bridge into the little town. Hilla is famous for its vermin, an uncleanliness that is abysmal even by Oriental standards, and a population whose fanaticism borders on madness. We stayed only long enough to satisfy some threescore beggars sitting by the wayside and hurried on toward the Tower of Babel,* which lies three-quarters of an hour's ride southwest of the town. The fact that Hilla occupies the approximate center of a still existing field of ruins will convey some idea of the huge area of ancient Babylon.

The sun was about to set when we saw the tower, which rises by the side of the Ibrahim Khalil ruin. It is surrounded by swamp and desert. What remains of it is probably no more than fifty meters high, and on it one can see a single shaft a little more than ten meters high which dominates the surrounding area. This is all that still stands of the "mother of cities," as Babylon was called, and even it has a deep crack running down the middle.

We stopped at the foot of the ruin, and while the others were preparing the evening meal I climbed the platform to look at the surrounding countryside. The sun was setting and its rays were saying farewell to the ruins of a giant city that was no more.

What had Babylon been?

Situated on the Euphrates and divided by it into two parts, the city, according to Herodotus, had a cir-

---

* This novel was written in 1882. More recent research dating from the year 1911 has shown that this identification is incorrect. While legend does tell us that the Birs Nimrud is the Tower of Babel, it is actually the remains of the step pyramid of Borsippa.

cumference of four hundred eighty stadia.* It was surrounded by a wall thirty-four meters thick and about a
hundred thirty meters high. For purposes of defense,
towers had been built at regular intervals and, in addition, a wide, deep moat protected it. A hundred gates
of ore led through this wall into the city, and from
each of them a straight road ran to the one on the
opposite side, thus dividing Babylon into squares. The
buildings had splendid exteriors and were separated
by open spaces. Squares and beautiful gardens where
a population of two million could stroll formed pleasing islands in this sea of houses. High, strong walls
also ran along the two banks of the river. Their gates,
which were closed at night, provided the only passage
if one wished to cross by boat. There was also a covered bridge ten meters wide and, according to Strabo,
one stadium long. Diodorus states that it took a quarter of an hour to cross it. Its roof could be removed.
To divert the river during its construction, a lake,
twelve miles in circumference and twenty-five meters
deep, was excavated west of the city. After the bridge
had been built, this lake served to absorb excess water
during floods and formed a huge reservoir from which
the fields were irrigated during droughts by means of
sluices. The outstanding structure of the city, however,
was the tower of which the Bible tells us. Holy Scripture does not indicate a precise height but merely
speaks of its top reaching heaven. Talmudists maintain
that it was seventy miles high. According to Oriental
traditions it exceeded sixty thousand feet, while others
speak of twenty-five thousand. A million workers are
said to have labored on its construction for twelve
years. Those are exaggerations, of course. It is a fact,
however, that a tower whose base had a circumference
of about one thousand paces, and which was between
six and eight hundred feet tall, did rise from the center
of the Baal temple. It consisted of eight superposed
sections of progressively decreasing area. A stepped
walk running eight times around the structure pro-

---

* A stadium is a Greek measure of length, approximately two
hundred twenty meters.

vided access to the top. Every section contained large, vaulted halls and rooms whose carved columns, tables, chairs, vessels, and other implements were of pure gold. Baal's statue, which weighed one thousand Babylonian talents and thus had a value of millions, stood on the lowest floor. The uppermost story contained an observatory where astronomers and astrologers worked. Xerxes stole all the treasures from this tower, which, according to Diodorus, had a value of 6,300 gold talents.

Oriental legend states that the structure also housed a well which was precisely as deep as the tower was high. Here the fallen angels Harut and Marut are suspended by their chained feet, and in its depth the key to all magic can allegedly be found.

Such was Babel! And now? With six hundred thousand foot soldiers, twelve thousand cavalry, and one thousand sickle chariots, plus thousands of camel riders, Cyrus conquered the city in spite of its fortified location and although it had a twenty-year store of provisions. Later, Darius had the walls torn down and Xerxes despoiled Babylon of all its treasure. When the great Alexander came to the city, he intended to rebuild the tower. He ordered no less than ten thousand workers to clear away the rubble, but because of his sudden death, his plan had to be abandoned. Since that time this gigantic city has been decaying more and more, so that today only an expanse of decayed brick can be seen, and even the trained eye of the geologist finds it difficult to orient itself.

To the right of the tower I saw the road leading to Karbala, to its left the one to An Najaf. I would have liked to stay here longer, but the sun had disappeared, and dusk soon drove me back to my companions. The women's tent had been set up and, except for Lindsay and Halef, everyone had gone to sleep. Little Halef wanted to wait on me, and the Englishman to exchange some ideas about our plans for the next few days. I put him off until the following morning, wrapped the blanket around me, and tried to go to sleep. But this was futile; a feverish restlessness allowed only a doze which tired me even more.

Toward morning I was shaken by chills which alternated with hot flashes; a curious pain throbbed in my limbs, and in spite of the darkness I felt as if my surroundings were whirling like a merry-go-round. I still did not believe that this was anything more than a fever which would soon abate, and took some more medicine, after which I felt a lethargy which resembled stupor rather than sleep.

When I woke up, things were already in full swing. It was nine in the morning and at that very moment the death caravan from Hilla, divided into two sections, one going to Karbala, the other to Najaf, was passing by. Halef brought me water and dates, but I could manage only a few swallows and found it impossible to eat. My condition was similar to a rather severe hangover. Summoning all my strength, I temporarily overcame my exhaustion and could even talk to Hassan Ardshir, who proposed setting out the moment most of the stragglers had passed. I urged him to be cautious and always to keep his weapons ready. He agreed with a gentle smile and promised to be back at this spot on the twentieth or twenty-first. He left toward noon.

As we were saying farewell, Benda, who was already in the sedan chair, gestured to me. "Effendi, although you are very worried, I know we will see each other again," she said. "To calm your fears, grant me a request: lend me your dagger until I get back."

"You shall have it."

It was the weapon Esla el Mahem had given me in exchange for my own dagger, and had these words chiseled on its blade: "Return me to the sheath when victory is won." I knew that the courageous girl would not hesitate to use it to defend herself, should that become necessary.

After Selim had called a few words of farewell to me, the small troop rode off and we followed it with our eyes until we could no longer see it. But then my strength was at an end. Halef seemed to notice it before I did.

"Sidi, you are tottering," he exclaimed. "Your face is purple. Let's see your tongue."

When he had examined it, he said, "It's blue, Sidi! You have a high fever. Take some medicine and lie down."

And this is precisely what I had to do, for once again I became so dizzy that I could not stay on my feet. Seriously worried now, I drank some water mixed with vinegar and wound a piece of cloth soaked in vinegar around my head.

"I suppose you won't be able to accompany me to look for a place where I might dig?" Lindsay asked.

"Impossible."

"Then I'll stay."

"You needn't. I have a fever but that's a common occurrence when one travels. Halef is with me. There is no reason you should not leave. But don't go too far away, for if you run into Shiites, God knows what may happen."

He left with his men and I closed my eyes. Halef was sitting by me, concerned, and kept dripping vinegar on the compress. I don't know how long I had been lying there when I heard steps and immediately thereafter, and very close by, the rude question: "Who are you?"

I opened my eyes. Before us stood three well-armed Arabs on foot, wild fellows with defiant faces that boded no good.

"Strangers," Halef answered.

"You are not men of the Shia! What is your tribe?"

"We come from far to the west and belong to the Sahara tribes. Why do you ask?"

"You may belong to them, but this other fellow is a Frank. Why doesn't he get up?"

"He is ill and has a fever."

"Where are the others that were with you?"

"They left for An Najaf."

"And the other Frank?"

"He is nearby with his men."

"Whose stallion is this?"

"The effendi's."

"Turn it over to us, and turn over your weapons as well."

He stepped up to Rih and seized the reins. Apparently that was an excellent cure for my fever, for in a moment all my weakness was gone and I was up on my feet.

"Stop and talk to me first! Anyone who touches that horse gets a bullet!"

The man stepped back hastily and looked anxiously at the revolver I was aiming at him. Here, in the vicinity of a city such as Baghdad, he had probably come to know this type of weapon and feared it.

"I am only joking," he said.

"Joke with whomever you please, but not with us! What are you looking for?"

"I saw you and thought I might be of service."

"Where are your horses?"

"We don't have any."

"You are lying! I can tell from the folds in your garment that you ride. How do you know that there are two Franks here?"

"I heard from pilgrims who met you."

"You are lying again. We told no pilgrims who we were."

"If you don't believe us, we'll leave." With greedy looks at our horses and weapons, they withdrew and disappeared behind some ruins.

"Halef, you answered unintelligently," I said. "Let's make sure they are really leaving."

We followed the three Arabs but only slowly, for now that my anger had subsided my weakness also returned, and my vision became so blurred that I could barely distinguish what I saw in front of me.

"Do you see them?" I asked when we had moved behind the ruins.

"Yes, they are running to their horses over there."

"How many animals?"

"Three. Don't you see them, Sidi?"

"No, I'm dizzy."

"Now they have mounted and are riding off at a gallop. Allah! What's that? There's a whole troop out there that seems to be waiting for them."

"Arabs?"

"I can't tell, it's too far."

"Then run back and get my binoculars!"

While the Hadji was running to the horse, I tried to

remember where I had heard the voice of the Arab who had talked to us. Its rough, hoarse sound was familiar. Now Halef was back and handing me the binoculars, but a blood-red, whirling mist rose before my eyes. I passed the glasses to him.

It took some time until he had made the proper adjustments, and then he exclaimed: "Those are Persians!"

"Ah! Do you recognize any faces?"

"No. They have joined up now and are riding away."

"They are quickly moving west, isn't that right?"

Halef confirmed this, and now I took a look. The dizzy spell was over. "Halef," I said. "Those Persians are Hassan Ardshir-Mirza's pursuers. Selim is in league with them. He left last night to tell them that we would separate here. They sent those three to find out if Hassan Ardshir had left, and now they'll make haste to attack him before he gets close to An Najaf."

"Then we must take off after them."

"Certainly. Get the horses ready."

"Should I look for the Englishman? He went in the direction of Ibrahim Khalil."

"Then we'll have to do without him. We'd lose too much time. Hurry!"

I looked through the binoculars once again and clearly saw the troop gallop west. Then I tore a leaf from my notebook, wrote down a few lines to advise the Englishman of what had happened and what I intended to do. I suggested that he leave the tower and await our return along the canal near Anane, since he might be attacked here by the tower if I did not succeed in preventing it. I placed this note among the rubble in such a way that Lindsay could not overlook it. Then we mounted and rode off.

# 10 : In the Clutches
# of the Plague

The power of the mind over the body is a remarkable thing. My sickness seemed completely gone, my head felt cool, my vision was undimmed. We reached the pilgrims' route, passed stragglers who made way as they insulted us, fled past beggars whose imploring gestures we ignored. Now, a fallen mule was lying in our way and two men in tatters were attempting to wrap a half-rotten corpse into a felt blanket that had burst open. The stench was horrible. An overwhelming, uncontrollable nausea seized me.

"Sidi, you look terrible!" Halef shouted as he took the reins of my horse. "Hold on or you'll fall!"

"Forward!"

"No! Stop! Your eyes are fixed as if you were insane. You are reeling!"

"Forward," I wanted to shout but did not hear the word. I could not articulate but only stammered incomprehensibly as I urged my horse on to greater speed. But not for long, for suddenly I felt as if I had taken a strong emetic. I had to give in to the irresistible urge and stopped. As I noticed the slimy, bilious excretion and considered that I had not felt the slightest pain in my stomach, the fear of death seized me.

"Halef, go on! Leave me!"

"Leave you? Why?" he asked, startled.

"I have the plague!"

"The plague? Allah kerim! Is that true, Sidi?"

"Yes. I thought it was a fever but I see now that it is more serious."

"That's horrible."

"Go on! Look for the Englishman! He'll take care of you. He is either at the tower or in Anane." I could only stammer these words.

Instead of letting himself be sent away, Halef took

my burning hand. "Sidi, do you think I would leave you?"

"Go on!"

"No! May Allah's curse devour me if I leave you! There is a dark coating on your teeth, and you are stammering. Yes, it is the plague, but I don't fear it! Who will be with my Sidi when he suffers? Who will bless him when he dies? Sidi, my soul sobs, my eye weeps. Come, hold on to the saddle. We'll look for a place where I can take care of you."

"Will you really do that, my faithful Halef?"

"I will not abandon you, Sidi."

"I will always remember that, but perhaps I can hold out. Come, let's follow the Persians!"

"Sidi, that's impossible now."

"Forward!"

I spurred Rih and, whether he wanted to or not, Halef had to follow. But soon I had to slow down. Everything went dark before my eyes and I had to rely on Halef, who took over without wasting words. Every hoofbeat of my horse felt like a blow on my head. I could not tell whom we were passing; I let go of the reins and held onto the saddle with both hands.

After a very long time we finally caught up with the caravan and I made an effort to distinguish individual groups. Soundlessly we flew past, through hellish vapors, but I did not see the people we were looking for.

"Didn't you spot Hassan and his men, Halef?" I asked as we reached the head of the procession.

"No."

"Then let's turn left and return by the same route. They cannot have gone off to the right. Do you see those birds over the caravan?"

"Yes, vultures, Sidi."

"They smell the corpses and are looking for cadavers. Watch if one of them flies left in our direction. I am helpless and have to depend on you."

"But what if we have to fight?"

"Then my will must and shall conquer my sickness. Ride on!"

The caravan disappeared on our left. We were riding as rapidly as Halef's horse could manage, although it was only with an extreme effort that I stayed in the stirrups. Now the Hadji pointed upward.

"The bearded vulture."

"Is it circling?"

"Yes."

"Ride so that we are directly below it. It's looking for prey."

Ten minutes passed. I sensed that a decision was approaching, and since I would be unable to hit anything from any distance at all, I pushed the hunting rifle aside and picked up the carbine. I noticed now how weak I had become. The heavy hunting rifle which I normally handled with one hand seemed to be weighing hundreds of pounds.

"Sidi, there are bodies lying there," Halef shouted as he raised an arm.

"Are there any living among them?"

"No."

What we saw a moment later is indelibly engraved in my memory. I counted five motionless shapes widely scattered over the ground. In the most intense excitement, I jumped off my horse and knelt down beside the first. My pulse was hammering and my hand trembling violently as I removed the corner of the coat that was covering the face of the man. It was Saduk, the mute who had escaped from us in the Kurdish mountains. I hurried on.

Here lay the old female servant, struck in the temple by a bullet, and at that moment, Halef exclaimed in dismay, "The Persian's wife!"

She also had been shot and beside her, with outstretched arms as if he still wanted to protect her in death, lay Hassan himself, covered with dust and sand. His wounds showed that the encounter had been fierce. Even his hands were cut.

"My God, why didn't he believe me," I shouted, overwhelmed by grief.

"Yes," Halef said with a dark look. "He trusted the traitor more than he did you. But there's one more over there."

Far from the others another female figure lay in the sand that had been kicked up by the horses. It was Benda.

"May Allah damn this Selim; he killed them all!" the Hadji shouted.

"No, Halef. Don't you recognize the dagger in the girl's heart? I had to lend it to her. Her hand is still clutching the handle. Selim pulled her away from the others; here you see the prints her feet left when she was dragged through the sand. Perhaps she wounded Selim; in that case she killed herself when she could no longer offer any resistance.—Halef, I am also going to die here."

"Sidi, these people are no longer living. We cannot bring them back, but we can avenge them!"

I did not answer. My head was on fire, the blood-drenched plain was circling around me, and I seemed to be spinning on my own axis. My hands, which had been resting on my knees, let go and I slowly slid to the ground. I felt as if I were sinking deeper and deeper into a misty and ever blacker abyss. I found no support, there was no end, no bottom, the depth was infinite, and as though from an enormous distance I heard Halef's voice.

"Sidi, wake up so we can avenge them!"

Finally, after a long time, I realized that I was sinking no further. I had reached a place where I lay firm and secure, a place where I was being held by two strong arms. I touched those arms and saw the man they belonged to. Great heavy tears were falling on me.

I wanted to speak but could only manage with considerable effort: "Halef, don't cry!"

"Sidi, I thought you were dead, that you had died of the disease and the pain. Hamdulillah, you are alive! Pull yourself together. There are the tracks of the murderers. We'll pursue and murder them. Yes, murder them, by Allah, I swear it!"

I protested weakly. "I am tired. Put the blanket under my head."

"Can't you ride, Sidi?"

"No."

"Please try!"

My faithful Hadji thought he had to stir my vitality by the thought of revenge, but he hadn't succeeded. He threw himself on the ground and beat his forehead with his fists. "May Allah destroy that wretch I am not allowed to catch! May Allah also destroy the plague which is sapping the strength of my incomparable Kara Ben Nemsi! I am a miserable worm that can do nothing. It will be best if I also lie down here and wait for death."

Laboriously I pulled myself up. "Halef, is the vulture to devour the dead?"

"Are you going to bury them?"

"Yes," I panted.

"Where and how?"

"Where else except here, in the sand."

"That's hard work, Sidi. I'll do it. But the vulture shall feast on this Saduk who played dumb to destroy his master. But first I want to check if the dead have anything left on them."

This search was fruitless. The victims had been stripped of everything. What wealth must have fallen into the hands of those devils! But it was surprising that they had not taken the dagger from Benda. Perhaps the murderers had hesitated to loosen the stiff fingers of the girl by force. I asked Halef to leave the dagger in the girl's heart. It would have been impossible for me to ever touch the weapon again.

We now began to dig. Because we had no tools and had to use our hands and knives, this depressing effort proceeded slowly, and at a depth of one foot the sand became so hard that we would have needed an entire week to dig a sufficiently large hole.

"It's no good, Sidi." Halef groaned. "What now?"

"We will return to the tower. It's hardly more than two hours."

"Wallahi, that hadn't occurred to me. We'll bring the Englishman with his workers and his tools."

"And in the meantime the vultures will have their meal."

"Then I'll go by myself and you will stay here."

"You will fall into the bandits' hands. They've accomplished their purpose, and I imagine they have gone to the tower to steal our horses and weapons."

"I'll strangle them."

"All by yourself?"

"You are right, Sidi. Besides, I mustn't leave you; you are too ill!"

"So both of us will go."

"And the dead?" he asked.

"We'll place them on the horses and walk alongside."

"You are too weak for that. Look how digging in this loose sand has exhausted you. Your legs are trembling."

"Let them. They'll carry me. Come along!"

It was both a disheartening and a difficult task to place the bodies on the two horses. Since we did not have enough straps and rope, I had to cut up my lasso which had accompanied me for so long on all my travels. But why hesitate? It was fairly certain that the hand that had thrown it would be rigid in a few hours. We fastened the dead so that one was suspended from each side of the horses; then we picked up the reins and set out for our destination.

I shall never forget that walk. Had I not had my faithful Halef along, I would have collapsed more than once. All my efforts notwithstanding, my knees kept buckling. I had to stop at short intervals, not to gather strength, for that was impossible, but to summon the will to go on. The two hours stretched into many. The sun sank. Instead of leading the horse, I was hanging onto the bridle, half pulled by Rih, half pushed by Halef.

We were also delayed because we had to carefully avoid any encounter, and we did not arrive at the tower until late at night. I would never have thought that I would end my turbulent life at this place!

We stopped where we had camped the night before. There was no trace of Lindsay. The note was gone. It had to be assumed that he had read it and followed my instructions by immediately leaving for the canal. We took the dead off the horses, tethered the animals, and lay down, for nothing more could be done that evening.

"I know we will see each other again," Benda had said. Yes, it was certainly true that I had seen her. Although I was dead tired and found it difficult to think clearly, I started reproaching myself bitterly. I should have stood up more vigorously for my view and opposed Hassan's carelessness with force if necessary. Since my illness had left me enough strength for our brisk ride and the sad walk back, it would also have been possible to put Selim out of action.

I spent a bad night. Although my skin temperature was almost normal, my pulse was rapid and uneven, I was short of breath, my tongue was hot and dry, and my dreams were full of disquieting images which tormented me so much that I called Halef repeatedly to determine what was imagination, what reality. Often I was also awakened from this light sleep by pain in the armpits, the neck, and the back of the neck. Because of this state, which I describe in all this detail only because the plague is unknown at home, I was awake at dawn, earlier than Halef, and noticed now that I had boils below the shoulders and along the neck, a carbuncle on the back of the neck, and red spots the size of pinheads on the chest and the inside of the arms.

Believing that I was done for, I roused the Hadji. He was startled at my appearance. I asked him for water and then sent him to the canal to get the Englishman. Three hours which seemed like three eternities passed, and then Halef returned alone. He had searched for a long time and found nothing but a pickaxe near which a great many hoofprints were visible, the obvious indication of a struggle. The pickaxe, which he had brought along, belonged to Lindsay. Had the Englishman been attacked? Halef had seen no bodies, no trace whatever of any wound. There was nothing I could do about any of this. I was incapable of even the slightest effort.

Apparently I looked even worse now, for Halef's anxiety about me intensified and he urged me to take medicine. But what? Quinine, chloroform, ammonium chloride, arsenic, arnica, opium, or the other things I had bought in Baghdad would be useless. Being a layman, I knew nothing about remedies for the plague. I thought that fresh air, a thorough cleaning of the skin by frequent bathing, and an incision into the carbuncle would do the most good, and since our safety demanded that we not remain where we were, I deliberated with the Hadji. There surely had to be a spring or a small body of water somewhere, and as I looked east it seemed to me that water would most likely be found beyond the ruins in the south. I therefore asked Halef to go look in that direction.

The obliging little fellow was immediately willing but did not leave me without some concern, and this concern was to prove well founded. Halef must have been gone about half an hour when I heard the hoofbeats of several horses. I turned and saw seven Arabs, two of whom seemed to be wounded. The three who had spoken to me yesterday were among them. When they saw the bodies they hesitated and stopped to counsel softly with each other. Then they came closer and surrounded me.

"Well now, are you going to give us your horse and your weapons today?" asked the man who had done the talking yesterday.

"Go on, take them," I answered with equanimity.

"Where is the other one?"

"Where are the four you attacked along the canal?" I asked.

"You'll find out when we have your animal and your weapons. Turn them over. But take care! There are six rifles aimed at you, and if you should decide to resist you are done for."

"I wouldn't dream of it. I don't mind in the least giving you what you want. I could kill only one of you, but all of you will die the moment you dare touch my horse or any of my belongings."

The man laughed. "These rifles are not going to fire at us all by themselves."

"Try it! Here, take them!" I sat up laboriously, offering him the revolver in my right hand but opening my garment with my left so that those scoundrels could see my neck and bared chest. Immediately the leader pulled his arm back and jumped toward his horse with a gesture of great fear.

"You are dying," he shouted as he leaped into the saddle. "He has the plague! Flee, you believers, flee quickly from this accursed place, or it will be your undoing!" He galloped off and the others followed.

These charming sons of the Prophet were so horri-
fied that they forgot the teaching of the Koran, that
everything is written in the Book and that they could
not escape their fate by flight.

Half an hour later Halef was back, beaming. I had
guessed correctly. He had found a small brook whose
clear water flowed into the Euphrates and which had
some bushes along its banks. I told the Hadji about
my encounter with the Arabs and he was annoyed at
not having been there, swearing that he would have
shot all of them.

Before we left the tower we had to bury the dead. I
dragged myself to the western side of the ruins where
Halef carried the bodies. Then he opened a deep,
wide hole in the wall, not a difficult job because the
brick was full of cracks. He placed the dead inside and
set about closing the opening. Neither the Persian nor
the three women touched the earth.

During this time I was sitting opposite the opening,
impressing the victims' faces on my memory. Benda
was leaning against the brick of Babylon. Her abundant hair was touching the ground and her right hand
still clasped the dagger in her cold heart. Muhammad
Emin had been buried in just this way, his face turned
toward the Kaaba. They had been with us during that
burial, and Hassan Ardshir had recited the sura. Who
could have prophesied that they would suffer the same
fate as the old sheik of the Haddedihn, death in battle?

When only the faces of the dead were still to be
covered, Halef said his farewell, and I also staggered
closer to the grave.

"Sidi, let me recite the prayers today," Halef said,
and did so.

Should I feel ashamed of the tears that were running down my cheeks? I said a Christian prayer to
send them on their final journey. They had not
reached Najaf, their goal, but had set out on a higher
pilgrimage to the city of clarity and truth, where error
does not exist and happiness and joy reign from eternity to eternity.

The grave was now closed, and we could leave.
Slowly we rode past the ruin and the southern edge of

the field of rubble to our left. I had to make every effort not to fall from the saddle, and thus more than an hour went by until we came to the place Halef had found earlier in half that time. I saw a brook which came from the west. By many twists and turns it was flowing toward the Euphrates and was edged on both sides by densely growing willows and bushes.

First Halef prepared a place for me to lie, shading it from the sun with a light roof of branches. I then bathed and stretched out on the foliage which was to be my sickbed. My dark red tongue had turned black and become cracked toward the middle. Because of the fever I felt alternately hot and cold. I saw Halef's movements as through a dense fog and heard his voice as if in a dream; it sounded like a ventriloquist's. The small red spots spread and the swelling increased so alarmingly that toward evening, when I was momentarily free of fever, I asked Halef to make an incision in the carbuncle. To avoid a dangerous narcolepsy during the night, I instructed him to shake me awake and to douse me, should the dreaded rigor set in.

The night passed, and morning came. I felt a little better and Halef left to hunt some game. It did not take him long to come back with some fowl, which he roasted on his spear. I could not eat a single bite and watched him quietly and in a melancholy mood. How sad was this hour along the Euphrates, the river of Paradise! Dangerously ill, without help, with the pestilential miasma filling the air, among half-savage, fanatical fools against whom we had no other weapon but the plague. We could not go to Hilla or anywhere else, for we would have been murdered on the spot. What would have become of me, here, without my brave Halef who left nothing undone to show me his love and loyalty?

Today was the fourth day of the disease and I had heard that it was the decisive one. I continued to expect salvation from the water and the fresh air, and although my body had suffered considerably from the exertions of the recent past, I believed that I could rely more on my remaining strength than on any medicine about whose application and effect I had no precise knowledge.

Toward evening the fever moderated and the swelling became less painful. For a while during that night I had a refreshing sleep, and when I showed Halef my tongue the next morning he told me that the black coloration had almost disappeared. I now began to hope that I would recover but was not much startled when my loyal servant began complaining about a headache, dizziness, and chills that afternoon. During that night I had already felt certain that he had been infected.

I saw the little fellow walking toward the river to get me some water; he had trouble staying on his feet. "Halef, you are falling," I exclaimed.

"Oh, Sidi, things are going round and round."

"You are sick with the plague."

"I know," he moaned.

"And I infected you."

"It was Allah's wish; it was written in the Book. I shall die and you will go to Hanneh and console her."

"No, you won't die! I shall nurse you."

"You? You are fighting death yourself."

"I am already on the road to recovery. I shall do no less for you than you did for me."

"Oh, Sidi, what am I compared to you? Leave me here to die!"

It was remarkable how much the depression characteristic of the plague had already taken hold of Halef. He had probably been fighting it for some time to keep his condition from me as long as he could. Now the little fellow was at the end of his strength, and a few hours later he was raving. Perhaps he had contracted the disease in Baghdad, at the same time as I, and what developed now was the most severe, the bilious form of the plague, in which all attacks are more violent.

It was only with an extreme effort that I could pull myself together for short periods to give Halef the care I still stood in need of myself. It is a time I remember with horror, and whose description it is best to omit here.

Halef also was saved, but on the tenth day of his illness he was still so weak that I had to keep picking him up, and I was not yet strong enough to fire my hunting rifle and hit what I was aiming at without a support for my arms. In view of all this it was lucky that our camp was not discovered. When I saw my reflection in the water for the first time, I was frightened by the heavily bearded skull that was grinning at me. No wonder the vultures were circling above us, and the hyenas and jackals that emerged from the ruins on their way to the watering place looked through the reeds to see if we were ready to be devoured. They always had to beat a hasty retreat because my dog was not very hospitable.

My first walk took me to the grave of the Persians. I spent about an hour sitting near the tower. Suddenly the dog barked. I turned and saw a troop of eight horsemen with some falcons and a pack of dogs. They had already noticed me and were coming closer.

"Who are you?" the man who seemed to be in charge asked me without a salute.

"A stranger," I answered even more briefly.

"What are you doing here?"

"I am mourning the dead that lie buried here."

"What illness did they die of?"

"They were murdered."

"By whom?"

"Persians."

"Ah! By Persians and Sobeid Arabs. We heard about them. They also killed some men along the canal."

This startled me. Those men could only be Lindsay and his escort. "Are you quite certain?"

"Yes, we belong to the Shat tribe and were taking pilgrims to Karbala. That's where we heard about it."

That was certainly a lie. The Shat live far to the south and have to be extremely careful when venturing into these regions. And the fact that these men were hawking made it abundantly clear that they could not be far from home. But I concealed my suspicions.

The man now rode up close to me, and said, "Let me see that odd-looking rifle."

He stretched out his arm but I stepped back. "This rifle is dangerous for anyone who doesn't know how to handle it."

"Then you'll show me how."

"Of course, if you dismount and walk some distance with me. No one will surrender his rifle unless he is certain he can do so without risk."

"Give it to me! It's mine!"

The bandit again stretched out his hand and pulled up his horse at the same time to ride me down, but at that moment Dojan jumped, clamped his teeth on the man's arm, and pulled him to the ground. The Arab who was holding on to the dogs gave a shout and released them. They immediately charged Dojan.

"Call back your dogs," I commanded as I raised my rifle.

No one obeyed, and so I fired three or four shots, every one of which killed one dog. But I had not paid enough attention to the leader, who jumped up, seized me from behind, and pulled me down. I was much too weak to offer sustained resistance. In spite of his wounded arm, he overpowered me and held onto me until the rest could help him. The rifle and knife were torn from my hands and then I was tied and propped against a pile of bricks. Meanwhile Dojan was fighting the remaining three uninjured dogs. His fur was scratched and he was bleeding from several wounds but fought valiantly, never exposing his throat.

Now one of the Arabs took his old rifle, aimed, and fired. The bullet hit Dojan in the ribs; he collapsed and was torn to pieces by his half-savage enemies.

I felt as if a friend had been shot. This cursed weakness! Had I been my normal self, the old piece of rope tied around my arms would never have held me.

"Are you here by yourself?" the leader asked.

"No. I have a companion," I answered.

"Where?"

"Nearby."

"What are you doing here?"

"We got the plague and stayed where we were." This honest answer was the only chance to get away from these men. I had hardly uttered the last word when the rascals shrank back with shouts of terror.

But their leader had not moved. He said with an angry laugh, "You are clever, but you won't trick me. No one survives the plague."

"Look at me," I countered simply.

"It's true that you look pathetic, but you don't have the plague, you just have a fever. Where's your companion?"

"He is lying—There he is!"

From far away I heard a voice screeching "Rih!" "Rih!" in a piercing falsetto. A moment later my stallion was rushing toward us across the debris and the ruins. Halef was lying on Rih, his left arm around the neck of the horse, the right between his ears. He was holding one of his pistols in his hand while the rifle was hanging from his shoulders.

The Arabs now turned their attention to this curious spectacle. How had the utterly exhausted Hadji managed to get on the horse? He did not have the strength to make it stop, and it dashed past us.

"Stop, Rih!" I shouted as loudly as I could. Immediately the intelligent animal turned back.

"Take your hand away from the ears, Halef."

He obeyed, and Rih stopped before me.

Halef fell to the ground, and though he could barely manage to sit up, he asked angrily, "I heard shooting, Sidi. Whom should I kill?"

The sight of the sick Halef did not fail to convince the Arabs that I had told them the truth. "It's the plague! May Allah protect us!"

"Yes, the plague," the leader joined in. He threw the carbine and knife away and leaped on his horse. "Flee, men! But you, you dogs who are infecting us, may you go to hell!"

He aimed at me, and another of the men at Halef. Both fired but the leader's hand had been immobilized by Dojan's bite and the hand of the other was shaking with fear of the plague. Halef fired his pistol but his hand was trembling like a branch in the wind. He also missed. When he wanted to raise his rifle he was too weak, and the Arabs were already safely beyond reach.

"They are getting away! May the devil overtake them!" Halef wanted to shout angrily but could only produce a mutter. "What did they do to you, Sidi?"

I told him and asked him to cut the rope. His arm was barely strong enough. "How did you get on the horse?"

"Very easily, Sidi. I heard shots. Rih was lying on

the ground. I untethered him and lay down on his back. I knew where you were and had to come and help you. You had told me the secret of your horse and so he carried me here quickly."

"Your appearance was all that was necessary. The fear of the plague is stronger than any weapon. Those men will mention this encounter and so I think we'll be safe from other visitors for as long as we stay here."

"And Dojan? Are those his limbs?"

"Yes."

"What a terrible pity! Sidi, it's exactly as if something had happened to me. Did he die fighting?"

"Yes. He would have defeated his enemies, had he not been shot. But we have suffered an even more serious loss. The Englishman and his men have been murdered."

"Who told you?"

"The leader of those bandits. He claimed he had heard about it; for all I know, he was one of the murderers."

"Then we must find the bodies. As soon as I can walk again, we'll look for them. This Englishman was an unbeliever but he loved you and therefore I loved him. Sidi, dig a hole for the dog. He should rest here, near the Persians. No vulture or jackal must devour him. And then take me away. I am so tired, I feel as if I had been hit by a bullet."

I did as he asked. We buried Dojan in front of the Persians' grave as if, even in death, he was to protect their safety. Then I placed Halef on the horse, picked up my weapons, and slowly returned to the river. I felt a need to leave this area as quickly as possible. It was a field of ruins where much had also come to dust for us. There was no question now of making the journey to Hadramaut, as we had planned at an earlier time.

# 11 : In Damascus

The view from the summit of the Djebel Kassjun es Salehije is indisputably one of the most magnificent on earth. The picturesque mountains of the Anti-Lebanon rise high into the sky behind the traveler, and the plain of Damascus, a natural paradise highly praised by the Muslims, spreads before his eyes. El Ghouta, a flatland densely covered by fruit trees and flowers, extends for miles along the mountains. It is irrigated and freshened by eight small streams and rivers seven of which are tributaries of the Barada. And behind this ring of gardens the city sparkles, a Fata Morgana become reality for the pilgrim as he draws near from the desert.

Here the wanderer finds himself on historic soil where legend also has flourished. Toward the north lies the Djebel Kassjun, where, according to Oriental tradition, Cain murdered his brother Abel. Arab lore tells us that the tree of knowledge under which the first sin was committed once grew in el Ghouta, and in Damascus itself there stands the famous mosque of the Umayyads onto whose minaret Christ will descend on the Day of Judgment. Thus the history of Damascus stretches from the beginning of the world to its end, and is unique in this sense among cities. Such, at least, is the claim of the proud and fanatical inhabitants of the "City on the Barada."

Damascus is one of the oldest towns on earth, but the time of its foundation cannot be precisely determined because Muslim historiography has confused rather than developed the threads of tradition. Holy Scripture mentions the city repeatedly. David conquered it, and it counted among the most splendid pearls of his crown. Later, Assyrians, Babylonians, Persians, the Seleucids, Romans, and Arabs ruled here. During the time of Paul's conversion it was under Arab domination.

Damascus has often been conquered and destroyed but always rose again with renewed vigor. It suffered most severely under Tamerlane, who let his wild hordes murder in the streets for ten days in 1399. When the silence of death had settled, a fire destroyed what had remained untouched. Under Osman rule the city increasingly lost importance. The former cosmopolis became a provincial town, the seat of a governor, and everyone knows that these administrators are expert at impoverishing the richest country on earth.

Today it is said that Damascus has some two hundred thousand inhabitants, among which there are a little over thirty thousand Christians and five thousand Jews. No Muslims, not even those living in Mecca, equal the Damascenes in fanaticism. The time is not long past when a Christian was not allowed to ride a camel or a horse; he had to walk if he did not wish to use a donkey. This fanaticism which so readily leads to excess is still as virulent today as it was in 1860, when six thousand Christians were massacred.

The horrible prelude to this event began at Hasbeya, on the western slope of Mount Hermon, south of Beirut, and in the coastal city of Sidon. On the ninth of July 1860, when the muezzin had just proclaimed the hour of the noon prayer in Damascus, the armed rabble, led by Bashi Bosuks, stormed the Christian quarter. Every man and boy was slain, and the women and girls either suffered a worse fate or were sold into slavery. The governor Achmed Pasha calmly looked on, but a man who had spent his life fighting them, Abd al Kadir, rose in defense of the Christians. This Algerian Bedouin hero had left his native country to seek obscurity in Damascus. He opened his house to the Christians who came to him for protection and patrolled the city with his Algerians, leading those who had escaped the mayhem into the old citadel. When some ten thousand Christians had been taken to safety there, the murdering rabble was about to rush the place. Clad in his armor and helmet, Abd el Kadir rode his horse into the crowd and told his men to lay fire to Damascus at the first sign that the citadel might be stormed. He prevailed. It is remarkable that such nobility should have been shown by a man whom the French had held in illegal imprisonment for five years after the treaty of Kerben.

From Damascus the great caravan route runs to Mecca, which is reached in forty-five days. It takes caravans between thirty and forty days for the journey to Baghdad, but postal service by dromedary covers the distance in only about twelve. I also had come to Damascus from Baghdad, but I had not taken the route by which the mail travels, and this for a very good reason.

After the events just reported, we had had to spend another six days along the brook until Halef had recovered sufficiently for us to return to Baghdad. Before we had set out, we had once again searched for Lindsay and any possible trail along the canal but found nothing. When we were back in Baghdad the Pole told us that he had neither seen nor heard anything from the Englishman, and I therefore reported his disappearance to the British authorities. I was promised a speedy investigation but it was fruitless, and so I decided to leave the city.

By way of Samarra we rode to Tikrit and then turned west to the Tharthar, to avoid the tribes whom we had battled earlier in the Valley of the Steps. A day's journey from the famous ruins of El Hadr we encountered two men who told us that the Shammar had withdrawn from their pastures and moved south toward Es Der on the Euphrates to elude the hostility of the governor of Mosul. We rejoined them there without any further interruption of our journey. Our arrival created both sadness and joy among the Haddedihn. Amad el Ghandur had not yet come back. The entire tribe had been deeply concerned about us but hoped for our safe return. News of the death of Muhammad Emin caused profound grief, and there was a huge celebration to honor his memory.

But the reunion with Hanneh was a moment of pure joy. Jubilantly she threw herself into her Halef's arms, and his delight redoubled when she led us into the tent to show him the little Hadji who had come into this world during our absence to set out on his earthly pilgrimage.

"And do you know what name I gave him, Sidi?" she asked me.

"Well?"

"I named him after you and his father—Kara Ben Halef."

"You acted wisely, you pearl of womanhood," Halef exclaimed delightedly. "My son will be a hero like his father, for his name is longer than the spear of his enemy. All men will honor him, all young women will love him, and all his enemies will flee when the name Kara Ben Hadji Halef Omar Ben Gadji Abul Abbas Ibn Hadji Dawuhd al Gossarah resounds in battle."

Sheik Malek was pleased to see us again. He had acquired considerable influence among the Haddedihn and it seemed probable that he would soon advance to the rank of leader. Should that happen my loyal little Hadji could count on being a Shammar sheik at some time in the future.

With a numerous escort we revisited all the places we had come to know during our first stay, and spent the evenings telling our adventures to the attentively listening Haddedihn, Halef never failing to emphasize how well he had protected me on our long travels.

Bill, the Irishman, and his friend Fred were still in the camp. During our absence they had gone "native" and learned enough Arabic to communicate with their hosts. Nonetheless, they yearned to leave, and when they heard that they could not count on their lost master they asked me to take charge of them. I agreed, for such had been my intention in coming here.

I had decided to travel to Palestine and from there to Istanbul by ship. But first I wanted to see Damascus, the city of the Umayyads, and in order to avoid any unpleasantness originating in Mosul, I determined to cross the Euphrates south of Es Der and make a sufficiently long detour to approach Damascus via the Hauran.

But the Haddedihn would not consent to my leaving after such a short stay, and Halef insisted on accompanying me to Damascus. I could not deny him that wish, and since I had to allow him some time with his family, my stay became much longer than I had intended. Weeks passed, but when the brief cold season had come and then drawn to its close, I would not tarry any longer. We left.

A great many Haddedihn accompanied us to the Euphrates, on whose left bank we separated, Halef for a short while and I forever, as I then believed. Amply provided with all necessities, we crossed the river and soon found ourselves far beyond it. A week later we saw the heights of the Hauran before us, but an encounter two days earlier was to shape future events significantly.

During the morning we had seen four camel riders ahead of us who seemed to be traveling in our direction. Since the Bedouins of the Hauran cannot be trusted, companions would have been welcome, and we therefore increased our speed to catch up with them. But when they noticed us they also urged on their animals, though this did not keep us from drawing ever closer. Recognizing this, they stopped and moved off to one side to let us pass. The group consisted of an older man and three younger, sturdy companions. They did not look very warlike but had placed their hands on their weapons to inspire respect.

"Selam," I called out as I reined in my horse. "You have no need of your weapons, we are no bandits."

"Who are you?" the older man asked.

"We are three Franks from the Occident, and this is my servant, a peaceful Arab."

The man's face lit up, and to make sure that I had told him the truth, he asked in broken French, "What country do you come from, Monsieur?"

"Germany."

"Ah," he said naïvely, "that's a very peaceful country whose citizens spend all their time reading books and drinking coffee. But where are you coming from now? Are you a merchant, perhaps, like me?"

"No, I travel to write books about the countries I visit, and those books are then read at coffee time. I am coming from Baghdad and am going to Damascus."

"But instead of writing implements, you are carrying a great many weapons."

"Because I could hardly use such implements to defend myself against the Bedouins who make this route unsafe."

"That's true." This man seemed to have conceived of a writer as someone with a gigantic quill behind his ear, a desk before him, and huge inkwells suspended from either side of his horse. "The Aneseh have pulled toward the Hauran, so one must be cautious. Shall we travel together?"

"Gladly. Are you also going to Damascus?"

"Yes. I live there. I am a merchant and join a caravan every year to trade with the Arabs in the south. I am just returning from such a journey."

"Are we going to cross the eastern Hauran or do we stay left, close to the road to Mecca?"

"Which is better?" he asked.

"The latter, without a doubt."

"I agree. Have you been here before?"

"No."

"Then I shall guide you."

The merchant's earlier suspicion had wholly disappeared. The man being frank and talkative, I soon discovered that he was carrying a rather substantial amount of money with him. For while the Arabs had paid him largely in natural products, he had been able to sell these advantageously.

"I also do a good deal of business with Istanbul," he said. "Are you going there as well?"

"I am."

"Then you could perhaps take a letter there for my brother. I would be very grateful."

"Of course. Will you permit me then to visit you in Damascus?"

"You will be welcome. My brother Maflei is also a merchant and has far-reaching connections. He might be useful to you."

"Maflei? I have heard that name somewhere before."

"Where?"

"Let me think. Yes, now I remember. In Egypt I met the son of a merchant from Istanbul whose name was Isla Ben Maflei."

"Really? What an odd coincidence! Isla is my nephew, my brother's son."

"If it is the same Isla."

"Describe him."

"Perhaps it would be better if I told you that there, along the Nile, he rescued his bride, who had been abducted from her parents."

"That's right. What was the girl's name?"

"Senitza."

"Everything checks. Where did you encounter him? Where did he tell you all this? In Cairo, perhaps?"

"No, at the very place where it all happened. Do you know the story?"

"Yes. Isla later came to visit me on some business matter and told me about it. He would never have found his bride again had he not met a certain Kara Ben Nemsi, an effendi—ah, that effendi was also a writer of books! What's your name, Monsieur?"

"In Egypt and beyond, I was called Kara Ben Nemsi."

"What a miracle! So it's you!"

"Ask my servant, Hadji Halef Omar, who helped free Senitza."

"Then you really must stay at my house in Damascus, both you and your companions. My house and everything I own are yours."

The merchant then cordially invited my companions to be his guests. I had to translate our conversation for the little Hadji. "Do you still remember Isla Ben Maflei, Halef?"

"I do. He was the young man whose bride we got out of Abrahim Mamsur's house."

"This man is Isla's uncle."

"Allah be praised! Now I have someone to whom I can tell everything that happened back there. A good deed must not be allowed to die; it must be recounted to remain alive."

"Yes, tell me," the Damascene said in Arabic.

Now Halef let loose, reporting the occurrence in the most flowery Oriental style. I was the most famous Hekim-Bashi on earth, Halef the most courageous hero, Isla the finest Istanbul youth, and Senitza the most splendid haura of Paradise. Abrahim Mamur was described as a true devil, and we had accomplished a deed which was already being talked about by all the peoples of the Orient.

When I tried to curb his exuberance and present matters in their true proportions, he said quite decisively, "Sidi, you don't understand that sort of thing. I know better, for I was your aga at the time, I had my whip of rhinoceros hide and had to handle all these things for you."

Orientals are incorrigible in such matters and so I bowed to the inevitable. The Damascene, however, seemed to enjoy Halef's storytelling. The little Hadji rose in his esteem, and he took him to his heart.

We reached the caravan route without incident and entered the suburb of El Meidan, where during the time of the Hajji the great pilgrims' caravan to Mecca gathers. The Barada flows through the town proper and feeds any number of canals. Large crowds surge through the famous bazaars or enjoy coffee in shaded cafés. The abundance of water all around the city favors the planting of large orchards. The Arab, who thinks of paradise as a large garden with trees, therefore sees Damascus as a reflection of the heavenly gardens.

The Christian quarter lies in the eastern part of the city and begins at the Thomas Gate, the starting point of the Palmyran caravan route. South of it, beyond the "street called Straight," is the Jewish quarter, while the western half of the city belongs to the Arabs. Here one finds the most handsome buildings: the citadel, the magnificent bazaars, the great Khan Assad Pasha, and, above all, the mosque of the Umayyads, which Christians are unfortunately not permitted to enter.

This mosque is one hundred thirty-one meters long and thirty-eight wide, and stands on the site of a pagan temple which the emperor Theodosius destroyed. The emperor Arcadius built a Christian church here which was dedicated to St. John. It contained the shrine where the severed head of John the Baptist was kept and which Chalid Ibn Welid, the conqueror of Damascus, is said to have found there. Chalid, whom the Muslims call the "Sword of God," turned half of the church into a mosque, a rare occurrence which had a specific reason. The besieging army was made up of two parts: one of them, commanded by Chalid, was massed outside the East Gate while the other, under the mild Abu Ubaida, was at the West Gate. Furious because of the length of the siege, Chalid swore not to spare a single inhabitant. Early in 635 he finally passed over the walls by the East Gate and ordered the massacre to begin. The western part of the city then quickly concluded an agreement with

Abu Ubaida. Its population agreed to voluntarily open the gate, provided he spared them. He consented. Both armies approached each other from opposite points along the "street called Straight" and joined near the Church of St. John. Because of Abu Ubaida's representations, Chalid ordered an end to the massacre and agreed that one half of the church should continue to serve the Christians.

For about a hundred and fifty years Christians and Muslims thus prayed in the same church, until it occurred to Welid the First to lay claim to the entire building. Although he did offer the Christians another place of worship, they did not trust his promise and opposed his proposal. There was a prophecy according to which the person who interfered with the building would become incurably insane, and it was believed that this would deter the caliph, but that did not happen. Rather, Welid was allegedly the first to pick up a hammer to smash the magnificent altar picture. Then the entrance of the Christians was walled up. The church, now wholly a mosque, was given closed halls of Corinthian columns and decorated with mosaics and six hundred hanging lamps of pure gold. For the work of rebuilding, some twelve hundred Greek architects and artists were called from Constantinople. The most beautiful columns of Syria were transported to Damascus, and tradition reports that eighteen beasts of burden carried the bills when the caliph wanted to examine them. Welid paid and then had the bills burned, because he meant the huge cost to remain an eternal secret.

Quite near this mosque, along the "street called Straight," was the house of the man I had just met. The entrance was in a narrow alley into which we now turned, for I could not possibly reject his hospitality. We stopped by a tall brick wall which showed no opening except for a not very sizable gate. In answer to some raps with the iron knocker it was opened a few moments later and a Moorish face, shining like ebony, appeared.

"Allah! The master!" the black exclaimed and opened the gate wide.

The merchant gave a friendly answer and gestured

us to follow him. After I had told Bill and Fred to take the animals inside and to stay with them, Halef and I stepped inside.

We found ourselves in a long, narrow courtyard and in front of a second wall whose gate had already been opened. When I had passed through it I was standing in a large, square yard paved with marble. Arcades, their openings hidden by large quantities of lemons, oranges, pomegranates, and figs all growing in tubs, gave onto it on three sides, the fourth being the wall through which we had just come. It was covered with jasmine, Damascene roses, and red-and-white Syrian hibiscus. The center of the court was occupied by a granite basin in whose water fish shimmered like gold and silver and at whose every corner stood a fountain which fed this basin. The arcades supported a gaily painted story to which a wide staircase amply decorated with fragrant flowers provided access. There was a large number of apartments and other rooms here whose windows were covered by silken curtains or ornate wooden grills.

A group of women was resting on soft pillows by the basin. They had no sooner seen us than they uttered fearful screams and scurried toward the stairs to disappear into their chambers. Only one remained. She also had risen but came toward the merchant and kissed his hand respectfully.

"Welcome, Father," she greeted him.

He embraced her warmly and said, "Go and tell your mother that God is blessing my house with cherished guests. I will take them to the selamlik and then come to you."

He had spoken Turkish, like his daughter. Perhaps he had lived in Istanbul at an earlier time.

The daughter left and we slowly followed her up the stair where we came into a corridor with many doors. The master of the house opened one and we entered a large room which received colored light through a domed roof whose openwork apertures were covered by glass of various colors. Tall, wide velvet cushions were arranged along the walls. A grandfather clock was evenly ticking in a niche, a gilded lamp with many arms was suspended from the dome, and numerous paintings in valuable frames hung between the silken wall coverings, looking down at us. They were the sort of amateurish productions "smart" business-men lavish upon the world: Napoleon in emperor's garb but with the vermillion, puffed-out cheeks one sees on trumpet-blowing angels; Frederick the Great with a wispy goatee; an enormous bouquet of sun-flowers, cornflowers, and bluedrops; Lady Stanhope with beauty spots; Washington wearing a gigantic wig; a Hercules with Saint George's dragon at his feet; and finally the storming of Sagunto, with cannon bar-rels projecting between its crenelles and thick violet gunsmoke settling over its demolished walls. The Orient is the only market for such ineptitudes.

Low, small tables with metal tops had been placed in front of the cushions and filled pipes and dainty coffee cups had been put on them. And—I hardly dared believe my eyes, though surely they weren't de-ceiving me—there was actually a piano, apparently still in tolerable condition, sitting in the middle of the room! I would have liked nothing better than to open it right then and there, but had to preserve the dig-nity I owed Kara Ben Nemsi Effendi.

We had barely entered and taken our seats when a handsome boy came in with a basin of glowing coals to light our pipes, and some minutes later a second one arrived with a silver coffeepot from which he filled our cups. After the first puff from his pipe our host again bade us welcome, and when he had finished the con-tents of the small bowl he requested permission to leave us for a short while to greet his family.

We continued smoking and drinking in silence until our host returned and asked us to follow him. He took us into a very amply furnished room which was to be mine, the adjoining one having been set aside for Halef. He also promised to see to accommodations for Fred and Bill. We then followed him downstairs, where, with incomprehensible speed, a bath had meanwhile been prepared for us. Two sets of gar-ments, from a red fez to a light babouche, had been laid out for us and two domestics were awaiting us to offer their services.

This was typically Oriental hospitality, and I was

truly grateful for it. When we had left the bath and changed, we returned to the selamlik as rejuvenated human beings. Our attentive host must have had someone report this, for we had barely entered the room when he rejoined us.

"Effendi, you have brought great joy to my family," he began in Arabic. "When I told them who you are, they asked for permission to appear before you. Will you permit it?"

"It would make me very happy to be able to talk to them."

"They will not come until the afternoon, for they are busy now preparing a meal. Today they will allow none of the servants to touch it.—Have you ever seen such paintings?" he now asked, for without meaning to I had been eyeing the Hercules.

"They are quite rare," I said evasively.

"They are. I bought them in Istanbul and paid a high price for them. No one else in this city owns such valuable works. Do you know what they represent?"

"I don't really think so."

"I had it explained to me. The first is Napoleon, the second the intelligent Emir of Alamanlar, then comes the Queen of England and the Shah of the Americans. Next is Hercules killing a sea lion, and finally the battle scene, the storming of Jerusalem by the Christians. Aren't they beautiful?"

"Magnificent. But what is this here in the middle of the room?"

"Oh, that's my most valuable possession. It is a musical instrument I bought from an Englishman who lived here and then moved away. May I show it to you?"

"Please do."

We walked up to it and opened it. The inscription above the keyboard read: Edward Southey, London," and a glance at the insides of the instrument showed me that while some strings were broken, it was generally in tolerable condition.

"I'll show you how it is done," he said. And our host started banging the keys with his fists in a way that made my hair stand on end. But I forced myself to make an admiring face and then asked if there was something else to go with the piano.

"The Englishman also gave me wire and a hammer to make music so that one's hands don't hurt. I'll show you."

He left and soon returned with a small box that contained strings and a tuning hammer. He took that hammer and noisily struck at the keys. It seemed that the charming Englishman had played a joke on our host by telling him that this was the proper use for it.

"Do you also want to make music?" he asked me. "No one is allowed to touch this instrument, but you are my guest and shall have permission to beat it a little." And with these words he handed me the key with a patronizing smile.

"You just showed me how music is made in Damascus," I said. "Now I will show you how we use this instrument in the Occident. But first you must permit me to make some improvements, for its condition is no longer what it ought to be."

"Effendi, surely you aren't going to ruin it?"

"No, you can trust me." I replaced the missing strings and then made a seat for myself from some cushions and began to tune it.

When the master of the house heard my fifths and octaves, he was delighted. "You are even better than I am."

"That isn't music," I said. "I am merely giving this wire the right tone. Didn't that Englishman show you how this instrument was to be played?"

"His wife made music, but then she died. He used to bang it with his fists and that pleased him so much he'd laugh."

"Then I'll show you how it should be done." In earlier days, as a poor student, I had often tuned pianos to earn some pocket money and so I did not find it difficult to put the instrument into a halfway playable condition. But there was no time for a thorough job.

While I was thus engaged, the door opened and all the women I had seen earlier in the courtyard entered. I heard an admiring whisper and occasionally even an exclamation of delight. How undemanding they were! Finally I was done and closed the lid, whereupon my audience disappeared.

"Won't you go on?" my host asked. "You are a great artist and the women are so pleased with this music they will spoil our dinner."

"I have to let the instrument rest now, but after dinner, when your family comes, I will play them some music they have never heard before."

"I have some female guests. May they also hear it?"

"Of course," I answered politely.

I was curious to see what effect a dashing waltz would have on these ladies, but self-interest militated against my distracting them from their culinary endeavors at this moment. And this circumspection bore fruit, for in expectation of the enjoyment awaiting them, they apparently worked more quickly than usual and soon an ample meal was served that was a credit to the house.

We had hardly finished when our host asked if the women might join us, and when I agreed the little boy who had brought us coffee ran out to get them.

The mistress now entered with two daughters and a son of about twelve. There were four more women, friends of our hostess. All of them wore veils. They quietly sat down on the cushions, and when I noticed how frequently their heads were turning toward the piano I got up to appease their impatience. It was amusing to observe the impression the first full chord and a vigorous run made on them.

"Mashallah," Halef exclaimed, startled.

"Look, look!" the head of the family shouted as he jumped up and raised his arms in amazement.

The women were so astonished that they drew back, shouted with surprise, and imprudently stretched out their hands so that the veils were momentarily pushed aside and I could see all their faces.

After a short prelude I started in on the smartest waltz I knew. At first my audience was rigid, but soon the rhythm began to exert its irresistible force. The stiff figures began to move, the hands twitched, the legs rebelled against their unnatural position, and the bodies were swaying back and forth. Our host got up, walked over, and stood behind me to stare at my fingers.

When I had finished he took my hands in his and examined them. "Effendi, what fingers you have! It was like an ant heap. I have never seen anything like it."

"Sidi," Halef said, "the only other place one can hear such music is where the spirits of the blessed dwell."

The women did not dare articulate their feelings, but their lively gestures and admiring whispers convinced me that they had not been bored. I continued playing and my audience did not tire of listening to sounds they had never heard before.

"Effendi, I never suspected that this instrument contains such pieces," the old merchant commented when I stopped.

"Oh, it contains even more magnificent ones. You just have to know how to elicit them. Where I come from, there are thousands of men and women who are much better at this than I am."

"Women too?" he asked in surprise.

"Yes."

"Then my wife will have to learn to make music on this instrument, and she will have to teach her daughters." The dear fellow had no conception of the difficulties that stood in the way of realizing his sudden decision here, in Damascus, and I did not feel it necessary to enlighten him on that score.

Now Fred and Bill were sent for, and I played a number of dances which the two performed with such enthusiasm and to such acclaim that it seemed as if the Damascene women would have liked nothing better than to join in.

After a while I felt I had done enough. The women thanked me cordially and retired, and our host told us that he would have to attend to some business matters. I informed him that Halef and I would go out for a while to look at the city and he immediately ordered two donkeys to be saddled. A servant would accompany us.

In the courtyard we found two white Baghdad donkeys for us and a gray one for the servant, who had brought pipes and an ample provision of tobacco

along. We lit the pipes, mounted the beasts, left the
courtyard and took an alley by which we reached the
"street called Straight." With slippers on our bare feet,
turbans on our heads, the pipes in our hands, and looking stately, like Turkish pashas, we rode down the
crowded street toward the Christian quarter. Leisurely
wending our way, we noticed that most of the crowd
was moving toward the Thomas Gate.

"There must be something going on there," I said to
the servant.

"Yes, a great deal. There is a festival today with an
archery contest. Anyone looking for amusement visits
the tents and gardens outside the city to share in the
joys Allah has prepared for him."

"It's early, so why not join them? Do you know
the place?"

"Yes, Effendi."

"Then show us the way."

Soon we had passed through the gate and out into
the Ghouta. There was much hustle and bustle everywhere. It was a fête open to members of all faiths, but
the servant could tell me nothing about its origin. All
available space was taken up by tents where flowers,
fruit, and various kinds of food were being sold. Rope
dancers, Indian magicians, fire eaters, snake charmers
were everywhere. Begging dervishes hampered our
progress, children were playing noisily, porters were
quarreling, camels screaming, horses neighing, dogs
barking and on top of all that, all sorts of instruments
were being blown, scraped, and beaten. We were
riding past a long row of fruit vendors when I suddenly
stopped my donkey to listen. Had I heard right? A
crowd had gathered in front of a large tent, and from
inside came the sounds of violins and harps, and then,
when the music had stopped, a worn-out soprano
began singing in the purest Erz Mountains dialect.

We dismounted, paid the admission, and entered.
More than a hundred Arabs, Turks, Kurds, Jews,
Christians, and others were sitting closely packed on
benches and at tables, drinking coffee, smoking, or
chewing fruit and pasteries. In back, on a stage, sat
two violin players, two female harpists, and a female
guitarist, all in Tyrolean costume.

The guitarist had meanwhile stopped singing, and I asked her, "In what language did you sing?"

"In German."

"Are you a German lady?"

"I was born in German Austria."

"In what town?"

"Presnitz."

Up to this moment I had spoken English and French, but now I switched to German and said, "Ah, Presnitz, near the border of Saxony, close to Jöhnstadt and Annaberg?"

"Right!" she exclaimed. "So you speak German too?"

"As you hear."

"In Damascus?"

"In Damascus, and everywhere else."

It was delightful to hear my native language once again, but this nostalgic moment was short-lived, for suddenly Halef nudged me and nodded toward the entrance. I followed his glance and saw a man we had often mentioned during recent days but whom I would never have expected to see here. Those handsome features which were yet so unpleasant in their disharmoniousness, the scrutinizing, piercing glance, those dark shadows which hatred, love, revenge, and unsatisfied ambition had left on his face were too familiar to be hidden under the heavy beard the man was now wearing. It was Dawuhd Arafim, who had called himself Abrahim Mamur back in the house on the Nile.

He was surveying the crowd and inevitably his glance fell on me. I saw him start, turn quickly, and leave the tent.

"After him, Halef. We must find out where he lives."

A moment later Abrahim was galloping away on a donkey, its owner clutching its tail as he ran behind it. Our servant had momentarily left us, and when we found him again in the tent of a storyteller it was too late to catch the fugitive.

This put me in such bad humor that I decided to return home. The moment I saw this man I had had the feeling that somehow I would cross swords with him again, and now I had missed the chance to find out where he was staying in Damascus. Halef also cursed into his small beard, then suggested that we return home and make some more music. We were riding back along the same route when someone called out to us in the "street called Straight." It was our host, who was standing at the entrance to a jeweler's shop with a young man, a servant and a donkey.

"Won't you come in, Effendi?" he asked. "In a little while we can all go back home together." We dismounted, entered the store, and were greeted with great cordiality by the young man.

"This is my son, Shafei Ibn Jakub Afarah," our host introduced him. This was the first time I had heard the name of the man in whose house we were staying, and this sort of thing is not rare in the Orient. He then introduced us to his son, and went on: "This is my store, which Shafei runs with the help of an assistant. You will have to forgive him. He cannot accompany us now. He has to stay here because the assistant left to have a look at the festival."

I looked around the store. It was small and rather dark but contained such quantities of valuables that, poor as I was, I found it unsettling. I made some comment to that effect and was told that Jakub owned several more stores in other bazaars, where he kept rugs, valuable smoking utensils, and delicacies. After we had had a cup of coffee, we left. Dusk was approaching, and we had been back home for only a short time when evening fell.

During my absence my room had been festively decorated. Hanging lamps filled with fragrant flowers had been suspended from the ceiling and tall vases placed in each corner. What a pity that I did not understand the language of flowers, otherwise I might perhaps have interpreted all this as a touching appreciation of the concert. I stretched out on the cushions to spend some time in idleness, but my thoughts kept returning to this Abrahim Mamur. What was he doing here in Damascus? Was he planning another abomination? Why had he fled when he saw me, since I had had no further dealings with him? And how could I set about discovering where he was staying?

As I lay there pondering these matters I became aware of the activity that was developing along the corridor. Some time later there was a knock at my door and Jakub entered.

"Effendi, are you ready for dinner?"

"I am at your command."

"Come along, then. Halef is already there."

He did not take me to the selamlik as I had expected, but across two corridors to the front side of the house, where we entered a large room. It was brightly lit by many candles, and quotations from the Koran in black embroidery hung from the silken walls. The room had been partitioned by an iron rod from which a heavy velvet curtain hung to the floor across the entire room. A meter above the floor a number of peepholes had been cut into the velvet, so I assumed that the women would take their seats on the far side of it. Some twenty men stood up as we entered. Among them were two sons and three assistants of Jakub.

During our conversation, which was somewhat halting at first, aromatic liqueurs were drunk and the obligatory pipes lit. Then a meal was served which included not only the dishes I was already familiar with, but stewed Indian figs and myrtle, a salad made with a red root similar to our turnip, fried garlic, and fried lizard, whose meat I found quite palatable. When one journeys into distant parts of the world, one learns to free oneself of prejudices.

After dinner the dishes and containers were removed and the piano carried in. An entreating glance from Jakub Afarah made clear what was expected of me, and I did my duty unhesitatingly. I did, however, make it a condition that the curtain be removed. My host looked at me, startled.

"Why, Effendi?"

"Because this velvet absorbs the sound, and you won't hear anything beautiful."

"But there are women on the other side."

"They are veiled, aren't they?"

Only after prolonged discussion with his guests did he muster the courage to push back the curtain, and I saw some thirty female figures crouching on soft mats on the floor. I did my best to entertain them, and even sang some songs, translating the text into Arabic as best I could.

When I stopped, Jakub took me to the small barred window which gave on to the "street called Straight." Down below I saw a tightly pressed crowd taking up the entire width of the street, and I wondered what must have gone through the Damascenes' heads as they heard me sing. Certainly the invited company did not feel that I was mad. These men were already too enlightened to spoil their pleasure by narrow-minded doubts, and when they left the house toward midnight it was with every intention of returning in the near future.

Jakub took me back to my room and was pleased when I permitted his son Shafei to accompany us. Shafei expressed his regret that his assistant from the jeweler's shop had not been at the concert.

"You would have given him great pleasure," my host remarked. "He loves music and is an intelligent man. He could have spoken Italian, French, or English with you."

"Is he from Damascus?" I asked politely.

"No. He is from Edirne, and my uncle's grandson. His name is Afrak Ben Hulam. We had never seen him. He arrived here with a letter from his father and a note from my brother Maflei in Istanbul to get some more experience in the business."

"Why wasn't he here tonight?"

"He was tired and did not feel well," Shafei said. "When he came back from the fête, I told him that Kara Ben Nemsi Effendi had come and would make music. He wanted to come but was ill and looked deathly pale. But he did hear the playing, for his room is close to the one where we gathered."

After a little while the two left and I settled down. How much better one slept on these cushions than on the sand of the desert!

When I woke up in the morning I heard a nightingale, which was sitting on a branch outside my window. When I entered Halef's room he was already up, drinking coffee and eating pastry. I joined him, and then we went down into the courtyard. After I had

had a look at the horses we smoked a pipe by the basin.

Before he left, Shafei invited us to visit the bazaar. He had to spend all day there because his cousin and assistant was feeling worse and would have to stay at home.

"Effendi, I know that you are a physician," he said.

"Who says so?"

"You helped many sick when you were on the Nile; Isla told us. So I asked my cousin just now to talk to you, but he refuses. He told me that his illness came frequently but always passed after two days. Won't you have a look at him?"

"No. Afrak doesn't want me to, and besides, I am not a real doctor."

After a while I asked that three donkeys be saddled so that Halef and I might make some small purchases. Since we were in no hurry and were curious, we rode through some alleys and even into the congested Jewish quarter. What an abundance of ruins, what misery! Dilapidated hovels among the remains of what had once been splendid buildings; men dressed in worn-out caftans that had burst at the seams, children in rags and tatters, women parading their genuine or imitation jewelry over their faded finery.

As we rode past the bazaar of the jewelers and goldsmiths on our way back, I wanted to stop at Shafei's but saw to my surprise that the store was closed. Two policemen were standing guard. When I asked what they were doing there I was given such a boorish answer that I hurried on. Back at Jakub's I found everyone in a state of extreme excitement. At the gate I ran into Shafei, who was about to leave the house in a great hurry but stopped when he saw me.

"Effendi, do you know what happened?" the young man called out excitedly.

"What?"

"There has been a terrible theft!"

"I heard nothing."

"Ask my father; I have to leave."

"Where are you going?"

"I don't know myself." Shafei was about to rush past

me but I stopped him. Whatever had happened was making it impossible for him to judge the situation calmly, and any rash action on his part therefore had to be forestalled.

"Wait!" I begged him.

"Let me go! I must pursue him."

"Who? The thief? Who is he?"

"Ask my father." The young man wanted to free himself but I slid off my donkey, pulled his arm under mine, and forced him to accompany me. He submitted and let me up the stairs into his father's apartment. Ready to go out, his father was standing in the room loading a pair of gigantic pistols.

When he saw his son he burst out angrily, "What are you still doing here? There's no time to waste! Hurry! I am leaving too and will shoot this man wherever I find him."

The rest of his family was standing around him, their wailing making a bad situation worse. I had trouble calming them and getting Jakub to give me an explanation. Afrak Ben Hulam, the sick assistant and cousin from Adrianople, had left the house after us, gone to the shop, and told Shafei to immediately join his father, who was negotiating a large purchase in the Khan Assad Pasha. Shafei had done so but had not found his father, although he had looked and waited for him for some time. Finally he had hurried back home and been startled to find his father resting under the arcades. Jakub had told him that he had not given Afrak any message, so Shafei returned to the bazaar and found the shop closed. He opened it with a second key he always carried on his person and saw immediately that a large number of valuables, his most precious possessions among them, were gone, and so was his assistant, Afrak Ben Hulam. Shafei then quickly informed his father. Fortunately, in spite of his dismay, he had been circumspect enough to lock the door and to post two policemen in front of the store. His report had caused an uproar in the house, and when I arrived with Halef, Shafei had been on the point of hurrying off again though without any clear idea where to. Jakub also wanted to shoot the thief but had not bothered asking himself where to look for him.

"You will do more harm than good with this mind-less haste," I said in an effort to soothe them. "Sit down, so we can deliberate calmly. A hasty racer is not always the fastest horse."

I finally got them to accept my point of view. "What is the value of the things that were stolen?" I asked.

"I don't know yet for certain," Shafei answered, "but probably thousands of piasters."

"And you believe only Afrak could have stolen them?"

"No one else! The message he gave me was an invention, and only he had the key and knew where the most valuable things were kept."

"All right then, he's the only one we have to deal with. Was he really just a relative of yours?"

"Yes. We had never seen him but we knew he was coming, and the letters he brought were genuine."

"Was he a jeweler, a goldsmith?"

"Yes, and a very good one."

"Does Afrak Ben Hulam know your families and circumstances?"

"Yes, although he often made slips."

"He was at the fête yesterday, and you said he had been pale. Was he already pale when he arrived or did he become pale when he heard that Kara Ben Nemsi was your guest?"

Shafei looked up, startled. "By Allah, what do you mean, Effendi? I do believe he only turned pale when I told him about you."

"That may be a clue."

"If that were only so, Effendi."

"Afrak was startled when you mentioned me," I went on. "He did not come when I played the piano. He gave the excuse that he was ill because he could not leave while I was in the courtyard. I would have seen him. So he left after I did. Halef, do you know who this Afrak Ben Hulam is?"

"How should I know?" the Hadji answered.

"None other than Dawuhd Arafim, who has also called himself Abrahim Mamur. I already suspected this last night, but it seemed so improbable I couldn't bring myself to believe it. But now I am convinced it was he."

My listeners were mute with astonishment, and it was only after an extended pause that Jakub said emphatically, "That's impossible, Effendi! My relative never called himself Dawuhd Arafim or Abrahim Mamur, and never was in Egypt either. Did you see this Abrahim Mamur here yesterday?"

"Yes. I forgot to mention it because I was thinking about the music. Describe your relative for me, and describe the clothes he wore when he rode to the fête."

They did, and everything checked. Afrak Ben Hulam was Abrahim Mamur. But the two merchants refused to believe it. "Afrak was never in Egypt," they kept repeating. "And how would a stranger get hold of the letters he had with him?"

"Those are the only two things still unclear. But what if this Abrahim took them from the real Afrak?"

"Allah kerim, then he would have had to kill him to avoid all risk to himself."

"That will have to be looked into. I think the man is capable of anything. But you see now that calm deliberation is preferable to unthinking haste. Either the thief is still in Damascus or he has rushed off. You must be prepared for the second eventuality. What would you do, Jakub Afarah, if he should already have left?"

"If I knew the direction, I would pursue him until I found him, even if that meant going to the ends of the earth!"

"Then quickly send Shafei to the police. He should make a report so that men can be posted at the gates and patrols sent through the Ghouta. He should also pick up a passport for you, which should be valid throughout the realm of the Padishah, and ask for an escort of mounted policemen on whose assistance he can rely."

"Effendi, your speech is better than my anger was. Your eye is keener than mine. Will you continue helping me?"

"Yes. Now take me to the thief's room."

Shafei hurried away while the rest of us went to the apartment of the false Afrak. It became evident that he had left with the intention not to return. But otherwise we could discover nothing to go on.

"That was a waste of time," I said. "We must try to find other clues. The three of us will split up and see if we hear something at the city gates or from the guides and the places where animals are rented."

Jakub Afarah and Halef agreed to my proposal, and a bare two minutes later I was riding the donkey to one of the gates. I had decided against taking Rih because I did not know whether I might have to make more urgent demands on him later. My efforts were fruitless. I inquired and investigated wherever I believed I might obtain information; I roamed the Ghouta and encountered police who had already been dispatched there, but found no trail and returned three hours after noon, perspiring heavily. Jakub had been back several times and had left again. Halef also had found nothing definite but at least had heard something that might lead somewhere. He had gone to the northern part of the city and passed the tent where we had listened to the singer the day before. The woman had recognized and called out to him. She had noticed that Abrahim Mamur was the reason we left so precipitously, and she told Halef that I should come and see her if I wanted information about the man.

"But why didn't she tell you then and there, Halef?"

"Sidi, she doesn't speak Arabic, and I don't know much Turkish. I could hardly understand her pronunciation. I even had to guess at what she told me today."

"Then we'll ride there immediately but we'll take our horses. The donkeys are tired."

It was the final day of the five-day festival. The tent was less crowded than on the previous day and because the musicians were taking a break, I could talk to the woman singer without having to wait.

"Why were you in such a rush yesterday?" she asked me.

"Because I wanted to follow the man who left the tent immediately after entering it. I wanted to find out where he lives."

"He won't tell anyone."

"Ah, you know that?"

"Yes. Yesterday was the third time he came here. He

: 233 :

was sitting close by with an Englishman whom he didn't tell where he lives either."

"Did he speak English, or did the Englishman speak Arabic?"

"They were speaking English, and I understood every word. The gentleman hired him as his interpreter."

"You don't say! For here, or for a journey?"

"A journey."

"Where to?"

"I don't know. I only heard the name El Salihia."

"And when are they leaving?"

"As soon as the interpreter has finished some business which brought him to Damascus. I believe he mentioned a shipment of olives to Beirut."

That was all the woman knew. I thanked her and gave her a present. Not to leave Jakub in the dark, I sent Halef back while I circled the city to get to El Salihia, which lies to the north of Damascus and is really a suburb. It is the starting point of the trade route to Beirut. When I arrived it was almost dark. I was uncertain whether I would obtain any useful information, for the houses there face away from the street and thus cannot be observed as closely as in the West. But then I saw some lepers, those unfortunates who are banished by society and only survive through others' mercy. Clad in rags, they were lying about a short distance from the street and raised their voices begging for alms when they saw me from far off.

I rode toward them but they ran off immediately, for they must not let a healthy person come close. Only because I repeatedly assured them that I was from the Occident and not afraid of their disease did they finally stop running. But even then I had to stay about twenty paces away.

"What do you want from us, master?" one of them asked. "Put your gift on the ground and leave us quickly!"

"What would you prefer? Money?"

"No. That's of no use. No one would accept it from us. Give us something else: a little tobacco, bread, meat, something to eat."

"Why are you out in the open?" I asked compassionately. "There are hospitals for lepers in Damascus."

"They are overcrowded. We have to wait until death makes room for us."

"Can you tell me something about some people? I will give you tobacco for several weeks and other things as well, but you will have to wait until tomorrow morning. I have nothing with me."

"What do you want to know?"

"You must have seen everyone who came by here. Were there many?"

"Many went to the city because of the festivities. But from the city there were just some mules and, shortly before noon, an Englishman with two others accompanying him."

"How do you know it was an Englishman?"

"Anyone can recognize an Englishman! He was wearing gray clothes and a tall hat, and had a large nose with two blue glasses on it. One of the men with him had to explain what we wanted, and then he gave us a little tobacco, a few small loaves of bread, and many little sticks to make fire with."

"Describe the person who was serving as his interpreter."

Their account was an accurate portrayal of the man I was looking for.

"Where did they ride?"

"We don't know. They were taking the road to Beirut. But the children of old Abu Medshach will be able to tell you. He was their guide. He lives in the house next to the large palm tree over there."

"Thank you. Early tomorrow I will come by here and bring you what I promised."

"Oh, master, your compassion will find grace in the eyes of Allah! Could you perhaps also bring us some pipes? They only cost a few para."

"You'll get them, I promise."

I entered El Salihia and found out in the guide's house that the Englishman had wanted to go to the valley of Es Sebedani. Old Abu Medshach had been hired only to take him to that point. That was certainly a precaution on the part of the interpreter, who wanted to make possible inquiries more difficult by this maneuver. But I knew enough now, and returned to Damascus.

My host was waiting for me in a state of considerable agitation. His own investigations had been fruitless but Halef's report had given him hope. Jakub Afarah already had a passport and a second document addressed to all police stations of the entire Damascus region. In addition, ten well-armed, mounted policemen were awaiting the order to leave with him.

I reported everything I had found out. Since evening had already come, I considered it best to wait for morning, but the impatience of the thief's victims did not permit such a delay. Jakub sent for a guide who would be able to find the way even in darkness. In his feverish restlessness, nothing could be done quickly enough, and I had barely mentioned my promise to the lepers when he gave orders to assemble the materials.

Nonetheless, some hours passed after my return before we were ready to leave. Jakub preferred renting horses, two for himself and a servant, and a third for whatever baggage was required. Since he could not tell where our expedition would take us or how long we might be gone, he had also provided himself with a rather substantial sum of money. Our farewell was brief. A full moon was in the sky as we rode down the "street called Straight" with the guide in the lead and the owner of the rented horses followed by Jakub, his servant, Halef, Bill, Fred, and me. The policemen made up the rear.

# 12 : In the Ruins of Baalbek

Because we were escorted by police, the guard at the gate did not stop us and we rode quickly past. Beyond El Salihia I left the road to look for the lepers. Our arrival roused them from their sleep and they were pleased with the large package I placed on the ground for them. Then we continued along the Barada. Before entering the mountains I turned to look back at Damascus. Shining in the light of the moon, surrounded by the dark ring of the Ghouta, the city looked like a residence of spirits. I had not anticipated that my stay there would be this brief.

We reached Dummar, a good-sized village where we made our first stop. With the assistance of the police, we roused the village elder to obtain whatever information we could. Thanks to his inquiries we learned that four riders had galloped through the village late in the afternoon, and that one of them had been an Englishman in gray clothes and blue glasses. They had taken the route to Es Suk, and we moved on without delay.

It was dawning as we rode across the El Djedeida plateau. We then passed left of the spot where the capital of old Abilene once stood, and on the other side saw the mountain where Abel supposedly lies buried. There followed several small villages whose names I have forgotten. We had to stop in one of them to allow our fatigued horses some rest. By this time we had covered a distance which would normally have required a full day. If we went on straining our animals in this fashion, we could be certain that they would not take us very far. We also heard from some people who were kind enough to make us an ample present of fruit that a small troop had passed through the village late in the evening.

After the horses were rested, we set out for Es Suk but could discover nothing definite there. On the far side of the village a single rider came toward us. It was an old Arab with a white beard whom our guide greeted cheerfully and introduced to us with the words: "This is Abu Medshach, the guide who escorted the Englishman."

"That's good luck," Jakub Afarah said. "Where did you leave him?"

"In Es Sebedani, master."

"How many men were with him?"

"Two, a dragoman and a servant."

"Who is the dragoman?"

"He claims to be from Konya but that's a lie. He

does not speak like the inhabitants of that town. He is a liar and a cheat."

"Why do you say that?"

"He is cheating the Englishman. I was perfectly aware of that although I could not speak to the foreigner."

"Do they have a great deal of baggage with them?"

"Only the Englishman. He owns the pack horses, but the dragoman only has a few big boxes which he seems to think are very valuable."

"In what house did they stay?"

"They didn't. I was paid in Es Sebedani and free to return home, but they went on although their horses were almost collapsing. I stayed with an acquaintance to rest, and am now on my way back to Damascus."

I was anxious to hear some details about the Englishman's appearance, and because I had incomprehensibly failed to ask about it in the tent in Damascus, I now said, "Didn't you hear the Englishman's name?"

"The dragoman always called him 'sir.' "

"That's not a name, it means 'master.' Try to remember."

"Occasionally he used another word but I am not really sure. It sounded like 'Liseh' or 'Lindseh.' "

I pricked up my ears. Could this be? No, it was impossible. Yet I asked, "Lindsay, perhaps?"

"Yes, yes, that's the word!"

"Describe the man."

"He was wearing gray clothes and his hat also was gray, and so tall it came up to here," he said, pointing to his knee. "He wore blue glasses and always had a hoe in his hand, even when he sat his horse."

"Ah! And his nose?"

"Very big and red. He had an Aleppo boil on it. His mouth was also big and wide. Two fingers were missing from his left hand."

"It's he! Halef, did you hear? Sir David Lindsay is up there ahead of us."

"Hamdulillah!" the little Hadji exclaimed jubilantly. "Allah is great and everything is possible to him! He gives and takes life as he pleases!"

Jakub did not understand our delight, so I told him what he needed to know and then asked that we continue quickly on our way. It was disquieting to me to know that a man who had unexpectedly risen from the dead was in the hands of a scoundrel.

The old guide rode on and we trotted through some pleasant villages. But soon the charming green of the terraced gardens came to an end. We crossed the Barada on a bridge and on its left bank came to a defile just wide enough for the path and the river bed. The walls of the ravine rose steeply and, especially along the northern side, numerous graves had been cut into the rock to which steps had probably led at an earlier time but had collapsed. This pass was called Suk el Barada, and through it one reaches the plain of Es Sebedani, on which the village of that name lies.

When we had the pass behind us and came to the southern part of the plain, we passed through some more small villages and reached Es Sebedani after a laborious ride and in a state which precluded a continuation of our pursuit. My stallion and Halef's horse were tired, and the other animals were on the verge of collapse, as I had feared.

Es Sebedani is a handsome village with stately houses and fertile gardens, although it lies 1180 meters above sea level. Half of its population are Maronites. The policemen lost no time finding quarters for themselves and us. We heard that the guide Abu Medshach had spent the night here, but the village head sent a messenger to the next hamlet to obtain information, and when this man returned toward evening he reported that the Englishman had spent the night there and then left for Soheir, taking a local inhabitant, the servant, and the interpreter along. Whether or not he would continue from there, no one could tell us.

It was barely dawn the following morning when we were back in the saddle. As we were leaving the vineyards and mulberry trees, I remembered the singer's telling me that the interpreter had mentioned an olive shipment to Beirut. That transaction was an invention, but Beirut had to be his destination, since he could not have avoided telling the Englishman the truth about where they were going. That he should have chosen this route and avoided the road from Damascus was easily explained. His safety demanded it.

Some time later that morning, as we were riding down a sloping path, it became apparent that the horses of our police escort were bad. They had weathered the strain of yesterday's ride but would be incapable of a repetition of that effort. The animals Jakub had leased were no good either, and thus we kept slowing down from quarter-hour to quarter-hour. At this rate we would never catch up with people who had an eight- or nine-hour head start.

I proposed to Jakub Afarah that I ride on ahead with Halef, but he wouldn't hear of it. He insisted he needed us and said the police would not keep him from feeling deserted. I thus had to give up this idea but derived some consolation from the likelihood that Lindsay's passion for excavating would not allow him to be quickly lured away from the area around Baalbek. But how had the Englishman reached Damascus? How had he managed to cheat death along the banks of the Euphrates? I was eager to find out, and therefore became all the more annoyed with our snail-like progress.

Soheir is on a mountain stream which flows into the Jahfufe. Shaded by poplars and very pretty, it is a sizable village in spite of its name, which means "the little one." We soon heard that the men we were pursuing had come through and taken the direction toward the pass across the Anti-Lebanon. After a brief rest we resumed the chase.

We first had to cross an extensive plain and then came into a valley leading to the pass. We climbed for over an hour, precipitous rocks to our left, a deep abyss to our right. Having reached the top, we saw that the western slope of the Anti-Lebanon on which we now found ourselves was considerably steeper than the eastern. Our guide told us that Baalbek was some five hours away as the crow flies but that we would need considerably more time, since the route was tortuous and our horses in poor condition.

He was right. We had to cut through any number of lateral valleys, and when we finally saw the gigantic ruins of the sun city looking up at us, it still took us several hours to reach them. Because one of the policemen stated that his horse could not go on, the officer in charge gave the order to halt. No request, no promise was of any avail, and since Jakub Afarah felt that the police had been entrusted to him and he could not leave them, we had to give in. Fortunately I could persuade the officer to go at least as far as one of the small, picturesque villages lying below us, but he made that concession only because I promised him a baksheesh. When we arrived we heard that a gray Englishman had passed through and that he had quarreled with the dragoman. A short time later a rider who turned out to be Lindsay's guide came through the village. He told me that he had not gone all the way to Baalbek but been let go in the last village this side of the city. It was his belief too that some kind of dispute had developed between the Englishman and the dragoman. He said that the Englishman was a very cautious person who always kept his hands on his small pistols which had only a single barrel but could be fired several times without reloading.

During the night I became increasingly worried about my old friend. I found no rest and could not sleep. At the first sign of dawn I woke my companions and urged them to move on, a suggestion the police complied with only after having received a further baksheesh. In general, I had the impression that the assistance they would give to Jakub Afarah would be proportionate to his generosity. I called his attention to this and asked him to make clear to these men that it was their job to help him, not to deplete his resources.

We passed through several more small villages, and when the foothills of the Anti-Lebanon which we were riding behind and which kept obscuring our view finally opened up, we saw the famous valley of Baalbek before us. These impressive ruins occupy an extensive area, and there is probably no other city whose remains make as strong an impression. Just as we entered the field of rubble, we saw a quarry off to one side in which a gigantic block of limestone was lying. It must have been over twenty meters in length, four meters wide and of the same height. Such blocks constituted the building material for the huge structures of Baalbek. Since a single one of them must certainly have weighed hundreds of tons, one wonders how they could have been moved with the means available at the time.

The large temple buildings had once been dedicated to Baal or Moloch, but what still stands today is of Roman origin. It is known that Antonius Pius built a temple here and dedicated it to the sun god Jupiter, and that that building was considered one of the wonders of the world. It seems that in the larger of the two temples the throng of Syrian gods was worshiped and that the smaller one was reserved for Baal-Jupiter. To construct this edifice, a foundation was first laid which rose some thirteen and a half meters above the ground. Three layers of those gigantic blocks were then placed on top of it and it was on them that the powerful columns which supported the heavy architraves rested. The six remaining columns of what was once the sun temple have a height of nineteen meters and a diameter of more than two.

Since it lay on the road from Palmyra to Sidon, the city of Baalbek was important in its own right in antiquity. Abu Ubaida, who showed the Christians of Damascus such humanity and was Chalid's fellow fighter, also conquered Baalbek. The acropolis was turned into a citadel and the stones of the destroyed temples were used for walls. Later the Mongols came, then the Tartars, and what they left intact was devastated by an earthquake in 1759. What remains today affords only a faint idea of the former splendor and glory. On the terrain once occupied by the sun city there now sits a miserable village inhabited by fanatical and thieving Arabs, and the soldiers of the garrison make the area even more unsafe.

Looking through my binoculars, I surveyed the far-flung site. No human being anywhere. I later heard that the soldiers had granted themselves a furlough and the Arabs had neither the time nor the inclination to receive us hospitably. A single person could disappear in this debris like an ant. To find Lindsay more easily, I asked the officer in charge of the police, a sergeant, to circle the ruins with his men and then search through them, should that turn out to be necessary, telling him that we would help him. But he refused; his men and animals would first have to rest and eat.

When this had been done, the police still showed no signs of wanting to go to work. Jakub entreated them and became rude; I entreated them and became equally rude, but all to no avail. Finally the sergeant stated quite frankly that he would be willing to send his men out only if he were given an appropriate baksheesh. Jakub was about to reach for his money but I stopped him:

"Isn't it a fact that you were given this escort so that they might help you?" I asked him.

"Yes," the jeweler answered.

"What are you supposed to pay for this service?"

"Provisions for men and animals and three piasters a day per soldier, five for the sergeant."

"Very well. That's their pay because they serve you. But if they refuse they will get nothing. We are going to keep to this arrangement, or I am leaving. And you will inform the pasha when you return to Damascus what lazy fellows he gave you."

"What business is this of yours?" the sergeant asked angrily.

"Speak properly when you address me. I am not one of your men," I told him. "Are you going to get started now, or not? Over there, along that high wall to the west, we'll meet again."

The sergeant rose ill-humoredly and mounted his horse. His men followed his example and when he had given his orders the men rode off in various directions.

A brook meandered through the extensive field. I told myself that a stranger with horses would certainly stay close to the water, and so we split up to investigate the terrain adjacent to it. Halef went with Jakub, and I took Bill and Fred after we had agreed that we would fire our weapons if signals were to be given. We rode slowly along the bank. Turning around a broken column, I noticed a wall with a hole in it. Before it lay a man with a rifle in his hand. Farther upstream, at a distance of perhaps a hundred paces, I saw the tall gray top hat nodding rhythmically up and down above a freshly dug hole.

I hurried back behind the column, turned my horse over to the two men with me, and told them to stay hidden until I called. I then stepped forward from behind the column and walked toward the man lying on the ground. Because of his position he could not see me, but when he heard my steps he jumped up, aiming his rifle at me. He wore Turkish dress but called out in English, "Stop! No one may pass here!"

"Why?"

"Ah, you speak English! Are you an interpreter?"

"No. Lower your rifle. Is that Sir David Lindsay over there in the hollow?"

"Yes."

"And you are his servant?"

"Yes."

"I am an old friend and would like to surprise him."

"I should report everyone who comes by here, but I'll make an exception in your case. You seem to be telling the truth."

Stepping softly, I walked up to the edge of the hollow and, just as Lindsay was straightening up, reached for his hat and took it off his head.

"What the devil! Who is . . ." He turned, his mouth wide open, but could not utter another word.

"Well, Sir David, why didn't you wait for me along the canal?"

"Good heavens, you are supposed to be dead!"

"Yes, but I have come back as a ghost. Surely you are not afraid of the spirit of an old acquaintance?"

"No, no!"

With these words Lindsay leaped out of the hollow. Recovered from his surprise, he threw his arms around me.

"You are alive, old friend, you are alive! And Halef?"

"He's here. And two other acquaintances as well."

"Who?"

"Bill and Fred."

"Indeed? So you visited the Haddedihn?"

"For over two months. Who's the man by the wall over there?"

"My servant. I hired him in Damascus. Come along, we have a lot to talk about." He led me to the opening in the wall, entered, and came back out with a bottle and a glass. It was real sherry.

"Wait. The others have to join us." I called the two servants. They almost wept with joy, and Sir David made the most incredible grimaces to hide his feelings, as befits a man.

"And where is your interpreter," I finally asked.

"Interpreter? So you know I have one?"

"Yes. You hired him at the festival, in a tent where all that singing went on."

"Marvelous! Incredible! You are omniscient. Did you come here by chance, or did you plan this meeting?"

"I planned it. We followed you all the way from Damascus. Now what about your interpreter?"

"He's gone."

"Oh, no! Did he take his things with him?"

"No, they are still here."

"Splendid! Now tell me what happened."

"What do you want to hear? Everything?"

"Just about the interpreter. We are after him. There'll be time for storytelling later."

"Why are you after him?"

"Because he's a thief, and an old enemy of mine besides."

"Thief? You mean he stole jewels?"

"Yes. Did you see them?"

"I did. Here's what happened: I ran into a man in the tent with the singers. He had seen that I am English and spoke to me in English. He talked about a transaction involving olives and said he wanted to go to Beirut. I wanted to go to Jerusalem and took him on as interpreter. He promised to come with me and said he would then sail from Jaffa to Beirut. He also promised to provide a guide. I was done in Damascus and waiting. He came and picked me up. He hired a guide in El Salihia . . .

"I know. I talked to him."

"Well, he must have run into you. So we rode up the Anti-Lebanon. During the morning I noticed that we were going in the wrong direction, continued paying close attention, and quarelled with the fellow. At first he denied it, then he told me he wanted to go to Baalbek first. There are supposed to be winged bulls here so I agreed, but I remained suspicious. The man seemed to be on the run. He knew the area here. He rode straight to this wall and said the opening would be a good place to spend the night. I woke up because I heard noises, horses snorting, felt a hand in my pocket, sat up—my wallet was gone. It was dawn. I see the interpreter riding off, reach for my rifle, shoot. The horse collapses, the man tries to untie something from the saddle, doesn't manage, flees. I pick up the parcel and open it. It contains gold, jewelry, precious stones."

"What did you have in your wallet?"

"All sorts of valuables like bandages, thread, needles, that sort of thing. I keep my money elsewhere."

"Listen, Sir David, that's a stroke of luck. The owner of those jewels is with me."

"Call him, he can take them back."

"Where are they?"

Lindsay went into the aperture in the wall and returned with a parcel which he opened. In addition to an Arabic shirt and a turban it contained nothing but small boxes. I covered them and fired my rifle twice. Immediately, from fairly nearby, an answering shot came. I pushed Lindsay and the other three back inside the opening because I did not want to spoil the surprise. When Jakub and Halef joined me, they saw the package but nothing else.

"Did you find something, Sidi?" Halef asked.

"I certainly did. Jakub Afarah, why don't you take those things out of the turban?"

"Mashallah, my jewels!"

"See if they are all there."

"Where did you find them, Effendi?"

"It wasn't my doing. Thank the man in that hollow there. Get him out, Halef."

The little Hadji stepped inside and burst out, "Allah akbar, the Englishman!"

When some necessary explanations had been given, I entered the opening to have a look at the cave. I noticed an impressive archway which was blocked some distance down; one side had caved in to such an extent that after removing the debris it had been possible to open up a fairly large space. Lindsay's four horses and his things were kept there. The dead horse outside had been covered by rubble so that it would not attract those nauseating vultures, and that was the reason I had not seen it.

Jakub Afarah was happy to have recovered his treasure but extremely upset that the thief had escaped.

"I would give a great deal if we could catch him. Is that possible, Effendi?"

"If I were you, I would be pleased to have recovered my possessions."

"I'd be just as pleased if I had the thief."

"Hm. Perhaps we can get hold of him."

"How?"

"Do you imagine he will abandon all this loot without at least making an attempt to recover it?"

"That scoundrel is too smart to come back here."

"How does he know we are here? He certainly left Baalbek immediately and cannot have seen us arrive. I should think he would come back because he believes it won't be difficult to handle Sir David and his servant if he can take them by surprise. And that's when we might capture him."

"Let's! We'll stay here until we do."

"Then we and our horses must be out of sight, and the policemen have to disappear. It will be best if they go to the barracks. They'll like nothing better than a chance to rest. Our horses are in the way here, so we'll leave them in the village, under guard."

"I'll see to that. I'll speak to the village head—or the mayor, since Baalbek is a city—and make the necessary arrangements."

Jakub got on his horse and rode off. He had papers which any official had to honor.

As I left the opening and looked toward the wall which I had picked as a rendezvous point, I could not see a single policeman. I assumed that they had not even considered searching the terrain but had gone directly into the city to while away the time in a coffeehouse and brag about their chase of a criminal.

Only now did we have the chance to discuss earlier events, and I began by telling Lindsay how we had fared.

"I thought you were dead," he said when I had finished.

"Why?"

"Because those scoundrels who caught me told me you were."

"So you were captured?"

"Yes."

"By whom?"

"I left with the workers to do some digging; one of them was a tolerable dragoman. We found nothing but I did come across the note you had left. We followed you and went to the canal, and that was an awful stupidity."

"Because you were taken prisoner?"

"Yes. We were lying there, sleeping . . ."

"So it was in the evening?"

"No, it was still daylight, otherwise someone would have stood guard. So we were sleeping. Before we knew what was up and could defend ourselves, we had been tied up and our pockets emptied."

"Did you have a great deal of money with you?"

"No. We were going to return to Baghdad."

"Who were the robbers?"

"Arabs. From the Shat tribe, they said."

"Then they must have been the same who later ran away when I told them I had the plague."

"Probably. We stayed hidden in the ruins for a few days. They gave us nothing to eat, and then they moved us."

"Where to?"

"I don't know. I saw nothing but swamp and reeds. The scoundrels had no interest in harming us, all they wanted was money. I had to write a letter which they proposed taking to Baghdad to pick up twenty thousand piasters. So I wrote a letter but made sure nothing would be given to them. They were told by the addressee to come back in three weeks, that he did not have that sum of money on hand."

"But that might have become dangerous for you."

"On the contrary. It turned out for the best. They

took us closer to Baghdad, where they had an encounter with a hostile tribe. There was some fighting, and I imagine the bandits won because there were more of them, but while that was going on we fled and hurried back to Baghdad. Sometime, when there's a chance, I'll tell you about all this in greater detail."

"Did you go to the apartment?"

"Yes. You had gone to visit the Haddedihn, so what could I do? I had to get to you and Bill and Fred. I sold the yacht and hired a man who spoke English, joined someone from the postal service, and crossed the Tigris near Tikrit to look for you. But the Haddedihn were gone. They had moved, and you were dead."

"Who told you that?"

"Abu Salman Arabs had robbed some travelers and killed them. The description fitted you. I was angry and upset, but what was the good of that? I didn't feel like getting killed myself, so I went on to Damascus. From there I sent the interpreter back and stayed for three weeks. I roamed the streets from morning to night. Had you stayed in the Christian quarter, among Europeans, we would have run into each other. You've heard the rest. Do you want more details?"

"No, that's enough. It was rather daring of you to ride from Baghdad to Damascus the way you did . . ."

"That was nothing. You did the same thing."

At this moment I saw a troop of men ride past at a considerable distance, moving in the direction from which we had come. When I looked more closely I saw that they were the policemen. What were they up to? Why didn't they come to the wall as I had told them? This question was to be answered shortly, for the jeweler was returning from the city on foot, bringing the mayor along. He was a venerable man, with an appearance that inspired confidence.

"Good morning," he greeted as he entered. When we had returned his greeting he said,

"I am Mustafa Effendi, the mayor of Baalbek. I came here to see you and smoke a pipe with you."

Lindsay offered him some tobacco and lit his pipe for him.

"Greetings, Effendi," I said. "Will you permit us to spend a short time in the district you administer?"

"Stay as long as you care to. I hear that you are Franks. I have also read the letter of my superior and therefore came in person to inform you that I will do everything I can to fulfill your wishes. I hope you don't mind that I sent the police back to Damascus."

"You did?"

"Yes. I was told that they were sitting in the café blabbering about your affairs. Can you catch a thief when it is perfectly well known that that's what you are trying to do? Besides, Jakub Afarah told me that they did not obey him and kept asking for a baksheesh every time you told them to do something. That's why I chased them away and gave the sergeant a letter to his commanding officer so that they will be punished. The sultan, whom Allah may bless, wants order in his land, and we must desire the same."

This was an honest official, a rare thing in the Turkey of that time. He was sorry that he could not be of direct use to us. We simply asked him to keep silent and to let us take care of the rest. "You can consider yourselves lucky that you did not go to another mayor," Mustafa Effendi remarked. "Do you know what he would have done? He would have asked for your money and your jewels to decide whom they belonged to. It must be shown that a theft has actually been committed, and who is the thief, who the victim. Weeks would pass, and during that period much can change, including gold and precious stones."

He was right. Jakub had reason to congratulate himself for having come upon this honest man. The mayor asked us to entrust our horses to him but to bring them individually so as to avoid attracting attention. Then he left, having first warned us about the subterranean passages and archways where, he said, it was easy to come to grief. These passages had served all manner of shady individuals as hiding places during the time of the Egyptian invasion, and today people who had reason not to let themselves be seen still lived there. Jakub had already left his horse at the mayor's house, and we now took our animals to Baalbek one by one.

The city seems small, particularly because the ruins

nearby have such enormous dimensions. The population raises silkworms and is famous for the handsome horses and mules they breed. The mayor's residence was one of the finest buildings and the stable into which we took our horses perfectly met our requirements.

We sat together for a while, after which I returned to the ruins but not by the route by which I had come. A single person would not arouse the suspicion of the thief, should he be on the lookout in some hiding place, and so I slowly walked through the ruins, abandoning myself to the impression they made on me. Snakes were darting about between the columns, a chameleon looked at me inquisitively, and high above the ground hovered a falcon, which then came down in a spiral to perch on one of the still upright pillars. He had his nest there.

Just then I had the impression that a shape had shot past, quickly and agilely, like the shadow of a cloud. It must have been an illusion, I told myself, but I slowly walked toward the point where I had seen it. A tunnel-like hollow behind a double column aroused my curiosity. What might the interior of one of those passages look like where once, in the light of burning torches, the victims of Baal had been butchered? There could be no harm in taking a few steps inside. If I made sure that I did not penetrate beyond the reach of daylight, nothing untoward could happen to me.

I entered the opening and advanced a few steps. The passage was wide enough for four people to walk side by side. The ceiling was supported by a heavy arch and the air was dry and pure. I looked and listened into the darkness and imagined how startled I would be if lights were suddenly to blaze in the distance and servants of the sun god came rushing forward to seize me and to drag me away, a sacrifice to Moloch.

I turned back to the entrance. How different the bright, warm light of day felt out here! In the radiance of the sun—but wait, wasn't something rustling behind me? I was about to turn, but at that very moment I received a fierce blow on the head. I remember that I staggered, quickly turned and stretched out my arms toward the man who had given it to me. Then all turned black before my eyes.

I don't know how long I remained unconscious. I recovered only slowly and it was some time before I remembered what had happened. I was lying on the ground, my hands and feet tied. Where was I? Darkness and silence reigned about me, but directly in front of me I saw two round, small spots with a curious shimmer which periodically disappeared only to return again. They were eyes observing me closely as their lids opened and closed.

Who was this? Certainly the man who had attacked me. But why? I was about to ask a question but the man began speaking: "I see you are finally waking up. Now I can talk to you."

Good Heavens! I recognized this voice. Having heard it once, I could not possibly forget its cold, piercing sound. The man who was sitting there, facing me, was none other than Abrahim Mamur, whom we had meant to catch. Should I answer him? Why not? Here, in this darkness, my facial expression could not convey that my silence was due not to fear but to contempt. I knew that something unpleasant awaited me but did not lose courage and would make no overtures. "Now I can talk to you," he had begun, and I sensed that he would do everything he could to torment me. But he would be in for a surprise.

"Speak," I answered briefly.

"Do you know me?"

"Yes."

"I don't believe so. How could you?"

"My ears tell me, Abrahim Mamur."

"You do know me then. But you will come to know me even better! Do you remember Egypt?"

"I often think of it."

"And Senitza, whom you took away from me?"

"Yes."

"The Shellal did not devour me when I fell into its raging waters. So Allah willed that I avenge myself."

"It was I who saved your life. So Allah wills I should not fear your revenge."

"You think so?" he murmured. "And yet it isn't good for you to have fallen into my hands. I searched for

: 252 :

you in Kahira and did not find you, but in Damascus, where I was not thinking of you, I saw you . . ."

"And fled from me! Abrahim Mamur or, rather, Dawuhd Arafim, you are a coward!"

"Go on and sting, scorpion. I am the lion that will devour you. I knew you would betray me. I left because I did not want you to cross my plans. You pursued me and took everything I had stolen. But I shall get back those jewels, depend on it."

"By all means."

"Yes. I will bring them here and show them to you, and that is the reason I did not kill you. You will die nonetheless, for you are the cause of all the torment I have suffered. You took away Senitza, through whom I would have become a different person. You hurled me back into the depth from which I wished to rise, and now you will be punished. You will die, but not quickly, by bullet or knife. No, slowly, and suffering untold pain. Hunger will tear apart your bowels and thirst will lick up your soul so that it hisses with pain like the drop of water the fire devours."

"I expect nothing else from you."

"Don't mock, and don't believe that you will get away. If you knew who I am, fear would petrify you."

"There is no need for me to know."

"There isn't? But I want you to so that you will abandon all hope, so that despair may grip your heart. Yes, you shall know everything so that you helplessly gnash your teeth. Do you know what a Tchuwaldar* is?" I did, having heard a good deal about this gang of outlaws which, not very long ago, had threatened Constantinople.

"Do you also know that they constitute a family that is run by a head?"

"No."

"Well then, I am that head!"

As he said this, I remembered that good friends in Istanbul whom I have mentioned previously† had told me that not only the capital of Turkey but also its

---

* A man who stuffs those he murders into a sack which he then throws into the water.
† See *In the Desert*.

European possessions, the Balkan countries, were ter-
rorized by a secret gang whose power reached as far
as the Black Mountains and down to the Albanian
coast. Incredible stories were told about this association, whose activities remained shrouded in mystery,
whose goals no one knew, but whose implacable ruth-
lessness was feared. Some considered them ordinary
criminals, others believed in a political conspiracy. But
all feared an encounter with this secret organization.
Could it be that Dawuhd Arafim was speaking about
this gang? If he did not exaggerate when he called
himself their leader, he certainly was a man to be wary
of.

"Braggart!" I answered his last words with a contemptuous laugh.

"Go on and mock! Didn't you see in Egypt how
wealthy I am? Where should this wealth come from,
since I am only an ignominiously discharged official?
The power of our league grows daily, and woe to the
person who crosses swords with us! He will die a piti-
ful death and his possessions become ours. Afrak Ben
Hulam from Adrianople was also stuffed into a bag
after one of my men had seen a great deal of money in
his hands. The letters he had with him were brought
to me. I opened them carefully, and after examining
their contents I decided to go to Damascus in his place
and to rob the shop of his honorable relative the moment an occasion offered. But then you appeared,
Giaour, and I had to be satisfied with a small fraction
of what would otherwise have been mine. For that I
hope the devil will send you to the hottest part of
hell."

"And even that small fraction you lost again."

"I'll get it back. But that will be the last thing you'll
see on this earth. I am going to take you to a place
from which there is no return. I know this area, for I
was born in Sobeir. My father lived in these passages
when the Pasha of Egypt came to Syria to conscript its
children. At that time I was still a boy. I was with my
father. We crawled and searched through this darkness and came to know every corner of these depths. I
know the place where your carcass will rot when you
have died in agony."

"Only Allah knows that place."

"But Allah won't help you, Giaour! The fate I have chosen for you will hold you as firmly as those ropes hold you now. There is no hope for you."

"Why not also tell me where that Barud el Amasat who sold Senitza to you is now?"

"I won't."

"You see, you coward. If you were certain that I would die here, there would be no reason not to tell me."

"That's not why I remain silent. It is simply that none of your wishes will be fulfilled. And now stop talking! I am going to sleep, for this night will demand much of me."

"You won't be able to; your conscience won't let you rest."

"A Giaour may have a conscience. A member of our association has nothing but contempt for it."

The rustling of his clothes told me that Dawuhd Arafim was stretching out on the ground. Did he really intend to sleep? Hardly. Or was this meant as a torture for me? Did he want to play with me, as the boy plays with the pet on his leash? I strained my eyes. No, the man had no intention of sleeping. He had closed his eyes but opened them from time to time to look at me, and did not do so sleepily or wearily. Those round dots were sparkling as they focused on me. Besides, he had not tied me securely enough to leave me to my own devices. He had put something around my ankles and wrists, but because I had my arms in front I could reach my feet without difficulty.

If only I had a knife! But Dawuhd had emptied my pockets. How lucky that I had had only a knife and two revolvers with me! If I was really to perish miserably in this place, at least rifles would not fall into the hands of this criminal; Halef would inherit them. But perish? Had it really come to that? Couldn't I defend myself? Since I could move my arms somewhat, it should not be impossible to take the knife away from him. If I succeeded in that, and then kept him away for as little as five seconds, I would be saved. And yet perhaps not entirely. At the moment I was down in these passages with no idea where this bandit had dragged me while I was unconscious. I might not find my way back to freedom unaided even if I did struggle free.

But this was for later. Right now I somehow had to take my mortal enemy by surprise, and do so without further delay. Some considerable time had surely elapsed since I had entered the passage, and it might occur to him to shoot me to make sure of my death. And if he had to leave me here, fettered though I was, he would not have that certainty. Dawuhd Arafim knew me a little. Only if I were dead would he be truly safe, and this meant that I had to free myself as quickly as possible.

I reflected. Could I slowly and carefully bend toward him and gingerly search his belt for the knife, using the tips of my fingers? That was impossible. Or could I throw myself at him and strangle him? But I could not get my hands sufficiently far apart to place them around a grown man's neck. Or should I attack with my feet? Perhaps try to kick him on the temple? That also was out of the question, for if I did not hit the right spot, all would be lost. If I did not seize the knife now, I would be wasting time, and my daring would be pointless.

I therefore attempted to raise myself gently to a sitting position. Not a single fold of my garment must rustle, and I also had to close my eyes so that the criminal would not notice my movements. If I could see him, the reverse was also true. After prolonged effort I managed to work my way into a crouch, only partly closing my eyes to keep observing my enemy's glances. Now he was looking at me again, and he had no sooner closed his lids than he uttered a shout: my right knee was pressing against his throat, my left against his chest. In sudden fear he jerked both hands toward his neck, and this gave me the opportunity to reach his belt with my fettered hands. I groped for the knife handle and pulled it out of the belt. He felt this and understood the danger. With a powerful heave, he threw me off and jumped to his feet.

"Son of a dog, you won't escape me!" he shouted and reached for me.

But only his finger tips brushed me. I knew that he

would now thrust his arm at the very spot where he had felt me a moment before. I stopped, stepped aside, and moved behind him.

"Ah, Giaour, where are you?"

He turned to the wrong side and this gave me a chance to cut the rope around my feet. I crawled a few paces farther. I had succeeded, and I breathed deeply. But now what? I must get away from Arafim to have time to think.

I scurried some distance farther and leaned against the wall. What should I do? Keep running down that passage? Mustafa had emphasized the danger of this subterranean labyrinth. Or was it better to overpower my adversary and force him to show me the way out? No. He was carrying firearms and no force would make him guide me back to daylight. Nor could I overpower him without killing him, and his corpse could not guide me.

It was an uncanny moment. My enemy also kept utterly still. Was he standing still, coming toward me, moving away? But surely these passages could not be all that extensive. I groped along in the direction I had taken, testing the ground with the point of my soft Arabic shoe before putting my feet down firmly. I had perhaps advanced some two hundred small steps when the air seemed to become damper and cooler. Extreme caution was necessary now and it came not a moment too soon, for a bare five paces farther the floor came to an end. I squatted down and lightly brushed the ground. The edge formed a large, round hole which took up the entire width of the passage. A well, no doubt, and with water in it, as the dampness proved. There was no telling its depth but no one who fell down there would ever come up again.

Judging by the circular opening, the well had a diameter of about one and a half meters. I could leap across, but I had no idea what would be on the far side. If the well were close to the end of the passage, with a wall directly beyond it, a jump would mean certain death. So I could not save myself in that direction. I had to turn back, and that was dangerous. The enemy was silent. Was he lying in wait where I had left him because he knew I would have to retrace my steps? Did he still believe I had escaped in another direction? Or had he simply hurried toward the exit, to be on the safe side, and decided to wait for me there? Whatever the case might be, I could not stay where I was. I took the knife between my teeth, lay down, and crawled back on my knees and the balls of my hands. I must not walk, but moving as I did I could test the space ahead of me with my slowly advancing finger tips, and then follow with the rest of my body. Thus I pushed myself forward—slowly, very slowly, but forward nonetheless. I had thrust my knees forward more than two hundred times and must already have passed the point where I had lain as Dawuhd's prisoner, but these two hundred paces had taken me far more than an hour. Another half-hour passed and the wall stopped on both sides but the floor continued. What was this? To the left and the right there was a corner, which meant that the passage I had been following up to this moment crossed another at right angles. Did it continue on the far side? If so, this intersection was a place where my enemy could be lying in wait.

I listened as hard as I could but there wasn't the slightest sound. Because I first had to establish whether the passage continued beyond the intersection, I pushed forward in the same direction, breathing calmly, my pulse beating no faster than normally. The greatest coolheadedness and circumspection were indispensable now. I got across the intersection without incident and determined that the passage continued. But which direction was I to take? Straight ahead, to the right, to the left? The air was stagnant everywhere, the dampness the same, the darkness dense and impenetrable. If Dawuhd was anywhere near, he would be somewhere along the passage leading out into the open. And if he wasn't, he would be at the entrance.

He was not at the beginning of the passage I had just discovered for I had moved my hands along the corners of the lateral walls. This left either side. I first turned to the left, pushing forward millimeters at a time. Some ten minutes later I knew that Dawuhd wasn't here either, so that he had to be somewhere in the passage to the right, and that is the direction I took.

I had advanced perhaps to the center of the intersection when I thought I heard a very soft, sustained sound. I strained my ears and moved half a hand's length forward. Yes; it was the ticking of a pocket watch, my own, which the criminal had taken from me. So I had finally found him, and also found the way out. But how was I to get there? Would I be able to get past him?

To determine that I had to discover my adversary's position: was he lying, sitting, or standing? I had to take an extreme risk, and move closer. To seize and wrestle with him was out of the question, for it seemed certain that he held a weapon in his hand and would be ready to fire. My hands pushed forward as cautiously and silently as the feelers of a snail. The ticking was becoming more audible and now the tip of my middle finger felt a piece of cloth. Dawuhd was directly in front of me. If he stretched out his hand he would touch me. In this dangerous proximity, another ten minutes passed and then I knew that he was lying across the passage.

Should I step over him? Or trick him away from there? I decided on the first alternative, which, though riskier, also offered a better chance of escape. Luck was with me; he had his legs crossed, which was better than if he had spread them far apart. I rose very slowly, stepped up to him, and raised one leg. What if he changed position at this precise moment? But he didn't, and I cleared the obstacle, one leg at a time.

The greatest difficulty now lay behind me. I need no longer crawl but could remain erect. As the distance from my enemy increased, I could put down my feet more firmly and make more rapid progress. After a little while, I was groping along at a normal walking pace and then I noticed that the air was changing. Finally I felt steps under my feet. As I climbed them it became lighter and lighter, and then I reached a small opening over which a dense juniper bush was spreading its branches. I squeezed through it.

Thank God I was free! But I found myself on an entirely different side of the sun temple. I would have to hurry now if we were going to seize the criminal, for the sun was already low on the horizon. I ran around the temple to the spot where my friends would be.

I was greeted with a flood of questions. I had been missed, they had tried to find me but without success. Even Mustafa Effendi had come to offer his assistance if the search for me was to continue.

I related my curious experience, which both dismayed and overjoyed my companions.

"Thank Allah," Jakub exclaimed. "Let's enter the passage and catch him!" Everyone picked up a weapon.

"Wait," Mustafa warned, "wait until I go into town and come back with some more men."

"There are enough of us," Halef contradicted him.

"No," the mayor answered. "These deep passages have their secrets. There are entrances and exits you don't know. We need at least fifty men to surround the ruins."

"There are nine of us, that's enough," Jakub said. "What do you say?" He addressed this question to me. I also felt it would be best to act quickly, and Lindsay, to whom I had explained the situation, agreed. We decided to take immediate action.

"What about lights?" I asked.

"I'll get some," the mayor said. "There's a dyer who lives over there in the ruins; he has a number of lamps." And Mustafa hurried off while we agreed on a plan.

Both the entrance by which I had come into the subterranean world and the exit by which I had escaped had to be occupied. At least three men would have to stay with our possessions. One would suffice for the exit, since that was where we would enter to make it impossible for Dawuhd to escape at that point. But by the double column where I had entered, we felt we should post two. That left four to go down and subdue our enemy.

How would these roles be assigned? I certainly had to go back down. Since Halef had experience stalking, I chose him to accompany me, and also decided to take Mustafa Effendi because of his position. Lindsay volunteered to be the fourth but I turned him down; I wanted him to guard our things. This entire enterprise had been undertaken to recover these valuables, after all. But the Englishman would not give in and the others persuaded me to let him come along. Jakub Afarah had to remain behind because the jewels were his, and so did Lindsay's servant. Bill and Fred were to post themselves at the double column and Jakub's servant would take up his position by the exit.

I borrowed a revolver from Lindsay, the only weapon I took besides my knife. Bill was given the carbine and Fred the hunting rifle, and then everyone went to his post. Half an hour after my return I was standing once more by the juniper bush. Mustafa Effendi and Lindsay were carrying the lamps, which were still unlit, and Halef and I took the lead. At the bottom of the stairs we took off our shoes and started crawling.

I had taken Halef's left hand. With his outstretched right, he was brushing along one wall while I was doing the same with my left along the one opposite so that nothing could escape us. Unfortunately, the mayor's ankle bones occasionally made a crackling noise behind us.

When we reached the point where the two passages intersected, I gave the men behind us a gentle shove as a signal to remain there. Then Halef and I stretched out on the ground to crawl to the place where I had left Dawuhd. We had agreed that each of us would grasp one of his hands, whereupon the others would quickly join us to tie him. We slowly reached the spot, but the criminal was gone. Now what? Had he stretched out in one of the other three passages? We investigated but could not find him. Yet he had to be in one of the three, though farther back. We returned to our two companions who had been anxiously await-ing our call.

"He's no longer there," I whispered. "Go back a bit and light your lamps. But hold them behind you. Their light must not fall into the other passages."

"What are you going to do?" Lindsay asked.

"We'll search the other three passages."

"Without a lamp?"

"Yes. Any light would endanger us. It would make it too easy for Arafim to shoot at us, and besides, he would be able to see us a long way off."

"But suppose you run into him and we aren't there?"

"We'll have to do what we can."

We went first into the passage where I had discovered the well. Taking up the entire width of it, we walked some two hundred paces without encountering a thing; then we had to be cautious. We got as far as the well without running into Dawuhd, and returned.

Next Halef and I crawled into the second passage. Here we had to be especially careful to avoid any unsuspected danger. We therefore moved very slowly and a quarter of an hour passed before we got to the end. We were standing before the foundation wall of the temple and again had to turn back without having accomplished a thing.

In the last remaining passage equal caution was called for. It was much longer than the earlier one and ended in a deep hole extending over the entire width. We turned back for the third time.

Our companions were amazed by what we told them. "He was there, so it follows he still is," Lindsay maintained. "No doubt about it."

"Dawuhd may have left while I was gone. Take the lamps. We'll have a look at the well first."

We turned left until we could go no farther. The well was very deep; its dark abyss showing nothing but blackness. Obviously the criminal could not have escaped that way, and we returned to the passage we had searched through last. When we reached the hole, we saw that it gave access to a staircase, but its first step was so far down that from where I stood I could not reach it with my outstretched arm.

"Are we going down there?" Mustafa Effendi asked with a slight shudder.

"Of course. It's the only way he can have escaped."

"But suppose he shoots at us from below?"

"You'll walk behind us. Let me have your lamp."

We stepped down. I counted some twenty steps. At the bottom there was a single long passage which ran along far below the surface and then ended at a set of steps which we climbed. At the top we found ourselves in yet another corridor. As we followed it we were led to an intersection similar to the earlier one, and now it was difficult to know what to do. We decided to split up.

Lindsay and the mayor kept one lamp and remained behind to guard the intersection while Halef and I took the second lamp and walked down one of the passages. It was also quite long, widening gradually and finally also becoming lighter. We hurried on and emerged in daylight near the double column behind which I had originally entered this labyrinth. But where were Bill and Fred?

"Sidi, Abrahim Mamur came by here, and they've got him," Halef suggested.

"Then they would have rushed to the other exit to tell us. Come, let's have a look."

We hurried to the other entrance and also found it unguarded. Jakub's servant had left his post.

"They took the fellow to the hollow where we camped, Sidi," Halef explained. "Let's go there."

"First we should get Lindsay and the mayor."

We ran back to the place where we had left our burning lamp and reentered the passage to get the two. When we came back out we extinguished the lamps and hurried to the camp site. Still some distance away, we saw Lindsay's servant speaking animatedly to Bill and Fred. Jakub's servant was also there but could not understand what they were saying. When they noticed us they ran toward us.

"Sir, he's gone!" Bill shouted when he was still some distance away.

"Who?"

"Mr. Jakub Afarah."

"Where to?"

"Where the other one went."

"Which other one?"

"The one we were after."

"I don't understand you. I thought you had captured him."

"We? No. He didn't come where we were. But we thought Mr. Jakub had caught him because we heard him shoot, and so we ran to help him."

"Why did he shoot?"

"Ask that fellow."

Bill was pointing at Lindsay's servant, who had stayed with Jakub Afarah, and what he told us was both astonishing and annoying. He had been sitting at the entrance to the hollow with Jakub, thinking that we would soon emerge with the thief. All of a sudden they had heard a cracking sound behind them, and when they turned they had seen that the rear section of the hollow was caving in. They thought the whole huge ruin would come tumbling down and ran as fast as their legs would carry them. But because the collapse they had feared did not occur, they slowly returned and were about to enter the cave to examine the damage when a man on horseback emerged from the hole. It was none other than Dawuhd Arafim. Startled, they fell back, and the criminal exploited this and galloped away. Jakub had quickly recovered from his surprise, picked up the first rifle he could lay his hands on, and pulled Lindsay's second horse out of the hollow to pursue the fugitive. He had fired twice and missed.

What an amazing story. I had trouble believing what I heard, but when we entered the hole it became obvious that the man was telling the truth. My first glance fell on the spot where the package with the valuables had been. It was gone. And so were two of Lindsay's horses, including the best one.

"He's gone," the Englishman said angrily. "After him, quick!"

He was about to jump on his third horse when I took him by the arm. "But where, Sir David?"

"After the criminal!"

"Do you know where he went?"

"No."

"Don't you think you should wait until Jakub comes back? We'll hear more from him."

"Sidi, what's that," Halef suddenly exclaimed, holding a small, square piece of paper out to me.

"Where did you find it?"

"It was sticking to the horse."

The piece of paper was still moist. It had been stuck to the horse's forehead and contained these words: "I listened and heard everything." How extraordinary! Here, in the hollow, Arafim could not have had the time to write this message; he must have done that earlier, an indication of how sure he had been when he devised the plan which had then succeeded brilliantly.

The passage had not collapsed of itself but had been deliberately filled with rubble. Boards had been placed across its entire width and the debris stacked against them to make it look like a cave-in. Near the bottom the mass had probably been three meters thick, but near the ceiling barely a quarter of a meter, and there may have been cracks up there through which one could survey the entire hollow and listen to everything being said. Dawuhd Arafim had known of this arrangement, perhaps from his father. He had probably soon become aware that I had got away from him and had then rushed into this passage to eavesdrop on us. The moment the two men guarding the valuables were left by themselves, he had broken through the thin layer of debris at the top. The hasty flight of the two had made it possible for him to escape with the jewels and a horse without a fight. The man really was a very crafty criminal.

The Englishman was standing by his two remaining horses, saddling them hastily. "That's a superfluous effort," I said.

"On the contrary, it's very necessary."

"You won't be able to follow your former interpreter today."

"But I will," Lindsay insisted stubbornly.

"At night? Don't you see that it's getting dark?"

"Ah! Hm. But he'll get away."

"Let's wait and see."

The mayor came up to us. "Kara Ben Nemsi Effendi, will you permit me to make a suggestion?"

"Of course."

"This fellow certainly took to the mountains where you can't pursue him now. But I have men who know every path between here and the sea. Shall I send off some messengers?"

"Do that, Mustafa Effendi. You'll be amply rewarded."

"Where shall I send them?"

"To the port cities from where he might escape by boat."

"That would mean Tripoli, Beirut, Saida, Es Sur, and Akka."

"Yes; the thief won't remain in the country. Do you have to give those messengers letters?"

"Yes."

"Write them quickly and then send the men here so we can give them money for their journey."

"I'll give them what they need and you'll return it to me. They would ask too much from you."

The honest man hurried back to town, and we had nothing better to do than to examine the passage by which the thief had broken out. We relit our lamps, left the servants with our things, and climbed across the debris. This passage was of the same length as the one we had searched through last, and led to the intersection from which I had then come to the double column with Halef. The whole thing was very simple but rather irritating to us.

After barely an hour Mustafa Effendi returned with five horsemen. He had already supplied them with provisions and money but Lindsay gave each a baksheesh large enough to satisfy them. Then they rode off.

It was not until late that evening that we heard the clop of a tired horse, and when we stepped outside we recognized Jakub Afarah, returning from his pursuit. He dismounted, entered, and sat down silently. We asked him no questions but waited for him to begin.

"Allah has deserted me. He has confused me."

"Allah does not desert a courageous man," I consoled him. "We'll catch the thief again. We have already dispatched messengers to Tripoli, Beirut, Said, Es Sur, and Akka."

"I thank you. But that would have been unnecessary had Allah not abandoned me. I already had him."

"Where?"

"Up there, on the far side of the village. The man who called himself my nephew was in such haste that he took a poor horse, while I chose that of the English effendi which was better than his, and so I kept gain-ing on him although he had a considerable head start. We were galloping north, rushing through the village. I had come so close to the rascal that I could almost have reached him with my hands . . ."

"Didn't you shoot?"

"I couldn't, because I had fired both barrels earlier. I was so angry I felt my strength redouble. I wanted to seize the impostor and pull him off the horse. We came to a number of walnut trees that were lining the route. He slipped from the saddle, threw the package over his shoulder, and fled under the trees. I could not follow him on my horse, so I also jumped off. I chased him for some distance but he runs faster than I. He made an arc and returned to the place where the animals had been left. He got there before I did, mounted the Englishman's good horse, and left me the poor one."

"That's unfortunate."

"I tried to catch him but couldn't, and it was getting dark. So I turned back, inquired the name of the village, and came here. May every stone Dawuhd Arafim stole become a rock of grief for him!"

I felt sorry that this decent man should have lost his property a second time. Nor was there any hope of making up for our mistake today. Judging by the direction he had taken, I felt certain that Dawuhd would go on to Tripoli. Since we could not take up the pursuit until morning, it would be impossible to catch him before he got there.

Lindsay was perhaps even more upset than Jakub. That the scoundrel should have stolen his best horse annoyed him profoundly.

"I'll have him hanged," he grumbled.

"The fellow who took your horse?"

"Who else?"

"Then it'll be our good Jakub Afarah that you'll have to hang."

"Why?"

"Because he had taken it but Dawuhd was smart enough to steal it from him." I told the Englishman what had happened, but instead of calming him it seemed I had poured oil on the fire. He grimaced in a way I had never seen before and shouted in great wrath, "So that's how it was? Terrible! He takes the good horse but doesn't catch him, and then lets himself be tricked out of it. Terrible!"

Jakub could tell from Lindsay's glances that he was the subject of discussion and had no trouble imagining what we were talking about. "I'll buy him another one," he offered.

"What's he saying?" Lindsay asked.

"Jakub wants to buy you another horse."

"Me? Buy me a horse? Me, David Lindsay? Things are going from bad to worse! First I was annoyed that the scoundrel took the best horse, then I was annoyed that he didn't have it, and now I am annoyed that David Lindsay is to be made a present of another. Miserable country! I'm leaving! Back to England! No intelligent people left here!"

That was precisely my impression, and I advised my friends to settle down for the night to be ready to set out early next morning. Lindsay asked Mustafa to procure him a man with two horses, and then we lay down.

It was past midnight when we were roused by a call. The mayor was standing outside with the man and animals Lindsay had hired. We got up. Jakub Afarah compensated the honest official for his trouble and expenses, and we set out. I cannot say that Baalbek was a pleasant memory. In the next village we were told that no stranger had spent the previous night there but that one of the villagers coming from Ain Ata had encountered a solitary horseman apparently riding there. In that place we were told that this horseman had come through and hired a guide who knew the shortest route to Tripoli.

We also took a guide and immediately continued our pursuit. Making inquiries as we went, we rode down the western slope of the Anti-Lebanon without stopping anywhere, resting only for brief periods during the night. This was not how I had imagined my journey across those mountains. I did not even have a chance to visit the famous cedar forest. Finally we had the first glimpse of the magnificent blue of the Mediterranean shimmering below us. Tripoli lies at the foot of the mountains and is called Tarabulus by the Arabs.

The town sits back somewhat from the sea, and only the suburb and port city El Mina is directly on the water. Between the two, splendid gardens exude their fragrance and enhance the pleasing impression the inner city makes on the visitor.

As we approached we saw a small sailing vessel leave the harbor. Was it already too late? Was the fugitive on board? We strained our animals and rushed downhill toward El Mina. Once there I observed the ship through my binoculars. It was still close enough for me to make out the faces of the men looking back toward the land. I saw him standing by the railing. I recognized Dawuhd Arafim clearly and stamped my foot in anger.

A Turkish sailor was standing nearby. "What is that ship?" I asked.

"Mashallah! A sailing ship," he answered, turning his back on me with the sailor's contempt for the landlubber.

Some distance away stood the port master, whom I recognized by his uniform. I asked him the same question and was told that it was the *Bouteuse*, from Marseille.

"Where is she going?"

"To Istanbul."

"Will another ship be leaving for there shortly?"

"There isn't any."

What should we do? The Englishman was cursing in English with his servants joining in, Jakub was cursing in Turkish, and I would have liked to do likewise if it would have done any good.

"We have to go to Beirut. We should find a vessel there that will take us to Istanbul," I suggested.

"Do you really think so, Effendi?" Jakub asked.

"I am sure of it."

"But you wanted to go to Jerusalem."

"There'll be time for that later. I will not rest until I know whether the jewels are lost to you or not."

Little Hadji Halef Omar now asked me if I would take him with me. Could I turn down this loyal companion? It was equally clear that Lindsay would not let us go without him. Jakub and the Englishman paid off the guide and the owner of the horses. Other guides and horses were taken and the next morning we got under way.

When we arrived in Beirut, we discovered that an American schooner was about to sail for Istanbul. We looked at it, felt it would get us there safely, and came to an agreement with the captain. Farewell, proud Lebanese mountains! I passed you unheeding, but there will be another time!

# 13 : Among the Dancing Dervishes

Two men, their faces pensive, were sitting in a room of the Hotel de Pest in Pera, drinking the excellent wine their host, Mr. Totfalushi, had poured for them, and smoking.

One could hardly have called them spick-and-span. One of them wore long, heavy boots of Russian leather, brown pants and a brown jacket, and had a sunburned face and the brown hands of a Bedouin. The other was all in gray except for a nose which seemed to be forever blushing.

Suddenly the gray fellow opened his mouth, shook his nose, and closed his eyes. He could no longer contain himself. An important thought had been gestating and was now being articulated in this weighty question: "Sir, what is your view of the Oriental Question?"

"That it should be phrased not as a question but as an exclamation," the fellow in brown answered.

His companion closed his mouth again, opened his eyes wide, and grimaced as if he had just been obliged to swallow a book of aphorisms.

The gray fellow was Sir David Lindsay, the brown one myself. I have never been passionately interested in politics, and considered the "Oriental Question" a genuine horror. The person who can elucidate the concept will have no difficulty providing a solution. Even in the liveliest company, that problem and the so-called "sick man of Europe" invariably cause me to lapse into immediate silence. Not having studied political medicine, I don't know from what disease this man suffers but would say that the conditions that prevail all around him cannot really be called healthy either.

Turks are human beings, and a human being cannot be cured by assembling his neighbors around his bed to hack piece after piece from his body—neighbors who call themselves Christians, at that. A sick man is not to be killed but made well, for he has the same sacred right to live as everyone else. One removes whatever harmful substances there are in his organism and supplies him with the remedies that will cure him and turn him once again into a functioning individual. Once the Turk was a rude but courageous nomad, an honest, good-natured fellow who begrudged no one what was his but also claimed a right to his own. Then his simple soul was ensnared in the dangerous web of Islamic fantasies and desires for conquest. He lost the clarity of a judgment that was untrained to begin with, wanted to find his bearings but merely lost himself more deeply. Now this grumpy fellow became angry, angry with himself and others. He wanted certainty, wanted to see if it was true that the word of the Prophet could be brought to the world by the sword. He slung his quiver over his shoulder, picked up his spear and bow, mounted his shaggy horse, and fell on whoever was closest. The Turk was victorious and kept being so, and began taking pleasure in this. As the victories multiplied, he felt his strength and self-confidence grow, and so moved boldly on. Thousands had been subdued, and though he could now wallow in gold and pearls, he went on eating his dry goat cheese and hard bread as he always had, for that diet strengthened his bones and gave him muscles of iron.

This continued until he became enmeshed in Byzantine hypocrisy. Fawned upon and adulated as a demigod, he was misled by honeyed words. Countless alluring vices were invented to corrupt him, and he was taught needs which could not fail to ruin him. His nature resisted for a long time, but once he began to ail, his decline was precipitous. And now he lies there, surrounded by selfish councilors who feel no hesitation about appropriating his legacy while he is still alive.

Why this introduction? Simply because I do not hate the Turks, I feel sorry for them because I am a Christian and because it always grieves me when I hear one of their enemies maintain that there is no help for them.

The *Bouteuse* was lying in the Golden Horn. Now at anchor, it had proven itself an excellent sailboat, having reached Istanbul a full day before we did on our American schooner. Once on land, I had immediately searched out the captain. He received me with the charming politeness so characteristic of social intercourse among the French.

"Do you wish to inspect my ship?" he asked me.

"No, Captain. I would like some information about one of the passengers on your last voyage."

"I am at your service."

"In Tripoli, a man came on board . . ."

"Yes, just one."

"May I ask what name he gave?"

"Are you a policeman?"

"No, an ordinary German. The man I am inquiring about stole valuable jewels from a friend of mine in Damascus. We pursued him but only arrived in Tripoli at the moment you were setting sail. We had to go to Beirut to find a ship to follow yours. Those are the reasons I came here."

The captain stroked his chin thoughtfully. "I am sorry for what happened to your friend, but though I should like to be of service, I don't know that I can."

"Did the man leave the moment you entered port?"

"Yes. And now it occurs to me that he gestured to a porter to come aboard to carry his things. There wasn't a great deal, he had just one parcel. I would recognize that porter. The passenger called himself Afrak Ben Hulam."

"That's an assumed name."

"No doubt. Come back. I'll talk to that porter if I see him."

I left. The others had been waiting at the quay. Jakub Afarah was going to take us to his brother's house but neither Lindsay nor I intended to accept his hospitality. We merely wanted to introduce ourselves.

Maflei, the wholesaler, lived near the mosque, in a house whose outside gave no indication of the extent of his wealth. Without having given our names we were taken into the selamlik and did not have to wait long for the master of the house. He seemed surprised about the number of his visitors, but when he recognized his brother he forgot the reserve customary among Muslims and hurried toward him to embrace him.

"Mashallah, my brother! May Allah bless you and your friends' coming!"

"Yes, these are friends I bring you."

"Are you coming to Istanbul in some business matter?"

"No. But we'll discuss that later. Is your son Isla in Istanbul or away on a journey?"

"He is here and will be pleased to see you."

"Your son will also be pleased about something else. Call him." Some minutes passed before Maflei returned. He was bringing Isla with him and I moved to one side as he entered. The young man embraced his uncle and then looked around. His glance fell on Halef, whom he recognized immediately.

"Allah, Hadji Halef Omar Aga, you here? In Istanbul?" he exclaimed. "Be greeted, companion of my friend. Did the two of you separate?"

"No."

"Then he is also here?"

"Yes."

"Why didn't he come with you?"

"Look more closely!"

Isla turned, and was embracing me a moment later. "Effendi, you don't realize the joy you are giving me. Father, look at this man! This is Kara Ben Nemsi Effendi whom I told you about, and that is Hadji Halef Omar, his companion."

The welcome was so sincere that even Lindsay's eyes shone. Servants had to scurry to bring pipes and tobacco, and Maflei and Isla immediately closed their shop to spend their time with us. Soon we were sitting on cushions telling our adventures.

"But how did you meet the effendi, uncle?" Isla asked.

"He was my guest in Damascus. We met in the steppe and became friends."

"Why aren't you bringing us greetings from Afrak Ben Hulam, my uncle's son?"

"I cannot bring you greetings but I do have news."

"News but no greetings? I don't understand."

"A certain Afrak Ben Hulam did come to my house, but he wasn't the real one."

"Allah! How can that be? We gave him a letter to take along. Didn't he give it to you?"

"He did. I took the man into my house as you had wished, and even took him into my heart, but he was ungrateful! He stole a great many bags full of jewels."

His relatives were so startled by this announcement that they were speechless. But then the father exclaimed, "You are mistaken! No one who has the blood of our ancestors in his veins would do something like that."

"I agree," Jakub Afarah said earnestly. "The man who brought your letter and called himself Afrak Ben Hulam was a stranger."

"Do you believe I would entrust such letters to a stranger?"

"He was a stranger who once called himself Dawuhd Arafim and then Abrahim Mamur and now . . ."

Isla jumped to his feet. "Abrahim Mamur? What are you saying? Where is he? Where did you see him?"

"He lived under my roof. I entrusted treasures worth millions to him without suspecting that it was Abrahim Mamur, your archenemy!"

"Allah Kerim! My soul is turning to stone," the old man wailed. "What misfortune my letter has caused! But how did it fall into his hands?"

"The criminal murdered our nephew Afrak Ben Hulam and took the letter. Remember that I did not know him! After he had read the letter he decided to come to me, pretend to be my relative, and plunder my shop. I owe it to Kara Ben Nemsi Effendi that that did not happen."

"What did you do with Abrahim Mamur?"

"He escaped and we pursued him. Yesterday he arrived here on a French ship, but we got here only today."

"Then I'll go right now and talk to the Frenchman," Isla said and got up.

"You needn't trouble yourself," I calmed him. "I have already seen him. The thief was no longer on board but the captain promised to help us. He invited me to come back."

"Then do not torment us any longer and tell us exactly what happened," Maflei asked.

His brother told him the story in considerable detail and caused great dismay. Maflei wanted to rush to the cadi and have all of Istanbul searched. He was pacing back and forth like a lion waiting for its enemy. His son Isla was also in a state of extreme excitement. Only after his anger had moderated somewhat could he think calmly enough to consider what steps to take. I advised against involving the police for the time being. I wanted to see whether I or someone among us might find some trace of the criminal. This view prevailed.

Maflei and Isla would not allow us to seek accommodations elsewhere, and insisted that we be their guests during our stay in the city. To ensure our privacy, a secluded garden house was placed at our disposal, and it would have offended them had we not accepted their offer. This house stood at the far end of the garden. Its rooms were well furnished and sufficiently far out of the way to allow us to live as we pleased. Now we could rest and discuss how to set about finding our enemy's trail. In Istanbul, where it is so convenient to merge into the crowds, that was no easy task. All we could really do was rely on luck as we methodically searched all the quarters of the city. But first I quickly paid a visit to the French captain to let him know that we were living at Maflei's. And this proved fortunate, for no later than the third day of our stay, the captain sent a porter to see us.

I asked him about the passenger whose baggage he had carried off the ship and was told that the man had gone to a house on Pera Street. The porter claimed that he could remember it perfectly well, and offered to take me there. I accepted immediately.

A broker who lived in the house remembered that a man had been there to inquire about an apartment for rent. Both had left to look at a number of houses but none of them had suited the stranger. They had parted company and that had been all. I could discover nothing further. But as though to compensate me for this lack of success, something significant happened on the way home.

I went into a café for a cup of Mocca and a pipe and had barely sat down when I heard someone call out in French, "Good heavens, is it possible? Is it really you, or someone else?"

I turned toward the speaker and saw a heavily bearded face which I seemed to recognize without being able to place it immediately. "Do you mean me?" I asked.

"Who else? Don't you recognize me?"

"I know I should but I don't. Why not refresh my memory?"

"Have you forgotten the Hamsad el Djerbaja who sang that pretty song to you on the Nile, and who later . . ."

I interrupted. "Of course! Your heavy beard confused me. Good day! Sit down here, or do you have some pressing business?"

"I have more than enough time if you'll be good enough to pay for my coffee. I am fresh out of money, as they say." He sat down next to me and we could converse without having to worry that we would be understood by the Turks around us.

"So you are broke? Tell me how you fared after we saw each other last."

"How else but badly! That Isla Ben Maflei whose servant I was discharged me because he thought he had no further use for me. I went to Alexandria and from there I accompanied a Greek to Kandia, where I hired out as a sailor to get to Istanbul, and here I made myself independent."

"Doing what?"

"Being an agent for any number of things—as a

guide through the city, as an occasional domestic, and doing temporary work. Anything to earn some money. But no one needs my services, they all go sightseeing without me; and so I go for walks and starve and listen to my stomach rumble. I hope you can do something for me, considering how I helped you out in the past."

"We'll see," I answered. "Why didn't you turn to Isla Ben Maflei here? He is in Istanbul, after all."

"No thanks. I don't want anything to do with him. He offended me; he attacked my honor and hurt my feelings. I don't want him to have the pleasure of seeing me in his house."

"I am staying there."

"That's too bad. Then I can't visit you."

"You wouldn't be visiting him, but me."

"Still! I wouldn't enter his house under any circumstances. But it would please me to be of some service to you."

"You can be. Do you remember that fellow Abrahim Mamur from whose house we rescued the girl?"

"Very well. His real name is Dawuhd Arafim, and he got away from us."

"He is here in Istanbul, and I am looking for him."

"I know he's here, I've seen him."

"Where?"

"Up in Dimitri where I ran into him. But he didn't recognize me."

Knowing that St. Dimitri was one of the most disreputable quarters of the city, I asked, "Are you often in Dimitri?"

"You might say so. I live there." That told me everything. This fellow had settled down among the Greek rabble in Dimitri, which is the most ignoble segment of Istanbul's population. It is a place where it is dangerous to be out at night, and even during the day; countless dens where vice celebrates its dissolute revelries and hideous diseases waste life never close their doors.

"So you live in Dimitri? Couldn't you have found somewhere else to stay?"

"Any number of places, but Dimitri is quite beautiful, especially if one has the money to enjoy it."

"Did you observe Abrahim Mamur for any length of time? I am very eager to find out where he is staying."

"I did no such thing. I was overjoyed that he didn't see me. But I do know the house he came out of, and I can make inquiries there."

"Why not show it to me now?"

"I don't mind."

I paid our bill and then we leased two horses and rode to Dimitri. It is said that Copenhagen, Dresden, Naples, and Istanbul are the most beautiful cities of Europe, and I have no reason to quarrel with this. But as regards Constantinople, I must say that that city can be called beautiful only when one looks at it from outside, from the Golden Horn. The moment one enters it, disappointment is bound to set in. The city is full of narrow, twisting alleys. Pavement is infrequent, the houses are mostly wooden, and it is their desolate, windowless fronts one sees from the street. At every step those ugly hairy dogs that devour the garbage no one else ever picks up get in one's way. Because the alleys are narrow, one must perpetually guard against being shoved into the filth by horses, porters, donkeys and other animals, or passers-by. All this was in evidence on our ride to Dimitri. The narrow streets were dirty, full of the refuse fish, meat, fruit, and vegetable vendors had thrown there. Quantities of melon rinds were rotting on the ground, large pools of blood around the butcher shops reeked revoltingly, and the cadavers of dogs, cats, rats, and disjointed pieces of horseflesh were giving off a sickening odor. Vultures and canines were the only creatures busy alleviating this unbearable condition. We barely managed to avoid being run down by porters carrying large rocks, boards, and beams through the neglected streets, and when a loaded ass, a fat Turk on horseback, or an ox-drawn chariot carrying women came toward us, it was no easy feat to get past them without being squeezed to death.

Finally we arrived in Dimitri, where we dismounted and returned the horses to their owner. First my fellow European showed me his apartment. It was the rear section of a half-dilapidated hut and resembled a goat pen rather than a habitation fit for human beings. The door consisted of some pieces of paper that had been glued together, the window was a hole punched through the wall, and—except for a handleless pitcher with a spider web across its spout—there were no pots or dishes of any sort. A torn piece of sail served as sofa and sleeping accommodation.

I inspected this depressing inventory silently and then followed the barber back into the street. He took me to a house with a forbidding exterior and an inside that confirmed the impression. It was one of those Greek bodegas where the value of a human life equals zero and the inhabitants and clients, their doings and dealings, are beyond description.

He led me into a back room where people were playing cards and smoking opium. The smokers were lying in a variety of positions and conditions on long, narrow straw cushions running along two walls. An old man, his skeletal shape erect in its greed, was just lighting some of the poisonous substance. His eyes, normally lusterless, were shining with desire and his hands were shaking. He made a horrible impression on me. Next to him lay a young man barely twenty years old. Unconscious, he smiled as if he were in Muhammad's seventh heaven. He was also already a slave to opium, that devil which will not readily let go of his victims. Near him a long, thin Dalmatian was writhing in the greatest ecstasy, and the disgusting grimace of a dissolute dervish was grinning at me from a few steps away. He had left his monastery and come to this den to sacrifice his remaining vitality to the mad images a deceptive trance provides.

"Do you smoke too?" I asked my compatriot suspiciously.

"Yes, but I haven't been doing it for long."

"For heaven's sake, then there may still be time to give it up! Don't you know the infernal effects of that poison?"

"Infernal? Hm, I don't think you know what you are talking about. It's heavenly, as far as I can tell. Would you like to try?"

"I wouldn't dream of it.—Can one get something to drink here?"

"Wine. I'll order some."

We were served a thick red Greek wine whose poor taste seems incomprehensible when one knows how delicious the large Greek grape is. So this was the house Abrahim Mamur frequented. I asked the owner about him, but because caution precluded the mention of any names and I was unaware by which one he was currently known, my inquiries were fruitless.

I therefore told the French barber to keep his eyes open and let me know if he found the man I was looking for. I gave him a small amount of money, but before I had closed the door of that depressing place behind me he had already joined the card players, where he would undoubtedly lose most of it gambling and then spend the rest on opium. I felt that the man was doomed to spiritual and physical ruin but promised myself to steer him back on the right track if I could.

The next day was a Friday, and Isla invited me to accompany him on a walk to Pera. On our way back we came to a mosquelike building near the Russian Embassy which had a fence running around it.

Isla stopped and asked, "Effendi, have you ever seen the dancing dervishes?"

"Yes, but not here in Constantinople."

"This is their monastery and service is about to be held. Would you care to go in?"

I agreed, and we entered a courtyard paved with wide marble slabs. The left side of the court was bordered by a cemetery which was also surrounded by a fence. A number of white tombstones in the shadow of tall, dark cypresses could be seen through the palings. They were decorated with a turbanlike crest. One side bore the name of the dead and a quotation from the Koran chiseled into the stone. Turkish women had chosen this cemetery as a place for their afternoon gatherings, and wherever one looked, one saw the shimmer of white veils and colored coats among the trees. Turks love to visit the places where their dead hold their everlasting kef.

A round structure with a cupola occupied the back of the courtyard, and to the right stood a second building, also crowned by a cupola. This was the monastery. The center of the court was taken up by a tall cypress with ivy entwining it along its entire height. The crowd of people in the court was surging toward the circular structure, but Isla first took me inside the monastery to show me what a Turkish dervish house looks like.

Dervish is a Persian word that means "poor person," the Arabic term being *fakir*, and is applied to every member of an Islamic religious order. There are a good many of these, but their members do not take vows. Promises of chastity, poverty, and obedience are unknown here. Dervish monasteries often have much real estate, money, and income, and it is generally true that the Turkish clergy does not live in penury. Most of the monks are married. Apart from common devotions, they spend their time eating, drinking, sleeping, playing games, smoking, and being indolent. The dervish once had considerable religious and political significance but no longer enjoys his former prestige, the lower classes now being the only ones that still show him a measure of respect. For this reason, dervishes practice ceremonies which give them the appearance of religious fanatics or miracle workers. They exhibit various skills and put on shows in which they perform curious dances or howl out their songs.

Behind the monastery gate we entered a tall, cool room which took up the width of the building. From here a corridor branched off to the left at a right angle, thus running parallel to the longer side of the building. The cells of the dervishes opened onto this corridor and their windows overlooked the yard. Since there were no doors, one could see into them as one walked along this passage. Their furniture was simple, consisting of nothing more than narrow cushions lying along the walls. On these the dervishes sat, wearing cone-shaped felt caps not unlike those used by clowns in European circuses. Some were smoking, others preparing for their dance, others still meditating and motionless.

From here we went to the circular structure, where we first entered a square vestibule from which we came into the large, octagonal main room. Its roof consisted of a cupola supported by slender pillars and there was a number of large, open windows along the back. The floor was mirror-smooth wainscot. Two rows of loges—one at floor level, the other halfway up the wall—ran along the eight sides of the hall. Some of the upper ones had gilded bars and were reserved for female spectators. Another loge at the same height accommodated the choir. All these loges were occupied, and so we sat down in one of the lower ones.

The performance, meant to be a religious service, now began. Through the main door, some thirty dervishes entered, with the head of the monastery in the lead. He was an old graybeard, dressed in a long black coat, while the rest wore brown cowls. But all of them had the tall conical caps on their heads. Slowly and with dignity they walked three times around the hall and then crouched down, the leader at the entrance facing the others, who had formed two half-circles to his right and his left. The music that now set in was so cacophonous that I feared my ears might be damaged, and the singing that went along with it could have "melted stones and driven men insane."

When these sounds had stopped, the dervishes made all sorts of bows and curious movements, now facing each other, now the leader. Sitting on their crossed legs, they swayed from side to side, or backward and forward, swiveled on their hips, twisted their necks, swung their arms, wrung their hands, clapped, threw themselves flat on the ground and struck it with their cone-shaped felt caps, making a considerable din.

This first part of this curious ritual must have lasted for about half an hour. Then the music and singing stopped. The dervishes remained in a crouch. The Turkish audience had observed this performance with rapt attention and amazement, and seemed pleased. Now the music began anew, but in a more rapid rhythm. The dervishes leaped to their feet and threw off their brown cowls, uncovering the white garments they wore underneath. Again they bowed to the leader and each other and then started in on the dance which has given them their name.

Actually, however, it is not a dance but a rotation. Each of them remained in place, turning slowly on his own axis, with one foot raised off the ground. At times they would cross their arms over their chests, at others they stretched their hands far forward, to the right or the left. Because the music became faster, the gyrations kept accelerating until the movement finally became so rapid that I closed my eyes for fear of becoming dizzy. This also lasted·about half an hour, and then one dervish after the other collapsed, and the show was over. I felt that I had had more than enough, but the audience was clearly pleased with what it had seen.

Isla looked at me and asked, "How did you like it, Effendi?"

"I almost became ill," I answered sincerely.

"You are right. I don't know if the Prophet commanded such exercises, and I don't know if his teaching does the country and the Ottoman people any good."

"I am surprised to hear that from a Muslim."

"Effendi," he whispered, "don't forget that my wife Senitza is a Christian!"

As we crossed the courtyard toward the exit, I felt a hand on my shoulder. I stopped and turned. A young man who had hurried after me was standing there. I recognized him immediately.

"Omar Ben Sadek! You here? Is it possible?"

"Praise be to God that he should give me the joy of seeing your face! My soul has longed for you many hundreds of times since I had to leave you so quickly."

It was Omar, the son of that Sadek who had guided Halef and me across the Shott Djerid and been killed by Abu en Nassr in the attempt.

"How did you get to Istanbul, and what are you doing here?" I asked.

"Don't you see that I am a porter? Come into a coffeehouse, I'll tell you everything."

In Egypt, Isla Ben Maflei had already heard about our Tunisian adventure and therefore knew Omar's name. He was happy to see the young man and gladly joined us in the first coffeehouse we came to.

Here I heard that the camel which the Wekil of Kbilli had so treacherously turned over to Abu en Nassr had been superior to the animal which Omar had been given by his friends. Nonetheless, he had not lost from sight the man he was pursuing until he came to Derna, on the Mediterranean coast. Here his camel had had to recover, and when he reached Bomba, still on the trail of the murderer, Abu en Nassr had already joined a caravan going to Siwa. Omar had had to wait for another opportunity and also trade his camel for a worse one because he needed money to buy food. It had not been until three weeks later that he joined a group journeying through the northern Barka desert and the Wadi Djarabub on its way to the Siwa oasis. Only after many inquiries and questions had he discovered there that Abu en Nassr had gone to Maghra and on to Birket Qarun Lake. When Omar had reached that point all his investigations were fruitless, and he had concluded that Abu en Nassr had taken a different direction and perhaps proceeded by a more southerly caravan route, passing through the Baharieh and Farafra oases on his way to Dakhla. He therefore went to those three places but found out nothing. Only in Tahtah, where he went subsequently, did he infer from some hints that the man he was looking for had gone down the Nile under an adopted name. Omar had then visited all the towns and villages along the banks of that river and finally arrived in Cairo utterly run-down and exhausted.

Quite unexpectedly, Omar had seen Abu en Nassr there, on Mehmed Ali square. He had followed him along the entire Mehmed Ali Boulevard but again lost sight of him. Without rest, he had roamed the city day and night and finally succeeded in finding Abu en Nassr in Bulak, but at the very moment the fugitive was boarding a vessel to leave the port. The captain had refused to take the penniless Omar and had not even allowed him to work his passage.

Burning with wrath and the desire for revenge, he had had to look on as his archenemy escaped him once again. Finally an Arab sheik whom he told of his situation gave him a horse and he followed the ship overland. He crossed the bridge over the Nile near Giza, and went on from there along the Rosetta. But then he recognized that the ship must have entered the Damietta. He rode to Kafr al Madshar and on across the delta and found out in Samannud that the ship had actually docked there and then gone on downstream. He followed this trail as far as Damietta, where he discovered too late that Abu had taken a freighter to Adalia, on the southern coast of Asia Minor.

Omar was now wholly without resources and first had to earn enough money by working in the harbor if he was to continue following his father's murderer, for what he obtained from selling his horse was insufficient. He finally managed to obtain free passage to Cyprus, where a fisherman took him to the mainland. He reached Anamur, opposite Cyprus, then walked to Selindi and Alajo and from there to Adalia. But here his investigations yielded no results. A long time had passed by then, and Omar had neither the means nor the experience to advance his search properly.

In spite of this, the young Arab did not lose the persistence the law of the blood feud prescribes. From the direction Abu en Nassr had taken, Omar judged that he intended to go to Istanbul, and therefore begged his way across Anatolia. This took a long time, and he became quite ill in Kutaiah. The hardships of his restless pursuit resulted in an illness of several months and he was lucky to be taken in by a Dervish monastery. Thus Omar arrived in Istanbul only after a great many months, a span of time during which I had journeyed very much farther. He still had not found the certain trail of the criminal but had not given up hope. To survive and put some money aside, he had become a porter, certainly a great sacrifice for a free Arab.

When I asked him how long he intended to remain in Istanbul when the situation seemed so hopeless, he answered, "Perhaps I will soon leave the city. Allah favored me, and I discovered an important name."

"Which?"

"Didn't you say on the Shott Djerid that Abu en Nassr's real name was Hamd el Amasat?"

"Yes."

"I found someone here who calls himself Ali Manach Ben Barud el Amasat."

"Really? Who?"

: 285 :

"A young dervish in the monastery you just visited. I was there to speak to him in his cell and to sound him out. Then I saw you and had to break it off."

"Ali Manach Ben Barud el Amasat!" Isla exclaimed so anxiously that I had to warn him that we were not alone. "So he is the son of that Barud el Amasat who sold my wife? I will return to the monastery and talk to him at once."

"Don't!" I cautioned him. "Amasat is not a rare name, and this dervish may be completely unrelated to the man you have in mind. But should things really be as you think, caution is imperative. Why not let me go instead?"

"Go on, Effendi. But now! We'll wait for you here."

I turned to Omar. "How did you find out that the dervish is called Amasat?"

"Yesterday I went to Baharije Koy by boat. He and another dervish were on board. They talked to each other and that's when I heard his name. It was already dark and I followed them. They stopped in front of a house. When the door was opened, a voice asked who it was, and they answered 'En Nassr.' I had to wait several hours until they came back out. Many men came and went there and all of them gave that password when they were asked. Do you understand that, Effendi?"

"Hm. Did they carry lanterns?"

"No, although no one is allowed to walk around without one in this city. There were no police to be seen. I followed those two as far as the monastery of the dancing dervishes."

"Did you understand the word 'En Nassr' correctly?"

"Absolutely."

Omar's report was food for thought. The words Dawuhd Arafim had said to me when he captured me in the ruins of Baalbek came to my mind. At that moment he had thought that I would no longer be dangerous to him and had bragged about being the head of a gang of murderers. Should that be true, this gang had to have members across a considerable area of Turkey, as his connections with Egypt and Damascus demonstrated. Istanbul is never without its criminal gangs, and at that very moment it was as unsafe as it had ever been. Houses had been found whose entire contents had been removed, their owners murdered or gone. Bodies giving every indication of having met a violent end could be seen floating in the waters of the Golden Horn and the Bosporus. At night, and at places quite distant from each other, fires broke out and pillaging and looting went on, and there seemed to be some connection between these events. After dark one encountered suspicious persons who did not carry lanterns and engaged the police in pitched battles when they were stopped by patrols. And it is incredible how the law dealt with such individuals. On one occasion an entire gang of the most dangerous criminals had been raided and the sultan had exiled them to Tripoli. After some time the captain of the ship that transported them returned with the report that he had been shipwrecked on the Tripoli coast and that all criminals on board had drowned. Some days later, and to no one's surprise, one could see those same "drowned" rascals running about the streets of the city.

For the time being I kept my thoughts to myself. Omar told me that the dervish Ali Manach could be found in the fifth cell from the entrance and I returned to the monastery. I crossed the courtyard, walked toward the gate, and entered the vestibule. The door to the corridor stood open and the dervishes had returned to their cells. I walked slowly down the long passage and then back again, to have a look at the cells and their occupants. No one paid any attention to me. A young dervish, perhaps twenty years old, was sitting in the fifth cell. He was looking fixedly up at the window and slipping the thirty-three beads of his rosary* through his fingers.

"Es-selam 'aleikum." I greeted him with a deep voice and dignified mien.

---

* The Muslims have thirty-three beads on their rosary. As each of them is passed through the fingers, one of Allah's attributes (the Compassionate One, the Merciful One, etc.) is named. Since there are ninety-nine such cognomina, the rosary must be gone through three times.

"We 'aleikum es selam," he answered. "What do you want?"

"I come from Baghdad and do not know the customs of this monastery. I saw your dance and would like to thank you for the edifying spectacle. Are you allowed to accept gifts?"

"I am. Let me have it."

"How large should it be?"

"Every para is welcome."

"Then take this."

I gave him according to my means, which were not large. But the dervish seemed satisfied, for he said, "I thank you. Is this intended for me or for the order?"

"Consider it a gift to you."

"Then tell me your name, so I will know whom I should thank."

"The Prophet says that an anonymous gift counts double. Permit me therefore to remain silent, but tell me yours so I will know the name of the true believer with whom I have been speaking."

"I am called Ali Manach Ben Barud el Amasat."

"And what is the place that witnessed your birth?"

"My home town is Scutari, in Albania." That checked! Isla had told me in Egypt that the Barud el Amasat who sold Senitza had lived in Scutari.

I asked, "Are the members of your devout family living there?"

"No," the dervish answered.

I could not ask any more questions because that would have made him suspicious. I therefore confined myself to a polite phrase and left.

Isla and Omar were impatiently waiting for me. "What did you find out?" Isla asked.

"Ali Manach is the son of that Barud el Amasat. He comes from Scutari, and unless I am altogether mistaken, Hamd el Amasat who calls himself Abu en Nassr is his uncle."

"He will have to tell us where his father is now, Effendi."

"Have to? Who is going to compel him?"

"The cadi."

"So Ali Manach will tell him the wrong place, or inform his father if he decides to tell the truth. No, we must be careful. First I want to have a look at the house where Ali Manach was yesterday. I'll go to Baharije Koy now with Omar, and then I may be in a position to advise you what to do."

"So be it. We'll separate, but bring Omar Ben Sadek back with you. I want him to stay at our house and stop working as a porter."

Isla went home and Omar and I rented a boat, went up the Golden Horn, and landed in Eyüp. From there we walked to Baharije Koy, the northwestern quarter of Constantinople. It was a laborious walk through filth and rubble, until we finally came to a blind alley.

Omar showed me the house as we passed, for we did not wish to stop and arouse suspicion. It was a narrow but apparently very deep building with a projecting upper story. Heavy sheet metal had been nailed to the door. In an otherwise bare wall there was just one tiny square hole near the entrance. The neighboring building also had an upper story and was equally narrow. A filthy piece of paper with the inscription "For rent" had been stuck on its door.

I opened and entered. Surprised at my lack of ceremony, Omar followed. We groped our way down a narrow, dark corridor until I found a door opposite the entrance. I opened it and came into a courtyard which was perhaps some five meters wide, like the house itself, but some ten times that long. The two sides and the rear were formed by three shedlike buildings in the final stage of dilapidation. Entrances to the right and the left of the courtyard door led into the two ground-level sections of the building. They had to be quite small. To get to the upper story one had to climb a rotten wooden staircase which had lost six of its original thirteen steps.

The courtyard was one huge puddle of mud which had been dried by the sun and transformed into a firm mass. A shapeless block of wood whose purpose it was impossible to determine stuck out from it. And on this mysterious chunk of wood something was sitting that would have been even more enigmatic had it not been smoking an old, filthy pipe. This object was ball-shaped and clad in a badly torn kaftan, and on this ball there sat what might once have been a blue or perhaps a red turban. Between turban and ball something like a human nose shone forth. When it noticed us, the hedgehoglike creature grunted. It sounded both contented and aggressive, after which it set about emerging from its kaftan.

"Selam," I greeted it.

"Sss—" it hissed and growled.

"Is this house for rent?"

All of a sudden the figure rolled off the chunk of wood and assumed an erect, humanoid position. "Yes indeed, to be rented immediately. It's a beautiful house, a magnificent house, a splendid apartment, almost too good for a pasha, and everything practically new. Would you like to inspect it, your eminence?" All this was uttered as rapidly as if it had come through a grinding mill. As tenants, we were clearly as welcome as we would have been undesirable had we had any other purpose.

The man was very short but made up for this with his bulk. Looking at him one saw nothing but a pair of worn-out slippers, the kaftan, the turban, the nose, and the pipe, but except for the nose all this seemed to date back to hoary antiquity. His ten toes protruded from the slippers, the kaftan was no longer cloth but filth, and the turban had the appearance of a huge, wrinkled dried prune. In the course of time the stem of the pipe had been chewed so thoroughly that only a bowl remained into which its fortunate owner had inserted a hollow vulture bone, less easy to bite through. I forgot to mention that the kaftan had lost its sleeves, and the fear with which the man pulled it around him and held on to its collar suggested that it was the only garment he had on.

He had addressed me politely, and I answered in kind. "Are you the owner of this house?"

"No, but your eminence can be assured that I am not one of those poor, shiftless . . ."

"Please," I interrupted, "answer my questions as succinctly as possible. Whose house is it?"

"It belongs to the wealthy baker Mehmed in Kassim Pasha; he inherited it."

"And what are you doing here?"

"I am the caretaker and am to wait for a tenant."

"What are you paid for that?"

"A piaster a day, and half a piaster's worth of bread."

"Is the house vacant?"

"Yes, I live next door."

"How much does the baker want?"

"Ten piasters per week, to be paid in advance."

"Show us the rooms."

He first opened the two doors on the ground floor. We saw two cellarlike caves full of vermin and filth but nothing else. We then climbed the stairs and came into three rooms which I would have called a dovecote, a chicken coop, and a rabbit warren respectively.

"This is the selamlik, this the living room, and this the harem," the old man explained with as much dignity as if he were showing a princely palace.

"Very well. And what do those buildings in the courtyard contain?"

"Nothing. They are for horses and servants."

"And what is your name?"

"I am Baruch Shebet Ben Baruch Chereb. I buy and sell precious stones, jewelry, and antiques, and should you be in need of a servant I would be willing to sweep your rooms every day, clean your clothes, and run all your errands."

"Where are your stones, jewelry, and antiques?"

"Eminence, it so happens that everything has been sold at the moment."

"Then go to your wealthy baker and tell him that I shall take the house. Here are ten piasters which he will receive each week, and here's another ten for tobacco for you."

"Eminence, I thank you," Baruch was delighted. "You know how to deal with a man whose only business is precious stones and jewelry. But the baker will ask me who you are. What should I say?"

"To begin with, don't call me 'eminence.' It's true that my clothes are new and without holes, but they are the only ones I own. I am a poor clerk, pleased when he can find someone who will employ him. And my friend here is a porter who doesn't earn much either. Both of us will live here, and perhaps we can find someone to share our expenses. I don't know yet whether I can use your services. We have to be thrifty." I told him that because this was a dangerous neighborhood and we would have to be as inconspicuous as possible.

The man answered, "Effendi, I don't need a great deal. If you pay me two piasters a day I will run all your errands and also take care of the house."

"I'll have to see if I can earn enough to let you have those two piasters. When can we move in?"

"Right away."

"We'll be back sometime today, and I hope the house won't be locked when we get here."

"I'll hurry to the baker right now and then await you here."

Back home, I told Isla, his father, and his uncle what we had done and proposed to do. They agreed to my moving into the baker's house with Halef and Omar. Lindsay wanted to come with us but I had to turn him down. His striking appearance would have been a liability. He was so annoyed that he said he could not remain at Maflei's by himself, and in the afternoon he really did move to Pera.

# 14 : In Darkest Istanbul

After we had discussed everything that required it, we collected our weapons and went to Baharije Koy. I left my horse at Maflei's. The caretaker was expecting us in our new residence. He had had it thoroughly cleaned by his wife and was delighted when I expressed my satisfaction. I asked him to get some bread, coffee, flour, eggs, tobacco, dishes, and three used blankets for us. After he had left we could unpack our rifles unobserved. They were taken into a room which no one but us would enter.

Baruch soon returned; his wife had helped him. The old woman—a mummy come back to life—invited me to join them for the evening meal. I accepted, since these two old people might be useful to me and I therefore wanted to keep them in good humor. That this proved successful was evident even before my visit, for without having been asked, they brought us some straw-filled bags to serve as a divan. True, they seemed to be largely holes and rips, but Baruch was poor. He thought we also were, and he meant well.

When the two had left, we lit our pipes and a small lamp, for meanwhile it had become dark. We agreed that during my absence Omar should keep our door slightly ajar and observe the comings and goings next door. Halef would go into the courtyard. The two houses were separated by a thin wall of boards, and when the little Hadji was in the shed, it might be assumed that he would hear something.

Baruch, who lived on the other side of the house, was waiting for me. The couple were the sole inhabitants of an ownerless hut, something that is fairly common in Istanbul. The purchases he had made for us had perhaps yielded him a small profit, for both were in excellent spirits and received me cordially if somewhat obsequiously. They may have felt a faint hope that our arrival might somewhat mitigate their unrelieved misery. The old woman was cleaner that I had imagined, so I could eat the small quantities I was offered without qualms. And when I made the couple a present of a little tobacco and coffee, they were overjoyed, as if they had received valuable gifts. I noticed again that the kaftan was practically Baruch's sole piece of clothing. Apparently he had no pants, and the jacket sleeves that protruded from the armholes of the kaftan were in pitiable condition. Some small help could do much here, and I decided to provide it. Obviously Baruch's jewelry and antiques were a fiction, but a harmless one. These poor wretches had had to survive on a piaster and a little bread a day, and so it really cheered them when I offered five piaster a day for their services.

During the course of our conversation, I casually asked about the neighborhood.

"Effendi," Baruch said, "only poor people live in this alley. Some are good and decent, others untrustworthy and malicious. You are a clerk and will not find work here. So you will have nothing to do with them. Yet I would ask you to be very wary of the house next door."

"Why?"

"It's dangerous to talk about it."

"I can keep my mouth shut."

"I believe you, but you might move out again immediately if I were to go into details, and I would regret that."

"I promise that I will keep this place. I hope we are friends, and so I think that you can be honest and sincere with me. I am not wealthy but even a poor person can be grateful."

"I have already seen that you are kind, and I believe your promise. Everyone living on this street knows that what goes on in the house next door is not good, but they don't concern themselves with it. Someone once sneaked in because he wanted to find out what went on inside. When he had not returned by the following morning, and his family looked for him, they found him hanging from a rafter. He certainly had not committed suicide."

"So you think my neighbors are criminals?"

"Yes. You must be careful of them!"

"But surely you can tell me who lives there?"

"A Greek with his wife and son. They serve wine and have a good many boys and girls living with them whom one never sees out on the street. Several men roam the city from morning till night looking for clients. People of some standing and ordinary folk, inhabitants of Istanbul and foreigners, are among the visitors. There is gambling and music, and I do not believe that everyone who goes there comes out again. Sometimes, at night, one can hear shouts for help, or the clatter of weapons, and when that happens one usually sees a corpse floating in the water the following morning. Not infrequently entire gangs arrive during the night, people who carry no lanterns but all sorts of things which are taken inside to be distributed."

"You say that no one wants to concern himself with what goes on there, yet you are very well informed. Have you ever eavesdropped?"

"Effendi, that is something I cannot discuss with anyone; it would mean my death."

"Not even with me?"

"You least of all, for you might do the same thing I did, and what happened to the man that was found dead might happen to you."

"Surely it's not as serious as all that."

"Effendi, I am not lying."

"I know you aren't, but perhaps you imagine things."

The old man did not care to be called a liar or a dreamer, and so he said, "All I am asking you is that you do not touch the board."

"What board?"

"Along the right wall of your selamlik there is a loose board. There's only a single nail along the top that holds it in place, so it can be pushed aside. Then you have a small gap and, behind that, the wall of the neighboring house. There is a nail loose there too, I pulled it out. If you push the board aside, you can look into the room where the opium smokers lie, and you can hear the tinkle of glasses and the laughter of the boys and girls I told you about."

"You were very reckless. Suppose they notice next door that the boards are loose?"

"But I wanted to observe what went on, and so I had to remove the nail. There was no other way."

"Yes, there was, an even easier one. You could have drilled a hole into the board, small enough to be overlooked."

"Then I wouldn't have seen enough."

"And why didn't you report what you saw? Wouldn't that have been your duty?"

"Effendi, my first duty is to stay alive. I don't want to be murdered."

"But surely the police wouldn't have betrayed you."

"You cannot have been living in Istanbul for long to talk as you do. When I looked through the crack I saw important persons. I also recognized dervishes and police. There are any number of high-ranking officials who receive no salary from the sultan and therefore live on the baksheesh they try to extort. And what is such a man to do if the baksheesh is inadequate? If someone were to denounce your neighbor, he might come before a police sergeant or a cadi who had been in that room himself, and that would be the end of him. No, I know what goes on in that house, and I won't bother about it any further. You are the only one I have told. Consider it a warning."

I had heard enough and thought it best not to press Baruch any further. I was convinced that my companions and I were in some danger. The Greek would certainly find out that he had new neighbors; he would presumably inquire about us and have us observed closely. That would be easy for him and could be accomplished without our noticing it, since only a wooden partition separated us. During the day we would have to be on our guard when we went into the courtyard, for someone who had known us in the past might spot us. It really was a good thing that I had hired Baruch as our servant. We would simply stay indoors.

Perhaps my companions had left the lantern burning. Through a crack its light might fall into the house next door. Or perhaps they were sitting and talking where they could be overhead. These fears made me restless, and I quickly returned after first having instructed Baruch how to conduct himself should someone inquire about us. He was to say that a poor clerk, a porter, and an even poorer Arab had taken the house —three men, in other words, who had their own problems. Since the two apartments adjoined, I would only have to knock on the wall when I needed the caretaker.

When I reached our front door, I found it ajar and Omar at his post. He told me that several people had already entered the house next door. Through an opening someone had asked them what they wanted, and they had simply answered "En Nassr." I asked Omar to lock the house and follow me. Halef was in the courtyard and he came with us. He had seen and heard nothing. There were no lamps burning in our shabby rooms, and I preferred to keep it that way.

After I had reported my talk with Baruch, I examined the right wall of the selamlik and found the board. I pulled it aside and reached inside. A beam's width away, I touched the wall of the adjoining house and also the loose board, which I then pushed carefully to one side. I could see that the room on the far side was completely dark. After I had put the board back in place, we pulled up our straw bags and blankets, waiting for the darkness, listening.

We had been sitting there for perhaps an hour, only whispering to each other, when we heard a noise on the other side. I was close to the board and pushed it aside. I could hear the heavy steps of several men, and a groan.

Then a voice said, "Over here! That's it! Hassan should get ready to go." After a pause the voice continued, "Can you write?"

"Yes."

"Do you have money at home?"

"You are asking for money? What did I do to you that you should lure me here and tie me up?"

"Do? Nothing! We have your wallet, watch, rings, and weapons. But that isn't enough. If you cannot give us what we ask, they'll find you in the water tomorrow morning."

"Allah kerim! How much do you want?"

"You are rich. Five thousand piasters isn't too much."

"It is! I don't have it!"

"How much do you have at home?"

"Barely three thousand."

"Will they be turned over to a messenger if you send one? Don't lie. I swear to you this will be your final hour if we don't get the money!"

"Allah! It will be given to you if I write a letter and seal it with my ring."

"I'll give you the ring. Untie his hands so he can write."

All was silent for a while. I lay down on the straw bag and reached into the wall. As gently and cautiously as possible I also moved the second board until there was a small crack I could see through. A man with his back toward us was sitting directly before it. His head was covered, his clothing torn, apparently damaged when he tried to resist. Three armed men were facing him—one, whom I took to be the owner of the house, in Greek dress, the other two in ordinary Turkish clothes. They watched as the prisoner sealed the letter on his knees.

I returned the board to its original position and continued listening. After a short while, I heard the Greek say; "Now tie him up again and take him next door. If he doesn't stay quiet, simply stab him." I heard a door being opened and people leaving.

It became quiet once more and I whispered to my companions what I had seen and heard.

"They are thieves," Halef said. "What do we do?"

"They are not just thieves but murderers. Do you really believe they'll let that fellow go? They would be signing their own death warrant. They'll wait until they get the three thousand and then put him out of the way."

"Then we must help him."

"True; but how?"

"We'll smash the boards and free him."

"That would make a noise and also go against our original purpose. A struggle might develop that would be dangerous to us, and even if we got the best of them, the criminals would abandon the house and all our trouble would have been for nothing. It would be better to bring the police here. But it may take too long to find them; a good deal could happen in the meantime. And who knows if the police would be willing to enter the house? It will be best if we detach one more board in our wall, and one over there. Then we can crawl through the opening. We'll bring the man here, replace the boards, and then decide what to do next."

"But we have no pliers."

"I have a knife. Above all, we must not be heard by those criminals. I'll start right now."

"Do you know where they are keeping him?"

"Yes. When they brought him in, they passed through the room where Baruch says the boys and girls are; that seems to be empty now. Opposite our wall there is a second room. I saw the door, and that's where he probably is."

I moved my hand along the wall and found that every board was attached by a nail at the top and another at the bottom. The one on our side seemed to be loose, and I only had to insert my knife between the board and the beam to loosen it carefully. Unfortunately, the opening turned out to be too small for a man to crawl through. But I could loosen a third board without making an audible noise. The boards could easily be slid upward. Once this was done, Omar held them in place. I now ran my hand over the wall of the adjoining house and noticed that the points of the nails were bent, which made my work considerably more difficult. I had to straighten them carefully and this could not be done soundlessly. My hands became so tired I had to switch from left to right repeatedly.

Some considerable time passed in this fashion, and I had just finished when I heard steps approaching. It was the Greek carrying a lantern. He opened the door opposite our wall but did not enter that room.

"Do you have the money?" I heard the prisoner ask.

"Yes," the Greek answered, laughing briefly.

"Then let me go!"

"Not just yet. You won't be set free until early tomorrow morning. I just came to tell you that some people will be arriving soon who must not know you are here. They won't come into this room but I don't want them to hear you. So I am going to tie you to a beam and gag you. If you stay completely quiet, you will be let go, but if you make a noise you'll leave this house as a corpse."

The prisoner again asked to be released and promised to tell no one what had happened to him, but in vain. Judging by the fear in his voice, he apparently suspected what the Greek proposed to do with him. He was tied up and gagged. Then the warder left, having first bolted the door from the outside.

We had to act quickly, before those people the Greek had mentioned started arriving. Luckily, I was ready. I picked up my revolver and knife, weapons I had bought in Istanbul, and crawled into the house next door. My companions did not follow me but held themselves ready to come to my help should I be attacked.

I pulled back the bolt and entered the second room. "Don't make a sound! I am going to free you," I whispered to the prisoner and ran my hand over his fetters at the same time. They were ropes, which I cut and put into my pockets. The gag was a piece of cloth which had been tied to his mouth and nose. I loosened it and also put it away.

"Mashallah!" the man said as he rose quickly. "Who are you and how . . ."

"Quiet!" I interrupted him. "Follow me!" I pulled him out of the room, bolted the door again, and then pushed him through the opening into our apartment.

"Hamdulillah, thank God!" Halef whispered. "I was worried about you, but it went faster than I expected."

I drove the corkscrew of my pocket knife into the second of the three adjoining boards in the opposite wall, thrust the dagger into the beam, and fastened the two handles to each other. In this way the boards held together in such a fashion that one could not tell from the opposite side that they had been pried loose.

We again heard steps on the other side. A drunk was brought in and placed on the floor to sleep off his stupor. I was certain now that no one would come back for some time, and I walked into our second room with my companions and the prisoner. There we made light and had a look at our involuntary guest. He was of medium height and probably not yet fifty, with an intelligent face.

"Welcome," I greeted him. "Fortunately, we witnessed the incident over there and considered it our duty to come and help you."

"So you don't belong to those scoundrels?" the man asked suspiciously.

"No."

"I knew they were going to kill me and thought you were sent because the time had come. Who are you?"

"I am a German, and these are my friends, free Arabs from the Sahara. This man, Omar Ben Sadek, has a blood feud against an enemy who seems to frequent that house. We rented this place to investigate." I intentionally said nothing about Abrahim or the jewelry theft; there was no need for the stranger to know. I continued, "We just moved in here today and Allah decreed that we should have an opportunity on our very first day to prevent a crime. May we know who you are?"

The Turk stared sullenly at the floor. Then he shook his head and answered, "I would prefer to remain silent. I don't want my name, which is known to many, to be mentioned in public in connection with this affair. You are a foreigner, and I can show my gratitude even if you don't discover who I am."

"I respect your wish and also ask you not to thank us. Did you recognize any of the men next door?"

"No. There are many guests, and many others who seem to be more than that. I'll have that den searched within the hour."

"But can you? I am sure that Greek won't discover before morning that you got away, so the police will take him by surprise unless he regularly posts guards. But I have heard that many policemen and officials visit that house, and so it seems doubtful that you will accomplish your purpose."

"Police?" he asked disdainfully. "I did see a room with police in it. But I won't go to the police. I am an officer, the rank doesn't matter. I'll get my soldiers and make short shrift here."

This was both welcome and unwelcome news. If the officer raided the gathering next door, it was likely that the very individuals we were looking for would not be there, and then we would have to start all over. But a chain of events was unfolding and there was nothing I could do to stop it.

"Then I ask that you let me see the prisoners you take," I answered. "We would like to know if the men we are looking for are among them."

"You'll see them all."

"And please let me say this: anyone who wishes to enter that house is asked what he wants and admitted only if he answers, 'En Nassr.' Perhaps that information will be useful to you."

"Ah, so that was the word my guide whispered into the opening by the door. But how do you happen to know that password?" he asked, suspicious again.

"Omar Ben Sadek heard it," I explained, and then told him the rest that he had to know. I went on: "It would be advisable to split up your men. Half of them can enter using the password, the other half can get inside through the opening by which you escaped. But no one must see the soldiers enter from the street until the rest are already here, for it must be expected that the guard who opens the door will shout a warning when he sees them, and give his accomplices the chance to get away."

"I can see that your intentions are honest. I'll take your advice. Does one of you have a fez? Those scoundrels even bared the head of a believer. I'll make them pay for that!"

"I'll lend you mine, and I'll also give you these pistols. You should not be unarmed."

"I thank you. All this will be returned to you. Be watchful. I'll be back in an hour at the latest."

I accompanied the officer to the door and he hurried down the opposite side of the alley.

"Effendi," Omar asked when I returned, "if Abu en Nassr should be next door, will they turn him over to me?"

"I don't know."

"But my revenge takes precedence."

"The officer might not agree."

"Then I know what I must do. Do you remember the oath I swore on the Shott Djerid, at the spot where my father disappeared? Look, I have let my hair and beard grow to this hour; the enemy who is so close today must not escape me." Omar went into the selamlik and sat down in front of the loose board. Woe to Abu en Nassr should the avenger find him tonight!

I put out the lantern and we followed Omar. Apparently a group was now in the room next door. I could hear the snoring and moaning typical of the early stages of opium intoxication. We kept quiet, and when three-quarters of an hour had passed I went downstairs to await the officer.

Far more than an hour had gone by when I recognized a long line of shapes silently approaching on the far side of the alley. They must have been given their instructions earlier, for the section in the rear stopped while those in front were led toward the entrance of our house. The officer, still in the clothes he had worn before, was leading them. He was more than adequately armed.

"I see you are waiting for us," he whispered. "Here are your pistols and your fez."

He took both from the man behind him, a captain. While I led the detachment—some thirty of them—he remained at the door. Our rooms were crowded when he rejoined us. In spite of the poor condition of the stairs, the maneuver had been performed without suspicious noise.

"Make a light," the officer said.

"Did you lock the door downstairs?" I asked.

"The bolt has been pushed to."

"And did you post a guard?"

"A guard?" He laughed. "What for?"

"I told you that this is my first day here. That means I do not know the place well and therefore have to allow for the possibility that the men you want to catch will rush into this courtyard and escape through my door."

"Let me worry about that," he answered condescendingly. "I know what I am doing."

When the light was burning, the Turkish officer placed it next to the wall and then ordered his men to start. The soldiers in front raised their rifles to knock down the wall. This was stupid, for before the first of them got across, those next door would have been warned. Only one of them acted more intelligently. The moment the first blow had been struck, he pushed the boards aside, pulled my knife and corkscrew out of the wood, and crawled through. He was long gone when the officer made his way across at the head of his men.

I followed the officer and the captain. Six or seven drunks and opium smokers were lying in the room. We leaped across them into the adjoining one and just caught a glimpse of the last man as he disappeared behind the door. We hurried after him.

Downstairs an enormous noise erupted, the soldiers having entered there as well. The room we now came into had two additional doors. We opened one and saw a room which had no other exit; it was full of boys and girls kneeling on the floor, stretching out their arms imploringly.

"A guard to the door!" the officer roared. He hastened to the second door, and I followed.

Here we collided with Omar, who had been coming toward us. "He isn't up here," he snorted. "I must get downstairs." The desire to avenge himself had driven him to the far end of the upper story before any of us had been able to reach it.

"Who's up here?" the officer asked him.

"More than twenty people, way in the back. I don't know any of them." Omar pushed us aside and hurried downstairs while we ran through several rooms all of which were lit up. The attack had been so sudden that in their fright people had forgotten to put out the lights. Later I heard that the guard at the door downstairs had immediately fired his pistol and disappeared in the dark corridor when he saw the soldiers coming. The smashing of the wall with the rifle butts had kept us from hearing that shot, but it had been heard by those living in and visiting the building. Since it had unquestionably been agreed upon as a signal warning of extreme danger, they had quickly escaped, and that was the reason we had found the front rooms empty when we burst into them.

Finally we came to the door of the last room, which had been barricaded from inside. While the soldiers were trying to knock it down with their rifles, I also heard a loud banging inside. The door was heavy and resisted too long. Having only my revolvers with me, I ran back into our apartment to pick up my hunting rifle.

When I returned with it, the door had only a small crack in it. It was very solidly made, presumably because the room behind it was the last refuge and therefore more adequately protected. And the wall was not timber but brick.

"Get away!" I ordered the soldiers. "Let me!"

My heavy hunting rifle was certainly a more adequate tool for breaking down a wall than the light rifles of the sultan's army. The very first thrust with the iron-plated butt made a breach. Three more powerful blows and the door had been smashed. But at that very moment a salvo of more than ten shots was fired at us. Several soldiers fell but I was unhurt because I had stood off to one side to knock down the door. I saw the officer enter the room with his weapon raised and was about to run in after him when I stopped to listen.

"Sidi, help, quickly, quickly!" I heard Halef's voice above the din. It had come from the courtyard.

My courageous Hadji was obviously in great danger and I must rush to his help. Was I to run back through all the rooms, into our apartment and down the stairs to the yard? That way was too long; as they were escaping, the criminals might kill my good Halef in the meantime. I now heard him call a second time, even more urgently. I jumped toward the wooden wall running along the side of our courtyard and knocked out some boards with my rifle.

"I'm on the way, Halef!" I called down.

"Quickly, Sidi, I've got him!" he shouted up at me.

The old, rotten boards flew down into the profound darkness fitfully illuminated by rifle fire. People were cursing. This was not the moment to hesitate, and so I jumped down, landing rather painfully.

I quickly picked myself up and shouted, "Where are you, Halef?"

"Here, at the door!"

And so he was. What I had told the officer the courageous Hadji had taken to heart. Instead of following us into the house next door, he had rushed downstairs to our entrance. The men who were packed into the room at the very back had knocked down the thin wall and jumped into our courtyard. Half of them had already got down there when I managed to smash the door upstairs. They had wanted to escape through our house but had run into Halef, who had not posted himself behind the door but was receiving them as they emerged. The shots I had heard had been fired at him. I could not tell whether he had been hit. He was standing erect, in any event, defending himself with the butt of his long rifle.

There is something special about a fight at close quarters and in darkness. One's senses become con-

siderably more acute, and one sees what would ordinarily escape one's attention. A certain instinct by
which one acts during such moments of danger has all
the qualities of a well-thought-out decision. My rifle
butt quickly extricated Halef from all danger. I saw
that his attackers were being beaten to the ground by
him or running off, but could think of only one thing.

"Whom have you got, Halef?"

"Abrahim Mamur."

"Where?"

"At my feet. I knocked him down."

"Finally! Bravo!"

The few who were still molesting us were quickly
scattered. I paid no attention to them but bent down
to have a look at the leader of the gang. A considerable tumult was still raging in the courtyard. Fleeing
from the soldiers, people were jumping down, but this
was no concern of mine. Dawuhd Arafim was more
important than all the rest.

I took out a match, lit it, and held it to the face of
the prostrate figure. "What a pity, Halef! It isn't he."

"No, Sidi? Impossible! I saw him quite clearly by
the flash of a shot."

"Then you mistakenly knocked down someone else.
The criminal has unfortunately got away. Where to, I
wonder?"

I got up and looked around the yard. Some of the
fugitives were climbing across the low planks which
were filling a gap between the house and the shed,
and that passage led to Baruch's courtyard. Halef had
also seen this.

"After them, Sidi," he shouted. "Abrahim crossed
there!"

"Of course. But we won't get him that way. He has
to pass by our front door, so let's hurry!"

I dashed along the corridor to our door and opened
it. Four shapes were hurrying past. They had emerged
from Baruch's house. A fifth, who was following them
and had not seen us, called out, "Stop! Stay together!"

It was the voice of the man we were after. Halef
also recognized it and was unintelligent enough to
shout, "It's he, Sidi! After him!"

Abrahim heard this and started running. We hastened after him. To get away from us he turned some corners and entered a number of dark, twisting alleys, but I was never more than fifteen paces behind him and Halef kept up with me. Apparently my leap into the courtyard had not been without consequences, for otherwise I would certainly have caught up with the fugitive. He was a good runner, and Halef was almost out of breath.

"Stop and shoot him down!" he panted.

That would have been easy, of course, but I didn't do as he asked. Others had a greater right to him than I, and I wanted to catch him alive. The jewels were uppermost in my mind. He must have hidden them somewhere. If I killed him now, and I well might in this darkness even if I didn't intend to, we probably would never discover what had happened to them. So the chase went on. Now the alley down which we had been running opened up and the water of the Golden Horn lay before us. Not far from the shore, the darkness of night notwithstanding, one could make out the chain of islands that lie between Baharije Koy and Südlüdje.

"To the right, Halef," I commanded.

He obeyed, and I jumped to the left. We now had the fugitive between us and the water. He stopped for a moment to look back at us and then started running toward the shore, jumped into the water, and disappeared in the waves.

"Waj!" Halef exclaimed angrily. "But this Abrahim will not get away!" He raised his rifle.

"Don't shoot," I suggested. "You are trembling from having run. I'll jump in after him."

"Sidi, when I aim at this scoundrel, I don't tremble," was the answer.

Now the head of the swimmer emerged from the water—Halef fired—a shout rang out, and the head disappeared in the gurgling waves.

"I hit him!" Halef exulted. "He's dead! You see, Sidi, I didn't tremble."

We waited for a while, but since Dawuhd Arafim did not come back up, we felt certain that the bullet had found its mark. We now returned to the scene of the skirmish.

Although I had paid attention to the direction we had taken while running and tried to memorize the number and location of the alleys we had rushed through, we did not find it easy to orient ourselves and it took some considerable time to get back to our house. There much had changed in the meantime. It had become fairly light in the alley, for the people living there and others from nearby streets were standing about with paper lanterns. Some of the soldiers had cordoned off the three houses and the rest were either looking for fugitives hiding in the courtyards or guarding the prisoners that had been taken. Every person who had been in the Greek's house on that day was considered a prisoner. The Greek himself was dead. The captain had split his head with a stroke of his saber. His wife was standing by the boys and girls who had been collected and shackled. The inebriated had also been brought there. In the tumult their consciousness had more or less returned. Some soldiers were dead, several wounded, and it turned out that my brave Halef's arm had unfortunately been grazed by a bullet and there was a luckily harmless stab wound right next to it. Of the prisoners, only four seemed to be members of the criminal gang. Six had been killed and the others had managed to escape. Omar, who had been boldest, was leaning against the stairs, in bad humor. He had not found Abu en Nassr and had not bothered with anything else.

Finally all the prisoners were fettered and ready to be moved, and the officer now permitted his men to ransack the Greek's house. They did not have to be asked twice: within ten minutes everything of value had been taken.

While this was going on I searched out the captain and I asked about his superior. "He's standing in front of the house," was the unfriendly answer.

I already knew that but wanted to find out something about the man. Initially I had respected his silence, but his subsequent conduct toward me had not been what I felt entitled to. Now that the fighting was over, he was ignoring me and so I no longer felt I need be considerate.

"What's his rank?" I asked.

"Don't ask," the man said rudely. "We are not allowed to tell."

But that was the very reason I had to find out. One of the soldiers had still been busy searching through Baruch's courtyard while his comrades had been looting. He had not done as well as the rest and was about to leave the house on his way toward the alley when I intercepted him.

"You didn't get anything?" I asked.

"Nothing," he grumbled angrily.

"I will give you something if you answer a question. What is the rank of the officer who led you tonight?"

"We are not supposed to talk about him but he didn't think of me either. Will you give me twenty piasters if I tell you?"

"Yes."

"He is a colonel and his name is . . ." He gave the name of a man who later played an important role in Istanbul and is still a high dignitary today. He is not Turkish by birth. Once the favorite of his former master, it was certainly not by his intellectual gifts that he rose to the rank he now holds.

I paid the sum asked for and then glanced out into the alley. The colonel was standing directly in front of the door and could not possibly fail to see me. As I expected, he came up to me and asked: "Are all Franks as fearful as you? Where were you when the rest of us were fighting?"

What a question! I felt like slapping him. "We also fought," I answered indifferently, "and those we fought are the ones you needlessly let get away. A wise man always strives to make up for the mistakes of others."

"Whom did I let escape?" he bristled.

"The majority of those you wanted to catch. You did not listen to me when I advised you to post some men at the door of this house, and my servant and I were unable to detain the larger number of those scoundrels while you were busy with a few. What's going to happen to the prisoners?"

"Only Allah knows. Where will you stay tomorrow?"

"Here."

"You won't go on living here."

"Why not?"

"You'll find out soon enough. Now tell me where I can find you tomorrow."

"At the house of the merchant Maflei."

"I'll send someone there." Without a farewell he turned away and signaled. The soldiers surrounded the prisoners and marched off.

I returned to the courtyard and saw why I would not live in that house tomorrow. The charming officer had had the Greek's house put on fire and the flames were already licking the roof. What a convenient way of disposing of a far from creditable episode!

Without sounding the alarm I rushed up into our apartment to pick up our rifles and the few belongings with which we had moved in. I carried everything down into the yard. By now the flames had leaped up high enough to be seen from the alley. The tumult which now erupted cannot possibly be described. One has to have witnessed a fire in Constantinople to have some idea of the utter confusion a conflagration creates here. No one thinks of putting it out but only of getting away. Since most of the houses are wooden structures, such a fire often consumes entire sections of the city.

Old Baruch was speechless with fear, and his wife unable to move. We consoled both as best we could, packed their few possessions, and promised they would be kindly received by Maflei. Some porters soon turned up and thus we left an apartment we had inhabited for less than a day. For the wealthy baker the building was certainly no irreplaceable loss.

At this late hour Maflei's house was locked but someone soon answered our knocks. All family members gathered. They were very much disappointed when they heard how our enterprise had ended, and would have preferred having the murderer of their relative in their power, but finally consoled themselves with the belief that he had met his reward in the waves of the Golden Horn. Baruch and his wife were welcomed and the master of the house assured him that he would take care of them.

After we were told that we would find our garden house waiting for us, Isla said cheerfully, "Effendi, during your absence today we had an unexpected, dear visitor. You have not seen him yet but I have told you about him. I'll call him and you can guess who it is."

I was rather curious about this guest, for he had to have some connection with our adventures. After a few moments Isla came in with an elderly man. He was wearing the customary Turkish dress but had nothing about him that could have given me a hint. His sunburned features were boldly chiseled. The lines in his face and the long, snow-white beard gave him the appearance of a man bowed down by grief.

"Here he is, Effendi," Isla said. "Who is he?"

"I don't know him."

"But you will guess his name nonetheless." And turning to the stranger he asked, "Address him in your mother tongue."

"Your devoted servant, honored sir."

This polite greeting in Serbian immediately put me on the right track. I stretched out both hands and answered, "It's father Osko! Welcome!"

It was Osko, Senitza's father, and everyone was delighted that I had recognized him by his greeting. To retire for the night was out of the question now—I first must find out how things had gone with him. Since the disappearance of his daughter, his only child, he had been roaming restlessly. Here and there, now and then, the Montenegrin had believed that he had found some trace of her but had invariably come to the conclusion that he was mistaken. During these wanderings—largely through Asia Minor and Armenia —he had suffered no want, for his resources had been ample. In typically Oriental fashion, Osko had sworn that he would not return to his country and his wife until he had found his child, but finally the futility of his efforts had compelled him to go to Constantinople. Such an odyssey is possible only in the Orient.

The reader can imagine the joy the Montenegrin felt when he found that his daughter had married the man for whom he had intended her. And he had not merely found his daughter but also his wife, who had followed the daughter to Istanbul. As a result of all he had been told, Osko was now thirsting for revenge. He had decided to force the dervish Ali Manach to tell where his father was and I had some difficulty persuading him to leave that visit to me.

Only then did we settle down for the night. Because of all the exertion, I fell asleep immediately and might not have waked up early the following morning had I not been roused. Maflei had me wakened with the message that someone urgently wanted to see me. Since one sleeps in one's clothes in the Orient, I lost no time answering this call. A man had come who first asked my name and then asked me to go to the bodega in St. Dimitri where I had been before with the French barber. It seemed that the barber was anxious to see me.

"What does he want?" I asked.

"I don't know. I live nearby and the landlord asked me to come and see you."

"Tell him I am on my way."

I paid the man for his trouble and he left. Five minutes later Omar and I followed. Because there is a risk in visiting a tavern in a disreputable part of the city, I felt I should not go alone but did not want to trouble Halef because he was wounded. With the owners of the animals we had rented behind us and clutching their tails, we made fairly rapid progress.

The innkeeper met us at the door, greeted us in a servile manner, and asked, "Effendi, are you the German who was here with Hamsad el Djerbaja a few days ago?"

"I am."

"He wants to talk to you."

"Where is Hamsad?"

"Upstairs, in bed. Your companion can wait for you in the tavern."

"In bed" suggested either illness or an accident. While Omar entered the tavern, I walked up the stairs with the owner. He stopped at the top and said, "Don't be alarmed. He is ill."

"What's wrong?"

"Nothing of consequence. A small knife wound."

"Who did it?"

"A stranger who's never been here before."

"Why?"

"At first they were sitting together talking. Then they gambled, and when your friend was supposed to pay up he had no money. They quarelled and drew their knives. Hamsad was drunk and got stabbed."

"Is it dangerous?"

"No, he's still alive." Apparently this fellow believed that a knife wound was dangerous only when death was instantaneous.

"I assume you detained the other man?"

"How could I?" the innkeeper asked. He seemed embarrassed. "Your friend had no money and was the first to draw his knife."

"Do you at least know the culprit?"

"No. I just told you he had never been here before."

"Did you send for a physician?"

"Yes. I sent for a famous hekim right away. He bandaged the wound. I expect you will reimburse me for what Hamsad owes for that visit, and also for what he drank? And I had to give the stranger what he had won from him."

"I'll think about it. Take me to Hamsad."

"Go in that door. I must get back downstairs."

As I walked into the room, which contained nothing but a sort of mattress, I saw that the barber was deathly pale and his features sunken. It was perfectly clear that the wound was dangerous, and I bent over him.

"Thank you for coming," he said laboriously.

"Are you allowed to talk?" I asked kindly.

"It can no longer do any harm. I am going to die."

"Take courage. Didn't the doctor give you hope?"

"He's a quack."

"I'll have you taken to Pera. Do you have some sort of document from the French envoy?"

"No. I didn't want to be known as a Frenchman."

"Who was the man you quarreled with?"

"Don't you know? You asked me to look for him. It was Abrahim Mamur."

Hearing that name made me recoil. "That's impossible! He's dead!"

"Dead? I wish he were" It was odd. Now, on his sick- or deathbed, the barber was no longer speaking his customary dialect but the purest French.

"Tell me what happened."

"I was here quite late at night when Abrahim Mamur came in, drenched, as if he had been in the water. I recognized him immediately, but he didn't know who I was. I sat down at his table and we started drinking. Then we gambled and I lost. I was drunk and may have mentioned that I knew him and was going to question him. I had no money, and so we started quarreling. I wanted to do you a favor and kill Abrahim, but he was faster. That's all."

"I won't reproach you. That would be useless and you are ill besides. Could you tell me if Abrahim Mamur knows the innkeeper?"

"They seemed to know each other well. He gave him dry clothes without being asked. Please don't ask me any more questions now. Are you really going to have me taken to Pera?"

"Yes. But first I want to send you a decent physician to find out if you can be transported. Is there anything you want?"

"Have them bring me some sherbet, and don't forget me."

The wounded man had spoken with effort and many pauses. Now he closed his eyes and lost consciousness. I went downstairs, gave the innkeeper some instruc- tions, and promised to repay his legitimate expenses. Then we quickly rode to Pera and I went to the French legation. The official in charge listened silently to my brief account and then promised in the most amiable manner to have the wounded man seen to. He said he would send a physician and merely requested that I leave Omar as guide. While this did not relieve me of all worry about the barber, I could now return home with an easy conscience, knowing that he was in good hands.

# 15 : At the Tower of Galata

Directly upon my return I sought out Isla to tell him that Abrahim Mamur was still alive. The young merchant was in a room filled with books and all sorts of merchandise samples, apparently his office. He was not precisely cheered by the news but calmed down when he considered that we might still be able to capture the fellow alive. He did not feel sorry for the barber, telling me that he had discharged him because he had repeatedly stolen from him.

As we were talking I kept looking at a book lying open before him. It seemed to be an account book whose content did not concern me. Isla was aimlessly turning its pages when my glance suddenly fell on a line. Quickly I put my hand on the page. I had seen the name "Henri Galingré, Scutari."

"Galingré in Scutari?" I asked. "Do you have business connections with a Galingré in that town?"

"Yes. He is a Frenchman from Marseille from whom I buy merchandise."

"From Marseille? How extraordinary! Have you ever seen or spoken to him?"

"More than once! He's been here and I have been at his home."

"Do you know anything about him or his family?"

"I inquired about Galingré before I did any business with him, and later he told me things. Originally he just had a small business in Marseille but that didn't satisfy him. So he went to Istanbul and then to Edirne. That's where I became acquainted with him. But for about a year now he has been living in Scutari and is one of the wealthiest men there."

"And his relatives?"

"Henri Galingré had a brother who did not like it in Marseille either. The brother first went to Algiers and then to Blida, where he did so well that Henri, who was in Edirne at the time, sent him his son to help him run the business. This son married a girl from Marseille and then returned to his father, where he took over the business years later. He once had to travel to Blida to discuss a rather important transaction with his uncle, and while he was there the uncle was murdered and all his money stolen. Suspicion fell on an Armenian trader, and the younger Galingré left home because he felt that the police weren't making sufficient efforts. He never came back. His father became the uncle's heir and thus doubled his fortune, but he still mourns his son and would give a great deal if he could find a trace of him."

"Well, I can put you on the trail."

"You?" Isla asked, astonished.

"Yes. I don't understand why you did not mention all this before. I told you in Egypt that the Abu Nassr whom Omar is looking for killed a Frenchman in the Wadi Tarfaui, and that I took possession of his things. Didn't I also tell you that the name of that Frenchman was Paul Galingré?"

"You did not mention the name to me."

"I still have his wedding ring on my finger. The other things were in my saddle pouch and unfortunately were lost when my horse sank into the Shott Djerid."

"Surely you will let the old man know of his son's death, Effendi?"

"Of course."

"Will you write him?"

"I'll see. A letter would be too sudden, but on my way home I may pass through that region. I'll have to think about it."

After this conversation I went to look for Halef, who at first refused to believe that his shot had missed but finally admitted the possibility. "Sidi, my arm must have trembled after all," he said apologetically.

"No doubt about it."

"But the man in the water uttered a shout and disappeared. We did not see his head again."

"That was probably deliberate, and smart. He must be a good swimmer. And I should say, my dear Halef, that we acted very foolishly. Do you really believe that a man who is shot through the head can still shout?"

"I don't know, Sidi," he grumbled. "I have never been shot through the head. Should that happen, and I pray to Allah it doesn't, for Hanneh's sake, I'll try it. But tell me, Sidi, do you think we'll find the trail of that dog again?"

"I hope so."

"Through the innkeeper?"

"Through either him or the dervish, for I suspect Ali Manach and Abrahim know each other. I am going to talk to that dervish before the day is out."

I also visited Baruch, who was occupying a small room in our garden house with his wife. He had resigned himself to his changed circumstances and no longer complained about the minor losses yesterday's fire had caused him. He knew that the wealthy Maflei would keep his promise. During my absence in St. Dimitri and Pera, Baruch had already been back to Baharije Koy. He told me that many houses had been destroyed by the flames. We were still talking when a black servant of Maflei's came to tell me that an officer was there to see me.

"What is his rank?"

"Captain."

"Let him wait."

I did not consider it appropriate to go to any trouble because of this man and therefore did not go to the main building but into my own room. Halef was there and I told him about the visitor.

"Sidi," he said. "That captain was rude to you. Are you going to be polite?"

"Yes."

"You think that will shame him? Very well, then I will also be very polite. Permit me, as your servant, to receive him."

Halef stepped outside while I sat down on my divan and lit my pipe. After a few moments I heard steps and then the voice of the little Hadji, who was asking the black servant, "Where are you going?"

"I am supposed to take this aga to the foreign effendi."

"You mean to the effendi from Almanja. It's a good thing you ran into me first. You don't seem to realize that one cannot simply barge into the room of such a gentleman as one can into that of a shoemaker or a tailor. The effendi whom Allah gave me as master is accustomed to the greatest politeness in those who have dealings with him."

"Where is your effendi?" I heard the imperious voice of the captain.

"Permit me, your eminence, first to ask who you are," Halef answered politely.

"Your effendi will discover for himself who I am."

"But I don't know whether the effendi will consent to see you. He is a strict master and I cannot let someone see him without first asking his permission."

With some amusement I pictured to myself the humble amiability of the little rascal as he stood up to the grim and gruff officer who had to execute the order of his superior and could not turn back, although he would probably have liked nothing better.

"Is your effendi really such a great and important person? People like that don't live in the sort of place we saw last night."

"The effendi did that because it amused him. He was bored, and decided to see how entertaining it might be when sixty brave soldiers capture twenty boys and girls but let the grownups get away. The effendi really enjoyed that, and he is now resting on his divan, holding his kef, which I would prefer not to disturb."

"You are wounded. Weren't you there yesterday?"

"I was. It was I who was standing downstairs by the door where a guard should have been posted. But I see that you would like to converse with me. Permit me to bring you a chair, captain."

"Wait. I really think you are serious. Tell your effendi that I wish to speak to him."

"And if he asks who you are?"

"Then say that I am the captain from last night."

"Very well, I will ask him to let his kindness shine on you and to permit you to enter. I know how far one may extend oneself for a man of your dignity."

Halef entered and closed the door behind him. He was beaming. "Should he sit by your side?" he asked softly.

"No. Take those cushions over there and place them

close to the door, but with the greatest politeness. And then you will bring him coffee and a pipe."

"Do you also want coffee?"

"No. I am not going to drink with him."

The Hadji opened the door. With a humble "the effendi permits" he allowed the waiting officer to enter.

The man inclined his head slightly and began: "I have come to . . ."

A quick gesture of mine made it unambiguously clear to the officer that I wanted him to be silent. He did not seem to feel that a polite greeting to a Frank was called for, and so I was going to show him that even a Christian may be used to respect.

The captain was still standing by the door. Halef placed the cushions directly before his feet and left the room. The captain's face was a study in conflicting emotions: indignation, surprise, and shame were all struggling for supremacy. But he submitted to the inevitable and sat down. To take his place at the door of a Christian clearly required a considerable effort of self-control. Because there is always a ready supply of boiling water in the Orient, Halef soon returned with coffee and fire. The Turk drank the coffee and allowed his pipe to be lit. Halef posted himself behind the guest and the conversation could now begin.

"My son," I began in a friendly, paternal fashion— although this undoubtedly sounded rather strange since I was no older than my visitor—"My son, I ask that you remember a few of the things I am going to tell you. When one enters the residence of a cultivated person, one greets him, for otherwise one will be considered either mute or ignorant. Nor should one ever be the first to speak but wait until one is addressed, for the master of the house has the right to decide when a conversation should begin. Judging another without knowing him entails frequent error, and often it is only a small step from error to humiliation. You will take these well-meant words to heart, for experience has an obligation to instruct youth. And now you may tell me what request you would like to make of me."

The man had lowered his pipe and was so dumfounded by my manner that his mouth fell open. Then he burst out, "It is not a request I am conveying but an order!"

"An order? It is always advantageous to speak slowly, my son, for that is the only way to avoid saying things one has not considered beforehand. I know of no one in this city who could give me orders. You must mean that you yourself were given an order and therefore came to me, considering that you are a subordinate and I a free man. Who is sending you to me?"

"The man who was in command yesterday."

"You mean Colonel . . ." I added the name which the soldier had given me the evening before.

The captain made a gesture of dismay and exclaimed, "You know his name!"

"As you hear. Does he have a request to make of me?"

"I am to order you not to look for him and not to discuss last night's events with anyone."

"I have already told you that no one may give me orders. Tell the colonel that the incident will be written up in tomorrow's paper. Since I accept no order, our conversation has come to an end. May Allah be with you."

I got up and walked into the adjoining room. The captain was so dazed that he continued sitting there silently, and it was only a while later that Halef told me he had left, cursing loudly.

It was practically certain that the colonel would send another messenger almost immediately. Since I had no inclination to wait for this, I got ready to leave for the monastery of the dervishes to speak to Ali Manach.

When I arrived the dervish was sitting in his cell, praying. When he finished he looked up. Judging by his expression, my visit was not agreeable to him.

He politely answered my greeting and asked, "Are you bringing me another gift, perhaps?"

"I don't know yet. First of all, tell me how to address you—Ali Manach Ben Barud el Amasat, or 'En Nassr'?"

He jumped up from his cushions and stood directly in front of me. "Don't talk here," he whispered fearfully. "Go out to the cemetery. I'll join you in a moment."

So far so good, I told myself. But I also realized that I would have to make up some misleading phrases if I did not wish to show my hand. I left the building, crossed the courtyard, and entered the cemetery by the gate. I had not gone far when I saw the dervish approach. Seemingly meditating, he walked to a remote corner where I followed him.

"What message do you bring?" Ali Manach asked me.

I had to be cautious, and so held back. "First I have to get to know you. Are you reliable?"

"Ask the usta.* He knows me well."

"Where do I find him?"

"In Dimitri, at Koletis'. We were in Baharije Koy until yesterday but were discovered and driven away. The master was almost shot. He saved himself only by swimming."

Thus Dawuhd Arafim was the leader of the gang, and had spoken the truth in Baalbek. But the dervish had mentioned someone who brought to mind an earlier experience. Hadn't the Greek whom I had captured during the battle in the "Valley of the Steps" been called Alexandros Koletis?

"Is it safe in Koletis' house?" I asked.

"Perfectly. Do you know where it is?"

"No. I haven't been here long."

"Where do you come from?"

"Esch Sham, where I met the master."

"He was there but he was unsuccessful. A Frank recognized him and he had to flee."

"I know. He did not get all of Afarah's jewels. Have they been sold?"

"No."

"Are you certain?"

"Quite. My father and I enjoy his confidence."

"I came here to discuss these jewels with him. I know a dependable person who will buy all of them. Can he lay his hands on them quickly?"

"They are hidden at a safe place in the tower of

---

* Usta means leader, chief.

Galata. You may be too late, for Koletis' brother also found a buyer who promised to come tonight."

This troubled me. "Where is your father? I have an important message for him."

"In Edirne, at the merchant Hulam's."

This startled me—there was obviously another bit of mischief in the making—but I controlled myself. "I thought as much," I said with an appearance of confidence. "This Hulam is a relative of that Jakub Afarah in Damascus, and he is also related to the trader Maflei here."

"I see you know everything. I can trust you."

"You might tell me where I can find your uncle, Hamd el Amasat."

"You know him too?" The dervish was obviously surprised.

"Very well. He has been in the Saharah and in Egypt."

His surprise grew. He seemed to take me for an important member of his charming gang, for now he asked, "Are you the leader in Esch Sham, by chance?"

"Don't ask questions now. Just answer mine."

"Hamd el Amasat is at present in Scutari. He is staying at the house of a French merchant called Galino or Galineh."

"You mean Galingré?"

"It's amazing how much you know!"

"Yes, except for one thing. What does the usta call himself now?"

"He is from Konya and calls himself Abd el Myrhatta."

"I thank you. You will soon hear from me again."

The humbleness with which Ali Manach answered my farewell proved to me that I had succeeded in deceiving him. Now not a moment must be lost, otherwise my present advantage might come to nothing. Without returning to Maflei, I rode to Dimitri to inquire about Koletis at the tavern. The innkeeper wasn't there but his wife was. I first asked about the barber and was told that a physician had come and applied a fresh bandage. Then, a short while ago, the wounded man had been picked up. I then inquired about Koletis.

The woman looked at me in surprise: "Koletis? That's my husband's name."

"I didn't know that. Is there a man from Konya here whose name is Abd el Myrhatta?"

"Yes."

"Where is he now?"

"He went for a walk to the tower of Galata."

"By himself?"

"With my husband's brother."

What a lucky coincidence! Were the two conspirators on their way to pick up the valuables? I had to follow them. As I rushed out the door, I was told that they had left only a short while ago and that Omar had still been at the tavern. He had left the house shortly after they had. I got on my horse and trotted down to Galata. In the dark streets of this quarter, full of sailors, soldiers, filthy potters, porters, importunate shipmasters, and other hurried individuals, it was not easy to make one's way. But the crush was even denser at the tower.

Something unusual must have happened, for the pushing and shoving was almost dangerous to life and limb. I paid the owner of my rented horse and moved closer to inquire. A boatman who was working his way out of the crowd told me, "Two men climbed up on the platform of the tower and fell over the railing. Their battered bodies are lying on the ground."

This was disquieting. Omar had followed the two men. Had he perhaps had an accident? Relentlessly I pushed forward. Inside a tight circle formed by the crowd I saw two horrible-looking human bodies. The platform of the tower of Galata is forty-four and a half meters high, and the reader can imagine what these corpses looked like. I could tell from the clothes that Omar was not one of them. The face of one of the men was uninjured and I recognized immediately that it was the same Alexandros Koletis who had escaped from the Haddedihn. But it was impossible to tell who the other one might be. He had had a horrible death, as someone who had seen the accident told me. As he was falling he had managed to clutch onto the lower section of a bar but been able to hold on for barely a minute. Involuntarily I glanced at his hands and no-

: 323 :

ticed a cut running across his right one, certainly the hand by which he had tried to hold on. So this had been no accident; he had been thrown.

But where was Omar? I pushed toward the tower, went inside and paid a baksheesh for permission to climb it. I rushed up the five sets of stone steps through the five lower stories, then the following three wooden stairs. As I arrived at the coffee bar I saw only the Kahwedshi; there were no customers. One hundred forty-three steps had led up here, and I now climbed forty-five more to the belfry, which is covered by sheet metal and slopes steeply. From there I vaulted out on the gallery and examined this area, which is some fifty paces long. There were several spots of blood on the side overlooking the ground where the dead were lying. A struggle had taken place here before they had been thrown down, a struggle at this height, on a smooth, sloping floor, and, as I suspected, of two against one. It was dreadful.

Without stopping at the coffee bar, I quickly rushed back down and home. The first person I ran into in the selamlik was Jakub Afarah, who was radiant.

He embraced me and exclaimed, "Effendi, share my joy! I have my jewels back!"

I was amazed. "How is that possible?"

"Your friend Omar Ben Sadek brought them."

"Where did he get them?"

"I don't know, Effendi. He gave me the package and then hurried into the garden house and locked himself into his room. He won't open for anyone."

"Perhaps he'll make an exception in my case."

Halef was standing at the door of the garden house. He came toward me and asked in a whisper, "Effendi, what happened? Omar Ben Sadek came home bleeding. He is washing his wound."

"He ran into Abrahim Mamur in Galata and threw him off the tower."

"Mashallah! Is that true?"

"I am merely guessing, but pretty sure. Of course no one must know about this. Don't speak of it."

I walked to Omar's room and loudly gave my name. He opened immediately and also let Halef enter. Without being asked he reported what had happened.

Omar had come to Koletis' with the physician whom he had escorted and then returned with the porters who went to pick up the barber. He had seen Dawuhd Arafim and Alexandros Koletis, whom he did not know, quietly talking to each other. He had understood a few words they said, become attentive, and got up and left the room but entered an empty adjoining one by the next door along the corridor. Because the two men believed they were alone, they had begun talking more loudly, and Omar had heard their conversation.

They had discussed the jewels from Damascus which they wanted to pick up at the tower, where one of the guards was a member of the gang. Halef had told Omar about the theft in Damascus, and now he realized that one of the men he had just seen was Dawuhd Arafim, or Abrahim Mamur, as we called him. The further course of the conversation confirmed this hunch, for Abrahim recounted how he had fled across the Golden Horn the evening before. Omar went back to the other room and decided to follow the two to the tower. When they left he followed surreptitiously. They spent considerable time with one of the guards on the filthy ground floor of the tower, which served as a chicken coop, and then went up the stairs. Omar followed them. Each of them had a cup of coffee, and then Abrahim and the Greek resumed their climb. The guard remained behind. As Omar entered the belfry, the conspirators were standing on the platform, their backs turned toward him. The package containing the jewels was lying in the belfry. Omar moved closer to them and then out on the platform. At this moment the two men saw him.

"What do you want?" Abrahim asked. "Didn't I just see you at Koletis'?"

"What business is that of yours?" Omar answered.

"Are you eavesdropping on us, you son of a dog?" When he heard this insult, Omar remembered that he was a son of the free and brave Uelad Merasig, and this gave him the pride and courage of a lion.

"Yes, I eavesdropped on you," he said boldly. "You are Abrahim Mamur, a kidnaper of young girls, and Dawuhd Arafim, the jewel thief whose hideaway we smoked out yesterday. Revenge is about to be taken on you. I bring you greetings from the German effendi who took Senitza away from you and drove you out of Damascus. Your time has come!"

Abrahim Mamur stood there as though petrified Omar seized him with lightning speed and swung him over the railing. Koletis screamed and unsheathed his dagger. But the struggle lasted only a moment. Omar had been scratched quite deeply in the back of the neck, and the pain redoubled his strength. The second man was also sent flying over the railing.

Then Omar noticed that Abrahim was holding on with one hand. He slashed his enemy across it, and Abrahim let go.

All this had happened much more quickly than can be told. Omar had returned to the belfry, picked up the package, and left. Although a great many people had already gathered around the two bodies, he had managed to slip away unnoticed.

The young Arab recounted all this as casually as if it were an everyday occurrence while I bandaged his harmless scratch and refrained from pointless comment. Then he went with us to the main building, where his report found an entirely different response. Maflei, his brother, and Isla jumped up and rushed off to have a look at the corpses. On their return they told us that the bodies had been taken to the ground floor of the tower for the time being, that no one had been able to identify the dead, and that they had not let on that they could.

I asked Halef if he wasn't curious to have a look at his old friend, the Greek interpreter Koletis, but he answered contemptuously, "If it were Kara Ben Nemsi or Hadji Halef Omar, I would go. But this Greek is a toad, and I don't want to see him."

Maflei and his relatives needed some time before they could express themselves calmly about the death of the leader of the gang. "That was no adequate punishment for Abrahim Mamur," Isla said. "To feel the fear of death for a short instant is not sufficient retribution for all he has done. What a pity he wasn't caught alive."

"There are still the two Amasat," his father added. "I

wonder if each of us might not perhaps get his hands on one of them?"

"Barud el Amasat should be enough for you; the other did you no harm," I said. "If you promise me to do nothing violent but to turn him over to a judge, I'll get him for you."

This caused more excitement, but although I was assailed by questions and requests, I remained firm and said nothing until they had given me the promise I demanded. Then I told them about the talk I had had with the dervish that day.

I had barely finished when Jakub exclaimed, "Allah kerim! I can guess what those people want. They are after our entire family because Isla took Senitza from Abrahim Mamur. Our relative, Afrak Ben Hulam, was murdered. Then I was to be made a poor man, but that failed. Now they are going to Edirne, and after that it will be Maflei's turn. They have already begun with his business friend. We must write immediately and warn Hulam and Galingré!"

"Write?" Isla asked. "That's no good! We have to travel to Adrianople ourselves to catch this Barud el Amasat. Effendi, are you coming with us?"

"Yes. It's the best plan, and I'll go with you, since Edirne lies on the route I have to take back home."

"You are going home, Effendi?"

"Yes. I have stayed away much longer than I had intended."

This decision was opposed by everyone. But when I explained my reasons more thoroughly all conceded that I was right. During this friendly dispute only one person remained silent, and that was Halef. But I could tell from his contained agitation that he had more to say than the others.

"And when are we leaving?" asked Isla, who was in very much of a hurry.

"Immediately," Osko answered. "I don't want to lose a moment's time until I lay my hands on this Barud el Amasat."

"Certain preparations are necessary," I said. "If we set out early tomorrow it won't be too much of a delay and we'll have all the daylight. How are we going?"

"We'll take our horses," Maflei decided.

"And who is going?"

"I! I!" everyone shouted.

After some deliberation it was agreed that the following would go: Jakub Afarah, who really had no business with Barud but wanted to use this opportunity to visit his relative; Isla, who would not hear of missing a chance to seize his wife's tormentor; Osko, who wanted to avenge his daughter's kidnapping; Omar, who had to go from Adrianople to Scutari to settle with Hamd el Amasat; and finally myself, who was eager to return home. It was difficult to persuade Maflei to stay behind, but he had to see to his affairs.

Halef still said nothing during all this. When I asked his opinion, the loyal little fellow said, "Do you perhaps think I would let you go alone, Sidi? Allah brought us together, and I shall stay with you."

"But think of Hanneh, the flower of womankind. You are moving farther and farther away from her."

"Be still. You know that I always do what I plan. I am coming along!"

"But the day will come when we will have to separate."

"Sidi, that will be soon enough, and who knows if we will ever see each other again. This way I will at least not say farewell before the others, and until I know that you are quitting the land of the padishah." The Hadji rose and left the room to cut off further objections, and so I had no choice but to take this loyal servant who had become my friend even farther away from his home.

My travel preparations were simple. Halef and I merely had to saddle the horses and we were ready. But I did have one obligation before leaving, and that was to look up Lindsay to tell him what had happened and what our plans were.

He welcomed me, half pleased, half sulking, and said, "What a bad fellow you are, moving to Baharije Koy without taking me along! What did you come for, eh?"

"Sir David, I must tell you that I am no longer living in Baharije Koy."

"Oh? All right, move in with me."

"Thank you, but I am leaving this city tomorrow. Do you want to come along or not?"

"That's a bad joke."

"I am serious, I assure you."

"Are you really? Why this hurry? You just got here."

"I know Constantinople as well as I care to, and though I am leaving earlier than expected, I don't regret it." I now told him in some detail what had happened.

When I finished he nodded, satisfied, and said, "Splendid that this criminal met with his reward. You'll get the other two as well. I'd like to join you but I can't. I have certain obligations."

"Of what sort?"

"I was at the consulate and ran into my cousin. He wants to go to Jerusalem, knows nothing about traveling, and asked me to come along. Too bad you can't join us! Well, I'll look in on Maflei tonight and say my goodbyes."

"That's what I wanted to ask of you, Sir David. In the course of a few months you and I have experienced more than others during a lifetime. That brings people close. I have become fond of you and leaving you grieves me, but one must bow to the inevitable. There is the hope that we will see each other again."

"Yes, well. But I really don't care for this separation," the Englishman said in an uncertain voice as he raised one hand to his nose, the other to his eyes. "And there is something else that occurs to me. What's going to happen to Rih?"

"What do you mean? I am taking him."

"Hm. From here on? Are you taking him back to Germany?"

"I don't know yet."

"Sell him, sir! You'll get a good price. Think about it. And if you need him now, you can send him to England later. I won't quibble, I'll pay whatever you ask."

This was a troublesome topic for me. What was a poor writer going to do with such a horse? My circumstances did not permit me to keep him once I was back home. But sell him? The precious gift of the

Haddedihn sheik? I would not be able to keep Rih, but neither would I sell him. This splendid animal that had carried me through so many dangers deserved a master who knew how to treat him. He must not perish in the cold north but return to the pastures of the south, the country of his birth, the camps of the Haddedihn.

Lindsay ordered a bottle of wine and we talked for a while about the "Oriental Question." Then I left, because Sir David intended to pay a visit to Maflei that evening. I went to the French legation, where I again saw the official in charge. He told me that the so-called barber would no longer be any trouble to anyone, since he had died. He had had to reveal his identity and thus it had been learned that he was an escaped criminal. I felt sorry for this young man whose exceptional gifts might have opened up other prospects than a miserable death in a foreign country.

That evening all of us, including Senitza, had dinner together. Being Christian she could let her face be seen at home, though Isla did not permit her to go out unveiled. Once again she spoke to us of her experiences, the grief she had felt during her captivity, the happiness when she was liberated from Abrahim Mamur's power.

Finally Lindsay took his leave. His boil was almost gone and there was thus no reason why he should not return to London after his journey to Jerusalem. I went back with him to his apartment, where he uncorked a bottle of wine and assured me that he loved me like a brother. "I am very pleased with you," he said. "There's only one thing that annoys me."

"And what's that, Sir David?"

"I've let you drag me around and I never found a single winged bull. It's vexing!"

"I think you can find them in England, and without even having to excavate. I should think any number of them would be running around there."

"You don't mean me, by any chance?"

"I wouldn't dream of it, Sir David."

"Very well. Have you thought about the horse?"

"I have. I won't sell."

"Then keep him. But you must come to England

nonetheless. I'll be back home in two months. And here's one more thing: you have been my guide, and I haven't yet paid your wages. Take this."

He pushed a full wallet toward me.

"No jokes, Sir David Lindsay." I laughed as I pushed it back. "I rode with you as your friend, not as a servant to be paid wages."

"But, sir, I think . . ."

"Think what you please but not that I would take money from you," I interrupted him. "Farewell!"

"Come and take this money!"

"Farewell, Sir David." I embraced him quickly and hurried out, ignoring his shouts. It had not been difficult for me to turn down the money the goodhearted Englishman had offered me. My watch and a bag full of money which I had lost in the subterranean corridors of Baalbek had been in the package Omar captured at the tower of Galata. Besides, I had carried an adequate sum sewn into a sleeve of my jacket.

When the run rose in the east, we had almost reached Tshataldsha, which lies on the road leading to Andrianople.

# 16 : In Edirne

Adrianople, called Edirne by the Turks, is the second most important city of the Ottoman Empire, after Constantinople. Here the sultans from Murad the First to Mehmed the Second held court. The latter conquered Constantinople in 1453 and moved the seat of government there, yet Edirne continued to be the favorite residence of many sultans, especially Mehmed the Fourth.

Of the more than forty mosques in the city the "great mosque" built by Selim the Second is well known. Even larger than the Hagia Sophia in Constantinople, it is the work of the famous architect Sinan. Like an oasis in the desert, it stands among a conglomeration of wooden buildings whose many-colored walls rise above the filth and debris scattered along the streets. On the inside its splendid cupola is supported by four massive pillars while four miraculously slender minarets, each with three ring-shaped balconies for the muezzin, enliven its exterior. The structure contains two sets of circular walks, built of the most valuable marble, which receive their light from two hundred and fifty windows. During Ramadan, the month of the fast, more than twelve thousand candles burn here.

We were coming from Kirk Kilissa and had already discerned the slim minarets of the mosque from a considerable distance. Seen from afar, Adrianople offers a splendid sight, but when we had reached it and were riding through its streets, our experience was the same as in all other Turkish cities: they lose their beauty seen close up.

On our way to Hulam, who lived near the mosque of Murad the Second, we finally came through a crowded alley and stopped by a two-story wall which was also the street side of the house. At head height, behind a circular opening in the gate, a bearded face appeared when Isla rapped the knocker.

"Do you still know me, Malhem?" the young man asked. "Open up!"

"Mashallah!" we heard from inside. "Is it really you, master? Hurry in!"

The gate was opened and we rode through a kind of passage into a fairly large courtyard which was framed by the arcades of the house. Everything here, including the number of servants rushing toward us, gave evidence of great wealth.

"Where is the master?" Isla asked the man who had greeted him with profound respect and was, as I learned later, the major-domo.

"In his study with his books."

"Take these men into the Selamlik and see that they are well served. The horses must also be taken care of."

Because it was their sad duty to inform their relative of the death of his son, Afrak Ben Hulam, who had been murdered by Dawuhd Arafim or his accomplices, Isla and Jakub Afarah went to the study. The rest of us were taken into a room with the dimensions of a small hall; its anterior section was open and supported by pillars while the other three walls, gold on a blue background, were decorated with quotations from the Koran.

Dusty as we were, we settled down on divans covered in green velvet. Each of us was given a water pipe and coffee in small cups resting on silver tripods. Everything we saw gave an impression of solid wealth. After some time Jakub Afarah and Isla Ben Maflei came in with the master of the house. Hulam's appearance was such that it would have been unthinkable to remain seated even if custom and his grief-stricken face had not demanded a show of deference.

"Es-selam 'aleikum!" he greeted us, raising his hands as though in blessing. "Welcome in my house! Consider it yours!" He greeted each of us in turn and then joined us with his two relatives. They also were served coffee and given pipes. Hulam signaled and the ser-' vants withdrew. Then Isla introduced us to him.

"Perhaps you don't realize yet that you are well known to me, Effendi," the master of the house addressed me. "Isla has told me a great deal about you. He is very fond of you and so you are also very dear to me although we have never seen each other."

"Your words ease me," I answered. "We are not in the desert or on the pasture of a Bedouin tribe, and so it is not always certain that one will be welcome."

"True. Year by year the fine customs of our fathers are losing ground. They are disappearing in the cities and withdrawing to the desert in sorrow. The desert is the birthplace of need, but Allah allows the palm of brotherly love to grow there. In the great cities the stranger therefore feels more lonely than in the Sahara where no roof hides Allah's sky from him. I have heard that you have been in the Sahara. Haven't you found that this is so?"

"Allah is wherever man believes in him. He lives in the cities, and looks on the Hammada. The Omniscient wakes over the waters and rustles in the darkness of the jungle. He creates in the interior of the earth, and in the air. The All-knowing guides the flight of the glowworm and the course of the shining sun. You hear

Allah in the exultation of pleasure and the call of pain. His eye shines in the tear of joy and shimmers in the drop with which grief moistens the cheek. I have been in cities with a population of millions, and I have been in the desert, far away from all human habitation, but I was never afraid of being alone, for I knew that God's hand held me. And it is also God who supports those that are struck by sorrow and gives them the strength to continue with their life and to give it new meaning."

"Effendi, you are a Christian, and yet a devout person. You are worthy of being a Muslim and I respect you as if the teaching of the Prophet were yours. Allah gives joy and grief, and we can only calmly accept both, for we are powerless to change what was decreed at the creation of the universe. Afrak, my son whom I sent to Esch Sham to further his knowledge and thus to become a better councilor in my house and during my old age, is dead—murdered by a scoundrel who lusted after his possessions. But the murderer was also overtaken by a just fate. Allah kerim—God is merciful, and His mercy should be a consolation to us."

Hulam fell silent, and in our silence we respected the wordless grief of this old man to whom the firmness of his faith gave an almost incomprehensible composure.

After a while he went on, "Isla told me that you have come to preserve me from great loss. Speak for the others."

"Then Isla did not tell you all the circumstances?"

"No, we spoke only of Afrak and his murderer."

"Then tell me if a stranger has been living in your house for some time."

"A stranger does live here, a devout person from Konya. But he is not in Edirne today. He rode to Tatar."

"From Konya? And his name?"

"Abd el Myrhatta. He has visited the grave of the famous Saint Myrhatta to fulfill a vow, which is the reason he calls himself Myrhatta's servant."

"Why is he staying in your house?"

"I invited him. He intends to buy a large business in Brussa and will make considerable purchase here."

"Is there a second stranger living here?"

"No."

"When will your guest return?"

"Tonight."

"Then he will be our prisoner tonight."

"Allah kerim! What do you mean? This devout Muslim is a man God takes pleasure in. Why should you wish to take him prisoner?"

"Because he is a cheat, and worse. He saw that you are a devout servant of Allah and hid behind a mask of piety. He is the man who kidnaped Senitza, Isla's wife. Ask Isla to tell you."

Hulam was startled, and when Isla had made his report the old merchant still could not believe he was dealing with a hardened criminal. He could not take in that someone might wear a mask so skillfully.

"You should first see and talk to him," he said, "and then you will agree that you are mistaken."

"There is no need to talk to him," Osko said. "We have only to see him, for I know him and so does Isla."

"You need neither see nor talk to him," I added. "I am certain that it is Barud el Amasat. Abd el Myrhatta is also the name Afrak's murderer used in Constantinople."

"But my guest could be the genuine Abd el Myrhatta," Hulam objected a little stubbornly.

"That is possible but not likely. We will have to wait until tonight."

There was nothing further to be said or done in this matter. According to ancient custom, each of us was given a room and, after a bath, we put on the clean clothes that had been laid out for us. Then we all gathered for a meal that was in keeping with the wealth of our host. Hulam did not refer to his son's death again. He was too considerate a man to wish to afflict us with his grief.

Impatiently we waited for evening, trying to kill time talking and playing chess. It was not advisable to go outdoors, since I considered it probable that Barud el Amasat had lied about riding to Tatar. He certainly had accomplices in town who required his presence more urgently than anything in that small place where he probably had no business whatever. Finally, darkness fell, and we withdrew into Isla's room because we wanted to stay together. Hulam had told us that he and his guest would have dinner in the selamlik and we had decided that Isla and Osko would surprise the impostor during the meal while the three of us made sure he could not escape.

Another two hours passed before we heard hoofbeats in the courtyard, and a quarter of an hour later a servant informed us that the master and his guest had sat down to dinner. We went downstairs. The gate was locked and the guard had been instructed to let no one out. We quietly moved toward the selamlik, which was now brightly lit by a Turkish hanging lamp of colored glass. Standing behind the pillars we could hear every word the two spoke during the meal. Hulam, who was paying close attention, had become aware of our approach and gave the conversation a skillful turn.

He began speaking of Constantinople, and asked, "Have you often been in Istanbul?"

"A few times," his guest answered.

"Then you know the city somewhat?"

"Yes."

"Do you also know a quarter called Baharije Koy?"

"I believe I have heard the name. Doesn't it lie above Eyüp, on the left side of the Golden Horn?"

"Yes. Something rather curious happened there recently. They took an entire gang of criminals and murderers prisoner."

"Allah!" the man exclaimed, startled. "How did that happen?"

"That scum owned a house to which people were admitted only if they knew the password 'En Nassr,' and . . ."

"How can that be?" his guest interrupted. The tone with which these words were uttered did not convey the revulsion of the impartial listener but the fear of someone that is implicated.

I was convinced now that this man was the one we

were looking for, and Osko, who was standing beside me, whispered softly, "It's Barud el Amasat. I see his face clearly."

"Some people overheard this password," our host went on, "and so got inside." Hulam then recounted the circumstances and his guest listened with considerable agitation. When the story had been told, Barud el Amasat asked with a trembling voice; "and was the usta really dead?"

"The usta? Who is that? Who goes by that name?"

"I mean the leader whom you called Dawuhd Arafim and Abrahim Mamur."

By using the term "usta" the criminal had given himself away.

Even Hulam could not but be aware of this, though he did not show it but answered, "No, not at first. He made believe he had been hit by a shot. But fate overtook him the following day. He was hurled from the platform of the tower of Galata."

"Really? How horrible! Did he die?"

"Yes, and a Greek by the name of Koletis was also thrown down and died with him."

"Koletis? Who killed them?"

"An Arab from Tunis, from the region around the Shott Djerid, who is carrying out a blood feud against a certain Hamd el Amasat. This Hamd el Amasat murdered a French merchant in Blida and later also killed the father of that Arab on the Shott. The son is now searching for the murderer."

"Allah kerim! What evil people there are in the world! That's because no one any longer believes in the teachings of the Prophet. Will the Arab find this Hamd el Amasat?"

"He's already on his trail. The murderer has a brother who is just as big a scoundrel. He kidnaped the daughter of a friend and sold her into slavery. She was taken away from the buyer, who was none other than this Abrahim Mamur, and Isla Ben Maflei, a relative of mine, married her. He has set out to find and punish this Barud el Amasat."

As he listened to this, Barud had become increasingly fearful. He had lost his appetite, his agitation was growing, and his glance was fixed on the lips of his host. "Will Isla Ben Maflei find the abductor of the girl?"

"No doubt. Isla is not alone. Osko, the girl's father, is with him, and so are the Frankish physician who freed Senitza, his servant, and also the Arab who hurled Abrahim Mamur from the tower."

"Are they already on his trail?"

"These people know the name Barud el Amasat is using now."

"No! What does he call himself?"

"Abd el Myrhatta. The usta in Istanbul also went by that name."

"But that is my name!" The man sounded terrified.

"Yes indeed. God knows how they happened to hit on the name of such a devout person. May their punishment be twice as severe because of it!"

"And how was this name discovered?"

"I'll tell you. Barud el Amasat has a brother in the monastery of the dancing dervishes in Pera. The Frankish physician went to see him and made him believe he was a member of that gang. The young man let himself be taken in, gave him the name, and also told him that Hamd el Amasat is staying in Scutari, at the home of a merchant called Galingré."

Now the man could no longer sit still. He got up and excused himself. "This sounds so terrible, I cannot go on eating. And I am very tired from riding. Permit me to retire."

Hulam had also risen. "I can readily believe that you no longer feel like eating. Anyone who has to listen to such talk about himself must choke with fear."

"About himself? I don't understand you. Surely you don't believe that I am that Barud, just because the criminal took my name?"

"I don't believe it, I am convinced of it, you scoundrel!"

Taken by surprise, the man pulled himself together. "You are calling me a scoundrel? Don't ever do that again, otherwise . . ."

"Otherwise what?" said a voice from close by. Isla had jumped forward and was standing next to Barud.

"Isla Ben Maflei!" the unmasked criminal exclaimed in dismay.

"Yes, Isla Ben Maflei, who knows you and whom you cannot deceive. Look around. There's someone else here who has something to say to you."

Barud el Amasat turned and saw Osko standing before him. He realized that he was lost unless he could flee quickly. "The devil brought you here! May you go to hell!"

With this shout, he pushed back Isla and was about to run. He had already reached the pillars when Halef stepped forward and tripped him. As he fell to the ground, we seized him and took him back into the selamlik. The man was a coward. Seeing himself surrounded, he did not offer the slightest resistance but quietly let himself be tied up and placed on the floor.

"Do you still believe in the piety of this man?" the little Hadji asked our host. "He was going to rob you, and then flee."

"You were right," Hulam admitted. "What's going to happen to him now?"

Osko stretched out his arm. "Barud el Amasat abducted my daughter and drove me out into the world to look for her. I have suffered much grief and pain. He is mine, according to the laws of the Black Mountains."

"Those laws have validity only in the Black Mountains, not here," I interposed. "Besides, the prince of your country has rescinded those laws. You promised me to turn this man over to a judge, and I hope you will keep your word!"

"Effendi, the judges here are disreputable," the Montenegrin objected. "They will accept bribes and give Barud an opportunity to escape. I demand him for myself."

"What will you do with him if we turn him over to you?" Hulam asked.

Osko drew his dagger. "Barud will die by this blade!"

"I cannot allow that. He has spilled no blood."

"He was a member of the murderous gang in Istanbul."

"That's the very reason you must not kill him. Is his son to escape with impunity? And are all the rest that could not be caught to escape although they were among those who know the password 'En Nassr'? He must stay alive so he can tell us their names," said our host.

"And who will guarantee that my daughter's abductor will be punished?"

"I will. I shall immediately go to the judge so that he can arrest and incarcerate this man, and I swear to you by Allah and the Prophet that the cadi will do his duty."

"Go on, then," Osko grumbled darkly. "But I tell you that I shall hold you to your promise until I have been avenged."

Barud el Amasat was locked up and the fierce Osko insisted on being locked up with him. Hulam went to the official and we waited for the news he would bring. He returned with several policemen. Barud was handed over to them, and when the policemen left we could settle down for the night, knowing that we had preserved our host from harm and put an end to an evil man's machinations.

The judgment of a Turkish cadi is never delayed for long, so we decided to wait until sentence would be pronounced. This gave us a chance to do some sightseeing in Adrianople.

The following morning we visited the mosques of Selim and Murada, and a Turkish seminary. We then strolled through the famous Ali Pasha bazaar and finally took a barge down the Tundzha River on which the city lies. We went back at noon. The cadi had sent us a summons, and we soon appeared before him.

The interrogation was public, and a fair number of spectators had come. Each one of us had to make a statement in the presence of the prisoner, who was there to hear the charges.

When all of us had had our say, the cadi asked the accused, "You have heard what these men said. Is it true or not?" Barud did not answer, and after the cadi had waited a few moments he continued, "You can advance nothing to refute the accusation of these men, and so are guilty. Since you are a member of the gang that was active in Istanbul, I must take you there. In that city you will also be punished for the abduction of the girl. But because you had the temerity to plan a crime here in Edirne, you will be given one hundred strokes on the soles of your feet. This will be done immediately."

He signaled to the policemen standing near him and ordered them to get the board and the sticks. Two of them left to bring these implements. At that moment a movement developed among the spectators which, though insignificant, could not escape an attentive observer. A man was slowly making his way from the rear. I looked at him. He was tall and emaciated and wore the clothing of an ordinary Bulgarian, but I did not believe he was one. His long neck, his hawk's nose, the narrow face, the drooping moustache, the swelling chest, all suggested that he was an Armenian. Why was this man pushing his way forward? Merely because he was curious, or for some other reason? I decided to observe him closely but unobtrusively.

The policemen returned. One of them was carrying several of those dreaded cudgels indispensable· for a bastinado, the other a board with slings of hemp at one end and the center with which the arms and legs of the culprit are fastened. In back was a simple device that served to keep the legs raised, thus bringing the bare soles into a horizontal position.

"Take off his shoes," the cadi ordered.

As the officials stepped up to Barud to carry out this order, he finally showed that he was capable of speech. "Stop!" he shouted. "I will not let myself be caned."

The cadi's eyebrows contracted. "You won't?" he asked. "Who will forbid me to have you bastinadoed?"

"I will."

"You son of a dog! How dare you speak to me like this? Do you want me to double your punishment?"

"You may not even have me struck once! You spoke and inquired about a number of things but forgot the most important. Or did you perhaps so much as ask what and who I am?"

"That isn't necessary," the judge replied. "You are a murderer and a thief, that suffices."

"So far I have admitted nothing. And you cannot have me bastinadoed in any event."

"Why not?"

"Because I am not a Muslim but a Christian!"

During this exchange Barud el Amasat had become aware of the stranger, who was drawing closer. The man was careful not to make a gesture which might have made others suspect that he was in league with the accused. But his look and stance were calculated to attract Barud's attention and to give him courage.

"One could tell that the last remark had made some impression on the cadi. "So you are a Giaour?" he asked. "Perhaps even a Frank?"

"No, I am Armenian."

"But then you are a subject of the padisha, to whom Allah grants a thousand lives. And so there is no reason why you should not be bastinadoed."

"You are mistaken," Barud insisted, assuming as confident a posture as he could manage, and trying to give his tone a hint of pride. "I am not the sultan's subject, nor the patriarch's. I was born an Armenian but became an evangelical Christian and am employed as an interpreter at the English legation. At this moment I am a British subject, and I call your attention to the responsibility you assume if you treat me as the sultan's, let alone have me caned."

The cadi looked disappointed. He had wanted to be of real service to Hulam, a man of considerable standing in Adrianople, but the Armenian's statement seemed to thwart this intent.

"Prove it," he said ill-humoredly.

"Inquire at the English legation in Istanbul."

"It is not I but you who must furnish proof."

"I can't, since I am a prisoner."

"Then I will send a messenger there. But you will be given twice one hundred strokes should you have lied to me."

"I am telling the truth. And I am certainly not under your jurisdiction. If I am to be questioned by a cadi, the court must be properly constituted."

The judge was looking very annoyed now, and his eyes were flashing angrily. "Giaour," he exclaimed. "You know the laws, yet you infringed them! I'll see to it that your punishment is tripled!"

"Do as you please, and see if you can! In the name of the British envoy, I protest against the caning to which you have sentenced me!"

Embarrassed, the cadi looked at each of us in turn and then said to the prisoner, "The law obliges me to listen to what you are saying. But don't think that this will give your affair a more favorable turn. You are a murderer and have forfeited your life. Take him back to prison and guard him ten times more closely than the rest."

Barud was led away but not without having cast a glance of complicity at the stranger, who returned it, though this exchange had not been observed by anyone except me. Should I call the cadi's attention to this man? But what good would that do? Even if the prisoner knew the stranger, there were no reasons to take official action against him. Besides, I did not feel that the cadi was the man to deal with such wily individuals, and so I decided to quietly attend to this man myself.

The session was over and the spectators were dispersing. The cadi came up to Hulam to offer his apologies, and Osko turned angrily to me. "Didn't I predict, Effendi, that things would turn out this way?"

"I must confess I had not expected this," I admitted. "I am no cadi and no Muslim legal scholar, but I do believe that the judge could not have acted differently."

"Does he have to inquire in Istanbul whether this man told the truth or not?"

"Yes."

"And how long will that take?"

"There's nothing we can do about it."

"And suppose the criminal really is a British subject?"

"He'll be punished all the same."

"And if he isn't?"

"Then he lied and the cadi will do what he can and give him the severest possible sentence. In any event, I don't think there's a word of truth in that story about his being British."

"I wonder. Why should Barud el Amasat invent such a lie?"

"To escape being bastinadoed, to begin with, and then to gain time. We have to make clear to the cadi that the prisoner must be very tightly guarded. I am convinced he will do everything he can to break out."

"Don't you think you should speak to the cadi, Effendi?"

"You do it; I don't have the time. There is something urgent I must see to; perhaps I'll tell you about it later. We'll see each other at Hulam's."

The stranger whom I took to be an Armenian had left the court. Wanting to find out about him, I went after the man. He was walking slowly and thoughtfully, and I followed him for about ten minutes.

Suddenly he turned and saw me. I had been a conspicuous participant during the interrogation. He had seen me there and now recognized me immediately. He walked on but then turned into a narrow alley. I decided not to let him out of my sight and assumed the manner of a person immersed in my own affairs and heedless of others. The Armenian in Bulgarian garb had walked perhaps half the length of the alley when he turned again. I was still behind him, and this had to seem odd to him. We walked thus down several alleys. Occasionally he would turn to look at me, and I did not let him out of my sight. I was so intent on this that I no longer cared that he was aware of me. His trying to lose me confirmed my conviction that he did not have a clear conscience.

He probably realized this, for when he had once again turned into a small alley and I came around the corner half a minute later, he suddenly stood before me, looking at me with flashing eyes. "Are you following me perhaps?" he grumbled.

"What do you care where I walk?"

"I care a great deal. You seem to be taking the same direction I am."

"In that case there is no reason to worry, for I am walking a straight path."

"Do you mean to say that mine isn't?"

"I don't know yours, and have no dealings with you."

"I should hope not," he said sarcastically. "That's why I want you to walk ahead of me now."

"As you please," I answered curtly.

I walked on without turning my head, but my ears were sufficiently well trained not to be deceived by him. At first he kept behind me, but then the sound of his steps died away. Though they were meant to be inaudible, I could still hear them.

When I no longer did, I quickly turned and ran back. I had been right. Already some distance away, the man was entering into another alley. I followed, he was again turning a corner. A few moments later I stood at the same spot and saw him entering the Ali Pasha bazaar. The man assumed that I would lose him in the crowd, should I still be behind him, but actually nothing pleased me more than his decision, for precisely because of the bustle I could get close without being noticed, and this is what happened. I stayed hard on the Armenian's heels although he changed direction more than ten times. Finally, when we had just passed through the section where clothing is offered for sale, he walked toward a nearby caravanserai and entered it. If the place did not have a second exit, he would not be able to get away from me now.

But did he live here? I soon became convinced that he had merely been looking for a hiding place from which to watch me, for he had stopped behind the gate and was carefully scrutinizing the square out front.

I walked up to the nearest tradesman. "Do you have a red turban?"

"Yes, Effendi."

"And a coat?"

"As many as you like."

"I am in a hurry. I just want to borrow the two, not buy them. Quickly, give me the coat and the turban. Here is my watch and my arms. In addition, I'll give you my kaftan and five hundred piasters. All that should be enough of a guarantee that I will be back."

The tradesman looked at me in surprise. Most likely nothing like this had ever happened to him. "Why are you doing that, Effendi?"

To avoid further delay, I had to explain: "I am following a man who must not recognize me. Quickly, otherwise he'll get away!"

"Allah! Are you the secret police?"

"Don't ask questions, hurry! Or don't you know that the sultan demands your assistance when a fugitive criminal is to be arrested?"

By now the tradesman was convinced I was a policeman. I walked into the back of the open shop and took off my kaftan. The tradesman threw the coat over my shoulders and tied the turban around my head. When I had given him my things as security, I stepped back out and waited. I had not let the Armenian out of my sight. He was still on the lookout behind the gate.

The tradesman followed my glance, and when he saw the man I was watching he asked, "Effendi, do you mean the fellow standing by the gate over there?"

"Yes."

"Who just passed by here?"

"Yes."

"And greeted me?"

"I didn't notice. Are you an acquaintance of his?"

"Yes, I bought some clothes from him. You think he's a criminal?"

"I'll find out. What's his name?"

"You are the sultan's servant, so I'll be honest with you. Tell me what you want to know."

"Were the clothes you bought from him new?"

"No."

"So he is no tailor?"

"Oh no! I had a big loss. The clothes were cheap, but I had to return most of them because they belonged to people who had been attacked on the street."

"Wasn't this man punished?"

"He is a stranger here and could not be found. And when he came back and was arrested, they did nothing to him because he has money."

"Who is he?"

"He dresses like a Bulgar but is an Armenian by the name of Manach el Barsha."

"Do you know where he lives?"

"He is the tax collector for non-Muslims in Usküb."

"Where does he stay when he is here?"

"When he is in Edirne, he usually stays at Doxati's inn."

"Where do I find this Doxati?"

"The inn is right next door to the house of the Greek metropolite."

I didn't know where the metropolite lived either, but was in no position to reveal my ignorance of local conditions. Manach el Barsha was now leaving the caravanserai. I thanked the tradesman and followed him. The Armenian looked back a few more times but did not recognize me. In my present disguise there was no need to be as careful as before, and finally I saw him enter a house.

A chestnut vendor was doing business nearby. I bought a handful and asked, "Do you know who lives in that big house to the left?"

"The Greek metropolite, Effendi."

"And next door?"

"A handshi, Doxati by name. Do you wish to move in there? It's cheap and comfortable."

"No. I am looking for the innkeeper Mavro."

"I don't know him."

To avoid suspicion I had chosen the first name that occurred to me. In any event, further inquiries were unnecessary at this moment; I knew enough for the time being. I took note of the location of Docati's inn and returned to Hulam's, where everyone was waiting for me. The outcome of the trial had disappointed all of them, and then they had been unable to account for my sudden disappearance.

"Sidi," little Halef confessed, "I was quite worried about you."

"Why?"

"Don't you know yet that I am your friend and protector?"

"But I do, my dear Halef."

"Well then, if I am your friend you should tell me where you intend to go, and if I am your protector you should take me with you."

"I had no use for you."

"No use?" he asked, plucking violently at his moustache. "You had use for me in the Sahara, in Egypt, along the Tigris, among the devil worshipers, in the ruins whose name I can't remember just now, in Istanbul, and everywhere else besides. And now you say you have no use for me? I can't believe it! Do you know that it is just as dangerous here as in the Sahara or the Valley of the Steps where we took all those enemies prisoner?"

"How so?"

"Because there are so many people here one cannot see one's enemies. Or do you imagine I don't realize that you left because of some new enemy?"

"Where did you get that idea?"

"I follow your eyes, and see what they do."

"And what did they do?"

"At the cadi's they observed a Bulgar who wasn't one. When we left, you hurried off."

"Really, Halef, you observed well. The man seems to be acquainted . . ."

"With the prisoner," Halef interrupted.

"You are right again."

"Perhaps he means to do something for him."

"No doubt. The stranger cast Barud el Amasat some glances to reassure him, and he certainly didn't do that without reason."

"So you followed him to find out where he lives."

"I did. I also found out his name, and what he does."

"What does he do?"

"His name is Manach el Barsha, and he is a tax collector in Usküb. He's staying at Doxati's inn."

"Would you want me to watch this Manach el Barsha?"

"You guessed it."

"But I can do that only if I stay at Doxati's too."

"You'll ride there as soon as it gets dark. I'll come along to show you the house."

At this point Osko came up to us. "I'll also watch, Effendi."

"Where?"

"In front of the prison where Barud el Amasat has been locked up."

"You think that's necessary?"

"I don't care whether it is or not. Barud sold my daughter into slavery and caused me great grief. He cannot escape my revenge. You stated that it is not mine but God's, and I went along with you and left Barud in the cadi's hands. But if the abductor tries to evade punishment, I will see to it that he does not also escape me. I am leaving now and will report when I see something of consequence." With these words the Montenegrin departed.

Halef now packed his few possessions and mounted his horse. He wanted to give the impression that he had just arrived in Andrianople. I accompanied him on foot, and waited until he had entered the gate. Then I returned to the bazaar to change back into my own clothes.

When I got back to Hulam's, Isla Ben Maflei suggested that we visit a bathhouse where good coffee and fine preserves were served and there was an excellent shadow play. We agreed.

So much has been written about Turkish baths that it would be superfluous to add anything. The shadow play was nothing special, and while the preserves may have been excellent, they weren't to my taste. When we left the bath, the evening air was so delightful that we decided to go for a long walk, past the city limits and along the bank of the Arda, which flows into the Maritsa here.

It was perhaps an hour before midnight when we turned back, but still fairly light. We had not yet reached the city when three riders came toward us. Two were mounted on white horses, the third on a dark one. As they trotted past us one of them made a very inconsequential remark. I heard it and stopped involuntarily.

"What is it?" Isla asked. "Do you know those people?"

"No. But I thought I recognized the voice."

"I dare say you are mistaken, Effendi. Voices often sound alike."

"That's true, and it reassures me. Otherwise I would have thought that one of the horsemen was Barud el Amasat."

"That would mean he escaped!"

"True. But how could that be?"

"And if it were, he would have taken the wide road to Philippopolis, and not this deserted, unsafe route."

"But precisely this route would be safer for a fugitive than the busy one."

It was as if an inner voice were telling me that I had

not been mistaken. I began walking more rapidly. Back home Osko had been waiting for us for some time, standing under the gate.

"Finally, finally!" he shouted. "I have been looking for you impatiently. I have the impression that something has happened!"

"What?" I asked tensely.

"When it got dark, I was at the prison gate. Someone came and asked to be let in. He entered and came back out again some time later with two others."

"Did you recognize anyone?"

"No. As they left, I heard one of them say, 'That was quicker than I expected.' I became suspicious and followed but lost them at a corner."

"And then what?"

"Then I came here to report the incident to you."

"Very well. We'll soon find out. Hulam can join us but the others should stay here."

With Hulam I hurried down the street to Doxati's inn. The gate was still open and we entered. There was a common room which opened to the courtyard but had no window on the street side. Remaining outside, I ordered one of the servants to bring the innkeeper.

Doxati was a little old man with a crafty look. He made a deep bow and asked what he could do for me.

"Did someone come here this evening?" I asked after I had returned his greeting.

"Several did, Effendi."

"I mean a small man on horseback."

"He is here. He has a beard as thin as the tail of an old hen."

"You speak rather disrespectfully of your guests. But it's probably the man I am looking for. Where is he?"

"In his room."

"Show us the way."

"Follow me." Doxati preceded us into the courtyard and up some stairs. At the top he opened one of several doors. A lamp was burning here but the room, furnished with nothing more than a single mat, was empty.

"Is this where the little Arab is staying?"

"Yes."

"But he isn't here!"

"Allah knows where he went to."

"Where is his horse?"

"In the stable in the second courtyard."

"Did he join the other guests tonight?"

"Yes. But then he stood under the gate for a long time."

"I am also looking for someone called Manach el Barsha. Do you know him?"

"Why shouldn't I? He stayed here today."

"Do you mean he's no longer here?"

"Yes; he left."

"Alone?"

"No, with two friends."

"All on horseback?"

"Yes."

"What sort of horses?"

"Two whites and a brown."

"Where did they go?"

"They were going to ride to Philippopolis and then on to Sofia."

"Did you know his two friends?"

"No. Manach el Barsha went out and then came back with them."

"Did he bring the three horses along?"

"No, only the brown one. He bought the whites here this evening."

Now I knew that my ears had not deceived me down by the river. Barud el Amasat had made his escape with the help of this Manach el Barsha. And who was the third? Perhaps the turnkey at the prison who had let the prisoner out and therefore been obliged to join the fugitives?

I asked, "And the Arab didn't follow them?"

"No."

"Are you certain?"

"Absolutely. I was standing by the gate when the three rode off."

Doxati now took us across the anterior courtyard and through a vaulted passage to a low building. Still some distance away, I could tell that this was the stable. Doxati opened the door. It was dark inside but a gentle snorting indicated the presence of a horse.

"Someone put out the light," the innkeeper said.

"Was there one burning here?" I asked.

"Yes."

"Were the horses of the tax collector Manach el Barsha also here?"

"Yes. But I wasn't here when he took them out."

"Let's light the lamp." I took out a match and lit the lantern hanging from the wall. I recognized Halef's horse and, next to it, on the ground, a shapeless lump wrapped into a kaftan and tied together with rope. I pulled the rope loose and removed the kaftan. It was my little Hadji Halef. He jumped to his feet and clenched his fists.

"Sidi, where are those sons of dogs who attacked me and then tied me and wrapped me up?"

"That's something you should know."

"How can I since I was tied up, like the Holy Koran that is attached by iron chains in Damascus?"

"Why did you let yourself be tied?"

Halef looked at me in surprise. "You are asking me that, you who sent me here to ..."

". . . demonstrate your intelligence," I interrupted. "You did not pass that test very well."

"Sidi, don't offend me! Had you been here, you'd understand."

"Perhaps. Do you know that Manach el Barsha got away?"

"Yes. May the devil devour him!"

"And Barud el Amasat with him?"

"Yes. May hell swallow him!"

"And that it is all your fault?"

"Then tell me what happened."

"Very well. When I came to this Doxati, who is standing here with his mouth wide open as if he were the devil about to devour Manach el Barsha, I heard that he had three horses because he had bought two white ones at dusk. That made me wonder. I observed him and saw him leave the house."

"Did you have any idea what he was up to?"

"Yes, Sidi."

"Why didn't you follow him?"

"I thought he would go to the prison, and Osko was watching there."

"Hm. That's true."

"You see, you have to admit I am right. I felt that Manach el Barsha intended to free the prisoner but I also knew that he needed his horses. In any event, he had to come back to the stable, and so I hid there to take him by surprise."

"You hid? But that wasn't necessary. You could have sent for some police or gone for them yourself. That would have been the safest way."

"Sidi, the safest is not always the most attractive, and I thought it would be really nice if I caught the scoundrels myself."

"And we have to pay for that now."

"Allah will return them to us. But back to my story: I was waiting, and there were three of them who came back. They asked me what I wanted. But Barud el Amasat had barely seen me when he recognized me, since I had testified against him at the interrogation. We started fighting and I resisted as best I could, but I was beaten down."

"Why didn't you use your weapons?"

"Sidi, six arms held me, and I have only two! Had Allah given me ten arms, I would have had four for my weapons. I was wrestled to the ground, wrapped in my kaftan, and tied up. And that's how I lay until you freed me. Now the criminals are gone. If we were in the desert it would be easy to find their trail, but here, in this large city, that won't be possible."

"I know where they went."

"Allah be praised that he gave you the sense which . . ."

". . . you lacked today! Unfortunately, the trail of a man isn't the same thing as the man. Bring the lamp over here. What's this?"

Halef bent down and picked up a rather large piece of cloth. He looked at it and said, "I tore that out of Barud el Amasat's kaftan. The pocket is still attached to it."

"Is there something in it?"

"A piece of paper."

I examined it by the light of the lantern. It was a tiny letter with a very large seal and contained three short lines in Arabic. But the writing was so small that I could not decipher it. I put it in my pocket and began looking for other traces of the struggle, but found nothing. It was incomprehensible that the three men had not taken Halef's knife and the two pistols in his belt. He had not had his rifle with him; I had seen it propped against the wall of his room.

"Had Manach el Barsha also taken a room in your inn?" I asked Doxati, who had looked on and listened in astonishment.

"Yes," he answered.

"Does he come here often?"

"Yes."

"So you know him well?"

"Yes. His name is as you say, and he is a tax collector in Usküb. But he isn't often at home. He travels a good deal to collect the taxes."

"Take us to his room."

Contrary to my expectations, I found nothing. I now sent the little Hadji back home on his horse, and he trotted off, dispirited, mumbling a thousand imprecations into his beard.

I asked Hulam to go immediately to the cadi with me. He had been silent so far, but now said, "Who would have thought this possible? And why see the cadi? Can he change what has happened?"

"We have to inform him of these events, and it is only through his help that we can know for certain that the prisoner is no longer in prison."

The official had long since retired and I had to use some strong language to persuade his staff to wake him. Then we were admitted. He was not precisely amiable when he received us and asked what we wanted.

"We turned Barud el Amasat over to you," I stated. "Did you see to it that he is properly guarded?"

"Did you come just to ask me that question?"

"I should like an answer."

"The prisoner is carefully guarded. You may go."

"We may go, but he has gone!"

"Allah akbar, God is great! He can understand you but I don't comprehend your words."

"Then I must be more explicit. Barud el Amasat has escaped."

The cadi jumped up from his cushions. "What are you saying? Escaped? From prison?"

"Exactly."

"How do you know?"

"We saw him."

"Allah! Then why didn't you detain him?"

"We didn't recognize him."

"Then how do you know it was he?"

"We didn't find out until later. A tax collector by the name of Manach el Barsha freed him."

"Manach el Barsha? I know him. He used to be a tax collector and lived in Usküb. But he no longer collects taxes and now lives in the mountains."

"Lives in the mountains" means "had to flee to the mountains," and so I asked, "Didn't you see him today during the questioning?"

"No. How is it you know him?"

"I found out his name and his local address from a clothes merchant. He took a room at Doxati's, bought horses, and left town this evening with Barud el Amasat and another man."

"Who was that?"

"I don't know, but I assume it was a turnkey from the prison."

We briefly told the cadi what had transpired. When we finished, he sent for his saber, ordered an escort of ten men, and accompanied us. The prison warden was not a little astonished at our late visit.

"Take us to the prisoner called Barud el Amasat," the cadi ordered. The official obeyed and was taken aback when he found the cell empty. The turnkey in charge of the prisoner had disappeared with him.

The wrath of the cadi was indescribable. This dignified judge used expressions unknown in any western language, and finally had the warden locked up. I tried to calm him by telling him that we would pursue the fugitive early in the morning, and he promised to send six policemen with an order for Barud's arrest. Then we left, relighting our lanterns in front of the prison; without one, one could not let oneself be seen, at least in the inner city, unless one did not mind being picked up by the police and spending a night in rather mixed company.

# 17 : Kidnaped

We had not gone far toward Hulam's when we turned a corner and ran into someone who, I thought, had come in a great hurry from the opposite direction. He bumped into me, jumped back, and exclaimed, "Watch out!"

"You should have said that earlier," I said, laughing.

"Mercy, mercy! I was in such a hurry my lantern went out. Would you be kind enough to let me relight it with yours?"

"Gladly."

He took the candle from his oil-paper lamp and lit it from ours while he explained as though by way of apology, "I have to find a physician, a barber or an apothecary quickly. We have a guest who suddenly became ill and speaks almost nothing but German."

This immediately aroused my sympathy. A countryman, suddenly taken ill, and practically ignorant of the language of the country! Wasn't it my duty to inquire about him, at least?

"What part of Germany is he from?"

"Bavaria."

That this might be a lie, a ruse, did not even occur to me. Who would know about Bavaria here? The chances were a hundred to one that nobody but a native of that country would know the name.

I asked, "What is his sickness?"

"Nervous fever." At that moment the implausibility of this answer did not strike me. All I could think was that here was a countryman in need of help.

"Who is he?" I asked.

"I don't know. He came to my master, a tobacconist, to buy tobacco."

"Do you live far from here?"

"No."

"Then take me to him."

"Are you a physician or an apothecary?"

"No, but I am also German and want to see if I can be of some assistance to a compatriot."

"Then follow me."

Hulam wanted to join me but I asked him to continue on his way home since I would not need him. I handed him the lantern and followed the stranger.

We did not have far to go. After a few minutes the messenger stopped in front of a door and knocked. Someone opened.

I was still standing on the street, behind my guide, when I heard the question: "Did you find a physician?"

"No, but a compatriot of the sick man."

"What good can he do us, or him?"

"He can act as interpreter, since we don't understand our guest."

"Then let him enter."

I came into a narrow corridor which led to a small courtyard. The light of the paper lantern barely permitted me to see three steps ahead. Oblivious to any danger, I was startled when I heard a voice: "Seize him! He's the one!"

Instantaneously the lantern went out and I was pounced upon from all sides. To call out for help would be pointless for the small courtyard was enclosed by buildings on all four sides. I would have to fend off the attackers and flee back to the street. Spreading my legs for a firm stance, I pushed my arms as far outward as I could, and abruptly pulled them back again. This created a jolt which shook off two of the enemy. But others were holding on to me both from behind and in front, and the two I had shaken loose quickly got their hands on me again.

This was certainly no mix-up; there could be no doubt that I was the target of this attack. They had lain in wait for me at the cadi's and then lured me into this trap. Words would be of no help, and thus a soundless struggle ensued. The effort I had to make was such that my chest threatened to burst, but it was fruitless. There were too many. I was pulled down and soon felt ropes being coiled around me. I was a prisoner, and fettered.

For the time being I was out of breath, but my adversaries were panting just as hard. I had had a knife and a pistol in my belt but they had been pulled out at the very start. There had been no chance to use my fists because some ten or fourteen arms had held me tightly. Now the scoundrels were cursing all around me, and it was so dark between those walls that one could not see one's hands in front of one's eyes.

"Have you finished?" a voice asked.

"Yes."

"Bring him inside."

They took hold of me and dragged me away. I noticed that I was taken through two dark rooms into a third, where I was thrown on the floor. The men left. Some time later two men entered the room. One of them was carrying a lamp.

"Do you still know me?" his companion asked. He placed himself so that the light from the lamp fell on his face. The reader will imagine my surprise when I recognized Ali Manach Ben Barud el Amasat, the son of the fugitive, the dervish with whom I had spoken in the monastery in Constantinople.

Silence would not benefit me. If I wanted to discover what plans they had for me, I had to talk. "Yes," I said.

"Liar! You were no Nassr!"

"Did I pretend I was?"

"You did."

"Not so. I simply had no reason to correct your misapprehension. What do you want from me?"

"We are going to kill you."

"Go ahead," I said, trying to sound as indifferent as possible.

"Don't pretend you don't love life. You are a Giaour, a Christian, and those dogs don't know how to die. They have no Koran, no Prophet, and no Paradise!"

"Whether or not I love life is of no moment now. What can I do about your wanting to kill me? I'll die calmly. Until then, leave me alone."

"No. I have to talk to you. Perhaps you'll be kind enough to smoke a pipe."

The boy's sarcasm made me angrier. "I've noticed that you are a good dancer," I answered maliciously. "But I had not thought you'd turn out to be an even better buffoon. Dancers don't usually have a sense of humor. If you really wish to talk to me, consider whom you are addressing. I am telling you that you won't hear my voice unless you show the respect the Prophet commands."

This was a deliberate insult. When a Turk uses the word "dance," he means the sensuous movements of a woman. The dance of the dervishes is something altogether different, and considered sacred. There was no greater insult for Ali Manach than to be called a dancer by me, and to have me deny the members of his order any sort of intellectual capacity. I was therefore surprised that he sat down calmly, although he did cast me an angry glance. The other man remained standing.

"If you were a Muslim, I would know how to chastise you," the dervish said. "But a Giaour can never offend a true believer. How could a toad dirty the sun? There are a few things I'd like you to tell me."

"I will answer if you ask politely."

"Are you the Frankish physician who foiled the usta in Damascus?"

"I am."

"Did you see the usta later in Istanbul?"

"Yes."

"Did you shoot at him when he jumped into the water?"

"That was my servant."

"Did you see the usta again at a later time?"

"I did."

"Where?"

"At the foot of the tower of Galata, where his corpse was lying."

"Then what this man here told me is true." Ali Manach was pointing at the fellow holding the lamp.

"Didn't you know that the usta was dead?" I countered.

"No. He had disappeared. Koletis was found dead and, beside him, a body no one could identify."

"It was the usta."

"You hurled him from the tower?"

"Who told you that?"

"This man here. I came to Edirne without knowing anything. I had been called to my father. I was looking for him at Hulam's without saying who I was, and that was when I learned that he was in prison. He was saved without my participation. This man here is his servant and lived with him in Hulam's house. Your friend and protector Hadji Halef Omar told him everything, that's how I know. Then I went looking for my father at Doxati's. He was already gone but you were in the stable. We observed you. I had found out that you are a German, and so one of us had to wait for you at the corner and tell you that a German had fallen ill. You walked into that trap, and are now in our power. What do you think we are going to do with you?"

This explanation was food for thought but there was no time for reflections now. I answered quickly, "I am not worried about my life. You won't kill me."

"Why not?"

"Because then you would have to do without the ransom I can pay."

His eyes flashed. I had made a good guess. After all, why not take the money and kill me afterwards? "How much will you pay?" he asked.

"How high do you estimate my value?"

"Your value is no greater than that of a scorpion or a snake. Both are poisonous and killed the moment one catches them. Your life isn't worth a tenth of a para. But what you have done to us demands atonement, and so you'll pay a ransom." That was clear enough: payment of the ransom was merely a punishment, and even then my life wouldn't be worth a cent.

It was foolish to go on negotiating, but I wanted to gain time and so I said with apparent seriousness, "You are comparing me with venomous vermin. Is that the politeness I made a condition? Kill me. I have no objections. I won't pay you a single piaster unless you change your tone."

"So be it. But the more politeness you demand, the greater the sum you will have to pay."

"How much?"

"Are you rich?"

"I wouldn't trade places with you."

"Then wait."

Ali Manach got up and left. His accomplice observed the most profound silence. I heard voices in the first of the three rooms but could understand nothing, though I noticed that the opinions exchanged differed. More than half an hour passed before Ali Manach returned.

"Will you pay fifty thousand piasters?"

"That's a great deal." For the sake of appearances, I had to resist a little.

He made a gesture of impatience, and said, "Not a para less! Will you pay? Answer quickly; we have no time."

"Very well, I'll pay."

"Where is your money?"

"I don't have it on me, as you can imagine. Nor even in Edirne."

"Then how can you pay us?"

"I'll give you a draft, payable in Constantinople."

"Made out to whom?"

"The Persian ambassador."

"The Persian ambassador?" he asked in astonishment. "The letter is to be presented to him?"

"Yes."

"Is he going to pay?"

"Do you think the representative of the shah is penniless?"

"On the contrary, he has a great deal of money. But will he be willing to spend it for you?"

"He is perfectly aware of the extent to which he will be reimbursed." Thus I was not telling a lie, for I was absolutely certain that the Persian would consider the bearer of my draft as mad as myself. The ambassador knew nothing of the existence of a German writer with my name.

"If you are all that certain, make out the draft."

"With what? On what? This wall?"

"We'll bring you what you need, and untie your hands."

This promise delighted me. Free hands! That might give me a chance to regain my freedom. I could seize the dervish and threaten to strangle him, and I could hold him by the throat until he let me go. But this extravagant idea could not even be put to the test. The dervish, who, incidentally, was not wearing the garb of his order now, was a cautious fellow. He did not trust me and thus returned with four men who, arms in their hands, sat down to my right and my left. Their faces were not precisely beaming good-naturedly. The slightest suspicious movement would have been the end of me.

I was given a sheet of parchment and paper for the envelope. Using my knees for support, I wrote as follows:

> To my brother Abbas Jesub Hamn Mirsa, the beam of the sun of Farsistan that is now shining in Istanbul:
> Give the bearer of this letter fifty thousand piasters for me, the unworthy reflection of your kindness. My cashier will repay you on demand. Do not ask the messenger who he is, where he comes from, or where he is going! I am the shadow of your light.
>
> KARA BEN NEMSI

I signed this name because I could assume that his father's servant had told the dervish that it was mine. After I had addressed the envelope, I handed both to Ali Manach. He read it out aloud and I was amused when I saw the satisfaction on the faces of these honorable bandits. I tried to imagine the ambassador's expression when he read my letter, addressed to a fictitious individual. Let the bearer beware!

The dervish smiled at me contentedly and said, "That's good! And you were smart to write the ambassador not to ask any questions. He wouldn't be told anything in any event! Now retie his hands. The Kiradshi is waiting."

I had to submit to this, after which the bandits left me alone in the darkness. I immediately tested the tightness of the ropes and soon realized that I could not free myself. Unable to use my hands, I put my intelligence to work.

Why had the dervish come to Adrianople? Certainly not to pursue us, for he had known nothing of our presence in the city. He had received a message from his father. Barud el Amasat had had his son called. Why? Did Ali Manach have to participate in the misdeed being planned? Or was it a new enterprise I knew nothing about? Where was I? Who were these people? Members of the farflung gang of the usta, no doubt. Or did they have. some other connection with Barud el Amasat and Manach el Barsha? The latter assumption was more plausible. Perhaps there was a similar criminal organization which committed its foul deeds in the Balkans. The four taciturn scoundrels who had been sitting next to me had certainly looked like Albanians. And their clothing suggested they were Arnauts.

The dervish had stated that the Kiradshi was already waiting, Kiradshi are carters who transport their wares by wagon or beasts of burden across the entire Balkan peninsula. The Kiradshi is everywhere and nowhere. He knows everything and everybody, and the answer to every question. Wherever he stops he is welcome as a teller of tales, and in the wild, rugged ravines of the Balkans there are regions no news would reach all year long, were it not for the Kiradshi who comes to see if the lonely shepherd has collected enough cheese for a load. Goods of considerable value are often entrusted to the Kiradshi without any security being demanded. The only guarantee is their honesty. Months, sometimes years later, they come and bring the money. If the father has died in the meantime, the son or the son-in-law will bring it, but it is unfailingly delivered.

The honesty of the Kiradshi long stood the test of time. Unfortunately, things seem to be changing. Newcomers exploit the customary trust and infiltrate the old and well-known Kiradshi families, reaping where honest folk have sowed. They are destroying the good reputation of the Kiradshi. It was such a man who was waiting. But surely not for me? Was I to be carted off somewhere? Here, in the middle of the city, it was reasonable to hope that I would be freed. If I was not back at Hulam's by morning, my friends, and especially my little Hadji, would leave no stone unturned to find me. When I thought of my companions and the six policemen who were to come to the gate before daybreak, I became so angry I felt as if I could burst all my bonds.

I had reproached Halef for his lack of caution but had been much more stupid myself. I had walked into an exceptionally crude trap. That it had been my good-naturedness that had been at fault was neither an excuse nor a consolation. What was important now was patience, awaiting what lay in store with sang-froid, and vigorously seizing any chance for escape.

Finally the four returned. Without a word they tied a cloth around my mouth, wrapped an old rug around me, and dragged me off, I couldn't see where. The cloth smelled strongly of garlic and, having trouble breathing, I gasped for air. That's how someone must feel who is buried alive and hears the first few shovelfuls of earth falling on his coffin. These men did not even seem to consider the possibility that I might choke under the cloth and the rotting rug.

The movement stopped. I felt firm support beneath me. I had been put down somewhere. Then I thought I could hear wheels creaking. I was shaken up and down and from side to side. Obviously, I was lying in a cart and being taken out of Adrianople. I could not move my limbs but it was possible for me to pull up and extend my legs. I did this, and repeated it until the rug became looser. Now I could at least breathe fresher air through my nose, and the terrible weight on my chest was gone.

Though I strained my ears, I heard no talk and thus could not determine whether I had been entrusted to a single person or a group. I rolled to the right, then to the left. There was not much room to maneuver. The cart seemed to be narrow, but what I knocked against was so soft that I assumed I was covered by straw or hay. By the kind of movement, I could tell that I was lying with my head toward the rear of the cart. If I could only manage to make myself fall off it! It was nighttime, and dark. I could roll far enough not to be found and would be safe. But perhaps not. How would I slip out of the ropes and the rug? I might perish miserably. Thus I had to abandon that hope.

A time, an eternity, passed. Finally, hands started busying themselves with the rug. I was rolled over and over until the package had been undone. I was lying in deep hay and saw that day had dawned.

Above me there appeared the face of Barud el Amasat's servant. "If you promise me not to say a word, I'll remove the cloth from your mouth," he said.

I nodded eagerly. He removed the gag and now fresh, pure air streamed into my lungs. Thank God! It was as if I had left hell and entered heaven.

"Are you hungry?" the man asked.

"No."

"Thirsty?"

"No."

"You will be given food and drink. We will not torture you as long as you keep quiet and make no attempt to loosen the ropes. But if you don't obey, I have been ordered to kill you."

The face disappeared. No longer wrapped inside the rug, I could now move more freely and sit up. I found myself in the rear section of a long, narrow cart with a canvas cover. Directly ahead the servant was crouching, guarding me, and up front two others were sitting. I was certain I had seen one of them; he was a member of the gang into whose hands I had fallen. The other was undoubtedly the Kiradshi the dervish had mentioned. All I saw of him was the fur which Kiradshis wear even in summer. This man in his filthy fur was very important to me. I could not imagine that a Kiradshi of the old school could be an accomplice of criminals, and it did not seem likely that this antediluvian fur was clothing a Kiradshi of the new type. I had to wait and see. Meanwhile I leaned against the rear panel, keeping an eye on the man.

Finally, after a long time, he turned around and glanced at me. For a few seconds his eyes were fixed rigidly on my face, then he turned away again. But before that he had found time to raise his brows and close his left eye. I immediately understood this sign. The movement of the brows meant that I should pay attention, the closing of the eye indicated the left side of the cart. But all I could see was a piece of string which was attached to the upper part of the ladder and hidden under the hay below. It was stretched taut, which meant that something was suspended from it. Was it this string he wanted to call to my attention?

As if my present position were uncomfortable, I slid farther forward. Now I leaned against the left side in such a way that I could examine the spot although my hands were tied. I had to make an effort to suppress an exclamation of joy, for what was suspended from the string was a knife! So the good Kiradshi had realized what was going on. He did not want to be a party to a villainy and had placed the knife there for my use. Fortunately, he had been smart enough to fasten it only by a loop which I could undo easily.

The next moment the knife had been detached from the string and was sticking in the shaft of my boot, the blade with the cutting edge turned outward and projecting beyond the top. I bent my knees and pulled them close enough to my body to reach the cutting edge with my hands. It was very sharp. Sawing back and forth four or five times sufficed to cut the ropes, and now I could easily free my feet. I breathed deeply. I was no longer a prisoner and the knife was a weapon I could rely on. All these movements had been made under the hay. No one could see that I was no longer tied. I raised one arm and the lower edge of the canvas a little to look out. Ali Manach Ben Barud el Amasat, the dervish, was riding out there. It seemed reasonable to assume that a second guard would be on the other side.

It did not take me long to make a plan. The escort would have firearms, which meant that I had to avoid combat and rely on cunning rather than strength. I moved back again, keeping my hands under the hay. Then I started cutting out the lower portion of the old, rotten panel, and a quarter of an hour later I had made an opening large enough to slip out of the rear of the cart. But all this had not been as easy as one might imagine, for the old rug got in my way and the guard occasionally cast a searching glance at me. Because of the hoofbeats, the screeching of the wheels, and the rumbling of the cart, it had luckily been impossible to hear the noise my knife made.

I waited until the guard had looked at me once again, burrowed under the hay, and crept, legs first, out of the opening. I touched the ground with my feet and then put my head out. Only now was I really free, and next I had to get hold of a horse.

We were on level terrain, on a little-traveled road with woods on either side. Ali Manach was on the left and a second man on the right, as I had suspected. The dervish's horse seemed better than that of the other rider. It had thick, strong hair, a magnificent mane, and a tail that almost touched the ground. Its pace was vigorous yet springy and light. Would it be able to carry two people?

I now took the knife between my teeth. The horseman was utterly unaware of what was going on behind his back. Trotting cheerfully alongside the cart, he could not be seen by the others. Only his toes were inside the stirrups. Because the horse was bridled in the Turkish manner, he was sitting firmly in the saddle, but a blow against the back of the neck would thrust his upper body forward and his feet would presumably be knocked out of the stirrups. Then he would have to be pushed to one side. During this maneuver it was essential that I stay firmly on the horse and avoid being thrown.

Some quick leaps brought me behind the horse, and the next moment I was kneeling on the rump behind the rider. Luckily for me, the horse was so startled by this sudden attack that it stood still. I struck the rider in the back of the neck and his feet left the stirrups. Seizing him by the throat, I rose from my kneeling position, pulled him up, and let myself fall into the now empty saddle without letting go of him. This was done just in time, for the horse was raising its front legs. I could barely take hold of the reins with my free hand to pull the horse around and ride off as silently as possible, back in the direction from which we had come.

Soon this path made a turn. Shortly before reaching it I looked back. The cart had kept rolling along; no one had noticed a thing because the wooden wheels on the wooden axles made an absolutely hellish screeching noise and the cart had been between me and the second rider.

I now placed the dervish across my legs and spurred the horse. We began galloping. Ali Manach had been so surprised, he had forgotten to cry out. Then I had squeezed his throat so that he could not shout but had only been able to produce a gurgling sound. Now he was lying motionless before me and I feared I might have strangled him. The horse was galloping so gently, evenly, and with such stamina that the second rider would never catch up. In any event, combat no longer presented a risk, for I also had firearms now, having appropriated the two loaded pistols in Ali Manach's belt. As we rode along I searched his pockets, where I found my watch and purse whose weight had increased since yesterday. Two linen bags serving as saddle pouches were suspended from the flanks of the horse. I stuck my hand into them and felt ammunition and provisions. Clearly, preparations for a longish journey had been made.

The forest came to an end and I saw an open plain with extensive fields of maize and rose gardens ahead. When I glanced back after some time, a horseman was galloping after me, presumably the man who had been riding along the right side of the cart. My escape had been noticed and he was looking for me. Although my horse was carrying a double burden, it was as fast as my pursuer's. A little later I had reached a busy road, and now felt perfectly safe. The man had reined in his animal and shortly thereafter had disappeared from view.

I stopped and dismounted to let the horse rest, but also for the dervish's sake. I laid him on the ground and examined him. His heartbeat was perfectly regular.

"Ali Manach, don't dissemble," I said. "I know you are conscious. Open your eyes!"

He disregarded this, but I knew what to do. "Very well," I said. "Then I should at least make sure you are dead. So I will thrust this blade into your heart."

I took out the knife, but the young man barely felt the point touch his chest when he opened his eyes wide with fear. "Stop, Effendi! Are you really going to kill me?"

"I don't enjoy killing someone, but a corpse cannot be harmed by being stabbed. If you wish to keep this knife away from yourself, don't try to make me think you have died."

He had been lying stretched out on the ground and now got up.

"Tell me, Ali Manach, where had you intended to take me?"

"To a safe place," he answered curtly.

"That's rather ambiguous. Was I to be safe, or were you going to be safe from me?"

"Both."

"You'll have to explain that for me."

"Nothing was going to happen to you, Effendi. We meant to take you to a place from which you would be unable to escape. My father wanted to gain time and make sure he would not be pursued. Then we would have let you go for ransom."

"That's very nice. Where was I going to be taken?"

"To a watchtower in the mountains."

"A watchtower? So you thought your father would make his escape more safely if I were your prisoner?"

"Yes, Effendi."

"Why?"

"Because you might have found out which direction he took."

"How could I have? I am not omniscient."

"Your Hadji Halef Omar told us that you can follow any trail."

"Hm. And how was I to find your father's in Edirne?"

"I don't know."

"Well, Ali Manach, I should tell you that I have already found it. Your father, the prison guard, and Manach el Barsha all rode along the Arda. They had two white and one brown horse."

The dervish gave a violent start. "You are quite mistaken," he tried to assure me.

"No. I hope that I will soon learn more. Where is the scrap of paper you took away from me?"

"What paper?"

"You yourself took it from my pocket. I hope you still have it."

"It didn't contain anything important, so I threw it away."

"I have the impression that it was very important, and I am going to look for it. Let's see your belt."

Ali Manach rose as if he wanted to make it easier for me to examine it, but I had barely stretched out my hand when he stepped back and ran toward the horse. This was not unexpected. Before he could put his foot in the stirrup, I had seized him and thrown him down.

"Stay where you are or I'll put a bullet through your head," I threatened. "You may have sufficient skill for the monastery of the dancing dervishes in Istanbul, but that isn't enough to get away from me!"

I searched him and then the saddle pouches but found nothing. Then I took out the wallet. It contained a quantity of gold coins which were not mine and also the scrap of paper with the three lines written in Nestaalik. This is a script that slants to the left, halfway between the hurried Nes'chi and the very slanted Ta'lik.

Because there was no time now to decipher it, I put the piece of paper back and said, "I believe these lines contain something of importance. You must know which direction your father took."

"I don't, Effendi! He was already gone when I arrived in Edirne yesterday."

"But surely you found out where he went. He must be riding to Scutari, where your uncle Hamd el Amasat is waiting for him." As I said this I pretended to be looking elsewhere. Something like satisfaction passed over his face. So his father had not gone to Scutari!

"Perhaps," he said. "I don't know. But now you should tell me what you intend to do with me, Effendi."

"What do you think?"

"You'll let me take my horse and go."

"Not bad! You don't merely want to be set free, you also want to ride away from here."

"But the horse is mine!"

"But you are my prisoner, so I get to keep the horse as well."

"I didn't do you any harm!"

"No harm? You will accompany me to Edirne, to the house you lured me to last night. I am curious to see who lives there. And the cadi will join us."

"You won't do that, Effendi. I know that you are a Christian, and that your Savior commands you to love your enemies."

"So you admit being my enemy?"

"I wasn't, but you became mine. I hope you are a good Christian and will obey your God's command."

"I am perfectly willing."

"Well then, why not let me go, Effendi?"

"Precisely because I obey the command, O Ali Manach. I love you so much, I am loath to separate from you."

"You are mocking me, Effendi. Let me go. I'll pay you a ransom."

"Are you wealthy?"

"No, but my father will be in the near future."

"He's probably stolen his wealth. I wouldn't want to touch that kind of money."

"Then I'll give you other money. You'll get yours back."

"Mine? Do you have money that belongs to me?"

"No. But the messenger has already been sent to pick up in Istanbul what you were going to give for your release. If you let me go, you'll get it back the moment it arrives."

"Oh, Ali Manach Ben Barud el Amasat, you danced away your reason in that city! Your messenger will not receive a single piaster. The name I gave you doesn't exist. And the Persian to whom the messenger may have been sent doesn't know me."

"So you deceived us, Effendi? We would have received nothing?"

"Nothing."

"That would have been your death!"

"I knew that. But I would also have died if the sum had been paid. In any event, I was not afraid of you and I proved to you that I was right. I am free."

"So you are really going to take me to Edirne as your prisoner?"

"I am."

"Then return the money I put inside your pouch."

"Why?"

"It's mine. I need it. I have to eat and drink, even in prison."

"They'll have to give you what you need, although it won't be delicacies. Besides, it won't do a dancer any harm to fast a bit."

"So you propose robbing me?"

"No. Look at me. When I struggled with you, my clothes were torn. I have to replace them. That's your fault, so I can take your money and still not be guilty of theft.—And that's enough chatter! We are leaving. Stretch out your hands."

Earlier I had seen some rope in one of the pouches and I now took it out.

"Effendi, what are you doing?" he asked, frightened.

"I am going to tie your hands to the stirrup."

"You can't! You are a Christian, I am a follower of the Prophet! You are not a policeman and do not have the right to treat a believer as a prisoner."

"Don't struggle. If you don't stretch out your hands right now, I'll knock you unconscious again. You are not going to prescribe to me how to treat you."

That did it. Ali Manach held out both hands and I tied them. I then attached him to the right stirrup and mounted the horse. And that was how we proceeded. I had not expected that I would be returning to Adrianople that quickly, and with a prisoner at that.

We soon came to the main route which leads to the famous Mustafa Pasha caravanserai. The many travelers we encountered looked at us in surprise but no one took the trouble to talk to us. Soon after we entered the city, I saw two policemen. I gave them a brief explanation and asked them to accompany me. I intended to first ride to Hulam's house to reassure my friends. The policemen helped me find the way.

In one of the streets through which we came, I noticed a man in the crowd who stood still and gave every indication of being frightened when he saw Ali

Manach, but then hurried on. Did he know my prisoner? I felt like sending one of the policemen after him to arrest him. What if this fellow warned the other members of the gang? But a mere hunch did not justify the risk of depriving a possibly innocent person of his freedom, not even for an hour. After all, I was a stranger, a Christian, in a Muslim country.

The gatekeeper at Hulam's uttered a shout of joy when he saw me. "Hamdulillah! Is it really you, Effendi?"

"Yes. Open up, Malhem!"

"I am coming! We were terribly worried about you. We thought you had had a mishap. But I see everything turned out well."

"Where is Hadji Halef Omar?"

"In the selamlik. They are all gathered there, mourning your disappearance."

"Wait," one of the policemen exclaimed. "Are you perhaps Kara Ben Nemsi Effendi?"

"That's my name."

"Wonderful! Then we have earned the three hundred piasters."

"What three hundred piasters?"

"We were sent out to search for you. Anyone finding a trace of you will receive three hundred piasters."

"Hm. Actually, it's I who found you. But you'll get your money. Come in."

The hoofbeats of the horse had barely become audible inside the courtyard when everyone came rushing out.

My little Hadji was the first. Taking all steps in one gigantic leap, he ran toward me, rejoicing: "Is it really you, Sidi?"

"It is, my dear Halef. Just let me get off the horse."

"And mounted? Have you been outside the city?"

"Yes. I had some bad luck, but also a lot of good luck."

Among the shouts of welcome, I heard an exclamation of surprise from Omar Ben Sadek: "But that's Ali Manach, the dervish!"

Up to this moment no one had noticed him. Now they all looked at him and saw that he was bound.

"Ali Manach, the son of the fugitive?" our host asked.

"Yes. He is my prisoner. Come inside and I'll tell you the story." We entered the selamlik and took the dervish along but had not yet sat down when the gate was opened again to admit the cadi. He was both pleased and astonished to see me.

"You are alive, Effendi? And here? Thanks to Allah! We thought you were dead, although I sent men out to search for you. Where have you been?"

"Sit down and you'll hear."

The prisoner had crouched down in a corner with Halef next to him. When the pipes were burning and we had had our coffee, I told my story to frequent interruptions. Then there were many questions and exclamations.

Only Halef maintained his calm. "Be silent, men!" he shouted. "There is no time now for talk. We must act!"

The cadi glanced at the little fellow as if to rebuke him but asked nonetheless, "And what should be done, in your opinion?"

"Ali Manach should be questioned now, and then we should go to the house where my Sidi was kept prisoner. And the cart in which he was to be taken to the watchtower should also be pursued."

"You are right. I'll have this son of the fugitive taken to prison immediately and interrogate him."

"Why not do that here?" I asked. "I would prefer leaving this very hour to pursue his father. Much precious time has already been lost. So it would be best if this man first tells us what he knows."

"Since that is your wish, it shall be done."

The cadi assumed a dignified expression and turned to the prisoner. "Your name is Ali Manach Ben Barud el Amasat?"

"Yes," he mumbled.

"So your father is Barud el Amasat?"

"Yes."

"He is the man who escaped?"

"I know nothing about that."

"Are you denying it? I'll have you bastinadoed. Do

: 374 :

you know the former tax collector Manach el Barsha?"

"No."

"You had this Effendi lured into a house yesterday to have him taken prisoner?"

"No."

"Son of a dog! Don't lie! The Effendi told us himself."

"He is mistaken."

"But you tied him up and carted him off today?"

"That isn't true either. I was riding on the road and caught up with the cart. I was speaking to the owner when I suddenly received a blow. I lost consciousness, and when I regained it I was the prisoner of this man whom I have done no harm."

"Your tongue is dripping untruth! But lying will only make your situation worse. We know that you are a Nassr."

"I don't know what that means."

"You discussed it with the Effendi in the monastery of the dancing dervishes."

"I have never been in a monastery of dancing dervishes."

The fellow thought he could save himself by denying everything, but the cadi burst out angrily, "By Allah! You'll be bastinadoed if you persist in not telling the truth! Or are you by chance a British subject, like your father?"

"I have no father who is a British subject. I notice that the Barud el Amasat whom you are talking about is not the same person as my father, whose name he improperly assumed."

"If you are no dervish, what are you?"

"I am a fisherman on a journey."

"From where?"

"Inada by the Sea."

"Where are you going?"

"I want to go to Sofia to visit relatives. I spent less than an hour in Edirne. I arrived here during the night, rode through the city and out the other side. Later, I came across the cart."

"You are no fisherman but a liar! Can you prove you live in Inada?"

"Send someone there, and you will be told that I spoke the truth."

This bit of insolence almost made the cadi speechless with indignation. He turned to Omar and asked, "Omar Ben Sadek, did you really see this man in the monastery of the dancing dervishes in Istanbul?"

"Yes," Omar answered. "It's he. I swear it by the Prophet and the memory of my ancestors."

"And you, Kara Ben Nemsi, you also saw him in that monastery?"

"Yes. I even talked to him there."

"And you maintain that he is that dervish?"

"Certainly. It's he. He admitted as much last night, and today. He thinks he can weather the storm if he denies everything."

"The young man will only make himself more miserable. But how are we going to prove to him that you are right?"

What a curious question!

"Isn't it his business to prove that we are wrong?" I asked.

"That's correct. But then I have to send him to Inada."

"Will you permit me to ask a question?"

"Speak," the judge said.

"You saw the scrap of paper which we found yesterday in the innkeeper's stable?"

"Yes, Effendi."

"Would you recognize it?"

"No doubt."

"Is it this one?"

I took the paper from the pouch and handed it to the cadi, who looked at it carefully and then said, "It's the same. Why do you ask?"

"You'll see in a moment. Hadji Halef Omar, do you know my wallet?"

"As well as my own," the little fellow said, smiling.

"Is this the one?"

"It is."

I was sure now I would catch the dervish. I asked him, "Ali Manach, tell us whom these gold coins in this wallet belong to."

"They are mine—they must be yours if the wallet is

really yours." I had almost caught him off guard but then he had seen the trap.

"So you lay no claim to the money?"

"What do I have to do with that money?"

The cadi shook his head. "Effendi, if I don't catch him, you certainly won't. I'll have him locked up and I'm sure I'll make him confess."

"But we can't wait for that. Let's take him to the house where I was attacked. The people living there will have to admit that he's the man we take him to be."

"You are right. We'll arrest all of them. Ali Manach, in what alley is that house?"

"I don't know it. I have never been in Edirne before."

"His lies keep getting bigger. Effendi, could you find the house?"

"Certainly."

"Then we should go there now. I'll send for some policemen. They'll follow us and arrest everyone. But your friend Hulam offered three hundred piasters. These men found you. Will they get the money, Effendi?"

"I'll give it to them now."

I was about to pay when Hulam took me by the arm. "Stop, Effendi! You are my guest. Will you dishonor me by not allowing me to keep my word?"

I saw that I had to make this concession. Hulam took out his purse and was about to pay the two policemen who, their eyes shining with pleasure, were lurking by the door, when the cadi stretched out his hand.

"Stop!" he exclaimed. "I am the superior of these officials. Tell us, Effendi, did they find you?"

I did not want to cause these poor devils to lose their reward, and so I said, "Yes, they did."

"Your words are very wise," the judge said, smiling. "But tell me now, would my men have found you if I had not sent them to look for you?"

"Hm. It's true that in that case the police would not have seen me."

"So who is it actually who is responsible for your having been seen by them?"

What could I do but go along with this conclusion? There was certainly nothing to be gained by alienating the judge, and so I gave the answer he expected: "Ultimately, it's you."

The cadi's smile became even more amiable as he went on: "So whom do those three hundred piaster belong to, Effendi?"

"Only you," I smiled back at this upholder of the law who was so intent on his own advantage.

"Then Hulam should give them to me. No one should be done an injustice. Even a cadi has to see to it that he gets what he deserves."

He was given the money and pocketed it while the two policemen made very disappointed faces. Unobtrusively I moved up to them, took two gold coins from my wallet, and gave one to each. This had to be done surreptitiously because otherwise the cadi might again have insisted that justice be done. The two men were happy with their present, and I suffered no loss since the money was Ali Manach's.

More police were sent for, and soon arrived. Before we set out, the cadi gestured me aside. I was curious what confidential communication he had for me.

"Effendi," he said pleasantly, "are you really certain that the man is the dervish from Istanbul?"

"I am absolutely certain."

"Was he there when you were taken prisoner?"

"Yes. He even set the amount of the ransom."

"And he took from you what you had in your pockets, including your purse?" I was beginning to suspect what the worthy cadi was after. When I recounted my experience I had truthfully mentioned that I had found more money in my purse than had been there before. It was this amount he wanted.

"Did Ali Manach have the purse in his pocket today?" he asked artlessly.

"Yes. I took it from him."

"And there was more money in it than before?"

"It contained some gold coins I had not put there."

"Then you'll admit that they aren't yours?"

"If they aren't mine, whose would they be?"

"They belong to the dervish, of course."

: 378 :

"That doesn't make sense to me. Why should he have put his money into my purse?"

"Because he preferred your purse to his. But no one may keep what doesn't belong to him."

"You are right there, O Cadi. But do you feel that I kept something that doesn't belong to me?"

"Certainly. The gold coins he put into your purse."

"But didn't you hear him deny that he did?"

"That's a lie!"

"That must be proved," I objected. "I don't know where that money came from."

"But you yourself say that it wasn't in your purse before."

"I admit that. No one knows how the money got there. But once there, it belongs to me."

"I cannot allow that! The authorities must confiscate it and return it to the rightful owner."

"Tell me first who owns the water that rains into your courtyard at night."

"What's the point of that question?" the cadi asked, annoyed.

"Do the authorities collect that water to turn it over to the rightful owner? During the night it rained into my purse. The water is mine, for the only person it might belong to other than myself renounced his claim to it."

"I see that you are a Frank and ignorant of the laws of this country."

"Perhaps. That's why I follow my own. Cadi, I am keeping that money. You won't get it!"

With these words I turned away, and the judge made no further attempt to make me change my mind. It was not my intention to use the money for myself but there would be something better to do with it than allow it to disappear in the bottomless pocket of this official.

Now, we set out. The police were ordered to follow at a distance to avoid attracting undue attention. We reached the corner where we had run into the man who allegedly had been sent for a physician. Hulam also remembered the spot very clearly. But from here on I had to be my own guide. Nonetheless, I had no trouble locating the house. The door was locked. We knocked but no one came.

"Those people are afraid," the cadi said. "They saw us coming and are hiding."

"I don't think so," I contradicted him. "I think that one of these conspirators saw me when I rode through the streets with Ali Manach. He saw that the dervish had been captured and that the attempt on me had misfired. So he immediately informed his accomplices and they ran for it."

"Then we have to break in."

After the cadi had instructed his men to tell the passers-by who had stopped to watch what was under way to move on, the door was simply knocked down. I immediately recognized the long, narrow corridor. The police quickly scattered into all the rooms but found no one. Various indications suggested that the inhabitants had fled in a hurry.

I searched out the room where I had been kept. When I returned to the narrow courtyard, the cadi had once again begun interrogating Ali Manach. The dervish now acted with even greater assurance than before. Perhaps he had been afraid that those living in the building might betray him, but that fear was gone. I had to repeat my statements; I had to point out the place where he had been sitting beside me, and also show the police the spot where I had resisted the numerically superior attackers.

"And do you really maintain that you don't know this house?" the cadi asked the prisoner.

"I don't know it," he said stubbornly.

"You have never been here?"

"Never," Ali Manach lied.

Now the official turned to me. "Surely no one can lie like this, Effendi. I am beginning to believe that you really are mistaken."

"Then Omar Ben Sadek and Isla Ben Maflei must also be mistaken when they claim they saw him in Istanbul."

"Is that impossible? Many people resemble others. This fisherman from Inada may be innocent."

"Will you step over here with me, cadi?"

"Why?"

"I would like to tell you something that I don't want others to hear."

"These people can hear anything you have to tell me, Effendi."

"Would you want them to hear things which you will find unpleasant?"

The judge considered and then said severely, "You would not dare say a single word I do not care to hear. But I shall be merciful and comply with your request. Come and speak." He moved a few paces away and I followed him.

"Why have you so suddenly changed your manner toward me, Cadi?" I asked. "How is it that you now believe in the innocence of this person, a man of whose guilt you were apparently convinced before?"

"I have seen that you are mistaken."

"No," I answered, keeping my voice low. "You haven't understood that I was mistaken but that you were."

"Mistaken about what? This fisherman?"

"No, mistaken about me. You thought you could take possession of my purse. You didn't succeed, and so the criminal is innocent."

"Effendi!"

"Cadi!"

He looked very angry. "Do you know that I can have you arrested for this insult?"

"But you won't. I am telling you that Ali Manach will confess everything if you make him believe he will be bastinadoed. I cannot tell you what to do, but it would please me to be able to say back in Germany that the sultan's judges are just men."

"And so we are! I'll prove that immediately."

He walked back to the others and addressed the prisoner: "Do you know the innkeeper Doxati here?"

Ali paled and answered uncertainly, "No, I have never been in Edirne before."

"And Doxati doesn't know you either?"

"How could he?"

"Ali Manach is lying," I interrupted. "Surely you can tell by looking at him, O Cadi, that he is not telling the truth. I demand that he be confronted with Doxati to—stop, get back, for heaven's sake!"

For no particular reason I had glanced up while speaking. We were standing in the small courtyard which was surrounded by buildings. Where I was looking now there was a kind of balcony, a wooden trellis through whose interstices I had seen two rifle barrels. One of them was pointed at me, the other at the prisoner. I jumped to one side and toward the entrance to protect myself, and at that very moment two shots were fired and someone shouted loudly for help.

It had been a policeman who uttered this shout as he threw himself down next to another who was lying on the ground in a pool of blood. One of the bullets had been meant for me, that much was certain. Had the shot been fired a moment earlier I would have been killed. The assassin had already been squeezing the trigger when I had jumped to one side, and the bullet had penetrated the head of the policeman standing behind me. The second bullet had found its mark. Ali Manach was dead.

That was all I saw. Obeying a momentary impulse, I leaped across the yard to the place where a narrow wooden stair led up to the trellis.

"Up there, Sidi! I am behind you!"

That was the voice of my brave Hadji, who was directly behind me. I entered the narrow corridor, which ended in some steps that were really holes. The corridor stopped at the lattice. Gun smoke was still in the air but there was no one in sight. Together with Halef I searched the rooms, but here also no one could be found. It was incomprehensible how the two murderers could have disappeared.

Now I heard hasty steps on the other side of the building. It had to be two people. The wall consisted only of boards. I noticed a knothole and looked through it. Two men, each of them carrying a long Turkish rifle, were hurrying across the courtyard next door.

I jumped out into the corridor and called down, "Quickly, into the alley, Cadi! The murderers are fleeing through the house next door!"

"Impossible!" he replied.

"I just saw them. Quickly, hurry!"

He turned to his men and told them with all the deliberateness imaginable, "Go see if he is right."

Two of them leisurely obeyed this order. What did I care whether or not the two were caught, I told myself, and climbed back down into the courtyard.

When I got there, the cadi asked, "Effendi, are you a hekim?"

"Yes," I said, because I did not want to waste time.

"Then check if those two are really dead."

In Ali Manach's case there was no doubt. The bullet had entered one temple and left by the other. The policeman had been shot in the forehead but was still alive.

"My father, my father!" the policeman leaning over him wailed.

"Why are you whining?" the cadi reproached him. "It is kismet. It was written in the Book that your father would die this way. Allah knows what he is doing."

Now the two guardians of public safety who had so indolently set out in pursuit of the two assassins returned.

"Well, was this effendi right?" the cadi asked them. "Yes."

"Why didn't you catch them?"

"They had already run some distance down the alley."

"Why didn't you follow them?"

"We weren't allowed to, Cadi. You had not ordered us to. You only ordered us to look and see if this effendi was right."

"You lazy sons of dogs! Go rush after them this minute and see if you can seize them!"

Now they took off at considerable speed, but they would undoubtedly slow down again the moment they were out of sight.

"Allah akbar, God is great!" Halef mumbled angrily to himself. "Those two scoundrels wanted to shoot you, and they got away!"

"Let them run, Halef. It isn't worth the trouble trying to do anything here."

"But what if one of the bullets had struck you?"

"That would have sealed their fate. You would not have allowed them to escape."

The cadi, who had been busy with the corpse of the prisoner, now turned to me: "Do you have any idea why Ali Manach was shot, Effendi?"

"Of course. The criminals thought he would betray them. He was neither courageous nor strong-willed. We could have found out everything from him."

"Kismet has punished Ali Manach. But why was this officer shot?"

"The bullet was meant for me, not for him. He was hit because I jumped aside at the last moment, and he was standing behind me."

"So the criminals wanted to avenge themselves on you?"

"Surely.—What will be done with the body?"

"I will not defile myself by touching it. This man has his reward. I shall have him buried, I can do no more. Ali Manach's horse is still at Hulam's; I shall have it sent for."

"And his father? Are we going to let him get away?"

"Do you intend to pursue Barud el Amasat, Effendi?"

"Certainly.—Do you still need us?"

"No, you may leave."

"Then we'll be on our way within two hours."

"May Allah be with you and give you success!"

"Yes, Allah should help, but I cannot do without your support."

"What do you mean?"

"Didn't you promise me an arrest warrant and six policemen?"

"I did. They were to be at Hulam's door at daybreak, but then I heard that you had disappeared. Do you need all six?"

"No, three will do."

"They'll be with you in two hours. Farewell. May Allah permit you to reach the country of your ancestors in good health."

The judge left. He had become a different man after I refused to turn over the money. His subordinates were also gone. Only the son was still kneeling by his father's side, moaning loudly. I took out my purse, counted out the money that had been Ali Manach's, and gave it to him. In spite of his grief, he was surprised.

"You want me to have this, Effendi?"

"Yes. Use it to have your father buried, but don't tell the cadi."

"Effendi, I thank you. Your kindness is balsam to the wound Allah has inflicted on me. My father had to obey his fate. I am poor, but now I can have the two tombstones placed on his grave so that visitors at the cemetery may see that a devout follower of the Prophet lies buried there."*

Without intending to, I, the Christian, had thus helped the dead Muslim to his tombstones. Would the dancing dervish's money have been better used had I turned it over to the cadi?

On our way to Hulam's house, we saw two policemen with Ali Manach's horse. What we would have considered impossible last night had already come about. I had asked, "Should Ali Manach not be punished?" Justice had been spared the trouble of searching him out in Istanbul; he had run into its arms.

All these events had made us lose an entire morning from our pursuit of the other criminals, and we now had to try to make up for this lost time. A council of war was held. Hulam began by asking who the people might have been who frequented the house where the dervish had died. He believed that there was some connection with the Nassrs in Constantinople. While this was not improbable, I also thought they were people of whom the inhabitants of the peninsula say that they have "gone to live in the mountains."

Now I had a chance to have a look at the scrap of paper which I had not yet deciphered.

"Can you read those lines?" Isla asked.

But though I made a considerable effort, I couldn't. The scrap of paper was passed around, but to no avail; no one could make it out. The letters were written clearly but made words which were incomprehensible

---

* On Muslim graves a larger stone is placed at the head end, a smaller at the foot end. When the grave is that of a man, the larger stone has a turban or a fez on it.

to all of us. I spelled the shortest of them—it made no sense. And here Halef showed the keenest intelligence.

"Sidi," he said, "Who do you suppose wrote that message?"

"Hamd el Amasat, I should say."

"Well, he had every reason in the world to keep what he wrote a secret. Don't you think that this is a secret writing of some sort?"

"You may be right. Hamd el Amasat had to consider the possibility that the paper might fall into the wrong hands. The writing is not coded but the combination of letters is unusual. 'As ila ni' is something I don't understand. 'Al' is an Arabic article, but 'nah' does not exist in any Oriental language, though when read backward it becomes 'han.' "

"Perhaps everything else is also written backward," Hulam suggested. "You read 'ila.' Read backward it would be 'ali.' "

"Correct! There is the name 'Ali,' but it is also a Serbian word meaning 'but.' 'Ni' becomes 'in,' which is Rumanian for 'very.' "

"Read the three lines from left to right, like the Franks, instead of from right to left as we do," Isla proposed.

I did this, but I had to expend considerable effort before I succeeded in grouping the letters so that real words resulted. What we finally arrived at was a sentence that constitued a deliberate mixture of Rumanian, Serbian, and Turkish, and meant: "Send news quickly to Karanorman-han, but after the fair in Melnik."

"That's right, that has to be right," Hulam rejoiced. "There will be a fair in Melnik in a few days."

"And Karanorman-han?" I asked. "Does anyone here know that place? Where could it be?"

No one had ever heard of it. Perhaps the word had been incorrectly spelled and ought to have read "Karaorman," the name of a village on the Bregalnitsa, as a glance at the map told me. The word means "black forest house" or "dark forest house." The place was small and lay in a forest.

"Let's stop trying to figure this out," I suggested. "The important thing is that the news is first to be taken to the fair at Melnik, then to Karanorman-han. The Serbian word *sa* means 'after' or 'behind.' I infer that the addressee of the letter is to visit the fair first and then go on to Karanorman-han. And I believe that the road the three horsemen took last night does go to Melnik. Isn't that so?"

"Yes," Hulam affirmed. "You are right. This Barud el Amasat has gone to Melnik. And one would be sure to run into him there."

"Then we should not waste any more time but leave as soon as possible."

"I agree. But before you do, have a meal here. And I must also have permission to supply you with whatever you may need."

Two hours later four people—Osko, Omar, Halef, and I—were in the courtyard, ready to move out.

"Effendi," Isla asked, "how long will you be gone?"

"I don't know. If we find the men we are looking for any time soon, I'll come back to bring Barud el Amasat to Edirne. Should the search be prolonged, it could be that we will not see each other again."

"That cannot be Allah's will. If you really do return home now, you must come back to Istanbul at a later time. Meanwhile you will send us your Hadji Halef Omar."

"I am going where my Sidi goes," Halef said, "and I won't leave him unless he sends me away."

At this moment the three policemen the cadi had dispatched came through the gate. I almost burst out laughing. They were sitting on nags none of which was worth a hundred piasters, were armed to the teeth, and looked like the most peaceful people imaginable.

One of them came toward me, looked at me closely, and asked; "Effendi, are you called Kara Ben Nemsi?"

"I am."

"I have been ordered to report to you. I am in charge of this detail."

"Did you bring the arrest warrant?"

"I did."

"Are you good horsemen?"

"We ride like devils! You will find it difficult to keep up with us."

"I'm glad to hear it. Did the cadi note down how much you should be paid every day?"

"Yes. You are to give each of us ten piasters a day. Here is the document."

This was not what the cadi and I had agreed on, and I really should have sent these three heroes packing. But a glance at them reassured me; I would not have to pay their wages forever.

"Do you know what this is all about?" I asked.

"Of course," the man in charge told me. "We are to seize three criminals you cannot catch and bring all of you back to Edirne."

What a remarkable way of putting the matter! Yet the three were to my taste, in spite of everything. I felt sure we would have fun with them, though Halef seemed terribly annoyed that the cadi should have dared provide such an escort.

The time had come to say our goodbyes. This was done in elaborate Oriental fashion but with the most sincere cordiality. It was uncertain whether we would see each other again, and I was leaving dear friends behind. But my favorite, my Hadji, was staying with me and that mitigated the melancholy mood a parting brings with it.

I had believed that I would be able to leave Edirne and go on to Philippopolis. Instead we were moving west, along the Arda, to face greater dangers and exertions than we suspected at the time.

# Editor's Note

*The Caravan of Death* continues the story begun in the first volume of the present series (*In the Desert*, series III, volume 1).

The action takes place in the 1870s, when the auto-biographical hero Kara Ben Nemsi and his faithful companion Hadji Halef Omar pursue an international ring of criminals through various countries of the Middle East. Their adventurous journey, which will eventually take them through the entire Ottoman Empire, is further described in the following volumes, also to be published by The Seabury Press: *The Secret Brotherhood, The Evil Saint,* and *The Black Persian.*

The present translation is based on volume 2 (*Von Bagdad nach Stambul*) of the latest edition of Karl May's Collected Works (74 vols.), published by Karl-May-Verlag, Bamberg, Germany.

E.J.H.

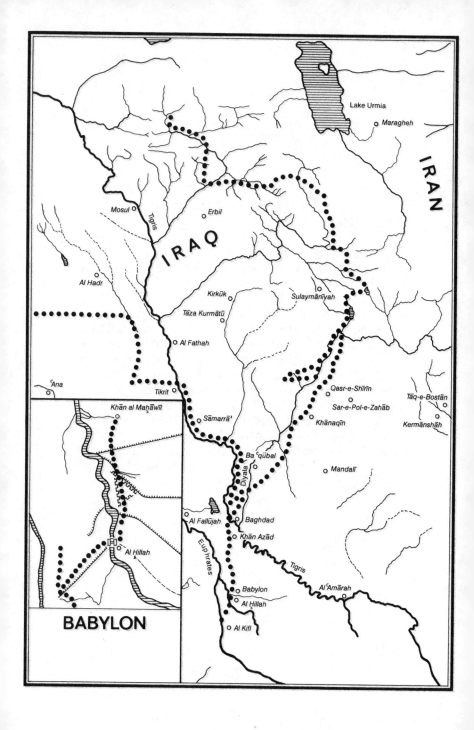

**BABYLON**